Captive Nights

Rachel surprised him, and ran her hands up his chest and locked them around the back of his neck. His eyes clashed with hers. "What are you doing?"

"I want to be in your arms."

"Why?"

"Because, I need you," she pulled his head down to hers and nibbled at his lips, then he parted his lips, and she deepened the kiss. Then he wrapped her in his arms, and cradled her body close to his.

Nick accepted what she offered. He plundered her willing lips as one hand traveled up her delicate back. He cupped her head, and held her still as he drank freely of her sweetness. Then he released her head, and ran his hands down her back to cup her gently rounded bottom. He pulled her tight against his raging need, and she answered his need by pushing against him. She wrapped one leg around his hips, and moved against the heat of him while her mouth did wonderful things to his. Nick groaned deeply, his heart was nearly beating him to death. He lifted her in his arms and took her into the shadows of the cave. He set her on her feet and took off his shirt. In the moonlit night they could see very well, and he was surprised when she took off her shirt. So, he unbuttoned his jeans and let them fall to the floor. He stood in only his boxers.

She unbuttoned the shorts she wore and let

them fall to the ground, then she kicked them off and straight into his arms. She giggled and it was the sweetest sound he'd ever heard. He dropped the shorts, her giggles had stopped and she stood with her fingers wrapped in the band of his boxers. He was standing in front of her, and he lifted her chin and brought her lips to his. It was a kiss full of sweet meaning and endless promise.

Forgive Me, My Love

A Novel by Dean King

ROGUE
A CALIENTE BOOK
WWW.ROGUEROMANCE.

A ROGUE® BOOK

COPYRIGHT © 2004 BY DEAN KING

Library of Congress Control Number: 2007901565
Publisher: BookSurge
North Charleston, South Carolina

ISBN 10:   0-9719751-6-7
ISBN 13: 978-0-9719751-6-3
THE NAME CALIENTE ® AND IT'S LOGO
ARE TRADEMARKS OF ROGUE.™
FIRST PRINTING: MARCH 2007
PRINTED IN THE UNITED STATES OF AMERICA.

PRINTED BY BOOK SURGE

FORGIVE ME, MY LOVE

MY LOVE

BY DEAN KING

EDITED BY ROBERT WAGNER
SHERYL MANBECK

Rogue

5

This novel is dedicated to all the people who stood by me. To those who believed I could do this, to those who tried to understand what I wanted to do, even when I didn't understand it. You helped me, you pushed me, you loved me. Thank you.

Forgive Me, My Love

 One

EYES HALF CLOSED, BIRTHDAY girl
Rachel McKinney felt her head slowly falling
back, and she let it. The loud thump echoed through bare
metal, and jarred her awake. Blinking rapidly against the
sting of salty sweat in her eyes, she had a desperate need
to lick her bound lips. It was hard to swallow with her
mouth stuffed full of some kind of disgusting rag, but she
tried anyway. The area around her reeked with the smell
of sweat from days of traveling, she didn't know how
long they had been in the van, but it was long enough. It
was dark, she could see an inch in front of her face. She
closed her eyes again and the relief was instant. The
constant strain of trying to see through the blackness
surrounding her was beginning to take its toll. Salty sweat
rolled down her forehead plastering her hair to her head,
neck and back. Her eyes stung and burned, she tried to
blink it away. Her skin was sticky and moist she felt
every fiber of her clingy orange dress. A soft whimper
came from her left, followed by the rustle of cloth. Every
now and again she could hear muffled crying. It came
from the far right corner of the hollowed out van. She
knew Bianca was some where in the tangled mix of

bodies.

Thank God I'm not alone. As soon as the thought ran through her beleaguered mind, she was filled with shame. It was wrong to wish this kind of thing on others and she immediately regretted it. She knew there were other women with her, all as unwilling as herself. But it would give them all a better chance at escape. She shifted her feet and a sharp pain shot up her legs, every muscle was screaming, an involuntary groan came from her dry throat. The intense heat and closeness of so many bodies was starting to make her woozy, sick to her stomach. She imagined the others were bound as tight as she was. Thick masking tape covered the rag in her mouth. Her arms cramped from being forced behind her back. The coarse rope binding her wrists rubbed deep sores as she constantly fought for freedom.

Was it only this morning that we had been carefree and incredibly happy? The morning had started so promising. Everything had been wonderful; the sky had been clear and bright as she and Bianca made their way back to school. They were ready to start the last semester of a long six years. They rode in her birthday present a brand new 2007 convertible sports car. The sun had just crept over the horizon, as they zoomed down the road. Pale shades of rose, peachy-orange and yellows streaked the soft blue of the sky as she zoomed by with the top down. She swore she could smell the clean, crisp morning dew that filled the air. Her thoughts had been so simple, even trivial. This was her last year as an intern, the last semester, she had just taken the bar and was waiting on the results, hopefully next year she would be a full fledge criminal lawyer. But her parents refused understand that she was an adult. She could take care of herself. They treated her like a child. Having just reached the age of twenty-four, she was ready to be on her own.

Rachel remembered basking in the caress of the wild wind and the sweet, warming kiss of the sun just breaking free of the night on her mocha skin as she roared down the road with the top down. Grinning from ear to ear, she had punched the gas pedal with her bright orange sandal. Texas A&M awaited her return. "Bea, are you ready for tonight?"

Bianca stretched and yawned in the seat next to her. "Did you say something?" It was more like a moan then actual words.

Rachel laughed and slanted her a quick look. "Wake up sleepy head. The fun is about to start. Just wait until we get back to the apartment."

"Oh God Rach," she groaned and clutched her flat stomach. "Don't you think we partied enough?"

"Excuse me! It's not everyday a girl turns twenty-four."

"Just let me catch up on my sleep then maybe I can keep pace with you tonight." She grumbled.

"Fine go back to sleep," Rachel let her eyes run over her best friend. Bianca's long frame was slumped down in the seat, lying as far back as it would go. Black sunglasses covered blood shot green eyes. Her long red hair was pulled back in a ponytail. A form fitting lime green dress clung to her thin body.

Last night, long after her parents had gone to bed, she and Bianca had gone out to a local nightclub and danced the night away. Rachel still didn't know how they had gotten up so early, having had only two hours of sleep.

"Bea?"

"Umm," came the groan of protest.

"Bea, look at me."

"What is it?" She turned and lowered the sunglasses, Bianca squinted at Rachel. "You know us old folks need our rest."

"What do you mean old?" Rachel laughed. "You are only two weeks older than me."

"Yeah, what do you want? I need to get some sleep if I'm going to be up all night again." Bianca announced.

"You weren't complaining when it was your birthday."

"That's because I didn't want to go anywhere, you forced me to go. And we only stayed out until two A.M. not five A.M."

"Well if I hadn't made you go celebrate what would you've done?"

"I would've been perfectly happy flirting with Stacy's boyfriend at our place."

"Ha, ha!" Rachel laughed. "He's too cute for her, maybe if she wasn't so mean he might stay with her."

"Yes, he is too cute," Bea was saying. "I heard he's about to dump her."

"I did too, but for who?"

"I don't know and I don't care," Bianca waved it off.

"But you should, maybe this is your chance. You haven't had a boyfriend in six months." Rachel insisted.

"And you know why," Rachel had been upset to see the glow leave Bianca's face as she settled back into the seat and put her shades back on.

"Yes, I know, but the Doctor said you are just a carrier for HIV. You don't have aids. There's only a small chance that you could give it to some one."

Bianca gave her the meanest look she could muster, but Rachel didn't cringe. "I'm a walking death trap. Any and everyone I touch could die Rach. Why would I do that to him? Why would I do it to anyone?"

"That's not true," Rachel declared hotly. "You know how to prevent contact, how to protect yourself and the person you're dating."

"It's not worth it," she sighed long and hard. "I'd rather be alone."

"Don't say that Bea," Rachel couldn't help but worry when Bianca started talking like this.

"I feel old. I'm about to finish my last year of college and yet my life is over before I can even live it."

"Your life isn't any more over than mine is."

Bianca gave a choked laugh and stared out the window. "My life was over that night we snuck out of your parent's house to meet those horrible guys."

"I remember like it was yesterday, we were only sixteen, it was so unfair, all we wanted was to have some fun."

"But you were smart Rach, you pushed your guy away and ran. But me," her voice wavered and her hand lifted to wipe at her face. Rachel clasped Bianca's hand and held it tight as Bianca continued. "I had to go all the way." She shrugged. "Maybe I was trying to prove something to myself. I still can't live down how bad I teased you for still being a virgin."

"You can't possibly know how I felt when you got sick two years later. If you hadn't had to have that blood

11

work done we would've never known. How I prayed they were wrong." Rachel was quiet for a moment and then said. "I wish I could take your place, you deserve so much more."

"And you don't?" Bianca snapped. "Stupidity runs in my family. I knew I was headed for rocky waters in my life. I just didn't know how I'd get there. I can't keep tagging along with your family."

"Why not, you are a part of my family."

"I wish that were really true."

"But it is, it's as if my parents adopted you."

"Simon hates me, but everyone else is great."

"Simon doesn't hate you. He's got issues that's all. I wish none of this had ever happened."

"Not any more than I do," she cried. "I wanted to kill myself when I found out, if you hadn't been in the car with me I would've run off the road and into that bayou by the church."

"I don't think you would've done that," Bianca laughed and Rachel cringed at the sound, it made her entire body hurt.

"You don't know what I'm capable of. You know my mother is a trailer park queen, and a drunken whore and I was headed to be just like her." Bianca had become thoughtful for a minute. Rachel wondered if Bea were thinking about what she'd told Rachel not long ago. Bea had tearfully explained her motives for pushing Rachel to make out with a strange man. Rachel knew Bea was sick with self-loathing and she wanted Bea to get over it. Bea had confessed to wanting to bring Rachel down to her level. She wanted Rachel to be trashy, to get drunk and prove that she was no better than them. Rachel was proud of herself for proving her wrong. She had gotten no further than one drink and a few kisses. Then she stormed through the door where Bianca was with and the other man and demanded they leave.

But instead of following her out Bianca had laughed and called her chicken and tried to tease her into being bad for once. But Rachel had looked down at her and said. "Being bad is one thing, being stupid is a whole different ballgame. I'm leaving, are you coming?"

It had made Bianca so mad that she had gotten up and slammed the door in Rachel's face, then continued with what she had been doing. Rachel remembered crying all night long.

"We've known each other since we were in daycare." Rachel was saying. "We were a year old and we liked each other from the start. Nothing could separate us Bianca. No man or anything else will come between us."

"Except my own arrogance and stupidity," Bianca had ranted, and Rachel's whole body tense and her fingers clamped hard onto the steering wheel.

"You are not a weak person and there is no way you are like your mother."

"You don't know Rach," Bianca sighed, and Rachel had wondered if maybe she didn't understand what Bea was going through. "My Daddy left because he knew, I look just like her. He knew I'd probably end up like her and I was well on my way."

"Stop it!" Rachel shouted and banged her fist on the steering wheel in frustration. "You stop that right now! That boy was your first and to this date he was the last guy you've slept with so don't go telling me you are some big whore! Tell it to someone who doesn't know you."

"Human Immune Virus has a way of defeating

you in so many ways."

"I'm sorry I mentioned it," Rachel frowned, and thought for a second about what she was about to say. Now wasn't the ideal time to tell Bianca, but she had to talk to someone. And she might as well get the fight over with.

Casting a hesitant glance at Bianca, she said. "Listen, I know you have issues with this, and I know you think I'm being stupid but, I'm going to give in to Richard and sleep with him."

Bianca sat up slowly; her movements measured, as if she were fighting for control. "What did you say?" Narrow green eyes stared at her.

"I said, since I'm going to marry him anyway, I might as well go all the way." Rachel had to look away from the fire in Bianca's eyes. "Don't look at me like that Bea. I know what I'm doing, I'm not sixteen anymore." She swallowed hard and steeled herself for the fight that was surely to come.

"No, you didn't just say that."

Rachel kept her eyes on the road, her nostrils flared, and her cheeks grew hot. "What's wrong with that? I told you I'm going to marry him. I decided yesterday that I wanted to."

"I knew it!" Bianca's palm slammed against the black leather of the dashboard. "I love your family but the minute you get around them you cave in."

"Stop it, I know what I'm doing." She'd been to angry to look at Bianca and now that she thought about, she knew it was because Bianca was right. "Richard loves me, he always has." Bianca was right in so many ways, and Rachel wondered at her own motives, she was not stupid. Richard wanted what her family could give him, but she held out some hope that he might, actually love her, and not just her father's money.

"The hell he does!" She riled tears glistening in her eyes. "You don't have a clue what you're playing with!" After long tense minutes, Bianca turned to Rachel. She caught her free hand and held on to it. "Honey you have known this man for thirteen months. I know your father introduced you two, and has made it plain he wants you two to get married, but sugar that doesn't make him right for you. For Gods sake Rachel, he's a liar and a cheat, and you know it."

"I know that Bea, but what man isn't? You said yourself that we have to train them. Besides, once we're married all that will change." Rachel didn't want to tell Bea the real reason she was giving in to Richard. She was embarrassed and ashamed of being a virgin. She was ready to become a woman in every sense of the word.

"Never in a million years will he change. The point is that he can't be trusted. You don't need a man you can't trust."

"So he slipped once, everybody does." Rachel shook her hand free and continued staring at the winding road ahead. She didn't want Bianca to talk her out of this, she was starting to feel like a fool, lying to everyone about her sex life or lack there of.

"You know it's more than once. You don't want a man you know lies flat out." Bianca continued. "For no reason at all he lied to your face, and he has cheated, not once, but twice. Tell your father he's wrong about Richard. Do you want to be like me and have to take AZT every day for the rest of your life?"

"Richard would never allow himself to become infected. I'm sure he has too much respect for me to let me become sick. As for Dad, I won't tell him that because I don't think he's wrong."

"Listen, Richard is an ass, and you know it. You have asked him to get tested, to respect your wishes and what does he do?" Now she was shouting, Rachel sighed as Bianca ranted. "He has cheated on you two times Rachel! Who knows what he has picked up from those girls."

"You are exaggerating. He only cheated once. And it was because I hadn't taken care of him, if I had he wouldn't have had to do that."

"I hear your father talking. Stop it Rachel!" She growled. "Just stop it. If you so much as think of giving in to him you can find yourself another friend. I won't stand by and watch this."

The tires screeched in protest as Rachel slammed on the breaks and skidded to a halt on the shoulder of the road. "What are you saying Bea?"

Bianca's green eyes turned stormy and she crossed her arms over her chest. "You are a sister to me, Rachel. Your parents have become my parents I call them Mom and Dad. You and your Mother are the only people alive who know my secret. I can't sit back and watch you fall into the same trap I did."

"But Richard isn't like Todd."

"Yes he is," Bianca grabbed Rachel's arms. "You don't see it but he is!" Tears filled Bianca's eyes, and she said. "If you do what I did, who's going to look after me when the time comes." Rachel immediately pulled Bianca into her arms and hugged her tight.

"Don't Bea, please don't do this," Rachel caressed her shaking back through her curly red hair. "I'm here for you honey."

"You don't know what it's like Rach," came the sob filled reply. "I'm lost and I'm selfish. I love you so much. I want you to find love Rachel. Find a man who loves you above all else and have his children. Then I can live through you. I'll make the best Aunt ever, I swear."

"You're wrong; I know exactly how it is, when this happened to you, it happened to me also." Rachel's arms tightened. "You'll find a man who loves you for who you are."

"And then I'll kill him and all my kids will die before their second birthdays." She cried in earnest her tears wetting Rachel's bold orange dress.

"Darlin' please don't," Rachel said stroking Bianca's shuddering back. "We'll both be happy, you'll see." Bianca nodded and pulled away, but Rachel wasn't fooled, but she would let it go for now.

After a last quaking breath, they each wiped their eyes. Leaning back Rachel looked into Bianca's red-rimmed eyes. "Together forever?"

"Together forever." They smiled at each other, and then got back on the road.

"Lets' go celebrate!"

"Let the fun began!" Their shouts rang out on the lonely stretch of road. Rachel turned up the music and punched the gas pedal. After another fifty miles she noticed the gas gage. "Damn! I thought it was filled up." But the thing read empty. Spotting a lone gas station off to her right, she cut quickly across the empty four lane high way and exited.

The place seemed deserted, but then it was still early. Rachel turned to Bianca, "You coming in?"

"Yes, I'm not staying out here," she hurried to open the door, shivering in the early hour.

They walked into the small shop, the heels of their pumps clicking on the hard wood floor. Loud cowbells rang out announcing their arrival.

"Geez," Rachel complained, looking at the large dingy brass bells that were hanging from the door. "You think that's loud enough?" She said to the old gap tooth man behind the counter.

"Gotta be, my hearing taint all that good these days," he grinned showing an incomplete set of dark yellow and black teeth, under a shaggy gray brown handle bar mustache.

Rachel went to the fountain drinks.

"I'm getting some coffee," Bianca announced going to the coffee pot in one corner. After getting a 44oz cup of tea, Rachel jumped when the bells rang again. Her hand flew to her heart and she shook her head, then looked over her shoulder. She found herself staring up into a pair of cobalt blue eyes. It was as if there was no space between them, she felt his presence like he stood inches from her and she shivered. The man looked like a cowboy in the worst way. His face had at least four days worth of black growth on it, but she could still make out the structure. It wasn't a handsome face, but it was very interesting. Black curls lay in wild abandonment all over his head. In his hand was a black cowboy hat, he smiled at her and nodded.

For an instant she was blinded, deep dimples carved into each cheek, he dipped his head to her again. Rachel caught her breath and looked away, she had been staring at him and he was laughing at her, mortified, she licked her dry lips and hurried to the counter with her purchases.

Bianca whistled low as she came to Rachel's side.

"Will you look at him?" She said eyeing his long form over the rim of her shades as he walked to the back of the store.

Rachel pulled on her arm, turning her until their backs were to the man. "Stop that," she hissed.

"Stop what?" Rachel's eyes followed Bianca's as they looked over their shoulders.

"Do you think he's a real cowboy?" Rachel asked, her eyes worked their way from the black curls on his gorgeous head, and down his tall form all the way to his boots. His entire body seemed to have a thin coat of dust all over it and his boots were creased with dirt, the spurs on them never once scraped the wooden floor.

"I don't know, but he's cute." Bianca whispered, and Rachel wanted to punch her. But sometimes she wished she could be like Bianca and flirt openly like that.

"How old do you think he is?" She asked and groaned as Bianca licked her pretty lips and batted her long golden eyelashes at the man even though he wasn't looking at them.

"I don't know," Bianca sighed. "Cowboys can be sixty and in those tight jeans they look thirty."

"I'd say he looks mid-twenties."

"I'd say you were right." Bianca cleared her throat. "Do you speak cowboy?"

Rachel frowned, tightly. "What the hell are you talking about?"

"You know, get'em up, and move'em out, git along little doggies. That kinda thing." They both giggled.

"No, I don't speak that." Rachel laughed.

"I bet he does."

"Come on lets git along outta of here. The last thing we want is for him to catch us staring." They were paying for their things when Rachel stiffened. The handsome cowboy came to stand behind them and proceeded to talk to the old man as if they weren't there. She felt the warmth of him against her back, she inhaled and her body tightened, he smelled so good.

"Hey, how you doing there Nick?"

Humm, Nick, nice name. She thought as her eyes roamed his incredibly masculine physic. *I wonder if it's short for something. He smells to good to look so dirty.*

"I'm fine Jeb. How's business?"

"Oh business doing fine, gets better later in the day. Say, I heard tell you was dead. Where ya been? Been pert near a year since I last seen ya." Jeb chatted away as he tallied up their purchases.

Rachel wished he would shut up. She wanted to hear the deep rich tones of Nick's voice again. But Jeb was finished ringing them up and there was no reason to stay. *Oh well. Maybe next time.* Mentally she shrugged it off, and grabbed Bianca's arm, nodded to them and left the store. She smiled as the heat of his gaze lingered on her back. Suddenly she was glad she had worn the pale sherbet orange dress. It clung to her shapely figure and the color made her amber skin glow. "Come on girl pick your tongue off the floor. We have some driving to do." Even the thought that he was probably looking at Bianca didn't spoil her mood.

"God Rach, he was beautiful," Bianca gushed leaning against the car as Rachel pumped the gas.

The door to the shop opened. Rachel had to agree, he was beautiful, she also admitted a man like that would never look at her the way they always looked at Bianca. Rachel glanced at the dirty big black truck next to her little red car. Rachel hoped he was getting gas too so she could check him out a little longer. She held her breath as he came out, then she stiffened when he walked straight to her. She swallowed hard, and her eyes widened.

"You forgot your change," he said and handed it to her. She tried to force her body not to flush but embarrassment always made her cheeks bright red and she could feel the heat rising. His lips lifted in a half smile and he tipped his hat to her. His velvet tones washed over her, and she knew her tongue had to be on the floor. His eyes ran the length of her and he winked. She wanted to say something smart and make him smile, but all she could say was.

"Thanks. I'm in a hurry."

He stepped aside with a cocky grin. "Don't let me stop you," he nodded, then turned towards his truck. The faded blue jeans hugged his slim hips as he climbed into the truck and left. Rachel couldn't take her eyes from him, she sighed and turned back to the business of pumping her gas. She tried desperately to ignore Bianca's drooling comments.

A sharp kick to the side of her leg brought her back to the present. She couldn't believe how easy it had been for them to fall into this trap. They had almost been to their destination when Sirens sounded behind them. She pulled over for the police to go by, but instead, they pulled in behind her. She knew she hadn't done anything. She looked at Bianca and found she was still asleep. Once the officer approached the car she knew right away something was not right, but she had done what he asked anyway. Getting out of the car was the last thing she remembered. Rachel sniffled and tried again to tease the ropes apart at her writs. Her fingertips were aching and sore but still she tried. Suddenly she froze. The van was pulling to a stop. Then she heard voices, speaking Spanish. Her heartbeat seemed to fill her head so much that she couldn't hear what was being said. Rachel strained, and then willing herself to calm down, she listened closely. "I got ta go pee."

"So do I, the Boss said never leave them."

"Fuck that! I have to go. They're all tied up. What harm can they do in five minutes?"

"You're right. But as soon as I finish I want…" Their voices faded as they walked further away.

Rachel went into action. Scooting as close to the back door as she could, she lay on her back. Ignoring the pain shooting through her body, she raised her bound feet and slammed them against the door. She screamed behind her gag. She didn't know how long she pounded, but her strength was starting to fade. The other occupants cried heaving sobs behind their gags and Rachel thanked God another captive was banging on the side of the van.

Suddenly bright light flooded the darkness, temporarily blinding her. For second she saw a head full of brown hair peak inside, then it was gone. But the door was left open and hope was there. She kicked with all her might, and the doors flew wide open. Rachel blinked her eyes free of the stinging sweat and spotted Bianca right away. She scurried towards Rachel whose feet had just hit the ground. Looking around she spotted no one. Rachel took one step and fell on her face. She had forgotten her feet were still bound. Tears welled up closing off her throat. Hot, dust filled her nostrils. Another thud landed beside her. Turning quickly to her left she saw Bianca struggling to get to her feet. Suddenly the sound of booted feet crunching gravel met her ears, her eyes widened. Frantically she rolled to her back. Her hands opened, flat on the gravel Rachel pushed herself into a sitting position, and then she brought her knees under her, and made it to her feet. The sound of a single gunshot whipped her around. There on the side of the store stood their abductors. The young man standing between them slowly slid to the ground, his mouth gaping, she saw stunned disbelief in his eyes as he turned to her. Then she was screaming through the rag.

"Christ!" The taller one shouted. "I thought you said the damned door was locked!" He yelled in Spanish as they ran towards the van.

"It was lock, I swear."

Rachel screamed and kicked as she was lifted off her feet and tossed back into the van followed by a franticly squirming Bianca.

They were moving again. She swallowed her tears. *They would have to stop again. Next time we will escape.*

Two

R**ACHEL** SHIVERED; SHE was thoroughly bound. This time she lay on something soft. She was in a room, probably on a bed, that much she knew. She had been awake for at least ten minutes trying to figure out her situation. She knew she wasn't alone, muted voices could be heard, and a few lewd chuckles. She had finally stopped gagging at the foul tasting rag that was stuffed in her mouth and tied tight behind her head. Some kind of cloth was wrapped so tight around her eyes it pulled her hair causing pain with every movement. They had made sure her eyes were covered and her hands and feet were still secure. There was movement on the other side of the bed and she froze. Then the faint fragrance of peaches hit her, she wanted to cry with relief, and sadness. It had to be Bianca. Rachel was sore, but what frightened her most was that Bianca couldn't get her daily shot, and that would surely kill her. It had already been, to her estimates two days. Her parents had to be worried, Rachel was sure the College had notified them when she and Bianca didn't show up.

"Ah Médico que usted está aquí," she stiffened as she heard the heavy British accent; speaking bad Spanish coming from her left. *Why did they need a doctor? Was Bianca hurt?* "Miguel, Santos ¡venga!," that voice, so cold and flat made her want to shrink away as other men were called into the room. She knew she could never let them know she was fluent in that language.

"Si Patron," there was a scurrying of feet, and then a door closed.

"El médico yo he sido aconsejado que la chica de McKinney es todavía una virgen. El pelirrojo no es," his voice changed direction, and Rachel tried to follow it, but she froze at the word virgin. *Why would they care if I'm a virgin?* The thought frightened her more than she already was. "You two, untie them, if I find that status has changed due to the recent trip here, someone will pay with his life."

Suddenly the ropes were being roughly yanked from her hands and feet, then the gag was pulled from her terribly dry mouth, peeling off a layer of skin from the inner lining of her dry cheeks and tongue. She cringed in pain, then lastly the blindfold was removed.

Rachel coughed, desperately trying to clear her throat, and then swallowed a few times to wet it. Blinking furiously, her eyes flew to the other occupants of the room. A cry of instant relief sprang from her lips as she spotted Bianca being untied. Rachel stumbled to her knees and crawled across the bed. "Bianca! Are you alright?"

"Rachel," Bianca cried. "Did they hurt you?"

Rachel pulled Bianca into her arms and both girls squeezed each other tight. "I'm fine," Rachel pulled back and brushed the hair back from Bianca's flushed face. "They don't know who they're messing with. You wait until Daddy finds out, there will be hell to pay."

"On the contrary my dear Rachel I know exactly who I'm messing with as you so quaintly put it."

Rachel turned quick, a gasp burst from her lips and sick dread formed in the pit of her stomach. Easing out of Bianca's arms, she slid off the big bed. "Mr. Henry?" Her brow creased in a tight frown, as she stared at the tall distinguished looking man. His black hair was nearly covered with gray and his face had a few extra lines creasing it then she remembered. He had been a constant in her family's home for years, then all of a sudden, nothing. "What is this? I thought you were friends with my father."

"You Americans, far too trusting my dear. Your father had been useful to me on occasion." He shrugged, and then walked closer to her; he lifted a stray curl from her shoulder and mused. "You are almost as pretty as your mother."

Her eyes narrowed, and she pulled away from him not liking the way his eyes roamed her body. "Since you know my father so well," she snapped trying to keep her fear at bay. "I'm sure you realized what a mistake it was kidnapping us."

"Oh no dear, there is no mistake. Your father owes me; you can leave when I get my money." The silky smoothness of his voice made her want to slap him.

"You can't do this! We're not back in the old west or in your case the eighteen hundreds!" She raged. "I demand you release us now." Rachel glared at him, fire flying from her eyes.

"Would you like to talk to your father?"

Rachel frowned at this sudden change, he sounded almost sympathetic. "Yes."

Henry snapped his fingers. "Miguel, get John McKinney on the phone."

"Si, si Patrón," the man nodded his dark head wildly.

Rachel turned to Bianca. "See, I knew he would

26

see things my way."

"Santos, bring the red-head to me." Rachel blanched as a huge, bald man headed for Bianca. Panic ripped through her and she jumped in his way, planting her feet in an attack mode, she had learned in karate.

"Don't you touch her!" Rachel slashed out at his massive chest, but he caught both her hands in one of his and flung her from him. She fell face first on the bed with Bianca's screams ringing in her head. She turned over quickly and shouted. "She's sick, she can't take much more of this!"

Bianca had jumped on the bed, and was now standing on top of it, she tried to run, but found she had no place to go. She removed the one shoe she still had, and waved the high heel like a weapon. "Don't you come near me; I'll bash your head in!"

Rachel rolled from the bed, jumped on his back, and sank her teeth into the flesh of his shoulder. He howled in pain, and she screamed as his meaty hand reached behind him and grabbed her dress. He pulled her from her perch as if she were a doll and tossed her to the bed.

"Si usted coloca una mano en el niña del Negro, yo dejaré le caer era usted se para!" The thunderous voice halted all movement. All eyes swung to Henry and the large black gun he held in a steady hand. Santos moved away from the bed to stand back against the wall, his large hands held up, and his dark brown eyes nearly black.

"Pero usted dijo obtiene el Patrocinador de chica," it was an unexpected whine from such a big man. If the situation hadn't been so dire Rachel would've laughed. To see that giant of a man squeaking like a little girl was amazing. *But you told me to get her.* He had squeaked and Rachel looked at Henry. *He can't have that kind of power. Can he?*

"Dije también que el negro no debía ser dañado en de todos modos. Si ella descubre una marca que usted pagará por lo." He said in low tones.

Rachel took some comfort in that comment; she didn't want to think of why she wasn't to be hurt; she hurried to Bianca and hugged her close. "Speak English you coward!" she sneered.

He smiled, but instead of being the friendly smile she remembered, this time it was sinister, it reeked of evil and her skin crawled. "I know all about Reds illness," he said in English and turned towards Bianca. "That was very careless of you little one. I am sorry for your fate, I made sure we had the meds for you. I don't know how long I will keep you alive." He glared at Rachel. "That depends on this little lady right here."

"Please, you have to let her go." Rachel said, her back straight, she stared at him. "She's not a part of this, apparently it's me you want, let her go."

He grinned and she wanted to shrink away. "I've watched you over the past five years. You are the type of woman who must be controlled. Your friend is only here to control you."

"I'll do whatever you say," Rachel cried, meaning every word. "I'll crawl, beg, plead, anything just send her home."

"You will, I know that you will. I have made sure of it." He assured her. "In her weakened state Bianca can't take much abuse, which means you will behave yourself and do everything I ask of you, or I can deny her the medicine she needs, or I can have her throat slit right in front of you. It is my choice to make."

"Aaahh!" Rachel screamed, and jumped back. "You black hearted monster! You wouldn't! My father would have your head on a platter! My brother is a Navy Seal, he'll find us and he'll rip your black heart out with his bare hands if you touch us!"

"Such fire!" He laughed, then he became quiet, his blue eyes nearly black with intent. "I wonder how much of that will transfer to the bed?"

She froze and her mahogany skin paled at the threat.

"Patron, I have the man."

A pleased smile lifted one corner of Henry's thin lips, but Rachel ignored it, she just wanted to hear her father's beloved voice. "By all means please put it on speaker phone."

"Hello?" Rachel gave a shuddering sigh, as that much loved voice filled the room. "Who is this?"

"Daddy!" She and Bianca yelled at the same time.

"Shut them up." Henry directed, and the girls were imeadately caught in hard arms, and held with hands over their mouths.

"Who is this?" The anxious voice said from the other end of the phone.

"John, John my old friend. Have you my money yet?"

"You listen to me Henry Dennison. I don't know what you are about, but I don't peddle drugs. I have no idea what happened to your diamonds! I doubt you even had any diamonds. Now, for the last time go fuck yourself, you insane bastard."

"It's Lord Henry, please do try to remember."

"You are no member of the peerage. I can't

believe I knew you all those years and didn't realize I was being set-up. You're lucky you got away or I would've taken pleasure in skinning your hide for what you tried to do to my company."

"Hey, when you sleep with dogs, you get fleas."

"I thought I was in with a friend. How dare you do this to me."

"I dare because I can, I want the money you owe me."

"I don't owe you a dime. I don't know how you got my signature on that invoice, but you and I know it's a lie. If you lost something, which I doubt, then it was your own fault."

"I need you to be more compromising than this John, after all we were friends. I could take you to court." He said with laughter in his tone.

"And do what? Slit your own throat? You don't have a case and we both know it. This harassment will stop, either you stop it or I'll stop it for you."

"I may not be a recognized member of the house of the Lords but make no mistake, I am of pure blood. You will respect me as such."

"Did you hear anything I said?" John gave a nasty chuckle. "I should've listened to my sons. They said something wasn't right about you. You keep your crazy ass buried deep in Mexico like you always have and everything will be fine."

"But John you didn't say this when we made the deal."

Rachel swallowed hard; confusion gripped her and her eyes stung with hot tears. "Daddy, tell him to let us go!"

"What?" John said in hushed tones. "Who said

that?"

"Bring Red to me," Henry said in his crisp tones.

"What are you talking about?" John's voice became an angry roar through the phone lines and Rachel shook when she heard the tremor in her father's voice. "Who is Red?"

"No!" Rachel screamed, "You said you won't hurt us, leave her alone!" She fought hard but the men were stronger by far.

"Noo, let me go," Bianca's eyes were wild as she fought them. "Please let me go!" She screamed as she was dragged to a far corner of the room.

"Daddy, help us!" Rachel screamed as she was held back by the man Henry had called the Doctor. "Daddy! Please."

"Oh my God!" Stunned silence came from the phone. "Rachel? Rachel, is that you honey?" She blinked back the tears of fear and tried to focus on his comforting voice.

"Daddy please, he has Bianca kneeling on the floor with a gun to her head, he's going to kill us!" Rachel screamed through her tears. Bianca knelt with her eyes closed tight, her arms were held behind her back.

"God damn you Henry, what have you done?" John thundered. "Let them go!"

A deep chuckle filled the room. "Who told you I would kill you sweetheart?" All was quiet, as Henry cooed. "I have much more interesting things in store for you."

"Don't you touch them Henry, or I will give you a war you'll never forget."

"John," that deceptively silky voice said. "I heard your beautiful daughter is still intact."

Silence fell. Then softly, "Please," John choked out, "don't touch her, she's just a child."

"So now you beg, and how nicely you do it." He grinned. "Are you on your knees?"

"Yes, anything just don't hurt her."

"Strip her."

"Nooo!" Rachel screamed fighting with every ounce of strength. But with both men ripping at her clothes she did not stand a chance.

Bianca turned soulful green eyes on Henry. "Please Mr. please don't do this, I'll do anything you want."

Henry looked into her eyes and caressed her wildly tangled red hair, he said. "How nice of you, but you will do what I say regardless dear." He murmured.

"Henry, please don't!" John begged tears evident in his voice. "I'll pay you anything you want! I can have the money to you in one week!" His voice broke, as Rachel's screams echoed through the large room. "Ssh, ssh baby-girl, it's okay, please Rachel darling."

"One week you say?"

"Yes! Twenty million dollars in small bills, I'll deliver it myself."

"That's fine. I tell you what; I will use her sweet little body until you get here."

"No! If you touch her the deal is off!"

"Now, why would you say that?" Henry chuckled. "Is a dead virgin better than a living non-virgin?"

"No, leave her alone, she's just a child! We are both grown men, don't do this to her."

"Hold her down."

"No, please dear God!" John's voice began to waver. "I'll kill you, you son of a bitch!"

Forgive Me, My Love

"Let me go!" Rachel fought with all her might, her teeth sank into the hand of one of her capturers. He howled in pain, and raised one meaty fist, he delivered a stunning blow to the side of her head sending her to the floor in an semi-conscious heap.

"God damn you Santos! Now you've ruined my show," Henry lifted the gun, he pointed it straight at Santos chest, and fired.

Bianca screamed as the sightless body fell forward only inches in front of her to lay next to Rachel. Hysteria held her in its' grip as she continued to scream.

"Oh, shut the hell up!" With the butt of the gun Henry brought it down on the back of her head. The sound of bone cracking brought a piercing cry from the phone.

"You bastard! If you hurt them you're dead!" John cried.

"I will call you with details of the delivery. I'll give you no longer then four days!" With that he hung up the receiver. "Now Doctor do your job, make sure she is still intact, I plan to make a lot of money off of her. I'll be in my study!"

*****

John McKinney fell into his chair, his skin felt clammy, and his heart raced with fear. He grabbed his chest, the pain was intense, blackness swirled in front of him. *My babies*. His mind refused to register what was happening. He'd just seen them, just kissed them good-bye. In his mind they were safe at College. His chest caved in, and fear tingled along the edge of his mind. His mouth opened on a silent cry that came from his soul, and

33

then hot tears raced down his weathered cheeks.

After a few minutes that felt like a lifetime, he collected himself. His face hardened, cold fury turned his eyes black. He picked up the phone.

"Tyrell," his voice was graveled, as he sought to control the emotion rolling through him.

"Hey, Dad what's up," he yawned, "It's kind of early isn't it?"

"Come home!" The steel in his voice could not be mistaken.

Tyrell was instantly awake. "What is it? What happened?"

"Call your brothers, and get Richard. Get your man to handle things for now."

"Alright," Tyrell hedged, "It'll take a day or two but I…"

"We don't have a day or two!" John growled. "Your sister and Bea have been kidnapped!"

*****

It was early for this part of the world nearly ten P.M. and he was neck deep in the Mexico badlands, in the cold, wet month of January. Dominick Rawlins lounged in the shadows of the glorified cantina. He hated places like this, it reeked of vile corruption. But it was a necessary evil in his line of business. And ever now and again he could find a sweet bit of fluff to take his mind off his troubles. The place was a contradiction in every way. Wealthy men dressed in suits and ties mingled with dirty, desperate men fresh off the road. If the money was right anyone was allowed inside this den of the damned. He had been here many times in his youth, it was some

34

sixty miles from his father's hacienda. Back then in was just a playground for a young man learning about life. Now he saw it through different eyes, the eyes of a bounty hunter.

He was hot on the trail of Jose Raphael Cortez, notorious bank robber and killer. After six months of tracking the bastard, he had finally gotten a good lead. Having to leave Houston in a hurry after the last robbery Cortez had had very little time to cover his tracks. Nick snorted; he probably didn't think he needed to, who would follow him across the Mexican boarder? Let alone deep into the wild woods of the backcountry. A crooked smile lifted one edge of his dry lips under his over grown mustache. With this one catch he could relax for a full year.

His sharp blue eyes scanned the crowded room. He'd thrown his dusty booted feet up on the seat in front of him, and pulled his battered black hat further down to cover his bearded face. He had very little time to make this catch. Bounty hunting was illegal in Mexico, if he were caught he'd find himself behind bars. The sooner he left these parts the better, besides that, if these people recognized him and reported it back to his father, he would be forced to leave without this fat purse, and that was something he had no intention of doing. Facing his father wasn't on his lists of things to do right now.

Nick thought back on the last time he had seen his father. Ten long years, what a child he had been. Once he'd found out his father was a drug lord, who owned almost everyone in the lower basin of Mexico, he'd been judgmental, angry, hurt and most of all disappointed. Two of his three brothers were key figures in the operations of the cartel, but one older brother had gotten away, never to be seen again. What made him angry was that no one seemed to think this was wrong. They operated as though it was the most acceptable thing in the world. To buy, sell, rape, kill and rip apart families was as natural to his father as breathing. So, Nick had left home calling his father every name in the book and swearing he would never come back. But after being persecuted by the very justice system he had fought so hard to protect, he now knew life was a bitch waiting to be fucked and anyone who believed other wise was a fool. The real world had proven his father wasn't all that bad, the law could be even worst. Corrupt and vengeful, it could turn on its best friend and you would find yourself in a cell with the very criminals you had put there.

Five years as a police officer in Texas, and he had been as green as they come. Believing in truth, justice and the American way. That last year he and his partner had stumbled onto a prostitution ring. Only this was a ring of officer's wives and run by the officers. Three Detectives and four Police Officers, all dirty and all up to their neck in crime. Then he'd found his partner dead, killed in an auto accident, so they said. It was just coincidence that they had planned to go to the Chief with their findings that next day. Soon after, Nick began to receive threatening letters telling him to keep his mouth shut. But with his incredible belief in right over wrong, he had gone to the Chief. Only to find the Chief was in it all just as deep as the others. After spending two years in jail, he was released and his name at the Police department was mud. His records were filled with malicious lies. Nick had resigned himself to a world where there was no absolute right or wrong. In this world it was who had the most money and power. Even though he didn't like what his father did, it was time to talk to him about what happened to his mother, Belinda. It was still a sore spot in his heart, nightmares till had him waking up in a pool of sweat. There had to be more to it then just her drug use. Why would a man send his wife away for her to die in the mountains?

Rowdy laughter pulled him from his morose thoughts. His eyes shot to Cortez who sat at the bar breaking a cardinal rule. His narrow back was to the room, anyone could sneak up on him. But Nick was no fool, he was sure Cortez had friends here, friends that wouldn't mind killing for him. This far into Mexico there were no holds barred, death came quick and usually ugly, suddenly there was a commotion near one of the entranceways.

"Don't you touch me!" A female voice rang out with unleashed fury. "Leave us alone you filthy bastard!" He stiffened at the sound of the girl screaming, then the ringing sound of a slap. He sucked in a sigh and shifted his gaze towards the struggling pair.

"You will do as you are told," instant recognition stiffened Nick.

"Christ," he hissed under his breath. "Why the hell can't things ever be simple?" he muttered.

"But I don't understand," the obviously black American woman was yelling. "You spoke with my dad. He said he would pay you. Why are you doing this?"

The man lifted a beefy hand and let it fall with stunning force across the redheads already red face. Nick was surprised the girl's neck didn't snap from the force. They looked like the girls he had past days ago at Jeb's. The one face he saw smiling at him every time he closed his eyes. They were dressed as Mexican peasants, their hair covered with multicolored scarves. Their feet bare, and bound with thick rope. Loose white shirts hung around their shoulders and long flowing skirts whirled around their trim ankles. The black girl snarled something he couldn't hear, then lowered her slim shoulder and rammed into Hectors unprotected stomach, sending both herself and him to the floor. The crowd roared with laughter. Hector pushed the girl off him, dumping her to the hard wood floor where she sat glaring at him.

"I told you not to hit her again!" The girl spat. "I'll kill you if you do it again."

Hector grabbed the girl's long black hair and pulled her to her feet. She cried out in pain, but once standing she sucked in a breath and let a huge wad of spit, it flew straight into his face.

"No, Rachel," the red head screamed, struggling with her captor. "They'll kill you."

The girl looked at her friend. "No they won't, they need me," her golden eyes shining like new coins. "If it's true then I for one would rather go out..." she never finished. Hectors meaty hand snaked around her throat cutting off her air, her eyes bulged then she was tossed over his shoulder where they disappeared in the back room behind the bar.

Nick became aware of many things. A stage was being pulled out. Chairs were being arranged as if getting ready for a show. Dread pulled at him. His stomach sick, he could only hope it wasn't what he thought it was. The soft background music stopped. Chuy, the proud owner of this establishment stood in the center of the stage calling for silence.

"El Favor de Por Senors, la calma por favor," he waved them all forward. "We have a rare treat for you tonight. Some of you were invited for just this occasion. This night we have a selection of fair beauties from around the world." There was a round of applause, as the man kept talking. "Some of our beauties are for sell. Others alas are only for use this night."

"What about the virgin?" Someone yelled from the crowd.

"Aah si le virgin," Chuy rubbed his hands together. "That one is feisty. That would be our own precioso Princessa. You see how she handled Hector no? She will give us a fine show. There is one special rule with that one. Her owner has asked that the man who beds her, share his treasure with us."

"No way," one man cried out, "if I get her I won't be letting everyone else have her."

"Yes," Cortez yelled, he raised his beer mug to the crowed. "I could careless who has her after I'm done."

"No, you misunderstand," Chuy said, "I mean you have to be man enough to let us watch you deflower that little dove," the man eyed the crowd. "Anyone who disagrees need not apply." He grinned. "The games will begin in one hour."

"Will they be drugged?"

"Oh no," Chuy said. "No, with this one the fight is half the fun."

"What about the red-head?" A man yelled, he looked like a college prep student. He and his three friends stuck out with their pale white skin. "Is she a virgin?"

Chuy shook his dark head, "No, but she can be just as wild in bed and they are both very young."

One man next to Nick rubbed his hands together. "After tonight they won't feel so young."

Nick wondered how these two had gotten into such a dire situation. For sure he wasn't going to be of any help to them. He couldn't get involved. He was a wanted man in these parts. He had been in Mexico more times then he cared to count. Just not this deep. If he were ever discovered there would be hell to pay, both from the law and his family. The day he left home, his father had let it be known that he was to be taken on sight and brought back to face his punishment.

Nick kept his eyes on his prey. He wouldn't be sidetracked. The girls were victims, but sometimes the innocent had to suffer, sometimes they just got in the way. There was nothing he could do, so he clenched his jaw against his self-ingrained principles, and his gaze hardened, as he turned his attention back to his reason for being here. He gave a mental shrug. *They might not even be the same girls, what were the chances?*

*****

Rachel past her tongue over her bruised and cracked lips. Only four days had gone by, and yet she felt like it had been an eternity. She had been poked, prodded and beaten. But no matter how hard she pushed them, they always managed to give pain without leaving a bruise. She wondered, not for the first time, if she and Bea would be alive by the time her father and brothers arrived. She had no doubt they were on their way, but would they be able to find them. They had been moved three times, and each place was nastier than the one before it. The only redeeming feature was that they needed her alive.

Whatever they had planned involved a living

breathing Rachel, and the only way they would get that was if Bea was in the same condition. Rachel refused to give them one inch. She fought them at every turn. And now she was afraid she was at the end of the journey. She was to be auctioned to the highest bidder, then used all night long.

She couldn't let that happen, anything but that. She scanned the darkness of what had to be a dressing room in the back of some theater. There were heavy purple drapes trimmed in gold tassels hanging from the ceiling, that pooled on the hard wood floors beneath her cold bare feet. It had a strange smell, like perfume, bees wax and sweat. There were spent candles in sconces with wax that dripped to the floor. And clothes littered the floor. The place was teamed with people, Rachel could hear the noise coming down the hallway and through the thin door of the room she was in. Fear for Bianca was the only thing keeping her in her seat. Already she had come up with a million ways to get out of here. But they had Bianca and she couldn't risk Bea getting hurt because of her own stupidity. Rachel glared down at the old woman who was roughly applying makeup to every part of her exposed body. Humiliated, she sat with her head held high, naked as the day she was born. Tears of shame pooled in her eyes, her lower lip began to tremble but she bit it hard. Instead of tears of pity she needed her anger. She needed it like she needed air to breathe.

"I wish you knew what I'm saying," she whispered to the old woman, but the woman never blinked. Rachel licked her dry lips; she couldn't take the chance. "Mi papa has tanto dinero; wealthy American. He will pay you well if you let me go." Still nothing. "Listen to me," she hissed, and took a frantic look around, "I can pay you, mucho dinero. Please Rosa por favor ¡socorro! My friend is sick, she needs her medicines. Rosa," against her will Rachel felt warm tears rolling down her cheeks as the woman applied red rogue to her areola. "Please don't let them do this to us."

Suddenly Rosa yelled. "Hector! Come here, this stupid bitch is crying, she is destroying my art work."

Rachel stiffened her spine, and cut off her tears as best she could, the door opened, and Hector walked towards her with what looked like a black leash in one hand, and whip in the other. Rachel cringed inside but she held his gaze and tried to stare him down.

"Well, well," he huffed, he was a big barrel of a man, and he smelled of greasy food. He was probably out of breath from just moving his bulk around, she thought scornfully. "Beautiful dove," he was saying. "I think I will ask Chuy to let me give you pleasure after the business part of tonight is done." He turned to Rosa and said. "Put her in the clothes Chuy gave you."

"Red or silver?"

"The red, bitch!"

Rachel was glad they would at least spare them some dignity and give them something to ware.

Rosa returned with a skimpy pair of sheer red pants and an equally sheer red top that billowed with the slightest breeze. Gold bangles were added to Rachel's wrists and ankles, and her hair was left down. And all she could do was let it happen. For the first time in her life she was glad her parents refused to let her cut the flowing mass of hair. It offered security and warmth, she almost cried thinking of home.

Her stomach dropped as her wrists were caught behind her back and tied together, but her feet were left free. Little red slippers were placed on them. She could've nearly swallowed her tongue when Hector hooked the leash to the collar around her neck.

"Ahora ramera de pequeño," Hector snarled close to her face. "Let's show the bidders how sweet you really are." Her eyes shot sparks at him, and she opened her mouth to give him a piece of her mind, but he cut her short by yanking on the leash, she stumbled against him. "You best remember, if you do anything. One wrong move and it's over for your little friend. She don't have no rich papa, she's just here to control you."

Rachel's stomach heaved at the smell of his breath, and she didn't stop it, she vomited all over him and herself.

"Why you little," he brought his fist down on the side of her head and all went black.

Dean King

Three

THE CROWD WAS GETTING ROWDY; Nick expected it to get real ugly very soon. With any luck it would give him the cover he needed to grab his prey and leave before the show could begin. His hopes were short lived, Chuy stepped on the stage, his grin just this side of sickening. He held up his fat hand. "Now, now, as you gentlemen know the bidding was supposed to start an hour ago but our prize had a little accident." Nick stiffened; his eyes became sharp as he scanned the area. He didn't want to think about what kind of accident.

Chuy clapped his hands once, and soft music started to play. "Aah, there is the signal we've been waiting for. Let's take a look at our first offering." A young Mexican woman was shoved onto the stage. Her long black pigtails covered her small breasts. If not for the smile on her face Nick would've felt sorry for her. She spread her thin arms and twirled teasing and taunting the rowdy men. She sashayed up and down the stage shaking her small bottom for the all to see.

Nick kept his face blank, but disgust rolled through him as the bidding picked up steam. After what seemed like hours of girl after girl prancing about offering their wares, Chuy motioned for silence.

"Now," he paused eyeing the crowd. "This next young lady is a prize. She has had the world's finest education."

"Who cares about that? Send her out," a man yelled.

With a flip of Chuy's head the man was removed from the room. Chuy cleared his throat. "This prize has culture and grace, the trapping of a real lady. She was raised to marry, and breed pure, but only a prince is worthy of her." Chuy laughed and shook his dark head. "How we came across such a treasure I will never know but we have her. In order to control her we must use our secret weapon." Chuy turned to the curtains. "Amigo's bring out the secret to controlling a tigress."

Nick straightened in his seat, his feet planted firmly on the floor. "What the hell?" he whispered, this was worst than he thought.

"This is our ace," the redhead struggled; her mouth was taped shut, her hands tied behind her head. "And what a lovely ace she is." She was stunning. Her pale skin glistened with a fine sheen of silver. She wore a sheer skirt that fell to her ankles and was lined with sparkling silver thread, the top was also sheer, leaving little to the imagination, and his heart stopped, every where he looked there was stunned silence. Her flaming hair danced about her in shimmering waves. Her big green eyes were wide with fear, and her long lashes were spiked with tears. It was the young girl he'd run into four days ago, he was sure of it. There was no way to deny it now. *How the hell did she fall into this hellhole?* Which led to another question. *Where is the other one?* Nick's insides froze as Chuy continued talking.

"Come Red," Chuy called her. The man behind her pushed her forward. Chuy grabbed her hands and cut the bounds, then he pulled the tape from her mouth and she winced in pain. "Take her and bind her to the pole."

"No," she whimpered, shaking her head. "No please." She cast those eyes on the crowd. "Somebody please help us!"

Chuy cupped her chin. "How prettily you beg, but lust rules this night. There is no help for you here. Do as you are told or your friend will die right here in front of you."

Nick growled under his breath, disbelief turned to anger as her head dropped, she nodded and allowed the man to pull her to the pole. Hector tied her hands above her head, and turned her to make sure she had a view of the stage. Nick knew what awaited the girl, he had no doubt her friend was either dead or about to walk out on that stage. Either way the night wouldn't end well for either of them, he also knew he couldn't let it happen.

"Now for the show," Chuy grinned, and clapped his hands once. "Bring out the Princess."

Nick held his breath as she emerged. He had held out hope that she had some how gotten away, but it had been in vain. His eyes were drawn to the open challenge on her lovely face. She glared at them all. There was no fear in this one. She would go down fighting. He felt a glint of admiration for her fighting spirit. He pulled off his hat and briefly ran his fingers through his too long shaggy hair, and his eyes traveled the length of her. Regal was the only word that came to his mind. Her chin was held high, her back straight, her nose was tossed in the air, contempt for her audience dripped from her. If she could've spat on them all he had a feeling she would've. She sparkled no matter which way she turned; every inch of her was covered in shimmering gold silk. Long black lashes never once fluttered as she saw her friend tied not ten feet from her. Her hair was piled high in a nest of curls and penned to her head. On her feet, barely visible under the gold confection she wore, were gold slippers.

"Now Princessa," Chuy was saying. "You will do as I say." His voice was deafening in the unusual quiet; even the musicians had stopped playing. Nick took a moment to look around, every mouth in the place was hanging open, he realized even he sat on the edge of his seat, quickly he put his hat back on and sat back folding his arms over his chest.

Her golden eyes were filled with scorn as her arms were released from the ropes. She briskly rubbed her wrists. "And if I don't?" Her voice rang out clear as crystal with the challenge.

Chuy lifted his hand and flicked it towards the red head. Hector raised the whip and slashed the tip of it across the girl's smooth bare stomach, they both stood stunned. A long thin red trail appeared on the girl's abdomen. Nick saw them look at each other. He clenched his teeth, the need to help them was about to force him into action. Then as he watched, the princess bent down and removed her shoe. Screaming, she ran at Hector, Chuy held up his hand preventing anyone from moving.

"You dirty, rotten bastard!" She screamed, beating the large man with the shoe. It seemed to have little effect on him. She must have realized she wasn't hurting him. Her eyes turned to golden bars, her hands clenched into fists and she stood tall, then rammed both fists at the same time into the sides of his throat, when he fell to his knees gagging and coughing, she drew back one fist and delivered a stunning blow to his bouncing Adam's apple. He fell like a ton of bricks. She twirled around to face her friend. Then she stiffened. There was another man standing next to the redhead, with a knife at her throat.

Chuy stood clapping. "Did I not tell you all, this one would be worth your money?" The audience clapped, and whistled. "Now Princess," he addressed the furious girl. "You will calm yourself."

"I will not!" Rachel shouted. "You have no right to do this to us!" She flung one arm out indicating to the audience. "Some of you men are Americans. For God sake act like it! Help us! My father…"

"Silencio!" Chuy grabbed a handful of her hair, but she rammed the heel of her shoe into his foot and he released her. She pulled away from him. "Kill Red slowly," he hissed staring into the girls' hard eyes.

"Noo!" She screamed, and ran towards her friend. "Please don't!" The girl stood between Chuy and her friend with her arms held out.

"Please Rach, let them kill me," Red begged. "I can't let them do this to you! Remember, I'm dead anyway."

"Shut the girl up," Chuy snapped. A thin line of blood ran down the redhead's neck. Nick stood up both hands on the butts of his guns. He wouldn't be able to take them all but maybe he could distract them long enough for the princess to grab the red head and get out of there.

"No wait," the Princess said. "I'll do whatever you want. I swear it."

"No! Don't do it!" The redhead screamed. "Let them kill me, please Rachel!"

"You said that before," Chuy snickered. "But you seem to like to do this the hard way."

"I said I'd do it."

"And what if I don't believe you?"

"You believe me." She challenged.

"Rach, listen to me, you can't do what he's asking. Please, think about the rest of you life. Think about what could happen to you."

The Princess turned to her friend. "Are you insane? Do you think we'll live past tonight?"

"You will, there has to be a way out of this for you."

"No, Bianca," The princess said. "You stop it! Your life is worth more than anything in this world to me. I won't let this scum take it. If we go, we go together."

"Is that so?" Chuy asked.

She nodded and tossed her head high. "I'll do what ever you want," then her eyes narrowed. "If you harm one more hair on her head all bets are off. You won't get any cooperation from me."

"You are in no position to bargain."

"Oh but I am," her lips lifted in a small sneer. "Your boss wants me alive, and without Bianca I'll kill myself, where would that leave you?"

Nick applauded her bravo, the girl had balls, and from the way Chuy's face drained of color he knew she had just pushed him too far. He lifted his hand and backhanded her, but she refused to grab her cheek or flinch.

"Let's get on with the show," Chuy yelled his eyes still on the glowering girl. "The princess will now disrobe for you. The bidding will start at thirty thousand dollars."

Rachel set her mind to what she had to do, then she looked at Bianca; the thin line of blood on her throat and stomach was frightening.

"Smile Princess, smile pretty for the bidders."

Rachel cut him a look that was meant to burn his

rotten soul. "You are a vile bastard, when I get out of this I'll slit your throat while you sleep." She promised Chuy through her brightest smile. She needed time to think. There had to be a way out of this. She spread her arms and let the material drape like wings around her, then she walked to one end of the stage and in one violent motion, she kicked off the one shoe she still wore. The men laughed when it hit one of them in the chest.

"Take off something," Chuy commanded, and even though it crushed her to do anything he wanted, she did it.

She stopped in the middle of the stage her mind working. Reaching up, she slowly removed the pens from her hair and let the mass tumble around her shoulders. Her stomach crunched at the catcalls that came from the room full of lechers. She felt hands at her shoulders but refused to flinch. She heard Bianca's whimper and made herself hold still as they disrobed her.

"Toss the pieces to the audience," the bids rose higher, and bile filled her throat. "See how god she smells?" Chuy laughed with the crowd. The screams of drunken male laughter and the giggling of girls made her want to throw up again but she held it in. She mustn't give up, she had to think positive, there had to be a way out. She just hadn't found it yet. She let the top fall from her shoulders to pool at her feet. Silence reigned, again. She tried to control her tears but then thought. *Why?* It made no difference, no one cared. Her tears only seem to drive them into a fury of excitement. The urge to cover herself was so strong she almost gave in until she heard Bianca sniffling behind her.

Nick tried to still the stirring of lust in his loins. They needed help, now wasn't the time for his body to betray him. But he was reminded of how long it had been since he'd held a bit of fluff in his arms. At that moment Cortez placed an eighty thousand dollar bid on the girl. And Nick tensed, he knew Cortez would kill the girl just for the fun of it. And from the looks of it, no one here would care.

His gaze went back to the stage, she stood with her arms high over her lovely head and her long golden legs swaying to the beat of the music, her body was sprinkled with gold dust and glittered in the spot light. She look like an angel cast down from heaven. Fresh tears ran down her caramel cheeks, but her face remained straight. He couldn't believe this was the same girl who had glanced so shyly at him at the gas station just days ago. The bidding had gone to one hundred thousand dollars.

"Dance for them Princess!" Chuy yelled, and Nick wanted to kill him. The girl had to be humiliated.

Slowly she began to move, her slender hips gyrating to the sensual music, her downcast eyes added to the allure of virtuousness.

"One hundred fifty thousand." Cortez snickered.

"One hundred eighty thousand." It was a voice Nick didn't recognize, but he couldn't let this go on.

"Two-hundred fifty thousand," Nick heard himself say and cursed under his breath, this wasn't going to help the girls. But it was the only way he could get close enough to help her.

Chuy perked up, "I hear two-hundred fifty thousand. Going once," No one answered the bid. "Going twice, sold to the man in the black hat."

Nick stood up and removed his hat.

Chuy grinned and wiped his hands on his already

stained shirt. "Cash?"

It was obvious Chuy didn't recognize him and that should've made him feel better.

This was one time when using his fathers name would surely help, but he tossed that idea aside. So many people hated his father that it might do more harm than good. Then again, they feared him enough to do anything for him. Nick walked up to the stage, the spurs on his boots jingling. "Check."

When he was close enough, Chuy said. "I remember requesting each bidder bring cash."

"I just stopped by, I wasn't really prepared for this but since my wife has been so frigid lately, I figured, why not."

"Hector, take him and verify the check is good," Chuy's eyes narrowed. "If it is not, kick him out. We will continue the bidding in five minutes."

"How about a credit card?" Nick offered.

The crowd laughed and Chuy shook his head. "You must really want this one. Why should I accept your plastic?"

"Because I'm paying more money than you ever thought you'd get. A credit card means instant money. You'd be a fool not to take it."

Chuy nodded to someone standing behind Nick. "Take him to the back, we'll wait."

Nick couldn't believe he was doing this, he had the money but this would eat up pretty much every dime he had and damn it, he had plans for that money. After his account was drained, they walked back to where the girl sat staring hard at him.

"It was bueno, Señor Chuy."

Chuy smiled, "I guess we have a winner. Come

and get your prize hombre."

"Princess," Nick called to her where she had been kneeling on the stage, and her head whipped around. "Pick up your robes. We're leaving."

"No, you can't," Chuy snapped and stepped in front of Nick. "Do not forget my rules."

"Fuck your rules," Nick growled, hoping his show of bravo would be enough to get them out of there. "I don't share my women. I believe I paid enough to have my privacy."

"You don't understand," Chuy was saying and Nick stiffened when he heard the sound of guns cocking. "The rules are the rules. Especially to strangers."

Nick looked around; there were three guns drawn, ready and aimed at him. Those he was sure he could take, but the other fifty or so men around them made his choices very limited. He cursed his rotten luck. "Look, I just want a quick lay not a god damned circus."

"Fine," Chuy said nodding. "Only my out of town guest will be allowed to watch."

"No," Nick growled but Chuy had turned away.

Chuy turned to the crowd. "If you are willing to pay six thousand American dollars you are invited to watch the princess' deflowering."

Seven men rushed to the stage.

Cursing under his breath, Nick went to the girl, he reached down and grabbed her arm, then pulled her to her feet.

"Please, you have to listen to me," she was saying, "This is wrong. I have a fiancé. He's waiting for me back home I can't go to him used."

"Why not?" Nick asked he tore his eyes from her trembling lips. "This is the twenty-first century most brides are not virgins when they marry."

"I don't care about most brides, I don't want to become a woman in the arms of a stranger," she snarled trying to pull away from him. "This is me, I live by my own rules. I'm asking you not to do this."

"And I'm telling you we have no choice," he growled into her up turned face. "They want a show. And if it means giving me a chance to save your damned life then that's what we are going to do." She stiffened and her eyes became hooded.

"What do you mean?"

"I mean, once we're done. I'll insist on staying the night with you, alone. Then I'll try to come up with a plan to get you out of here."

Hope blossomed bright in her eyes. "Oh my God thank you," then as quickly as it was there it was gone. "How do I know I can trust you? Why do we have to wait until we're done? What if after I cooperate with you, you leave me to the rest of those animals?"

"What other choice do you have?"

She shrugged, and her disheartened expression pulled at his heart. "You're right, but I won't leave without my sister."

He frowned, "The redhead?"

"Yes, I can't go without her."

"I can't get you both out," he shook his head, knowing it was impossible.

"Then you might as well leave me here," she crossed her arms over her chest. "Because, I'm not going without her."

"If I say you are, then you are," he snapped, not at all in the mood for this. "At least one of you will live."

"I won't," she pulled hard on the part of her arm

54

he held, catching him off guard, she turned and raced down the hall, only to run smack into a hard chest.

"Where do you think you are going?" She stumbled back, cringing at the disgusting leer on the man's face. She turned quickly to face her would be rescuer, he stood just where she'd left him, his arms folded over his chest watching her.

"I have to get out of here," she cried.

"I don't know about you," his voice came to her from where he propped himself up against the wall. "But if I were a woman I'd prefer one man over a hundred." He pushed off the wall and walked to her, then caught her around her waist. "Come on, let's get this over with."

She screamed and kicked, but he picked her up and tossed her over his shoulder as if she weighed nothing. "Be a good girl," Nick said. "You never know, you might just like it."

"Noooo," she wailed, trying desperately to free herself. "Pleaseee, stop!"

Nick closed his mind to the panic in her voice. He pushed the door open ever mindful of their audience, then tossed her on the bed. She fell in lovely disarray, but she didn't stay there. She was up and backed against the far wall staring at them all like an angry cat. Her eyes were shooting sparks, daring anyone to come near. Her chest heaved with every angry breath.

Nick stood near the door; there was a light tap on his shoulder. He flicked a look at the smaller man.

"Remember," Chuy said. "This is a show. Give the men what they paid for. So if she fights it is good, then she will use all her energy so the next man will be well satisfied."

Nick turned, he grabbed Chuy's loose shirt. "What

do you mean the next man? I bought her for the night."

"Oh no, I can't let you do that. This girl can make me mucho dinero esta noche. Besides, the girls were a loan, and the instructions were to make sure they were well used then returned."

"No," Nick said. "I'm drawing the line. She belongs to me. Tomorrow night you do what you want with her but tonight she's all mine."

"Amigo, I run this place. And you will do as I say, no?" The sleazy grin that crept across his face made Nick's skin crawl. "But I could change my mind, take your money then kill you and give her to someone else, who is to say you were even here?"

"Listen friend, I'm not an easy man to kill," Nick said with slow intent, his eyes were hard and unflinching. "You have the upper hand at the moment. But you don't want to fall into my lists of enemies."

Chuy paled under his sun darkened skin. "As you said I do have the upper hand." Suddenly he grinned. "Listen I am open to any suggestions. It is all about the money Señor, the girl will bring me much. I may not get another chance like this one."

"You've made plenty of money off me," Nick reasoned. "Why not give me a chance to enjoy what I've bought?"

"I wish I could, but…"

"But nothing, I paid, now you do your part."

"I tell you what," Chuy scratched his whiskered chin. "I will let you have your time, but only after the men have watched you deflower her."

"I need privacy." Nick insisted, "I won't share my…"

"It is for me to say what you will or will not do!"

"Fine," Nick said finally. "I'll accept your rule."

"You have no choice," Chuy turned to the eager group. "This way gentlemen, the room is small so we'll have to stand beside the wall. Everyone will have a good view." As Chuy gave the men their final instructions, Nick went to stand in front of the quivering girl who had plastered herself to a far wall.

"If it will make you feel any better, I'm not at all happy about this either." She let loose a wad of spit in the center of his dusty shirt. Nick looked down at it, then back at her. "I just wanted you to know I'll be as gentle as you allow." She bit her lip and looked away from him. "Listen to me," he caught her chin turning her towards him.

She pulled her chin away. "Don't you touch me! You keep your filthy hands to yourself."

"Listen woman, I'm trying to help you."

"Help me?" She sneered. "Help yourself is more like it. Look at you, what woman would want a man whose face she can't even see? Look at your clothes, and when was the last time you bathe?" Her voice choked on a sob. "I'm about to loose my self respect and you stand there saying you are helping me?" She threw her head back and gave a watery laugh. "I might as well..." her hand whipped out and snatched his gun from its holster. She held it with both hands and pressed the nozzle against his chest.

"What do you think you are doing?" Nick asked. If the situation weren't so grave he would've applauded her for getting the drop on him. But as it were, this was far from funny.

"I'm going to kill you," she hissed, her eyes intense. He stiffened, and his eyes narrowed. She had just enough fear and anger in her right now to do just that. "And as many of them as I can before I..." she motioned to the crowd behind him and he knew he had to take her off guard.

Nick let a slow grin ease to his lips. "Then what? You'll run out of bullets. Then they'll kill your friend, by the time they finish with you, you'll beg for death." The color drained from her cheeks, her eyes darted from him to her friend and then the men around them. "That's what they'll do you know." Nick continued, "Look over there in that corner," she looked around his shoulder. His hand whipped out and grabbed the gun pulling it from her startled grasp.

"I was going to give it to you anyway," she snapped, fury turning her face red.

"Everyone," Chuy said, with sadistic glee. "Take your places. Hector bring Red."

Bianca sniffled, wiping at her nose with her bound hands. "Please mister, don't do this."

"Red, I want you over here," Chuy stood at the end of the bed.

Bianca shook her head, "No, I won't," she planted her feet and refused to move.

"Si, you will," he hissed, "get over here."

"No," she brought her foot down on the heel of the man holding her and bit his hand. He screamed and she ducked under his arms and ran towards Rachel.

"Aarrugh!" Bianca screamed as she was yanked off her feet by a cruel grip on her hair.

"Do not disobey me again," Chuy's warm breath scorched her trembling cheek. "You I can do what I want."

#

"YOU ARE SICK, YOU asshole!" Bianca collected a wad of saliva and spit it at him but only succeeded in hitting his sleeve. It lodged there, slowly her defiant eyes rose to meet his amused gaze.

"Just for that the princesa will have to entertain every man in this room."

Her skin turned ashen. "No," she cried. "I did it, I spit on you. I'll take her place."

"I'm sure you would, but you are not worth as much to me as she is."

Chuy held her arms behind her back and forced her to stand in front of him at the foot of the bed. "Now," he scanned the eager men. "We are ready when ever you are Senor."

Nick hardened his heart to what he was about to do. She would hate him but she would be alive, that was what he would focus on. That and thinking of a way to get them out of here.

"Alright little darlin' it's time to get this over with."

Rachel thought she would die, her heart was beating so fast. In fact, she wanted to die, she wanted to make them so mad that they killed her but she had wanted that to happen before this defilement. Her gaze turned to Bianca. Her eyes were closed and her lips were moving in what was probably a silent prayer.

"Bea," Rachel said quietly. Bianca opened her eyes. "Together forever."

Bianca nodded and sniffled. "Together forever."

Nick recognized the tone in their voice. They were preparing to die together. While he admired their courage, he wasn't ready to let that happen. "Chuy, keep a tight grip on that one, I don't want any interruptions." The room erupted in laughter.

Rachel sighed in defeat, they had decided to die together a long time ago, if it came to that, which it looked more and more like it would. It was just sad that the moment wouldn't come before the moment of her humiliation.

Suddenly Rachel screamed as she was picked up and tossed to the bed. She landed on her back and before she could get herself together the man fell on her and settled himself between her thrashing legs. She lifted her hands and bared her nails like claws ready to rake his face, and then stilled as she looked into the same cobalt eyes she had seen days ago. She shivered with dread, and something she didn't understand. He grabbed both her hands and held them over her head, then his free hand began to travel her semi exposed body, the sheer material doing very little to shield her.

If anything it made her breasts tingle as his fingers manipulated the hard tips. Her breath was now harsh and hard to control, fear ran so high through her she couldn't think. The weight of his lower body pressed against her womanhood. And Rachel struggled to toss him off, she swallowed hard and tried to understand what was happening. She burned with a hate she never knew possible. Yet, her eyes threatened to close when his skillful lips teased her nipples until they begged for more. She closed her eyes against her body's betrayal and screamed high and long as she fought his movements. She raised her legs, kicking but it did no good. His big body forced her legs even wider apart and his coarse jeans were rubbing up and down her heated center and she wanted to grab him and make him move faster, harder anything to stop the bottomless spiral that was now in her stomach and traveling to her lower regions. *Why?* She wanted to scream. *Why is this happening to me?* Her fingers curled into claws, but he held her hands and she could do nothing, helplessness filled her and tears spilled from her eyes.

Rachel opened her eyes and stared into his. "I hate you."

"I can appreciate that," he nodded. "But your body wants mine just as much as mine wants yours."

"Why are you doing this?" She sobbed tears running down her cheeks. "Why can't you just do it and get it over with? Why shame me?"

He bent down just a bit and kissed her ear and she shivered, then his tongue lashed out, tickling the delicate shell and she nearly cried out as her body jerked with unwanted pleasure. He smelled so good, she almost purred against him. Then his voice intruded. "I have to get you wet and ready for me or this would be a thousand times worst for you Chica."

She turned her head away and ordered her hips to keep still; she wasn't supposed to feel this way. But as his lips made their way down her throat she felt a moan start deep in her stomach, and quickly squashed it. Then his strong hand was traveling over her body, and her skin burned everywhere he touched. She felt as if she were on fire and only he could put it out. Suddenly he lifted his lower half off her and she could hear the sound of his belt loosening and she froze, then the unmistakable sound of a zipper being pulled down. Fear came back full force and she pulled hard to free her hands, but he was too strong. Every time she tried to lift her legs to kick him, he just settled more deeply onto her.

Rachel tried not to look down, she was deathly afraid of the weapon he wheeled but she couldn't help it, her eyes drifted downward and an involuntary scream burst from her lips.

"No!" she cried. "Don't do this please." She sobbed fighting as hard as she could.

"I have to," he sighed, his forehead against her neck. "Do you think I want to do this?" he hissed. "Just like you, I have no choice."

When she lifted her legs to kick him off, he took full advantage of her openness and braced himself against her orifice and pushed. Rachel's eyes widened and she screamed at the top of her lungs, but he was kissing her neck, then her lips as she sobbed, her body shook, not from the pain, because most of that was gone, but from the humiliation of it all. She heard Bianca crying with her and that made it even worst.

"I hate you," she murmured through her tears. "I hate you, I hate you..."

"I know sweetheart," he said and he actually sounded like he meant it. "Look at me princess." She shook her head unable to answer him.

"Look at me Goddamn it!" He growled and her eyes flew to his face.

Rachel wanted to scratch his eyes out, but the look in them made her pause.

Forgive Me, My Love

"I'm so sorry," he whispered and she almost believed him, still she was unable to look away.

"Hold on princess, don't relax yet, I'm only part way inside you." Her eyes bulged as she looked at him through tear sparkled eyes. "Hold onto my shirt while I finish this."

Later she would be left to wonder why she did what he said, but as soon as he released her hands she grabbed his shirt and closed her eyes as his hips began to move. At first, the pain had started to come back and she whimpered, but then things changed as the movements of his hips turned slow and deliberate. Her body adjusted, and to her horror, began to accept his. Then his movements became more vigorous and demanding, she could feel the heat of him against her and she knew he had completed his goal, and her humiliation was absolute.

But her body began to tingle and burned with the heat he created. And all she could do was bury her face in his warm, strong neck. He wrapped her in his strong arms and soon she forgot the other people in the room, she was only aware of him, and what he was doing to her. He held her tight against is broad chest. Her hips rose all on their own to meet each thrust of his and the fullness of him made some crazy feeling inside her curl tight as a spring, then he took her lips in the first kiss since this started and she couldn't resist it. The taste of him was clean and fresh and it had her moaning as she rocked against him, then his movements became frantic and his kiss deepened and she fell into it, suddenly the bed was rocking and he had stiffened over her, his deep ragged groan flowing into her mouth. She opened her eyes to see his curly black head resting on her chin.

"Bravo," Chuy cried as the room erupted in

applause. "Now that my friend is worth the money."

"I'm next," one of the preppy boys stepped forward. "I always wanted a taste of dark meat."

Nick eased off her, her skin was a beautiful deep mocha, and Nick's eyes narrowed at the red marks decorating her neck and shoulders. His fury was so great he wanted to jump up and kick the crap out of every man in the room. Nick dropped a quick kiss on her shoulder. He wouldn't force her to look at him, the shaking of her shoulders told him all he needed to know. As he eased away, he closed her legs and pulled the sheet over her. She rolled to her side and curled into a ball. He put his clothes back together, then turned to Chuy.

Chuy had released her friend and now they sat hugging each other while they cried.

He felt like the worst kind of bastard. "You won't taste this girl, she's mine for the night." There was an outbreak of protest but Nick took Chuy aside.

"You know I can't let you have the girl Señor." Chuy was saying. "I need to make up the money I'm loosing here."

"You and I both know you have not lost any money. I've already paid you a king's ransom." Nick was about to play his last bargaining chip, and God help them if it didn't work. "How about I tell you how you can earn triple that amount?"

Chuy's blood shot brown eyes gleamed with greed. "If so I might let you have her."

Nick went on to tell Chuy about the bounty that was standing not four feet from them. Chuy nodded and scratched his chin as he contemplated the idea.

"I think you may have a deal. Mario, my brother, is going into Texas, he is to leave tomorrow. A citizen's arrest you say? America is so free with it's money, I think I will help myself to some of it."

Nick was so relieved he almost relaxed.

"You can have the girl for six hours only, then I have three others who are willing to pay and they have the money in hand."

It was more than he had hoped for. "Thanks, now get these people out of here."

"The red-head will be with me," Chuy was saying to one of his men. "Get her and follow me."

"Why can't I have them both?" Nick knew it wasn't going to happen but there was no harm in asking.

"You are too funny," Chuy said. "If anything happens to you this one will die, tell the princess to behave."

Nick ignored the sobbing girls as they were pulled apart and one dragged from the room. Soon the room became eerily quiet. He turned to find the girl sitting on the bed hugging herself with a vacant look in her golden eyes. He went to her, the moment he sat down she moved, rolling from the bed on the opposite side, she stood staring at him.

"Look we don't have much time," he said. "Chuy gave us six hours but it might be more like two, so we need to get out of here."

"What do you mean? I'm not going anywhere with you!" She snarled. "And where would we go? He'll kill Bianca if I leave. I can't!"

He rushed to her and put his hand over her mouth. "Shut up! Do you want them to come in here now and finish you off?"

"Why not," she cried and her eyes welled with tears. "Don't look at me. I might as well die! I'm nothing but trash now, dirty, soiled…"

He pulled her close and stroked her tangled hair. "You don't mean that," he felt her nodded against his shoulder. "What of your sister? We need to plan how we'll help her don't we?"

Slowly she lifted her head, then wiped at the tears on her cheeks. "I think I might know where they would have her."

"Where?" He left her and started moving around the room.

"It's me they want; she's just a means to make me do what they want." Rachel looked him over, he didn't look a whole lot like the man from the store, but she would remember that hair and those eyes. And he was so tall; the top of her head barely reached his shoulder. She wouldn't think about the things he made her feel, had in fact forced her to feel. "What are you doing?"

"I'm turning off the lights, just in case there are peep holes and such."

"Oh."

"Do you speak any Spanish?" he asked and she quickly shook her head. "It's just as well. If I can help it you two will be out of here soon and there would be no need."

*****

Nick sat in his truck with the motor running, staring at his childhood home. The fierce heat from the noon sun seared the skin of his forearm through the tinted windows of his quad cab pickup. It was still winter, but the rains hadn't started yet. And what little cold season they had hadn't put in an appearance. Still his feet refused to step towards that house. It's white washed walls were nearly blinding even from this distance. Only desperation could've brought him here of all places. Primal instinct had led him to the place of his birth, the place where his father had ordered the death of his mother. He had left with tears of self righteous anger burning in his eyes. He had been so sure he would show his father right from wrong. Nick laughed sourly. It was he who had learned the lesson. Life proved, there was evil and then there was greater evil. You pick which one you could stomach most and lived with it.

The rest of the world had demonstrated it was no better than his father; at least his father loved him. He clenched his teeth, anger still vibrated through him. Betrayal was something he couldn't handle. It was the worst thing in the world as far as he was concerned. At least his father was honest about what he did. He might be the lowest form of snake shit, but he was upright and up front about it. At lease with him he was.

Nick was still pissed at having spent two years in prison before he was paroled and then only because he said he didn't remember why he was there. Sometimes Nick wondered if maybe they knew who his father was, if maybe that was why he was allowed to live.

That was when he had become a bounty hunter, content to work out his anger on lawbreakers. That was something he could do something about, and earn a good living in the process. Some criminals met justice at the end of his shoulder-hugging guns; others actually made it to the courthouse. He didn't care any more.

And now he could count himself in the same league as the lowest vermin on earth. He turned and looked at the girl bundled so tight against her friend in the backseat of his truck. *Would she care that I did it to protect them? Probably not.* It didn't make him feel any better to know that he had done the only thing he could do. Now they would both have to live with the consequences.

He removed the black Stetson from his head and stared at the sweat-encrusted ring inside his favorite hat. Then he tossed the hat into the seat beside him, he was careful not to disturb the dog laying so peacefully on it. He looked into the back seat again, and sighed as the two battered women snuggled together in various pieces of his clothing. He reached down and pulled a blanket over them to hide them from sight. He needed a place to stash them for a few days, until he could get some money, after that he would take them back to Texas.

He turned to face the house. Getting them out of that hellhole had been brutal; he had killed six men and been grazed on the arm and not one word of thank you passed those girls lips. He lifted a tired hand and wiped the sweat from his forehead. The air conditioning had been turned off for only ten minutes and already he regretted it.

The rambling hacienda sat some twenty miles ahead of him, it had at one time been a haven for him and his three brothers. Buried deep in the heart of the Mexican mountains, Nick had been in love with Mexico, it was after all the only home he'd ever had. And now even after seeing most of the world he still thought there was no place like home, the closes he had ever come to feeling at home had been when he had lived in Texas.

He shook his head as sorrow rolled through him. At one time he had thought his parents were the proper English couple, but they had turned into... well, highly sophisticated criminals. He snorted, his family had always been criminals according to the stories his father told, proud drug dealers, cold-blooded killers, pirates and gun runners, all throughout history. And to this day no one had been able to stop them. His father had taught he and his brothers that crime does pay and you should do whatever you can to up hold the family legacy, without getting caught.

The day he had learned the real reason for his family being in Mexico was the day his childhood ended. He was ten years old. Life was harsh that year. It held lessons most kids couldn't understand and still others would never have to. The stars had been forcibly ripped from his eyes, and he saw the world as it was. Truth, justice, and honor, those were words that only applied to those rich enough to buy them. For the rest of the world you make do.

Nick jumped, there was a loud tapping on the glass of his truck window. An old Hispanic man stood staring at him, a large shotgun cradled in his arms. He motioned for Nick to roll down the window. He did, piercing the man with an intense look.

"Esto es la tierra de Dennison," the man snapped, his haggard face looked as if it were set in petrified wood. "¿Qué quieres?"

"I used to live here," Nick chuckled at the look on the man's weathered face. "Don't tell me it's been so long that you don't remember me old friend?" Nick pushed his hair from his face and smiled.

The man frowned deeply, then his face cleared and his dark lips split into a grin, his leathered face lightening. "What the hell?" The man clasped Nick's forearm through the opened window. "Dónde le tiene fue hombre?"

"Every where Miguel, I've been everywhere," Nick grinned. "¿Cómo estás?"

"Fine, fine, everything's fine," he paused, his lined face clouding. "Does you father know you are coming?"

"No, we need to talk," Nick sighed and looked at the house. "You know I didn't leave on very good terms."

"I know, I know but he loves you," Miguel cleared his throat. "He got in a new shipment."

Nick stiffened, his eyes shuttered. "What kind of shipment?"

"I'll tell you, but you know your Padre is just a business man. He is…"

"Just tell me Miguel," Nick sighed hard, knowing he wasn't going to like it.

"Is cocaine, girls, and…"

"Forget it, don't tell me," Nick closed his heart and ears. "I don't want to know. All I want is a place to lay low for a day or two."

"You will see your Papa no?"

"Yes, I'll see him. Is he here?"

"No, but he'll be back in a few hours. He will be happy to see you. You know Nicky," Miguel paused. "He is so proud of you, a lawman. He would always say how happy he was that one of his sons led a respectful life, poor but respectful."

Nick sighed, with a heavy heart, "I'm having second thoughts about my vocation."

"Well, this is the place to figure it all out."

"Is Tia Maria still here?"

"Si, she is in our casa out back."

"I'll see you later," Nick waved to the older man

and threw his truck into drive. As soon as he drove through the gate he felt suffocated, it was almost a trapped feeling. The house was surrounded by two foot thick white washed walls that were ten feet high. He drove around back and parked under a large tree draped in Spanish moss. It's twin sat in a courtyard in the middle of the house.

He left the motor on so the air conditioner would keep the girls and his dog cool. "You keep an eye on them for me old girl." Patting her head, he got out of the truck and hurried across the grounds to the small stucco home. He remembered Cara, Maria's daughter, crying until he thought she would be sick on the day he had left. He wondered how she was doing now. She had been a sweetheart as a child hopefully life had been good to her, but how that could be with her living here he didn't know. Maybe she had married and had children of her own and was happy.

He knocked lightly on the door and waited. He didn't want to think, not yet, not until he had those girls safely on a plane and headed for their home.

The door opened and a short round woman with long glossy black braids that were streaked with silver stood squinting up at him. "¿Te puedo ayudar?"

He grinned and took off his hat. "Tía Mía, I'm home."

Suddenly her eyes begin to sparkle and she grinned. "I tell you never call me Tía Mía you rascal!"

He laughed and scooped her up in his arms, then twirled her in circles until she laughed, her short arms circling his neck.

"I'm so happy you home little one! We feared you never come home." She laughed.

71

He set her on her feet and allowed her to drag him into her home; the cool darkness immediately eased him. This was home; he took a deep breath and smiled at the wonderful fragrance of the place, it was just as it had been when he'd left. This was where he had spent a good many years of his life.

"What have you been doing, de Jefe tells me you are a law man. That you have a great career and you have become a big man in your town."

"No no," he laughed. "I'm just a small fish in a big pond."

"But he say you getting to make very big name for youself."

"That might have been true for a while but things change." Nick shook himself, he didn't have time to socialize he had urgent this to attend to. "Tía, I need your help."

"Anything you need nacido," her wide curious eyes held his when he hesitated. "¿Qué quieres niño?"

"I have two young girls with me, I took them from Chuy's Cantina."

Her hand flew to cover her mouth as she let out a gasp. "Are they hurt," she lifted her hand and banged her forehead with her open palm. "How stupid, that was a loco question. If they were there I'm sure they need my care, where are they?"

"Asleep in my truck, they are American. They don't speak Spanish so please if you have anything important to say, say it to me not them."

"But why nacido?" she frowned. "They must be so very afraid why make it worst?"

"That's just it, I don't want them to get upset by anything they hear. Speak to them as little as possible, they don't need to know where they are."

Suddenly her brow cleared. "You don't what them to know this is you home?"

"This isn't my home," he snapped and immediately stopped at the look on her much loved face. "I'm sorry Tía, you're right but only because where I stand now is my only home."

Her face softened and she reached up to caress his bearded cheek. "You do not know how lost we have all been without you niño. Even your father has been worst than usual. Roberto is here."

"My brother is home? When did he come back?"

"De Jefe did a little pushing, and well," she shrugged her small shoulders. "He had to come home."

"I'm not going to say what I'm thinking, I just need to get through the next few days." Nick looked around. "Is Cara here?"

"No." Her voice didn't invite questions.

Nick didn't push it. "You said Robert is here?"

"Si, he came home three days ago and there is word that Tony and Blake are also on their way here, that is where *de Jefe* is going, to pick them up from the airport."

His heart gave an uneasy jump this couldn't be good. "Do you know what's going on?"

She shrugged her small shoulders. "I am not knowing this."

Nick didn't want to face everyone at the same time. Whatever they were planning he didn't want to be apart of it. "Change of plans. Could you get me some clothing? I'll take them to a hotel let them clean up there. Then I'll come back."

"No Nicky, please don't do this. I know you will

not come back. Stay here, it's been so long."

"I can't stay, something's going on, and these girls are soft, they are innocent and you know what happens to an innocent around here. I have to get them out of here."

"You are right," she grabbed his sleeve. "But please say hello to your Papa. If you make peace it might go easier for the rest of us."

"Has it been that hard?" His hand covered hers in a gentle caress.

Her eyes began to water. "You don't know how hard."

"Alright Tía, I'll stay, but just for one night. I'll try to make peace, then we'll leave."

"Thank you, thank you my boy."

"Come, help me get them."

"Oh," she paused, "I don't have room. Bonita is here with her dim-witted husband."

"She got married?" Nick smiled. "When I left she was still running around like one of the boys riding bulls and feeding the hogs."

"Yes, she married one of the ranch hands four years ago."

"I'll have to congratulate her. But I can't take the girls to the big house. I don't want them to get involved with whatever is happening in there."

She was thoughtful for a moment then smiled. "I know the perfect place. They will be safe, come on."

Nick opened the truck door as quietly as he could. "Julie, come here girl." The big German Shepard jumped onto the flagstone; tail wagging she stood by his side waiting. "Tía, this is Julie, she's been with me for eight years."

"Oh Nick, she is beautiful, you always did like

dogs." Her eyes turned glossy and he looked away. "You don't know how much we have all missed you."

He reached into the truck. "Red," he whispered softly trying not to awaken the other one. "Red, look at me."

Her head lifted and she brushed her flaming red hair out of her still swollen face, and dull green eyes slowly focused on him. He knew she was fully awake when she stiffened and pulled back from him. He motioned with his finger for her to keep silent. She nodded and blinked then took a hesitant look around.

"This lady's name is Maria, she'll get you two cleaned up and into some clothes. Then, after a good nights sleep, I'll take both of you to the airport and put you on a plane home." He turned away when her lower lip started tremble to and her emerald eyes turned bright with tears. "Look we don't have time for tears. Suck it up and come on." He knew he sounded harsh, but it had the desired affect. She straightened and her eyes cleared. "Don't move yet, I want your friend to sleep as long as she can. I'm taking you both upstairs." Nick ignored Maria who stood next to him with a look of displeasure stamped on her face.

Red nodded and gently untangled herself from her friend. Nick reached inside and as gently as possible, he scooped up the Tigress as he labeled her and cradled her close to his chest. "Alright Tía, lead the way." He said in Spanish.

Maria helped Bianca out of the truck and held onto her arm as the girl stumbled. Raw, red knuckled hands clutched the shirt she wore in one fist, while the other hand held onto Maria. Nick nodded in admiration, these girls maybe pampered princesses' but they knew how to hold their own in a fight.

"Sígueme," they walked across the flagstone walkway and through the arched wooden doors, the stout heel of his boots hitting against the limestone floor. The white stucco walls gave the interior a cool relaxing feel, for years coming home had been the farthest thing from his mind. And now he knew why, the instant he entered the house his body tensed, and his heart started to race, it was all he could do not to turn around and run for the nearest exit. The girl in his arms whimpered and he realized he held her too tight, he loosened his hold and concentrated on getting this night over with.

"Here, in here hurry."

He walked into the room and froze. "These are..." he looked at Maria.

"Si," she knew what he was thinking, in Spanish, she said. "Your Mother's rooms have been kept clean all these years, but de Jefe never steps a foot inside these doors. They will be safe here."

Nick inhaled deeply to cut off any emotion that would've taken him back to the child he had been, sneaking in here and sleeping in his mothers arms. But that was before she had become hooked on the drugs his father sold. He walked to the bed and lay his burden down, careful not to wake her.

"There is a restroom back there through the sitting room, use it. Maria will get clothing for you two and bring you food. Wash, get some sleep and in the morning we'll leave."

"I shouldn't be thanking you, after what happened."

"Save it!" He snapped.

"Did you have to kill them?" Red asked and Nick

bristled at the accusation in her tone.

"No," he said causally. "I could've let them keep the two of you and let you die after being used by hundreds of men. Thanks to my act of heroism I am now flat broke, almost penniless! All because I don't know how to mind my own business. So no, you don't need to thank me."

Her color, already shallow, blanched even more. "I understand, thank you. I'm sorry I..."

"Just be ready at four a.m." He left them to Maria's clucking and tender care.

Nick went further down the hall to his old room, opening the door he realized it had been preserved just as his mothers had been. Well tended and cleaned as if he was expected at any moment. He tossed his rucksack on the bed and went to the bathroom. He needed a bath in the worst way. He glanced into the mirror above the sink and grimaced. No wonder that girl put up such a fight with him on top of her. He looked like he had come straight from the pits of Hell. He took out his shaving kit and scissors; if he were going to face the dragon he had better make himself presentable.

RACHEL WAS SLOWLY BECOMING aware of her surroundings. She didn't want to wake up but she knew she had to. She was sure their rescuer was dead, he couldn't survive so many guns. Tears crept into her eyes and she shook her head as the memory of their escape came back to her.

The man yanked on her arm pulling her onto the ledge of the two-story building. As scared as she was she wasn't willing to stay in that room alone. Plastering herself against the rough wall she silently thanked him for the loan of his shirt. Being on the ledge was one thing but being naked on the ledge was a different story.

"Jump!" He hissed, and she didn't think twice. Taking a deep breath she jumped and landed hard on the ground, dust rose up and choked her, she rolled to her side then jumped to her feet and ran to the side of the house where she pressed herself tight against it. Rather than wait for him, she took off in the direction she knew Bianca was being held.

"Hey," his voice came in a low growl from behind her. "Where do you think you're going? Come back here," she heard him curse as she continued on, the rocks were cutting into her bare feet and she wanted to scream in pain.

Soon he caught up to her, "Woman!"

"Just shut up," she hissed. "Give me a weapon," she ignored his raised eyebrows and held out her hand.

"Why so you can kill me as soon as I turn my back."

"No," she snapped. "I'll save that for later, right now I need you."

"I need you to get to my truck and stay out of my way."

"No," she hissed. "I'm going with you. She's sick, she'll need me."

"You keep saying that, what's wrong with her."

"None of your business!" Rachel murmured. "Now give me a weapon, preferably a knife."

"I guess I don't have to ask if you can use it."

"I've never used one before but the way I'm feeling right now I could slit the throat of any man who crosses my path."

"That's what I'm afraid of," he snarled and she ignored it. "Lead the way and no, you are not getting a weapon."

They crept around the back of the building, careful to keep to the shadows. It was dark, the only thing they could see besides flat dusty land, maybe a few shrubs here and there, and that was limited by the small amount of light coming from the only light pole in the area. It was enough to see three men standing at the entrance of the cantina, all heavily loaded with weapons. They stood snickering and talking about what fun they would have when their turn came with the red head and Rachel's stomach turned, her skin became cold with sweat and she fought the need to rush in and kill them all.

"How are we going to get in?" As soon as the words were out of her mouth, the men were falling to the ground with a stunned look of disbelief on their faces, one clutching at his chest, the other two had blank looks as a dark stain appeared in the center of their foreheads. She looked at the man with her and was astonished to see a smoking gun with a silencer on it.

"Which way?" he asked, as if nothing had happened. For a moment she remembered she was afraid of him.

Rachel swallowed and blinked; she got up and ran to the cantina. Then posting up on the side of the cantina she took big steps away, and started counting. "There's a hole," she threw over her shoulder to him. "It's a hundred feet from the cantina, that's where they kept us." As she neared the spot, she fell to her hands and knees and began dusting off the area, soon her hand hit a latch. "Here," she whispered. "I found it."

He stood thoughtful for a moment, and then nodded. "This is what we're going to do. I don't know how many of them are in there but we need to bring them all out. When we do the whole cantina might hear us and fall right on top of us. I need you to be ready to run in there and grab your friend and start running in that direction," he pointed north towards the trees and the rocks beyond. She nodded.

"You ready?" She swallowed hard and nodded, her eyes wide. "Stay back, when I lift this lid they should all come running out."

Rachel was scared but not for herself, she was afraid for Bianca, what if they had already. *No.* She had to concentrate.

He yanked back on the lid throwing it open. "Prender fuego a algo e! Salir corriendo!" He yelled, and she smiled, yelling fire always worked. "¡vamos!,

¡venga!" Suddenly the air exploded as men came running from the hole and he picked them off one by one. The last one to emerge was dragging Bianca by her arm as she fought him.

Rachel screamed and ran forward, the man turned and she stopped in her tracks, she sucked in her breath as he raised his gun and fired. The sound echoed through the dark night as she waited for the searing pain to hit. Instead, he clutched his stomach and fell to his knees. Bianca shook lose of him and ran to Rachel.

"Now, you two," the man hissed. "Run!" They needed no second warning as they took off into the vast darkness. They ran hard and fast, fearful of the gunshots that rang out behind them, and then suddenly all had gone black.

"Rachel," she heard Bianca's soft voice and sniffles. "Come on Rachel you have to wake up."

Rachel opened her eyes and pulled herself into a sitting position, a smile eased onto her lips at the sight of Bianca. Other than a black eye and purple bruised lips, she looked fine. Her hair looked freshly washed and she wore a flowing white lace shirt tucked inside a pair of blue jeans that looked like Capri's pants, they were so short. "Wow, you look good."

"You will too once we get you in the tub," Rachel flushed darkly. "Come on, the water is hot and I picked out something for you to ware."

"Where are we, and how did we get here?" Rachel asked looking around at the beautiful room.

"That man brought us here."

"What man?" Rachel looked at Bianca's reddening face. "You mean the one who…"

"Yes," Bianca helped Rachel stand up and led her

into the bathroom. "You fell when we were running and hit your head on a rock. He found us and carried you to his truck." Rachel looked into the mirror and cringed, she looked like a psycho clown. Make up and bruises decorated her chocolate skin. A big red goose egg rested on the upper right corner of her forehead, she reached up and touched it then flinched, it was still painful.

"Where is our Hero?" Rachel was unbelievably happy that he'd made it out alive, but she was still angry with him, and tried to keep the tartness from her voice but couldn't.

"You have every right to be upset Rach," Bianca was saying as she got out towels and soap. "He's not here, I don't know where he went but he did say he would take us to the airport in the morning and give us safe passage home."

Rachel turned to stare at Bianca. "He said that?"

"Yes," Bianca sighed. "I believe him Rach."

"I don't!" Rachel snapped and began removing her clothes with angry, jerking movements. She took the towel Bianca handed her.

"He helped us as best he could. I think what he did was the only way out of this for us."

"He didn't do it to you!" Rachel fought it but the tears that were always there waiting to weaken her resolve took hold. Bianca was at her side in a heartbeat, taking her into her arms. "Richard won't want me now."

"I'm so sorry Rach," she cried. "I would've given anything to have taken your place."

Rachel got control of herself, and straightened. "What about you Bea, they had you down there for a while. Are you okay?"

Bianca let her go and walked away. "They were

playing some kind of game to see who would go first. By the time you two showed up they had gotten in line but that was as far as it went."

"Oh, thank God!" Rachel sighed. "I thought we might have been too late."

"No,"

"Oh, Senorita," Maria exclaimed as she came into the bathroom. "You are awake." Her eyes saddened as she took in Rachel's battered form and Rachel fought not to look away.

Bianca stepped between them. "Rach this is Maria she is helping us while we are here. She's sweet, you'll like her." Rachel's eyes flew from one to the other. "She helped me, she's really nice." Still, Rachel didn't move, she clutched the towel around her tighter. Bianca's eyes darkened, "Don't you trust me Rach?"

The pain in her voice was too much to ignore. Rachel swallowed hard and forced a tight laugh. "Of course I trust you Bea. I'm sorry Ma'am, it's just that so much has happened that my head is spinning."

"You poor Chica, come let me help you," Rachel glanced at Bianca, who nodded, and she went with Maria.

*****

Nick made sure his bag was packed and ready. One last tug on his long sleeve black shirt, he brushed at his blue jeans then adjusted his knife, it was snuggly attached to his belt behind him, while it's twin lay safe in his bag, then he headed downstairs. It was six p.m.; he had to go check on the girls. With any luck they should be well fed and fast asleep. They needed it, shit he did too but he needed to see his family first. Those few hours of the catnap he'd took would just have to do.

He hurried down the hallway and knocked quickly on their door, and then hurried inside.

"What are you doing in here?" He cringed at the sharp irritation in that feminine voice.

"I came to make sure you two were doing well," he let out a slow whistle as he took in their outfits. "I can see you've made yourselves at home." He leaned back against the door and stared at them. Both girls were tall and slender, but Red had cute brown freckles across the bridge of her sharp nose. Her long red-gold hair was freshly washed, and hung around her slim shoulders in big bouncing curls. Like the Tigress, she wore faded blue jeans that hung loosely around her thin hips and were just a tad bit too short, the white shirt was pretty, delicate lace trimmed the collar and the sleeves that were also too short. She looked like an over grown child.

His Tigress on the other hand was bursting out of her clothes, her bosom was only a handful but they seemed too much for the white shirt, the jeans were over lapped around her tiny waist and held in place by a belt. She looked just like a kid. A beautiful, enticing well developed child. Her thick black hair hung in wet waves down around her shoulders to the center of her slender back. Her slanted honey brown eyes never missed a thing and right now they were on him something fierce.

Rachel wasn't surprised by her violent reaction to the sight of him. Her stomach churned and she fought the urge to look away. She wanted to be repulsed, to hate him for what he had done, and she convinced herself that she did. It didn't matter that he was attractive; she resented his fine good looks. He had no right to be beautiful, rapists were supposed to be hideous creatures that preyed upon innocent women. Monsters that stole your soul and made you live in fear the rest of your life. But there he stood and her blood surged with the need to…to…well, the need to kill him. That was it, she wanted to rip out his soul stealing eyes and bury his hard body in the deepest darkest woods.

She hoped he could read the hate in her eyes as they raked over him. He had broad shoulders that were encased in a long sleeve black shirt, it was neatly tucked into trim fitting blue jeans. Yes, he looked good, but then her eyes found his face and she swallowed hard. He was so beautiful; there was just no way around it. Striking, stunning, and oh God those eyes, breathtaking, God could've been kinder to women and given this creep a scar or maybe a big hooked nose, or perhaps brown eyes. No, brown eyes would just make him more sultry possibly mysterious, therefore more deadly to female hearts. His hair was pitch black, it flowed in large loose ringlets at the back of his neck and hugged his temples in the front. Long black lashes curled over what could only be labeled bedroom eyes, and this man had taken her virginity. That thought stopped her cold.

"What the hell do you want? Haven't you taken enough?"

"Rachel!" Bianca cried. "Stop that. He saved our lives!"

Rachel hurried away to stand next to the wall and look out the window, her arms crossed over her chest. She wanted him to go away. He made her think and feel crazy things, things she didn't want to feel. Gratitude wasn't something she was prepared to give him right now.

"Hi, my name is Bianca," Rachel wanted to strangle Bianca for giving her real name. "And this is…"

"No!" Rachel snapped turning towards them.

"What are you doing?" She yelled at Bianca. "Why don't you give him our shoe size and blood type while you're at it?"

"Stop it Rachel!"

Rachel banged her head with the flat of her hand and turned away. "You've done it now! Why can't you just keep quiet Bianca?"

"There is no harm in telling the man who saved our lives what our names are. If anything you should be over here thanking him."

Rachel turned to stare at Bianca but she caught sight of his grinning face over her shoulder. "Thank him for what Bea? What do I have to thank him for?"

Bianca hurried to Rachel's side. "I know what he did was terrible Rach," she whispered. "But if he hadn't, where would we be right now?"

Rachel flushed and looked at the floor. "But you didn't have his hands on you, Bea and in front of all those people. He raped me and you all saw it."

Bianca caught Rachel's face between her hands and kissed her cheek. "I know honey and I suffered with you."

"You can't imagine this," Rachel cried softly and hugged herself as the memory of it came rushing back. The problem was, it wasn't that horrible. The memory of her body's betrayal and all the things he made her feel. Forced her to feel, was the problem.

"Rach, if not for what you did with him we would be dead right now. Don't you think we should thank him?"

"You're right," Rachel conceded. "But I just can't bring myself to do it just yet. I will when we get on the plane." They jumped at the sound of the door closing.

Forgive Me, My Love

Nick walked down the massive staircase that brought him into the foyer. The muted light from the sun was coming in from the many stain glass windows to bathe everything in a rosy glow of a kaleidoscope of colors. It looked more like a place of sanctuary rather then the den of horrors he knew it to be. He turned and went down the hall and into his fathers study, sitting in his father's chair he got comfortable, it would probably be a while before his father and brothers came in.

He let his mind slip to the Tigress. She was a beauty, pure and astonishingly spectacular. What he had done last night had been to save them but it was the best money he had ever spent. Even in that environment she had been wickedly wild, and deliciously timid all at the same time. At the time he could've sworn she had forgotten they were in a room full of people, he knew he had. From the moment he entered her sweet body to the very end nothing had existed but her and he had lost himself in her sweetness. His last thought before he drifted off into a light sleep, was of deep chocolate eyes, long sensual eyelashes and imploring pouting lips.

Nick snapped awake at the sound of voices raised in laughter. He straightened then blinked hard as bright light flooded the room and the laughter stopped.

He stood up and waited; uncertain of the reception he would receive.

"Dominick!" The happiness in his father's voice put him at ease, and the warm hug that he had never in his life experienced from this particular person thrilled him. He let his arms fold around the older man.

"Hola Papá," he said and his father pulled back, his blue eyes suspiciously shining.

"My son, my son," he caught Nick's lean cheeks

87

in his hands and squeezed shaking him. "You're home! Look, see Robert I told you he would come home."

Nick looked past his fathers beaming face to see his brothers standing as if in shock.

"Come here," Henry growled to them, and Nick wished he hadn't made them. It would've been nice if they came to him with open arms. "Say hello to your little brother fools."

They each came forward and Nick could feel the tension emitting from them.

"Hello Nick," Blake was saying, his cocky little grin giving Nick some ease. At least this one seemed happy to see him. "It's been a while big brother."

"You've grown." Nick hugged him close, and then patted his back. "Not that I doubted it, but you filled out nicely." Blake gave a full-blown grin and stepped back.

"What are you doing here?" Tony snapped, and received the backhand of his father across his left cheek. Tony turned and stalked from the room.

"Pay him no mind," Henry was saying. "He has always been too hot headed for my taste."

"Papá don't hog him," Robert yelled, coming forward. "I want to see the man this little one has become."

Henry stepped aside and Robert grinned into Nick's eyes. "Look at you! No longer the little one uh? You are taller than me, what are you six three, six four?"

"Six-three."

"Damn, I knew you would become a big one. When you were born you had such big hands, and those feet were almost longer then mine, and I was eight." He turned to Henry. "Didn't I tell you Papá? Come give me a hug pup."

Forgive Me, My Love

Nick hugged him, feeling relieved, this meeting was going better than he had hoped. "How are you Robert?"

"I'm fine! How is the police work? Do you like it? We have newspaper clippings of your success. You were becoming a big shot in Texas no?"

"I don't do that any more," Nick said quietly and looked at his father. There was something in the looks that past between his father and his brothers that gave him pause. It was as if they already knew.

Henry stepped forward. "What is this? Why not, what happened?" But his tone lacked sincerity and Nick wondered how much they knew.

"Let's just say life isn't what is seemed on either sides of the law. I had to learn that the hard way."

"So you are ready to forgive your father his supposed crimes?" Henry said with a grinning slap on Nicks back.

"I need some time on that one. Some of the things that happened here I can never forgive or forget. But I have learned more about what motivates people and that things are never just black and white."

Henry hugged him close and patted his back. "Tell me who I must deal with to get your job back."

"No Dad," Nick sighed, he didn't know whether to be touched or frightened by that remark. "Look, I'm leaving in the morning. I just stopped in to see you."

"No you must stay," Henry yelled. "You can't show up and give me hope, then leave. I may never see you again."

"I have to go."

"I need you here," Henry sighed, and for once he seemed older than his years. "Come everyone sit down."

89

They did as instructed. "The reason I have ordered you to come is because there is probably trouble coming. It has been almost a week and nothing has happened so maybe I am just jumping at shadows. But I believe in being safe, I want all my sons with me when this happens."

"What happened? Why do you think there will be trouble?" Robert asked.

"A business deal went bad. I haven't heard from Mario my spy, but that could mean anything."

"And it could mean nothing," Blake snorted. "You have been very jumpy lately."

"Those shadows could leap out of the dark and cut your throat when you least expect it."

"I'd like to stay," Nick said. "But I have a meeting I can't miss. I need to be on the first flight in the morning."

"Where you headed for?" Blake asked.

"Family comes first Dominick! You haven't figured that out yet?" Henry snapped. "You must stay."

"I can't, any other time I would…" Nick froze as a high-pitched scream vibrated through the hallways. He was up and running, he crashed through the doors and down the hall then froze.

Tony stood holding the arms of the struggling women. "What the hell is this?" He yelled and tossed the girls to the floor.

Nick didn't move. "They're friends of mine. I'm taking them to Texas with me."

"Then why hide them in Mother's room? I saw Maria sneaking out of there and then I heard these two talking. What the fuck is wrong with you?"

Henry stepped forward as the girls stood up, their faces white as sheets they stared at him. Nick felt the skin on the beck of his neck prickle. Something in the way they stared unable to utter a word shook him. He looked at Henry, his eyes were wide, then they hardened when they turned to Nick.

"You couldn't leave the cop behind could you?"

"What are you talking about?"

"Robert grab the girls. Tony, Blake strip him, look for any wires and cameras, anything he might have on him to incriminate us."

"What the hell," Nick yelled, but he held still letting them take off all his clothes. "What the hell are you doing?"

"I want to see where you hid the wires. I can't tell you how hurt I am at your weak attempt to frame me."

"Frame you?" Nick was confused. "For what?"

"You bastard!" The tigress was yelling at him. "How could you bring us back here?" She screamed. "Why not just kill us and let it be over with!" What she was saying registered in his mind. He looked at Henry.

"You stole these girls?" Nick couldn't hide the disbelief in his voice.

"Don't act as if you didn't know," Henry growled.

"Maybe he didn't," Robert suggested. "Look at his face; do you think he'd have come, if he knew what was going on?"

"Maybe you're right," Henry conceded. "Put your clothes on."

Nick was at a lost, he felt like the worst kind of fool. His father had kidnapped these girls and sold them to Chuy and he had brought them right back into harms way. "What have you done Henry?"

"Take them to the third floor."

Suddenly the glass above their heads shattered and

a bullet lodged itself in the wall opposite them. Chaos insued.

"Get out here Henry!" A voice yelled out of the darkness.

"Take the girls up stairs," Henry hissed. "The rest of you get your guns and turn off all the lights."

Six

SIMON KNEW A SENSE OF DREAD, it pulled deep in his guts. He and his brothers Tyrell and Ryan stood in the study of his fathers home, each deep in thought. It was a solemn group John, their father walked in on and he quickly closed the door. He moved past them and dropped into his chair.

"Boys take a seat," they did, each staring at him and waiting. He cleared his throat. "You boys know Henry Dennison?" They nodded. "Over the pass few years I've had dealing with him. I know he isn't the best person I could've picked to do business with but I was desperate. You didn't know this, but five years ago I was a hairs breath away from bankruptcy. I needed a quick injection of cash and he was there. Well, I have more than paid him back over the years and yet he still tries to keep his hand in my affairs. I had thought over the last year that I'd gotten rid of him, then he called. He needed help getting a shipment of pottery into the States, it was all legal but he needed some one over here to pick them up and take them to his warehouse."

"Dad," Tyrell was shaking his clean-cut head. "Tell me you didn't help him."

Simon looked at his father, his coffee eyes bleak. "If he hadn't there would be no need for us to be here." He waved John on. "Continue."

John nodded his face grim. "I thought fine, but this is the last time. We signed an agreement that cut all my ties to him and his company."

"Did you ever dapple in his chief export?" Simon asked his voice a low angry growl.

"Do I look insane to you?" John shouted. "No, I had nothing to do with his drugs." He exhaled loudly, and put his elbow on the desk and dropped his forehead into it. "What I didn't know was Henry had two papers, one on top the other. When I signed the first one it went through onto the other document."

"You know Henry is a snake, why didn't you let your lawyer or one of us look at it first?" Simon snapped.

"What is this about?" Ryan growled. "Simon, you act like you know the most, let me in on it."

"Shut up Ryan and just listen," Simon snapped, and Ryan fell back into his seat with a fierce frown on his rebellious young face.

"Oh God!" Tyrell moaned. "What did the document say?"

"Basically, it said I was accepting full responsibility for a shipment of diamonds. Not a lot, just twenty million dollars worth."

"Let me guess," Simon drawled. "The shipment got lost."

"Yes," John nodded.

"So why don't you tell him to go fuck himself?"

"I did," John lifted his head and speared them all. "Henry has your sister and Bianca."

Simon cursed under his breath and looked away. Tyrell just stared.

"What do you mean he has them?" Ryan wanted to know. "Is he holding them hostage?"

"That and so much more," John breathe, his voice soft with torment. "They plan to use the girls physically until they get the money."

Simon jumped from his seat and rushed to the door.

"Simon!" John jumped up. "Where are you going?"

He stopped but kept his back to them, reaching out he braced his hand against the door jam and tried to collect himself. Taking a shuddering breath, he turned to stare at them. "I'm going to get the girls back. If you three want to come you had better hurry. I'm leaving in two hours." With that he was gone.

*****

A mile and a half from Henry's hacienda, Simon calmed himself and controlled his erratic breathing. He stared into the darkening sky, the sun had just gone down, but the moon had yet to rise, and the darkness was complete. This had been the longest day of his life. It had taken them two days to get everything and everyone together, and then they had to bribe the guards at the boarder so they would be able to carry all their weapons into the country. He took a deep breath and closed his eyes for a moment. Rachel and Bea had been in there for one solid week, and there was no telling what condition the girls were in, but now wasn't the time to think of it, he could do that later, after he had killed everyone of those bastards who dared touch a hair on the girls' heads.

It was dark enough to see inside the well-lit hacienda, with high powered binoculars. The stained glass windows helped, he could watch every move. He looked at his father and Tyrell, both were breathing hard, they looked like they were about to faint. But Ryan was right beside him, ready to take on anything and everyone. Simon hadn't wanted to bring John and Tyrell but what choice did he have? He needed someone the girls trusted to take care of them while he killed every bastard that had done this to them.

He tried not to think about what the girls might have endured. He had seen women after they had been used and abused, raped by gorilla troops as they pillaged each and every village in Honduras and again in Africa. Bile rose in his throat and burned his stomach. He coughed and spit it out. But the turning wouldn't stop, visions of his sister and Bea dying such a horrible death wouldn't let him go. He couldn't forgive himself for not being there to protect them. He shook his head and took a drink of water. He sighed as his thoughts stayed on the girls. Rachel was the sparkle in his eyes, she made his life fun, every since she was born she had held the hand of her oldest brother and had never let it go. She had faith in him, when no one else had; she had trusted him, in his blackest moments. Now this, in the darkest time in her life, he hadn't been there for her.

Suddenly bright laughing green eyes flashed in front of him and he flinched. His heart actually shuddered and he couldn't bring himself to think of Bianca. Sweet, teasing Bianca who had already had more pain in her short life than anyone should. Yet she continued to fight, to be brave and look towards a bright future. The night he had learned of her illness he had left home, determined to never look at her again. She didn't deserve what happened to her and baring his heart could only make her life just that much worst. He swallowed hard and blinked away the pain that was trying to bring him down.

Forgive Me, My Love

"Dad," he turned to them, he hadn't wanted this to be a circus. This was reckless and stupid! His plan had been simple, take a few well trained men, his ex-military friends and sneak in, get the girls then come back and kill everyone in the house. But John was too angry to think, he brought the whole state of Texas down on the heads of these fools. There was no way this was going to end well. "I want you and Tyrell to stay by the truck. We will need a fast get away. Keep the lights off and the engines running. When you see two flashes of the flashlight that means we have them. I want you to drive like crazy to meet us."

"No," John spoke up. "I'm going with you."

"I can't let you Dad, either you stay with the truck or get in one of the helicopters. Help them spot anyone leaving the house."

"What do you mean you can't let me?" John roared, hearing only what he wanted to hear. "That's my child down there I have to be there."

"No!" Simon hissed. "I should've left you home to comfort Mom. You are a liability here." Simon didn't want to be harsh, but fear and anger pushed him. They were so close, and now to have this hold up was almost more then he could take. "How can I help them if I have to worry about you? What if your heart can't hold up? You don't know what we'll find in there, they may barely be alive, and if they are alive they'll be wishing they were dead. You've got to let us handle this, she won't want you to see her like this."

"He's right Dad," Tyrell chimed in. "He's got four other guys and Ryan, I'm sure they can get the girls. You and I can each get in one of the choppers and be a look out from the sky. We'll have one of the men stay with the truck."

"Fine, you go," John conceded, but Simon could tell by his flat voice that he was hurt. He would deal with it later. "But I have to confront Henry one way or another." John was saying. "Either I do it tonight or some other time. It doesn't matter, it's going to happen."

"Jesus Christ!" Simon cursed. "Dad, your pride is going to get someone killed. I'll handle Henry."

"Henry has to know I can protect my own. If they're hurt, I want to kill Henry with my own hands."

"Fine," Simon snarled. "When we get him I'll bring him out to you." Simon turned to one of his colleagues. "Jessie you stay here, same signal. Stay alert." He motioned for them to move out and they blended into the dark night and out of sight.

"Henry!" Simon yelled. "Send the girls out here and I'll let you live a while longer."

Henry smiled and Rachel tried to pull away.

"Do you have my money?" Henry shouted.

"Yes," he called. "Come and get it."

"You don't think I'm that stupid do you?"

Rachel's heart lurched at the sound of Simon's voice. She knew her father, her other brothers and Richard had to be with him. Simon probably brought his friends from the military with him. She looked around, feeling so much braver now; Bianca was sitting with her back against the stairwell. That blue-eyed Devil was kneeling a few feet away with his hands tied behind his back and his booted feet tied. Obviously they didn't trust him, and she damn sure didn't trust him either. It seemed as if they had been like this for hours, when the gunfire turned rapid and unceasing and her head began to ring. She also wondered why they were still in the hallway.

Forgive Me, My Love

It was dark inside the house and as silent as a tomb. Nothing moved. Henry had refused to give in; as luck would have it, most of his men were gone, only his sons were here to aide him. She still hadn't figured out why they were here. *How did Nick know Henry?* These men obviously didn't like him. The one named Tony actually took pleasure in hitting the bound man. Even though she didn't care for the blue eyed devil she didn't want him hurt.

"Hey, you big brute!" She yelled as Tony landed his fist in Nick's stomach for the third time. "I bet you wouldn't do that if he wasn't tied up." He stopped and looked at her. Rachel could almost feel Bianca shaking next to her.

"Can't you keep your mouth shut Rachel?" She hissed.

"You big ass chicken," Rachel taunted. "You could probably beat us too, we are bound and there's no way we could hurt you."

"Bitch, shut up before I," then his eyes took on a nasty gleam. "They want you, they can have you." He was walking towards her and she didn't like the look in his brown eyes. But one of the others caught his arm.

"What are you doing?"

"I'm going to kill her, who cares if I put a bullet right between her cat eyes?"

"Leave that girl alone." The young man grabbed his arm and thrust him away.

Tony stood glaring, his eyes filled with hate. "Since when is a number pusher allowed to tell me what to do?"

"What?" The other one said, and held out his arms. "You gonna shoot me?" He grinned, as if he had a secret. "I don't think so big brother, Dad needs me. If you kill me I don't think he'll be to happy about it, and you know what happens when dad isn't happy."

Tony grinned, too but his was evil and Rachel shivered. She moved closer to Nick. "I can't wait until dad is no longer happy with you," he rubbed his hands and Rachel shuddered with fear at the look in his eyes. "That lil' wifey of yours sure looks tasty, you wouldn't want to have to share her."

That received a fist to the face, and Tony went flying across the room. At that point Henry showed up.

"What the hell is going on? The fight is out there; stop this before I stop it for you."

Rachel's eyes went back to her blue eyed devil, he was working at his ropes and for a reason unknown to her, she had faith that he would save them. For a brief moment she wondered if he were trying to join this gang of thieves and maybe win their trust by bringing her and Bianca here. Maybe he thought this was the best way to get into their nest. *Dumb ass*, she sneered in his direction. She caught sight of Bianca, and frowned. *What is she doing?*

Every time she looked up Bianca seemed to be getting closer to Nick. Their hands and feet had been left untied. Suddenly, Bianca picked up a vase and threw it at the window above them, shattering it. A barrage of gunfire erupted, in the chaos allowing her to crawl to Nick, then she whispered something to him. Then she reached behind him and pulled out something. Rachel tried not to feel anything for him, she wanted to be able to dismiss him without a thought, but it wasn't happening. She wanted Bianca to stay away from him. But in the reflection from the light of the moon, Rachel noticed it was a large wicked, looking knife. Her spirits soared with relief.

Bianca sliced through the ropes binding him and flinched as he quickly grabbed the knife and her.

"What the fuck are you doing?" The one named Robert shouted.

"I'm ending this!" Nick yelled, as he backed to where Rachel knelt on the floor.

"Let her go, that girl is my property!" Henry yelled, his gun pointed at Nick as he and Bianca stepped in front of Rachel. "This is my war boy I'll handle it my way, that's part of the fun, and you are ruining my plans."

"Give them back. This can be over in no time." Rachel stood up and stepped behind him, she clutched the back of his shirt using him as a shield. "You can't use people like this."

"Yes Henry," Rachel sneered. "Let us go, you're fighting a loosing battle. Even if I die here I'll know my family served you the justice you deserved."

"Only justice being served today will be handed out by me!" Henry said.

"When we get to the end of the hallway," Nick whispered, and Rachel was inclined to listen to him. "I want you to run. I don't care which way you go just run and hide. You can escape later, but for now I want you out of harms way."

"This will never be over," Henry cried as he pressed a button and the floor at the end of the stairs opened up. Now Rachel understood why they were in the hallway. A secret room under the stairs. But Henry continued raving like a lunatic. "You think this man is just going to tuck tail and run as soon as he has his daughter? He'll try to kill us all and I'm not going to let you help him."

"You should've thought of that!" Nick snapped. "Is this fight worth the lives of your sons'? These girls are scared...haven't you proved your point? They're not badly hurt. We can give them back and..."

"And what?" Robert yelled. "Dad has made a mortal enemy, if those two girls were my children do you think I'd just let it go? If you hand them back to me do you think I'd say, 'Well thank you for giving them back.'? No, I'd want blood!"

"I'll take them to town and drop them off, they could call and let everyone know that they are fine. I don't want anyone to die here. This is stupid, senseless. Let me try to fix this. I know the ways of the law, maybe I can settle this legally for the both families." As he talked, he was slowly backing them down the hallway.

"Stop where you are," Rachel froze as the cold barrel of a gun was pushed into the back of her head. "I knew you were a trader, you pequeño bastardo!"

Her stomach plunged as Nick, held up his hands and let go of Bianca, she turned. Rachel turned fast and knocked the gun from Tony's hand. Nick drew back and delivered a blow to the man's head but they didn't stick around to see the damage. She grabbed Bianca's hand and they ran through the dark house with shouts and threats of death following them. Afraid to run outside for all the bullets flying, they took the first set of stairs they came to and ran as fast as their feet could take them. The sound of boots on the stairs forced them to run faster. They made it to the second floor and ran into one bedroom after another looking for a place to hide. They ran into one bedroom at the far end of the hall and Bianca hurried to a large window.

Forgive Me, My Love

"Rachel, come here I found a way out," Bianca turned the latch on the window and it sprang opened.

Rachel saw a brown travel bag on the bed, she went to it and dug around, her hand touched the cold metal, she pulled it out and stared at it. It was a very big gun. She wrapped her hand around the handle as she tried to decide what to do with it, then the door opened, and she turned and fire with vey little thuught. A sharp yell came from the man and he fell.

She picked up the bag and tossed it to Bianca who was screaming. "Stop that!" Rachel hissed. "You'll tell them exactly where we are, here take this, toss it down there then aim for it when you jump. It won't do much, but it will help soften the fall." Bianca nodded and concentrated on throwing one leg over the window seal.

"I'm sorry sweets, but you two aren't going anywhere." They swung around to confront that sneering voice and froze. There was a gun pointed right at them, and Rachel's eyes fell to the gun she'd just tossed to the bed. "You know we don't need two of you. Red, why don't you take a leap?" He cocked the gun and fired, then he was falling to the floor just as his bullet found its' target. Rachel watched in horror as Bianca was struck, and then she was falling.

"Nooo!" Rachel screamed, she ran to the window and threw herself half way over the rail reaching for Bianca. But Bianca hit the ground hard, her body twisted at an awkward angle and nothing moved. Rachel screamed over and over and tried to get over the ledge. But strong hard hands pulled her back, the bag was snatched from her hands and harsh breath was blowing in her face. She could barely make out what he was saying.

Nick delivered one good blow to Tony's stomach,

and watched as his brother lay groaning. He took off in the direction of the girls' frantic footsteps. He prayed he could get there before any of his brothers'.

Just as he rounded the corner he could make out the outline of a man and he was taking aim. Nick slammed the butt of his gun against the man's head, but from the sound of things he was too late for one of them.

He rushed into the room and grabbed the screaming girl, and he hated himself for being so relieved that his tigress was still standing. "Shut up!" he shook her hard. "Shut up damn it! Look at me," her frantic eyes rested on him for just a second then shot back to the window.

"I have to get her. I can't leave her. I can't leave her."

"You can and you will."

"No," she stormed and tried to pull away from him. Nick sighed hard and pulled back delivering a blow to the side of her chin, she fell without a sound. He tossed her over one shoulder and grabbed his bag. Hurrying from the room Nick took one of the hiding places he knew of and made it to the ground floor. He spied his truck and then cursed under his breath, the tires had been cut, and it was as flat as most of Texas. He knew in the barn some one hundred yards away would be horses. If he could get to them they could probably get safely away.

He snuck into the kitchen and non-to-gently laid his burden on the flagstone floor. After a brief search of the kitchen drawers, he found a roll of electrical tape. The first thing he did was tape her mouth shut, then he bound her hands behind her back and next her feet. After picking her up, he scanned the back porch and crept out the back door. Knowing they were probably being watched he clung to the shadows and hurried into the barn. Once there he breathe a sigh of relief, then started looking for two good strong horses. If he remembered correctly, Henry trained his horses to respond to voice commands at the drop of a hat.

The girl was starting to wake up, he had to hurry. He spied a big black already saddled, and then a brown and white beauty standing peacefully in the next stall. He quickly lay the girl on the ground, then hurried away, ignoring her furious thrashing, he set about putting a saddle on the little mare, then he hooked his bag on the saddle horn. "Come on hell cat, we have a lot of traveling to do." Nick picked her up and was about to toss her across the horse when a voice stopped him.

"You can just drop her right where you are."

Nick heard a gasp from the girl and she began to wiggle hard. He reached up and slapped her behind hard and she became still.

"You can let go of my sister right now and I might not kill you."

"What kind of a fool do you think I am?" Nick gave a hard sigh and turned to face the man. "As soon as I dropped her you'd gun me down."

"You're damned right," the man gave a nasty chuckle. "Ya know, after this stupid stunt I really thought you people didn't have a brain among you. I see you might have one after all, too bad you'll have to die."

"Listen," Nick tried, not sure if he could get the girl on the horse and not get shot in the process. "I don't want to hurt her. But if you come any closer you will make me do something we'll both regret."

"I'm not leaving without my sister." The man took a step closer. "Lay her down, and step away. And I might let you live."

"I'm not leaving without your sister." Nick clasped her legs to his chest as she started to wiggle hard. He held the man's glare but his other hand had sought out his knife, finding it, his fingers closed around the handle. He whipped it from its sheath and threw it with deadly accuracy. The man yelled out in pain and fell to the ground clutching his left side. Nick threw her over the side of the black horse, then pulled himself over, he grabbed the reigns of the mare, and burst through the doors at breakneck speed and into the darkness beyond.

*****

Simon was tired; this was getting them nowhere. They had already lost the advantage of a surprise attack. They had been shooting at the house for two hours, all because Ryan couldn't keep his head on straight. Simon signaled the men to come in, after changing tactics, he dispersed them to different areas of the hacienda. He crept along the left side to the back, careful to stay out of the now well-lit night, the moon had come out with a vengeance. Suddenly from above a piercing scream caught his attention, then not ten feet from him a woman's body landed with a dull thud. The woman's bright red hair and slim build caused him to freeze. For a second he couldn't move, his heart refused to beat. And then common sense kicked in and pushed him into action, he ran to her and pulled her into the shadows. Simon brushed the hair from her face and his breath caught, it was Bianca, and his world nearly caved in. Quickly he checked her pulse and to his great relief she started coughing and crying. He lifted his gaze heavenward, thanking God and all the angels and Saints. Then she was tearing at his shirt, fighting to get away.

"Let me go! Oh God let me go!"

"Bianca, it's me," Simon cried, he caught her frantic hands and held them to her chest as he held her tight. "It's me honey, stop fighting I have you." Then she was crying and she fell into his arms like she was always meant to be there.

"Simon," she sobbed against his neck. "I knew you'd come."

"Ssh, darling," he closed his eyes and allowed himself a moment to hold her close. "Of course I'd come. I couldn't let them get away with hurting you two."

"My arm," she wailed. "My arm hurts so badly."

He looked at it, and his insides churned with fury, she had been shot. Someone was going to pay and pay dearly. He looked down at her tear stained bruised face, and swore she was the most beautiful woman in the world. "I'll take you back to Dad, and then once we get Rachel, you two will go straight to the Doctor."

"Oh! Rachel is still in there," she tried to sit up. "They'll kill her Simon."

"Not while I'm alive they won't," he caressed her cheek, and then kissed her forehead. "Let me get you back to the truck." She nodded and let him lift her in his arms.

At the truck he handed her over to his father.

"Dad, Tyrell, keep Bianca safe. They still have Rachel." With that he was off, pointedly ignoring their questions.

Simon had just rounded a corner at the back of the house he saw his prey enter the barn. He followed; thanking God his sister was still alive.

Later, as Simon watched them ride away he pulled

himself into a sitting position and leaned against the side of the barn, he saw a shadow move. He cursed his rotten luck and couldn't believe he'd let that fool get the drop on him. The man just rode out with Rachel thrown across his lap and he had done nothing about it. *Why? How could that have happened?*

Finally, after twenty lengthy minutes he was able to recognize the shadow. "Ryan," he yelled, with his breath fast leaving him. "Come over here, I need help."

"What happened?" Ryan asked as he hurried across the stables and to Simon's side, then he helped Simon to his feet.

"Our prey went that way, and he has Rachel," he grimaced, the pain in his side was nearly unbearable. Simon slowly, and with great care pulled the knife out, he tossed it to the ground and held his hand over the oozing wound. The bleeding had to stop, he needed to go after that bastard. "Let's go get her."

"What about the men in the house?"

"How can you ask that? Rachel isn't in there, I saw him take her. Those fools can wait. We have to get her, once she's safe, we can come back and kill them."

"Fine, whatever you say."

"Go get the old man and round up the others."

"We need to get you to a Doctor."

"First things first, we have to get Rachel then I want you to take everyone home with you."

"What the hell are you talking about?" Ryan whispered furiously. "You can't even stand up. How will you find them? You don't know this land."

"I'll just sit and wait. When they think it's safe they'll bring her back here or they'll ride out to check on the merchandise. When they move I move and I am fluent in Spanish and my skin is dark, I could pass for an Native."

"We have to get you to a hospital."

"I can't waist a single moment. If I don't get on the trail now...I'll...damn...I...I"

"Stop talking, I'll be right back. They can get you to a hospital and I'll stay here and watch."

"No...me...I need..."

"I told you what you need, shut up. I'm going for Dad."

Dean King

Seven

NICK SWORE UNDER HIS BREATH, this wasn't the homecoming he had anticipated, far from it. This had been a long shot, a chance to tell his father he was sorry. *But now?* He looked down at the woman thrown across his lap and he couldn't comprehend it. It was still dark enough out to make their journey relatively safe. It had taken some doing to get away from the helicopters but he had done it. Now they were on their way to a place he hoped no one could find. They had been riding for six hours, she had stopped struggling an hour ago, but her tears wouldn't let up. She cried until his pant leg was wet. He had taken the tape off her mouth for fear she'd choke. There was no making her understand what happened back there; he didn't understand it himself. All she knew was that people she loved had died trying to save her and it had been in vain. He couldn't let her go now. He didn't know how many family members he had lost last tonight. The thought made him clench his fists on the reins. *All for what? Her? What is so special about her that father is willing to let his sons die to keep her?*

Nick felt hollow inside, drained of every emotion accept burning rage and a deep confusion. They took hold of him and refused to let go. He shook his head to clear it, he had to think. It was strange, but this crying girl brought out his baser emotions, the need to punish someone was riding him hard. She was the reason he had no family left and by God she would tell him what this was about!

After pushing the horses another four hours, he was relieved when they reached the rocky bluffs to the south of the Hacienda. He needed to find the caves that were tucked away in the hills. It was a place no sane person would ever venture into. If anyone did they would never be seen alive again, the wolves and bandits would make sure of that.

With a quick jerk on the reigns, he pulled the horse to a halt in a grove between a pile of large boulders. He knew how to cover a trail, but from the look of things there was no one on their trail. Nick caught the back of her shirt in his fist, and pulled. She flipped over, and was unceremoniously dumped to the hard cracked dirt. She lay there, her chest heaving and glared at him as if he were the bad guy, as if this were his fault. He jumped off the horse and looked around, and then looked up. The sky was just starting to turn pink. *This will be a good place to rest until tonight.* He looked at the hole in the rocks partially covered by brush. Then out of habit he looked back. Nothing and no one in sight.

His tired mind went back to the girl's brother, he was sick with the thought of what he'd done. He hated thinking he'd killed her brother, the man had only been trying to protect her, and shouldn't have had to die for that. At the time survival was the only thing on his mind. Nick looked around, his tired eyes went back to the opening of a cave. But he knew this area. Unwanted memories came flooding back, memories he'd never wanted to think of again.

But in his present state he couldn't prevent them

from drowning him. When he was ten years old, he'd found a cave like this. He had been out looking for his mother. He would never forget. It was at just this time in the morning when he had found her body, not ten miles west of here, mauled by wolves. She had died a horrible death. His only hope was that she was too high on drugs to feel any of it. After he'd buried her body, he had gone back home, only to be told he wasn't wanted. Nick had spent one week living at the edge of the hacienda, until Henry had finally given in and let him back into the house.

Later, this place had provided a much needed escape when he needed one, it was the only place he felt close to her, he was safe here.

"Come on boy," he patted the horses muzzle and walked him into the cool dark shadows of the surrounding rocks. He unsaddled the horse and grabbed a handful of crisp brown grass and proceeded to rub him down, then did the same to the mare.

Rachel lay on her back in the dirt where he had left her, not one place on her body was free of pain. Her hard gaze found the man responsible for this. Oh, how she hated him. Tears filled her eyes and she was surprised she had any left. She heard her father's voice, he had come for them and now he was probably dead. Physical pain hit her and she pulled her knees up to her chest. Then all she could see was Bianca's lifeless body on the ground so far below the window, and then Simon. She pulled her legs up tighter but it didn't help, the pain was so great, it was blinding. He had lain on the ground with that large knife sticking out of his stomach. She pulled her bound hands to her face and took a deep breath, then screamed her pain as loud and as long as she could.

Forgive Me, My Love

He came to her and grabbed her arms, he flung them from her face. "Stop it!" he yelled into her face. "Stop it right now do you hear me?" And then he squeezed her arms hard, and shook her until she thought her brain would scramble.

Still she screamed, her eyes tightly closed she refused to stop. Suddenly he dropped her arms and she landed back on the ground, then he walked away.

Rachel stopped only when her throat hurt so much she couldn't make any more sounds. Slowly, she turned until she was on her stomach, her face was hot and wet, she lay on the gravel but she didn't care about the rocks digging into her flesh, nor did she care about the large scorpion that was slowly making it's way towards her. What she did care about was the sight of her brother on the ground with a huge knife sticking out of him. She could still hear the sound of his yelling as they galloped past. She squeezed her eyes shut, and tried to block out the heart wrenching sight. Rachel's body jerked, she couldn't get away from it. Suddenly a swooshing sound filled her ears, her eyes snapped opened to see the same wicked knife that had probably killed her brother, sticking out of the ground not two inches from her face. She didn't even flinch when she saw the scorpion had been impaled.

"What the hell is your problem?" He yelled and she glared up at him as he came charging out of the entrance of the cave he had disappeared into. "Answer me woman!" he shouted, she had no intention of answering him. "What the hell is going on in that head of yours? Why didn't you scream or at least yell for help? Or are you all screamed out?"

She stared at him not really seeing his fury or caring. Then his face cleared of the massive frown. "Oh, so this is how it's going to be?" Still, she didn't answer. "Fine, suit yourself but make no mistake about it, you will tell me what I want to know." She stared; she would never tell him anything! He was lower than the lowest snake, and his bloodied hands and forked tongue would never have a chance to hurt her again.

"Come on, I need to get you inside," he reached for her and she tried to scurry away, but she didn't get far. "Stop that!" He snapped. She stiffened when he picked her up and slung her over his shoulder as if she weighed nothing and walked into the dark interior of the cave. Out of no where he smacked her bottom, it was a hard slap, a stinging pain rippled through her and her breath hissed through tight lips. He'd die for what he had done, that was the only thing she could grasp and hang onto. He dumped her on a smooth flat rock, and she flinched from the pain. "Now, you stay there," she hated the hard growl in his voice, he had no right to be angry. She would never grace him with the sound of her voice.

Nick cursed under his breath; she sat glaring at him as if this were all his fault. It was hers! She knew why Henry wanted her and by god she would tell him. Right now was as good a time as any to get to the bottom of this mess. He smiled, but it was a hard smile, one meant to intimidate. He reached out and brushed her wild black hair back from her sweaty, dirty face, and she didn't move, just sat there glaring at him with those hate filled golden brown eyes. He ran a finger over her velvety soft chocolate skin and still she didn't flinch or bat an eyelash.

"Do you know how pretty you are? So young, so sweet," he gave a chuckle, but it was low and ugly, it had the desired response, her eyes widened ever so slightly. He went to his knees in front of her, his eyes boring into hers. "You know what happened last night." It was a statement, and he eased closer, but she didn't draw back. "Tell me who those people were and why Henry wanted you?" He knew who they were, they were her family, but he wanted to start with something easy, just to get her talking. She lifted her nose high and turned slightly away. "Now how did I know that would be your answer?" He reached up and opened the first two buttons of her shirt. She gasped, and a look of fear jumped into her lovely eyes. "I'll ask again, who are they and what do they want?" He saw the muscles bulge in her jaw, and her nostrils began to flare. "Fine, have it your way, I was hoping you wouldn't talk. I'll enjoy making you." He loosened more buttons, and slid the shirt over her shoulders, and down her bound arms, baring her proud breasts. Her face flamed and she quickly lifted her arms to shield herself. But he held her hands to her lap with one hand, and with the other he clasped her jaw, and roughly turned her to face him. "You will tell me what I want to know or I'll have you naked and spread eagle on this ground available for my pleasure until you scream them at me."

Her lips started to move and he fought his disappointment, he had a fierce desire to taste her sweet charms again. But just as he began to smile, she let lose a wad of saliva, it hit him square in the face.

"You know," he growled low in his throat, trying to keep his temper under control. "I forgot you were a spitter. One of these days I'll have to teach you to swallow." He grabbed a handful of her hair and wiped his face with it. She lifted her bound feet and kicked at him, but he caught her feet and pushed her to the ground, then rolled her to her back. He whipped off her shoes, reached up and pulled down the zipper of her jeans, then he grabbed both sides and pulled.

"Noooo!" she screamed. "Wait! I'll tell you!" She sobbed. "Just don't hurt me again."

It took a second for him to realize she had given in, but he did, then he pulled her pants up, and sat her up. Yanking the shirt over her shaking shoulders, he snapped. "Go ahead, I'm listening."

Rachel gathered the shirt in her fists as best she could and looked away from him. "The man who owns the hacienda as you seemed to know is Henry Dennison," she paused.

"I know that!" he barked. "Get on with it!"

Rachel steeled herself, she realized she had no way to protect herself, and she was at his mercy. "His men kidnapped Bianca and I when we were on our way back to school." Nick flinched at the word school. *Is she really that young?* "Henry called my father, they spoke of some kind of shipment that was lost. Henry said my father had to pay for it, that he'd signed for it so he was responsible, but my father said Henry was full of crap and that he never did any such thing. Henry said the cost of the shipment was twenty million dollars, he said my Dad wouldn't see us again until it was paid, and if he didn't pay, then Henry would kill us."

Rachel watched him pace in front of her, one hand on his chin, the other folded across his hard stomach. She wished she knew what he was thinking. Maybe he would let her go, then again as black hearted as he was, probably not. Some how she had to get to a phone. Rachel frowned as frustration took over. She had no idea where she was and there was no way she could tell them how to find her; all she knew was that she was somewhere deep in the heart of Mexico. Her throat threatened to close as tears formed. She shot his pacing form a heated look, but he was so lost in thought that he didn't notice, which didn't help her dark mood.

So, she is innocent. Nick thought, as he stared at her. Not that he had doubted it, but he had to hear it from her lips. It did, however, make what he had done to her even worst. Nick looked out through the cave's entrance, bright daylight and stone met his gaze. Twenty million dollars was a lot of money. He had to get to Irapuato. The town was deep inside the state of Guanajuato. The problem was Henry owned everything that moved inside Guanajuato, if he were to go there he was as good as dead. Nick had to find a way to get in touch with Miguel, he would know what was going on. But could he risk the life of his old friend? Henry would surely kill anyone who defied him. Nick looked back at her. *What to do with her?* He couldn't leave her here, it wasn't safe. Could he take her with him? No, she'd run the first chance she got. He paced the cave, and then stopped to look at her again.

"I have some business to attend to, we're going into town for the night."

"Whatever you say Boss," she sneered, her cat like eyes raking him with distain. Nick didn't cringe, he could care less what she thought of him. His only goal was keeping them both alive.

"You don't have to like it. Just do as I say and you might make it to Mommy and Daddy in one piece. And don't think you can escape, this is the type of town that makes me look like an altar boy."

When she didn't say anything else, Nick went to his knees and rummaged through his bag. He knew there was no food, but he'd hoped for at least a candy bar. He sat back on his hunches when he came up empty handed. "I hope you are not hungry," he looked at her, and sighed when she turned away from him. "I don't have anything to eat." He moved to her and cut her feet free. "Come on, it's been a long time since I've been on a horse and I'm sor. Let's get some sleep."

"I'm not sleeping with you."

"I don't care what you do. But your hands will be tied, and one foot will be tied to mine. You make the most of that."

She struggled, but he lifted her and moved to a patch of grass and laid her down. After tying her to wrist to his, and her ankle to his ankle, he turned her to face him and pulled her close, then shut his eyes.

*****

Simon grimaced in pain. He reached up and caught Ryan's arm. "Don't let them leave her Ryan!" He rasped. "Please we can't lose the trail."

"I won't leave her," Ryan assured him, then turned to John. "Dad, I'll stay with Jessie, the rest of you can all go home."

"I'm staying with you." John said. "I'm not leaving her."

"You are the only one Simon will listen to, you have to go. I'll find her."

"You've never done this before. You don't know how to track anyone, you're just a snot nosed kid!" John said. "Go home, I'll stay."

"I'm not leaving, Simon needs you, Bianca needs immediate care. You and Tyrell have to take them home."

"He's right dad, we need to get them home. Trust

Ryan, if nothing else it'll make Mom feel better knowing he's still out here looking for her."

"I don't want to go, I need to stay."

"Look at Simon, Bianca is bleeding to death while you stand there babbling!" Ryan yelled. "Get on the chopper and get them to safety."

"Fine," John nodded. "But you keep in touch. "I wanna hear the minute you have her."

"You will Dad, I'll tare every inch of every town apart until I find her."

John hugged him then followed Tyrell, they jumped in the chopper and Ryan waved to them as they took off. He turned to Jessie. "Let's go find my sister."

*****

Nick didn't get any real sleep, but the rest did him well. He looked down at her, she was knocked out. Her head was cushioned on his chest, and one leg was tossed up over his. He had to admit she fit nicely in his arms. She was soft in all the right places. He felt his heart softening towards her, and he knew he couldn't afford to let that happen. He looked towards the opening and noticed the sun had gone down. It was time to get on the road.

Nick sighed, and pushed her off him. She screamed and was instantly awake. "Time to get up." He sat up and brushed off. "Did you know you drool in your sleep?"

She gasped and lifted her hand to her mouth. When it came away dry, her gaze narrowed at him. "Liar!" She snapped.

He laughed and cut her wrist free of his and then

freed her ankle. He quickly tied her feet together, then tied her wrists. "Come on, it's time for us to hit the road. He lifted her and walked out of the cave, he sat her on a rock. "Now, be a gook little girl and stay put. I'm going to get the horses together.

Once he was done he went to her and picked her up, then placed her on the mare. "Just hang onto her mane and you should be fine." He walked away, his mind already on other things, and then he jumped on his horse and grabbed the reins of hers, and headed due south.

He stiffened when her waspish voice rang out. "If my fiancé finds you, I'll laugh while he slits you from head to toe."

Nick didn't turn to look at her. "When you see him, give him my regards will you? Oh, and tell him, he doesn't need to thank me for breaking you in for him."

His horse nimbly dodged her well-aimed foot, and he laughed as she cursed under her breath.

Six hours later, Nick paused as they came closer to town, the night was quiet, which was unusual for a pay day weekend. It was black enough outside to let them pass without notice. Walking the horses to the back of a dilapidated hotel at the edge of town, he slid off his horse and tied it to a wooden bench. He didn't worry about running into that army her father had, Henry would keep them busy for at least another day. And if they were searching towns, this one wasn't on any map, they'd probably not find it unless it was by mistake.

Nick hurried to her horse and pulled her down, then before she could say anything, he quickly placed a piece of tape over her mouth. Then spun her around and lifted her, tossing her back over the horse so that her hair was dangling over one side and her legs on the other.

After securing her feet, he went around the other side, pointedly ignoring her muffled screams. If he were lucky Miguel would've made it to the cantina by now. In the old days, when ever Nick had a problem this was the little cantina he always went to, only Miguel knew of it.

"Now," Nick brushed her hair out of the way, and said into her fuming face. "I'm not doing this because I don't trust you," then he gave a small humorless chuckle. "Hey wait a minute. That's exactly why I'm doing it." Casting a quick look around, he spied a multi colored blanket not to far away, he hurried to it, and after a glance around, he grabbed it. Nick went back to her and lifted it then tossed it over her, making sure to cover her from head to toe. There were many horses lining the street, because of the mountainous territory horses were necessary. There were some places up here even the heavy-duty trucks couldn't get through. It gave the sleepy little town an old west look that was kind of creepy at night. He half expected someone to be waiting to gun him down in the middle of the street. "I'll be back in two minutes, be a good girl and stay put."

Just as promised, he was back in record time. "Come on Tigress, I found us a room for the night. It's not the Ritz, but it'll have to do." He threw the blanket off her, and grabbed her hips pulling her off the horse. He picked her up and again threw her over his shoulder, then marched into a back door of the Hotel.

Rachel had long ago given up trying to see any kind of land marks, she always seem to be in a prone position, with her hair falling to hide the world from her...

Suddenly, she found herself flying through the air, she landed with a painful jolt on what could pass only by the slightest margins for a mattress, but was most likely just blankets filled with cornhusks, and boy did it hurt. She moaned behind her gag, and closed her eyes, certain this nightmare would never end.

She heard a scratching sound, and then smelled an acid stench. And then his image flared to life in an orange glow. It was then that she noticed the candle he held, and she relaxed. He put the candle down and came to the bed. She tried not to flinch as he sat next to her, but she did scoot as far from him as she could get. Then she felt the warm adobe wall scratch at her back and knew she could go no further.

"I have to change, I can't go walking around in bloody, dirty clothes, you can watch if you'd like," he pulled off his shirt and tossed it on a ladder back chair, and then he stood up and reached for the zipper of his pants; she jumped and closed her eyes. She clenched her teeth as his chuckle reached her ears.

"I'm sorry, but there's no bathroom in here." He was saying. "If you have to go, there's a pot in the corner." Slowly she opened her eyes; he had already pulled on a clean pair of blue jeans and was now buttoning a white shirt. As luck would have it the bag she had grabbed must have belonged to him. She willed him to leave; it would give her a chance to get the knife she knew was inside and a sure chance at freedom.

"I don't want your death on my hands," he said and her hopes were dashed as he lifted the knife and tucked it into the waistband of his jeans. "So, I won't give you the chance to escape. I'll see you in a bit, lovely. I have some things to take care of."

Rachel fumed. *Why hadn't he turned on the light?* She was starving, her stomach felt like it was touching her backbone and he didn't care. The tape was starting to cut through her skin and she had to pee in the worst way. Tears wouldn't help, but she let them fall anyway. Everything felt so hopeless, then her eyes were drawn to the candle, he had left it burning, her eyes gleamed as an idea started to form.

Nick hurried across the narrow dirt street. The town was so isolated and small that he could see the beginning and end of main-street. It was a good thirty miles from his fathers Hacienda. When he and his brothers were young, this was one of the places they had come to party. But still it wasn't far enough to let his guard down. His father's people were everywhere; Nick wasn't stupid enough to believe they would ever be safe. If Henry were still alive he would hunt them down and kill them both.

Reaching the battered doors of the cantina that stood across the street and down some, he pulled his hat further down over his head to shield his eyes and pushed the doors opened. With a practiced eye, he scanned the room. It was crowded, most of the occupants were drunk and getting drunker. The music from an old time jukebox filled the room with eighties pop. Women floated from male to male showing they were more then willing to give pleasure for the right price. It was as if time stood still, the place looked as if it were a throw back from the 1800's.

Nick walked into the room, careful to keep his head low. He headed to the wooden bar and hailed the barkeeper. "Give me a cold beer." He had a desperate need to drink something.

"What kind?"

"You offer a variety?" Nick asked with surprise,

the man grinned.

"We have all the favorites even a few lites for the diet conscious. What do you want Amigo?"

"Give me a bud," the man turned, reached into a vat of ice and pulled out an aluminum can.

"That'll be three dollars."

Nick pulled out a credit card and looked at it. He debated using it, but it was all he had. The odds were that Henry didn't know much about him, so tracking his card wouldn't come into play. Anyway he had to get the girl something to eat. He shrugged and handed it to the man. He understood the risk in using it, but he was cash poor right now. Plastic was all he had left.

After three tries, the man tossed the card on the counter. "That card is no good. It has been reported stolen. If I were you mister I'd get out of here before I have to call the policía."

"Damn!"

"It's okay, Raul I'll pay for him."

Nick turned to find Miguel at his side. "My friend," they clasped hands and Miguel nodded. "Come my son, let us have a seat."

Nick grabbed his beer, and his card and followed Miguel to a chair in the far back. "I'd only hoped you could come, I didn't think you'd be able to get away this soon. I'm surprised you remembered which cantina I liked."

Miguel snickered, and wagged his bushy black eyebrows. "It wasn't hard to remember. There are three towns close to the hacienda. I just figured you'd go to the one you know best. They think I'm out looking for you, it gives me freedom."

Nick nodded. "Tell me what's going on? Is Tia

okay? She wasn't hurt with all the gunfire?"

"No, I got them out, they were in town visiting family."

"Good thinking."

"Sit," Miguel pulled out a ragged ladder backed chair and straddled it. "You took a chance coming here."

"I have questions." Nick said. "I didn't want you to track me down and get yourself in trouble or killed. But I have to know what's going on."

"I was careful. But niño it was a stupid thing to do. Why did you take the girl? You should've left her with Henry."

"And let him kill her? No, I couldn't do that, I owe her too much."

"She is dead anyway, and now, so are you."

"I know, but I have to give her a chance to live. I want to know what all this is about?" Nick settled into the wooden chair, careful to keep his eyes on the crowd. "Was anyone hurt?"

"You will not like my news."

Nick sat with his back to the wall, his eyes on the doors. "I already don't like it. Tell me."

"Roberto is in the hospital, he was shot in the stomach. Tony is hot on your trail, he thinks you may have gone to Jalisco. Your father," Miguel sighed and shook his head. "Henry swears you are just like your mother and must be treated the same. He means to kill you niño. The authorities across the country have been alerted. They have put warrants with both yours and the girl's pictures on them, and the fee as they are calling it, is half a million to anyone who finds you dead or alive."

"Geez!"

"No wait, there is more."

"I can't wait to here the rest."

"Her family is offering one million for her alive. If anyone brings her to them they will pay on the spot. They are saying she was kidnapped. Henry has spies everywhere. He is furious and he won't rest until he has you and the girl."

"Why, why can't he just let it go?"

"He won't, it is how he is."

"What about the others?"

"Blake is worried for you, he wants to help, he said if I were to find you, I was to tell him."

"Why?" Nick couldn't keep the sarcasm from his voice. "So he can prove what a big man he is and kill me in front of Father?"

"No, no, it's no like that anymore. Blake has grown into a fine man. He is honest, well as honest as any man can be that the line of work he does."

"And what does my little brother do now?"

"He is Henry's exporter. He has told Henry that he didn't want to know what was in the boxes, all he would do was send them where they needed to go."

"Turning a blind eye is not being honest."

Miguel shrugged. "He is more honest then the rest. He has a hacienda one hundred miles south of here, and he has two children. One boy and one girl, he married a real Spanish girl he met on one of his trips to Spain. She is beautiful, blazing wheat hair and the bluest eyes I have ever seen."

"So Blake is married. I would've never figured he'd be the first."

"He wasn't the first." At Nick's surprised look Miguel went on. "Robert was married, but it didn't end well. Never mind that. Like I said, Blake is a good boy.

He wants out of the business all the way, but he is afraid for his family. He thinks Henry will try to use them against him."

"He's probably right."

"Can I tell him I have seen you?"

"No, don't tell him just yet. I might need to drop in on him later, but for now let me lay low, maybe things will calm down abit."

"Don't bet on it," Miguel looked around and lowered his voice. "But I have the perfect place for you to hide."

Nick was instantly alert. "Where? And how long can we stay?"

Miguel chuckled. "You did not ask if it was safe."

"I trust you, why would I ask that?" Miguel's tired red veined eyes grew misty, and he nodded.

"I am glad to hear that, I would never let you down niño."

"I don't want any harm to come to you or your family for helping me old man. If Henry finds out, there will be hell to pay."

"He'll never find out," Miguel sounded so absolute Nick just nodded. "You can hide out with Loretta. Her place is just at the end of town to the north. She has a room that is hidden, it is for her special guests. Let me talk to her first, then I'll come and get you."

"Fine, that sounds perfect. Now, what can you tell me about the girl? Do you know if any of her people were hurt?"

Miguel shrugged. "I don't know that, but then I don't know much about the girl either, only that she was on her way back to school when they took her. Her father is a rich American, and from what I've heard, the man was raised in a barrio part of Houston and is not the typical rich man. It seems we have awakened the sleeping serpent. I don't think he'll rest until we are all dead. No matter what happens to his daughter, he will want revenge."

Nick's head had long ago dropped in his hands, and he groaned as Miguel continued. "What is it niño? You have ever reason to be distressed, this will get even uglier."

Nick put his hands down, and looked Miguel straight in his eyes. "Tell me I didn't have sex with a child?" His look was so tortured Miguel laughed and patted his shoulder.

"I can't tell you, because I don't know how old she is. But she has the body of a woman. Anyway, in my country at fifteen a girl turns into a woman. She has to be older than that."

"Have you seen her face?" Nick snapped. "She looks like she maybe in her last year of high school." He felt sick and his hands were starting to shake. "She's just a child, I may have ruined her life."

"No, no," Miguel said. "I tell you she is over fifteen and it is okay. You have made her a woman, it was time."

"If she were my child I'd kill the bastard who took her against her will. I deserve whatever they want to do to me."

"Don't say that, you paid…"

Nick slammed his fist against his thigh, and stared at the wall. "That makes it even worst." He whispered.

"Stop it," Miguel barked. "You did what you had to do to save her from Henry. You must look at it like that. What you did was wrong in her country, but here it is okay, you saved her life."

Nick nodded, but he knew this would haunt him the rest of his life. He had never thought to have children, but he knew if she were his child, he would want blood. Sitting there, he realized most of the violent rage he felt was directed at himself, it had nothing to do with the girl. She was a victim not only of Henry, but of Nick's lust as well. *Could there have been another way?* Maybe he could've talked Chuy into letting them be... He sighed and shook his weary head. There was no use going over it, nothing would've gotten them through that door alive. However, he didn't know if he could live with what he had done, he felt like the worst kind of pervert.

Finally when he was able to speak again he said. "Tell me what's going on, I got some of it from the girl but I need to know the rest."

"Henry has been losing money. I think it is because your brother Tony is stealing it, but that is no matter. The money is still gone, and it needs replaced. Henry saw a chance to rob the American and he latched onto it. He tricked the man into signing false papers, then accused him of losing the cargo. It had worked on many men, but this one is different. Henry saw how much the man loved his only daughter. So he steals her. What he didn't count on was the fighting spirit of the Texan. He thought they would bring the money for fear he would deflower the girl and her friend. I can tell you Henry was some surprised when the man came in with guns blazing."

"Jesus! Why didn't I figure it was something like that? That man doesn't have a truthful bone in his body." Nick shook his head in astonishment. "So what now? I have the girl. Henry wants her, her father wants her, and yet she isn't safe with either of them. As long as they're fighting she'll be in the middle of it. Henry won't rest until he has taken her again. Then her father will kill me because no matter how insane my father is, I won't let anyone kill him."

"You are gonna have to make the choice. Someone is going to die, if the girl was dead, they wouldn't have a pawn to fight with or for."

"It doesn't matter if the girl were dead or not," Nick insisted, all this talk of death was making him edgy. "There's still the little problem of the blackmail. I'm sure her father won't forget that."

"Maybe Henry will come to his senses and let well enough alone?" Miguel suggested, half heartedly.

"Henry?"

"Wonders do happen."

"I'm going to try to keep the girl out of this the best way I can. I need time to think, to get a plan together. I want you to tell everyone she's dead. That she died in the gunfight. Tell Henry I was severely wounded, and I didn't make it."

"And how am I supposed to have come across all this knowledge?"

"Tell him I came to you for help, and they buried us in an unmarked grave somewhere. I'll give you something of hers to validate the claim. As for me, they won't care."

"They will care," Miguel said abruptly, then he caught himself. "Sorry, but not only will they care, but they will want proof."

Nick let Miguel's outburst go. "Maybe we can find some bodies, it's a lively night in here, someone is bound to do some shooting."

"I'll set it up for you, it's as good as done."

Miguel assured Nick. "But I want you two to stay out of sight until things have died down."

"What about money, I'm broke, what happened to my accounts?"

"Henry froze your bank accounts. Your credit cards, he reported them stolen."

"Damn! How? It's not even been a complete twenty-four hours. He doesn't know anything about me."

"I hate to tell you this, but Henry has always known where you were. He knows how to find you at all times. He even got you out of jail."

"Why, how?" Nick sighed in frustration. "I knew he had something to do with that. He's got to have some ulterior motive; I know it's not love that made him keep track of me."

"He loves you in his own way hijo, he's all about family. If he hadn't stepped in, you'd be dead right now. Those cops had planned to kill you. He paid them to set you free. He thinks he raised you and your brothers to be a certain way. Just because you went the way of the law, doesn't mean he has lost you, it just means to him that you are strong, and that you can stand up for what you believe in, even if it is not right."

"So he thinks having law and order is wrong?"

"Let us not worry about what he thinks. Right now you are the only one who is important. You have an account that Henry started the day you left home. I hate to say it, but it is the place Henry hides his extra money from the government. It is very fat with cash. If you can stick around for a few days, I'll get you the account number and a check book. But you will only have one shot at getting the money. When he finds out you have used it, he'll know you are still alive and he will know someone is helping you. Close the account, get all the money, and then go into hiding."

"I will, but what about you?" Nick asked, fearing Miguel would die helping him. "Will Henry know you helped me? Will it be dangerous for you?"

Miguel shook his head. "No, I will be fine, he will not know it was me."

"How will you do it?" Nick caught Miguel's arm. "I don't want you to get hurt."

"I won't be hurt." Miguel shook Nickk's hold off, and patted his arm. "I will be fine, there has been so many things missing that this will just be one more."

"But when the account is empty, then what? He'll know…"

"He will supect," Miguel shook a finger at Nick. "He will not know."

"But will you get out of there?"

"As soon as I can, but Henry will think I'm out looking for you, how could I have taken his account information?"

Nick grinned. "As long as you are safe, then you do what you must."

"I'll be okay, but thank you for worrying. Now, I'll have Loretta put you up until it is done. But after that I want you to leave, forget you ever knew of this part of the world. Whatever you do don't tell me, I don't want to be forced to talk. I've seen some of the horrible things they do that will make people who don't want to talk spill their guts just to make the pain stop. If you want to keep the girl safe, you are going to have to disappear."

"Don't worry, I know," Nick assured him, "and I wouldn't put you or anyone in that position."

"You will do this? Take the girl and hide? It

maybe for a very long time."

"I have to," Nick gave a careless shrug. "If I don't, more people will die."

They sat in silence for a few moments each lost in the bad turn of events. "Miguel, where can I find some food at this time of night?"

"Loretta and her girls will feed you, but I'll give you what money I have, make it stretch. I'll try to make it back in a day or two."

Nick reluctantly reached out and took the offered money. "I'll pay you back as soon as I can."

"Naw, is nothing. You just come out of this alive. That is all the payment I need. Now you go, we shouldn't be seen together. I'll meet you in one hour to take you to my friend. I'll be around, don't think you are alone. I'll try to stay as near to you and the girl as I can."

"Thanks old friend," Nick stood up and left the room. He bought some beans, Spanish rice, tortillas and beef fajitas. The smell had his own stomach rumbling; it reminded him that he hadn't eaten in days.

Eight

HE HURRIED INTO THE HOTEL and down the hall. Nick had to admit he was eager to see her. He pulled out the key, and after a quick look around, he darted into the room. He pulled up short when he saw the girl standing with her bound hands extended over the flame that was coming from the single candle. He dropped the food and jumped into action when the tape burst into flames. He grabbed the blanket and threw it over her hands, then tackled her to the floor. She was screaming, but he didn't know if it was from burnt hands or her defeated attempt at freedom.

"Get off me!" She screamed.

Nick rolled to his side, and stared at her. "That was a damned fool stupid thing you did. You could've been killed."

"It was a chance I had to take."

"All you had to do was ask, I would've untied you."

"I'm not stupid. You're lying; you'd never let me go. My father won't give you any money you know, and I don't have anything left to give."

Nick stood up, and pulled her to her feet. "Let me look at those hands?"

She pulled away, and glared at him. "Did I say my hands hurt?"

Forgive Me, My Love

"You don't have to say it; I can see they have a burn or two on them."

"So, now you care?" She turned away from him, but he caught her arm and swung her back around to face him.

"I don't care, but I don't want you dying on me just yet either." He sighed and picked up the bags he dropped earlier, and slammed the door. "I brought us some food," her eyes brightened, but she tried not to show it, and he almost laughed at her defiance, but it only reminded him of how young she was. "Let's eat, then we can get some sleep, the morning will be a better time to talk."

"As far as I'm concerned we don't have anything to talk about," she said, but he noticed she took a seat at the wobble wooden table.

"It's a good thing it's not up to you isn't it?" She flung a hard look at him, then her eyes went to the bags, he felt a pang of conscious at having not thought of this earlier. She had to be starving, but she waited patiently as he opened the first bag and set everything on the table. Then she grabbed the bag closest to her, and ripped it open. She only glanced at him once before she was eating. Nick sat down opposite her, and watched, after the first bite she closed her eyes and released a sigh of pure heaven. Nick held in the urge to smile. When you are as hungry as she was, it was okay to let table manners go out the window.

He tore open the third bag and dove in. Food had no right to taste this good, he thought as he savored the seasoned beef wrapped in a warm soft tortilla.

After all the food was gone, they both eased back in their chairs and exhaled. Rachel looked away from him, her wrists were starting to hurt. But she wouldn't let him know it. He'd probably touch her burns just to make them hurt more. Hours alone in this dank little room had done nothing for her disposition; she was tired of all this abuse. And she wanted to go home.

"Let me go home?" Her voice must have surprised him from the way he looked at her.

"No."

His nonchalant answer irritated her. "Who were those people at Henry's house and why did you bring us back there?"

He slanted her a go to hell look and she gave in to the impulse and kicked his leg under the table. For all the good it did, he had boots on and her feet were bare. "Let me go damn you!"

"I said no," his voice had a soft, almost violent quality she didn't like. She knew he could be mean and she didn't want to test it to see how mean, but she had to get home.

"Look fella that was my Father and brothers back there. For all I know they could be dead right now. And Bianca's," she had to paused as a lump formed in her throat. "They have to get her body, she can't be left there she has a gravesite in our family plots. Someone has to bury her." Anger replaced her tears as she shouted at him. "This is entirely your fault! I have to know that they're alright."

"So what do you want me to do?" He just sat staring at her, and Rachel fought the urge to rip his beautiful eyes out. With eyes like that he couldn't possibly be this callus.

"I want you to let me go. Right now, you are innocent of all wrongdoing. I'll even let the rape charges go if you let me leave right now."

She clenched her fists as he threw his head back and laughed! He was laughing at her. "How dare you!" she screamed. "You are a vile, despicable, nauseating, disgusting…"

"Alright," he chuckled. "I know what I am, but that's not going to help you sweetheart. You and I are stuck with each other for a while."

"A while?" she said, and her eyes narrowed. She didn't like the look in his cobalt eyes. "How long is a while?"

"Until I say otherwise."

"You can't do this," she growled and stamped her foot on the dusty floor. "I'm leaving you at the first opportunity."

"Thanks for the warning."

"You'd be lucky if I don't cut you throat one night while you sleep."

"I'll remember that," he tossed a blanket at her, and it hit her square in the face. "Go to sleep."

"Where are you going?" She cried as he walked from the room.

Nick ignored her, he to had get their things ready for their trip to Loretta's. He shook his head and wondered why he didn't just give to girl back to her father, and let them work things out on their own. It would be so easy to just walk away.

*****

Rachel stretched and yawned, a smile bloomed on her lips as she inhaled the fresh clean scent of springtime. The sheets she lay on were soft and the bed was so supple she sank into its depths. It had all been a dream, no, a nightmare. Now she could open her eyes and be in her bed waking up from a night of partying after her birthday.

A sudden frown wrinkled her brow and her stomach tightened with dismay. Carlotta the housekeeper didn't use that kind of fabric softener, and her bed wasn't this soft. A chill raced through her and she slowly opened her eyes. Then a small scream escaped her as her eyes fell on the white canopy overhead anchored to a wooden beam in the ceiling.

She sat up quickly and looked around. On the floor beside the bed was his hat. Next to that were the clothes she had been wearing. Her hands flew to her chest and she gasped as she was met with bare skin. Suddenly the door opened and Rachel pulled the covers over her naked body.

"So, you're awake?" He stood with the door open grinning at her.

"Close the door you buffoon!"

He laughed and quietly closed the door behind him.

"What are we doing here? Where are we? And why am I without my clothes?" She demanded as she slid off the bed and gathered her things. "Why didn't you tell me we were moving? How did I get here?"

"You leave no bases uncovered do you?"

"Just answer my questions." She fought to put on her clothes while keeping herself covered.

Nick walked towards the bed, and then sat down. His hands braced on the bed behind him, as he admired her cute little bottom that she tried so desperately to hide. "We're in hiding. This is the safest place I could think of and your clothes are gone because the owner of this establishment wanted to see what I had to offer her as payment for letting us hide out here."

"What!" Her mocha skin paled, and her eyes stretched wide, he almost laughed. "People looked at my body without my permission?" She screeched and he covered his ears.

"All they needed was mine!" He shouted back, looking for the flames that were sure to start coming from her ears.

"You sick bastard!" She growled, as she shoved her legs one at a time into the jeans that were too small. "How could you, how dare you. Did you let them poke and prod me too?"

"Well," he hedged and she stiffened, glaring at him. "They wanted to, but I told them no. I told them I bought you, and you're my private property. No one could have that body but me, unless they paid a pretty hefty amount."

"Not even!" She stood fuming, her clothes forgotten. "You vile, arrogant, disgusting asshole!"

"As it turns out you are to be confined to this room. If you try to leave you could stumble into some very bad territory, you will get hurt."

"Is that a threat?"

"It's a promise." He could almost see her brain working. He was having fun just watching her. It was almost better then last night when he'd had to remove her clothes so that she could sleep in comfort. His body was still at attention as he remembered her sweet backside pressed against his hip as he had tried to ignore her charms. It was his own fault, he should've left her in the clothes, but she looked so uncomfortable and he knew this would be the last time she would have a real bed. In being nice he had caused his own suffering, now he couldn't look at her without the need to have her.

He had thought to relieve himself with one of the girls downstairs, but when he'd made it down there the need had vanished. And now here he was staring at the most beautiful, angry woman he'd ever seen, and he couldn't have her.

"You know I won't fall for that." Her eyes narrowed and he half expected her to stick her tongue out at him. "Your juvenile attempt to scare me is just sad."

"Fine," he leaned back on the bed and intertwined his fingers behind his head. "Help yourself." He waved her to the door.

She hurried and yanked on the last of her clothing, then looped her hair in one fist, then she caught it in a ponytail and secured it with something she must've found.

"I don't know what kind of game you're playing," she yelled, "but I'm going to check it out anyway. And if I find a way out of here, you better watch your back because I'll do to you just what you did to me."

He sat up, intrigued. "And what would that be?"

"Take away your free will." With that she was gone. Nick hadn't had a good night sleep since he realized how young the girl was. He stared at the door, and then a smile creased his lips. Her words sounded less like a threat and more like an erotic promise. He found he couldn't wait for her to make good on her threat. First he had to find out how old she was, but he doubted she would willingly tell him. If she were jailbait he would have to stay away from her, if she were legal, well that was a very different ballgame.

Rachel stood outside the door half afraid to let go of the handle. Her eyes bulged as she stared down the hallway. Garish red, gold tassels and dark hard wood beams were everywhere. With supreme effort she looked at the door behind her, and thought of the man lying so confidently on the bed. She couldn't go back in there, she had to try to find away out of here.

She pried her fingers loose from the doorknob, and hurried down the hall. Thick gold frame paintings of nude women were everywhere. She didn't have to ask where she was, this was obviously a house of ill repute. She hurried down the hall trying to look straight ahead, but just as she came to the top of the stairs, a door to her right opened. She stopped in her tracks. There stood a petite girl, with long dark hair and the face of an angel.

"You must be the new girl." The girl said in perfect Spanish. Rachel pretended she didn't understand. She turned ignoring the girl, and almost ran down the stairs, and then as she reached the bottom of the stairs, she found her arms caught in hard hurtful hands.

She jerked hard to get away. "Let go of me!" She yelled into the face of a hulking man, she hadn't even heard him step up behind her.

"Yes, she is the new girl," the man was saying. "Senor Nick said if she came into the halls it means she wants to join our staff."

"No!" Rachel screamed. She couldn't believe her ears. "What are you doing? Let me go." She pulled hard and caught him off guard, free for a moment she raced down the hall and grabbed the door handle, yanking it open she rushed into the room and slammed the door shut. She turned to glare at him, he was laughing holding his side. "What's so funny?"

"You, you should see the look on your face."

"Couldn't you find any other place? Why a whore

house?"

"What's the matter, your eyes too young to see that kind of thing?" He taunted, and hoped she would take the bait.

She frowned and his heart sank, it made her look even younger. "What?" She looked confused. "I have never been in a whorehouse, are you trying to say I have?"

"Oh for Christ sake," he sighed. "Just like a woman to go off in a totally different direction."

"Just what are you trying to say? Because you found me at Chuy's you think I sell my body?"

He ran his hand over his eyes. "Now that would make me stupid wouldn't it? Seeing as you were at virgin and I took your virginity."

"Well, if you have to say it, yes, that would make you stupid."

Now she was grinning and his eyes caressed her charming face. She really was a beautiful child. "You aren't even old enough to buy cigarettes why would I think you were old enough to have seen anything of the world?"

"How does this have anything to do with our conversation?" She didn't take to bait, which to him meant he was right, she was young, but he needed to know how young. "How old are you?"

She blinked and stared at him. "Why?"

"Can you just answer the question?"

"Again, why?"

"Because I want to know."

"Why would I give you more ammunition to use against my family?"

"How in the hell would I use that against your

family?"

She shrugged one slim shoulder. "I don't know, but you would find a way."

Then a thought hit him. "Listen child, if you fly into the United States from Mexico you need a passport. I need all your information in order to get you one. Can you wrap your brain around that?"

Her eyes narrowed, and then she folded her arms over her chest and leaned back against the door. "So why didn't you say that?"

"Just tell me?"

"Don't you need a pencil and paper to write it down?"

He chuckled softly and got off the bed, with slow deliberate movements, he walked to her. She unfolded her arms and stood straighter, as if preparing herself for a battle. The look she gave him was definitely hostile. Right now she didn't look like a child and his body didn't react as if she were a child. He leaned his hands on either side of her head, boxing her in. Then, staring straight in to her sultry eyes, he leaned forward until they shared the same breath. "I would never let anyone see you naked." Her eyes widened and her lips parted as if she was about to speak, but he hurried on. "Put my mind at ease," he said softly begging her to respond. "Tell me you are not a child, tell me I held a woman in my arms that night?" Ever so softly he brushed her lips with his, then his hand went to her neck in a gentle caress and her eyes closed. He kissed each eyelid, and then trailed kisses along the path his hand had taken.

"I'm twenty-four," she said softly, and he paused.

"I don't believe you, tell me the truth."

"I have every right to lie to you. But why would I

lie about my age?"

"I was told you were on your way back to school, you look like you maybe seventeen or eighteen. Which is it?"

"We were on our way to Texas A&M. I went home to celebrate my birthday. I just turned twenty-four, right now I'm in my last semester of law school. I've already taken the bar exam."

"If you are twenty-four, what are you, a career student?" His relief knew no limits, he could've kissed her right then, and there but there were still some things he needed to know and while she was in a talkative mood he intended to find out. "Why were you still a virgin?"

"Don't be an idiot, because I don't sleep around. You have heard of waiting until you get married to enjoy the pleasures of the flesh. Besides, Bianca is sick and possibly dying because of a mistake like that. It's been our mission to stop it from happening to me." She pushed at his chest until he released her and she moved across the room away from his magnetic presence. Rachel hated to admit she felt anything for him. It had to be her anger that wouldn't let his image be erased from her mind. Yes, she admitted he was a sexy beast, but did he have to act like it? Lust, was a base emotion, maybe that was what she felt. *No,* she thought, *not lust.* But why did her body tighten every time he was near? *Fear.* Yes, that's what it was. Some kind of crazy fear. Even though she could sware she wasn't afraid of him. It didn't matter that he had made her feel these crazy wild things, and at odd moments she tingled when she remembered them. What mattered was the here and now. "Until this happened I was engaged to a prominent lawyer. The son of a friend of my father's." She took a seat on the bed, her eyes carefully on him as he leaned against the door.

"So you could say I saved you in more ways than one."

"No, you couldn't say that." She snapped, hating the smirk in his smooth voice. "I was happy, I love him and he loves me, I just wonder if he'll be able to over look this, after he kills you, it shouldn't take him to long to recover from my shaming him."

"If I were him, I'd kick you to the curb and find myself another virgin." Nick said in harsher tones than he intended, an unwanted image of her in the arms of some suit angered him in too many ways to count.

"How dare you, you disgusting degenerate." Her eyes scanned the room, no doubt looking for something to hit him with. When she could find nothing she turned those hot eyes on him. "That just shows how shallow you are."

Nick gave a soft chuckle meant to piss her off. "Do you think some rich lawyer would bring himself down here, into the bowels of Mexico just to find his soiled girlfriend?"

"You don't know Richard." She said in an uppity little tone and it frayed his nerves.

"Oh, I think I do, I know his type, Dick's not coming princess so you can forget that thought."

"I won't listen to you, you don't know anything about my Richard. And don't call him Dick, he goes by Rich."

"I'll bet he does."

"Just keep his name out of your mouth. He'll come. He's brave and strong and he loves me."

"Fine," he sighed. "Believe what you will." He went back to the bed and took a seat and almost laughed when she scooted away from him, and went to stand by the door he'd just left. "So you were in law school?"

"Not all of us want to be criminals." When he didn't answer she continued. "Why do you live a life of crime?"

"It's easy when you're born into it."

"What does that mean?"

"None of your business. And who said I was a criminal?"

"Well, let's see," she held a finger to her chin and acted as if she were really thinking about it. "You've killed too many men for me to count. You've taken me against my will, and if I'm not mistaken you've kidnapped me. You know the most sinful corrupt man alive... Need I go on?"

He shook his head and sighed. "That's your misguided perception of things. You should be careful, things aren't always the way they seem."

"But you do know this house of ill repute well don't you?"

"What can I say?" he shrugged, and tossed her a grin. "They seem to like me."

"I bet!" She crossed her arms over her chest and paced the room. She looked at him. "I suppose you have total run of the place?"

"I do, but I did my running, now its time to relax."

"Relax? What do you mean relax? Shouldn't we find the airport? You said you would let me go."

"Things have changed."

"How?" She snapped. "You said I could trust you. You said you'd let me go home. What was all that about a passport?"

"That was when I thought I'd have some money.

Now, I'm broke so you have to stay with me. I'll take you to Texas, but it'll be the long way around."

"What long way?"

"By land," he heaved a tired sigh, and ruffled his hair.

"Okay by land," she shrugged. "We get a truck and go, it shouldn't take more than two, maybe three days."

"Horseback, over the mountains." At her disbelieving look he added. "You do know how to ride a horse don't you? Most princesses do."

"Stop calling me that!"

"Do you or don't you?"

"I do!" she shouted.

"I rest my case."

"You have no case, you are lying to me."

"It's the safest way to travel, so that's the way we are going."

"Why do I feel like you're lying to me?"

"Maybe it's your untrusting nature."

"Maybe because I've been lied to and abused for the last week?"

He stood up and walked to her.

She froze and looked around. "What are you doing?"

"I need to get some sleep."

"Don't touch me!" She yelled when he grabbed her hands and pulled her towards the bed. "I just got up. I'm not sleepy."

"I am and I don't trust you enough to let you roam free, you might get yourself into trouble." He tied her right ankle to his left ankle, and then pushed her down on the bed. Seeing her frightened look he said. "Don't worry, there are plenty of willing women in this joint, I don't have to force myself on one that isn't."

"Good!" She spat, and he lay next to her then placed his back to her. She could feel the heat coming from his hard body and she made herself remember he was the enemy. "Make sure you remember that."

Hours later Rachel gave a sleepy yawn and sighed with pleasure, her whole body trembled with need as a strong masculine hand traversed her very willing body. She tingled from head to toe with a violent need to erupt in a million pieces. She felt the tremors, then the hot harsh breath on her breasts and her blue-eyed stranger was the cause. Suddenly she gasped and her body tensed, then started to shake, and then her eyes snapped open! There he was, leaning over her his mouth locked on hers and she was kissing him back! Rachel screamed and bit down. He drew back quickly.

"What was that for?"

"What are you doing?" She screeched.

"What the hell do you think I'm doing?" He shouted. "I'm doing what you begged me to do."

Her eyes stretched wide. "What?" She croaked.

He leaned back and she gasped. Her eyes traveled his naked chest, then down to his waist and she refused to look further. She tried to jerk away but was surprised to find her hands were bound to the headboard. "What is this? Why are my hands tied?"

"Oh," he grinned. "I had to go to the restroom. I couldn't leave you by yourself so I tied you to the bed."

"Just that simple huh?" She sneered, trying hard to ignore her screaming body.

He shrugged, "You could say so."

"And since I was helpless you decided to take

advantage of me!"

"Hold on sister," he eased off the bed and walked to where his shirt lay. Rachel sucked in her breath and commanded her body not to react. But what ever he had done to her was already taking effect and her body was tense and straining for what he offered. She became so aware of his sculpted nakedness that she felt the wetness between her thighs and cringed with shame.

"One minute you blow hot, the next you blow cold." He shook his head and pulled on his shirt.

"You can't leave me like this," she whispered, in real agony. Humiliation forbad her to say more.

"Oh I'll untie you," he growled. "But the next time you grab my rod and tell me to love you I'm gonna tell you…"

"I did not say that!"

"The hell you didn't!" He yelled. "You think I would jump your skinny bones when I could have any woman I want down stairs?"

"Then go!" She screamed. "Go get some kind of disease! It's what you deserve. You are nothing but a dirty liar. I'd never ask you to make love to me you probably don't even know what love is."

"Oh," he said, one black brow lifted at her. "You think I don't?"

She knew better than to push him, just like any man he would want to prove her wrong. But her body ached to feel his, and she would die before she admitted it to him. "I know you don't," she sneered and braced herself. The look on his face made her blood surge with anticipation. "As a matter of fact, you did nothing for me at Chuy's, absolutely nothing."

"Really?" He started removing his shirt, and then

he walked to the bed. "Let's see what a good little liar you are." He reached down and ran his hand over her exposed body and she fought the shiver that raced through her. He laughed and stretched out beside her.

"Untie my hands." She whispered.

"Not on your life."

Rachel was shocked and a little frightened by her behavior. She almost purred when his hard body slid against hers. Then he cupped her face and tried to kiss her, but she turned away. She couldn't let him know how bad she wanted him. Instead he kissed her ear, then her throat, she cried out in alarm and struggled fruitlessly. She screamed in protest, but she knew she was only fighting herself, and tried to squirm out of his hold.

"Well, you gonna fight me now?" he murmured. "If you scream again, lovely, I'll leave you just like this, unsatisfied."

Her eyes wide with distress and confusion, Rachel could only nod. "What are you doing?"

"Ssh," he said again. "Just trust me, honey." He ran his fingers through her hair, and then trailed them down to her trembling lips. "Open your mouth," he demanded, but his voice was soft. She didn't want to comply, but her body had a mind of its own, she did as he asked. He put his fingertip between her lips, and touched her tongue, and she closed her lips around it. He groaned as he pulled his finger out and trailed it over her chin down to her neck, leaving a trail of wetness that gave Rachel chills.

He chuckled as he felt her shiver. And she hated him all the more. Then he ran a hand down her throat to one of her breasts, he gave it a gentle squeeze. Rachel uttered a soft cry of reluctant pleasure. Then he ran the pad of his thumb against her nipple, and it hardened involuntarily. He did the same to the other nipple, and Rachel writhed.

He laughed softly. "Don't worry, Tigress. I'll give you just what you want."

"Please," she whispered, and wondered if he saw through her plot to push him into doing exactly what he was doing. "Please, stop." The fight was out of her, and the last thing she wanted was for him to know it. She did not want this. She was certain she didn't want this. But even as he kept going, now flicking his tongue against her nipple, she moaned in defeat.

He was suckling her breasts with sweet determination, his hand slowly moving over her quivering stomach, then to the inner part of her thigh, and she gasped with a shameful eagerness. Then he slid his hand over her nether lips, slipping a finger inside to find that she was already wet.

"I knew you were enjoying it," he teased her; his breath hot against her skin. Rachel cried out with passion as he slid his finger against her love button. She hated his smugness, but she had begun to want him with an almost desperate need.

His head lowered, and all she could see was his black curls. "Oh, God!" escaped her lips, as she wondered what he would do next.

She stiffened and started to shake as his mouth enveloped her lower regions, and his tongue flicked deep inside her. Rachel moaned loudly, squirming beneath him, and lifted her hips to encourage him. He went on forever, licking, sucking, plunging with his skilled tongue, until she couldn't stand it and her body tensed, she screamed and her legs tightened around his head and she thought for sure she had died and gone to heaven.

Nick said nothing as she relaxed. Her whole body went limp and her head rolled to the side and she purred like a cat with a beastly smile on her beautiful face. He smiled, she probably didn't know what just happened, but he did. He knew and he wanted to get her there again. But this time he wouldn't use his tongue. He eased her legs down and gently pushed them as far apart as he could get. His body was a raging mass of wanting. When he had awakened to find her sweet hand on him, he had been shocked. Speechless, he waited, and then her hand started to move, she caressed him like a pro and he was afraid he would lose himself in his pants if she didn't stop. Her leg had been thrown over his and her pelvis pushed against his hips. He was lost. Her beauty was something out of a storybook, and her innocence drove him wild. The fact that he had been her first made him want to be her only. But he knew that wasn't going to happen, she would have other men in her life, but for now she was his. Nick looked down at his straining member and back to her drowsy face. He lifted one of her legs and placed the tip of him at her opening. Sucking in his breath he pushed in. Her face froze, and she turned to look at him.

"Don't worry, love. I promise I'll be gentle." He pulled out and she gave a small cry, then he slid his manhood against her opening, making her whimper. Then ever so slowly, he began to ease inside her again, and she gasped. His heart raced at the delicious feel of her. Then her other leg came up and she wrapped it around him trying to draw him nearer and he smiled a deeply satisfying smile. He lifted both her legs and surged forward, she cried out and pulled against her binding. Then he was fully sheathed, they both exhaled a low moan. He began to move, lowering his head to rest in the crook between her neck and shoulder.

Then sheer pleasure took hold of Rachel. She was rocking her hips against him with every thrust he delivered, crying out in rapture. She wanted more than anything for him to release her hands so that she could touch him.

"Please," she cried out. "Please untie me!"

He didn't stop, his thrusts were deep and sharp and his hips rose and fell against hers. His lips took hers in a greedy kiss, while his hands untied the rope. Rachel sighed with relief, but didn't waste time as she ran her hands up his chest, then wrapped them around his shoulders and pulled him tight against her. She nipped at his ear, and he picked up the pace. Her tongue flicked out to tickle his ear lobe, and he groaned deep in his throat. "I hate you so much." She hissed, then claimed his lips.

She pushed her hips against him and began to rock ferociously, digging her nails into the muscles of his arms, causing him to cry out with wild desire. She tossed back her head as she ground against him, and he groaned, his hands captured her bouncing breasts. Soon both of their moans were rising, until the two of them were screaming their release at the same time. Exhausted, Rachel didn't mind as he fell against her, his head on her heaving chest. They were both slick with sweat, breathing heavily. After a long, quiet moment, Rachel felt him gently roll off her until he lay beside her, and he pulled her until she was on her side, and tucked neatly into his arms. She lifted her eyes to look at him.

"This never happened."

"Hush," he whispered. "Don't say a word, it was only a dream."

Nine

J OHN STOOD NEXT TO THE HOSPITAL bed and stared down at his oldest son. Simon had been here recovering from the knife wound to his stomach for nearly two weeks. But now he was starting to wake up. He knew what Simon would do the minute his eyes opened, so in the interest of keeping his son alive he had the doctor sedate him a while longer. But the time John dreaded had come, it was time to let Simon heal on his own terms.

"John?" He turned as Dr. Joseph walked into the room.

"Hi Doc, how's my boy?"

"He's fine," Joseph cleared his throat and John looked at him. "I'm going to have to stop the sedatives."

John nodded. "I know, I just don't want to lose him."

"He's strong willed and he'll do what he wants. If he goes after Rachel he might kill himself."

"Can you be a little more uplifting?" Mockery dripped from John's lips before he could stop it.

"I know you're hurting John. I feel your pain as well as my own. I delivered all your children, and I know Rachel. She can survive this, she is a fighter, look at the rough boys she grew up with, and they taught her well. I know she's fine."

John looked away, tears pooled in his eyes. "But

she is innocent in so many ways, she doesn't know about men and how evil they can be. Underneath that tough hide of hers is a heart as soft as a baby's breath. She'll be a broken woman when she gets back."

"But she'll be back John," Dr. Joseph said with fierce conviction and John smiled. "I know she'll be back, you are having all of Mexico searched. Even though Henry has gone into hiding, you'll find him. It was sad that one of his sons had to die but…"

"What's sad about it?" Simon growled. They looked down to see his eyes opened and on them. "Is she back? Did you find her?"

John shook his head. "I'm not going to go into this with you. You need to rest and get your strength back."

"Is she here?" he rasped louder.

"Stop it Simon, you won't get any information from me." John barked.

Simon cursed under his breath and tried to sit up.

"No," John pushed him back down. "You are as weak as a kitten, I won't lose two of my children. You will stay in that bed until Doc thinks you're ready to leave it."

Simon lay on his back and stared at the ceiling. "You didn't find her." It was a simple statement, but John felt it like a needle jabbed in his heart.

"We're still looking."

Simon turned his face away and stared at the far wall.

"Promise me you won't leave this room without a Doctors okay." John pleaded.

"Like I promised her, I'd always protect her?"

"Simon don't do this, she loves you. Rachel knows we're trying, she knows we'll never give up. No matter how long it takes."

"Can you leave me alone Dad?" Simon whispered.

John looked at Dr. Joseph, and he nodded. They both quietly left, closing the door softly behind them.

Later, close to mid-night Simon pulled himself into a sitting position. He reached down and pulled the IV needle out of his arm and applied pressure to the area to stop the bleeding. He swung his legs over the side of the bed, and waited a moment while his body remembered how it was supposed to work. He pushed aside the gown and stared at the eight stitches in his lower right side. It looked angry, red and puffy, but he was sure it was something he could handle. Standing on shaky legs, he ripped off the hospital gown and made it to the closet. After dragging on his clothes, he sent a silent thanks to his mother for thinking of everything. He leaned against the sink and shaved, then combed his hair, and brushed his teeth. With all that done, he was sweating profusely, he sat in the chair beside his bed until he could recover. Once he had his breath back he picked up the phone and called a cab. It would take them a good thirty minutes to get there which gave him enough time to get down to the front of the hospital undetected.

He had to get back to the search, Rachel was counting on him. A sick twisting settled in his guts and he grew light headed, but he pushed on. She was out there and he would find her.

*****

Miguel had proven true to his word. Nick had enough money to be considered a rich man. He gave a humorless laugh as he remembered the look on the bank manager's face when he had told them who he was, and that he was here to close his account. It had almost been like robbing a bank, he had asked for cash, small bills and they had been horrified. But they had given him want he wanted. He borrowed a truck and had them pile the bags of money into the flat bed. It had been a stroke of bad luck that the bank was so close to the hacienda.

After buying some supplies, he sat in the truck he had borrowed from one of the town's resident. Sixty miles from the town next to a small graveyard, he waited for the sun to vacate the sky. When it was dark enough, he began to dig. Alone, it took six hours to get as deep and as wide as he needed. That done he took the wooden creates that he'd stashed the bags of money in, and tossed them in the hole. Twelve Dunlap bags holding five hundred fifty thousand dollars each. He made sure he kept two, then he covered the grave and placed a marker. It read Beloved Julie, may you rest in peace. With the date imprinted, he was satisfied with the nights work.

He looked up, the sun was about to rise again, and he felt a pang of sympathy for his Tigress. He had been gone all day and she was probably hungry. He would put a smile on her lovely face. He planned to buy some thing's for their long trip, a few women's personals and some lace would make her happy. He had left strict instructions that she wasn't to be disturbed and she wasn't allowed to leave their room. A smile tickled his lips as he thought of her, looking out the barred window and spitting nails. He jumped into the truck and hurried back to the hotel. He still got a sick twisting in his gut when he thought of her near miss with death. Nick still didn't understand why Miguel had done it, why hadn't he taken care of her? *Why leave her in such filth?* Nick had made the joureny to Blake's and back. He'd had to servey the area to make sure Blake's place was safe. He couldn't take the girl into another dangerous situation. His heart couldn't take it, she was in his care, it was up to him to keep her safe. But it had been long enough for his Tigress to get herself into some deep trouble. As terrifiying as that whole evnt had been, he still couldn't take the chance of taking her with him on this trip. So, now, hours later, most of the day was gone. And much to his annoyance he couldn't wait to get back to her. The hotel would be bustling by the time he got back, which was perfect, it would camouflage any screams she may be inclined to bellow at his head. After paying the man for the unexpected use of his truck, he went to the stables and prepared the horses, it was time to leave town. Henry would've been informed of the transaction and could even now be on his way. Besides, they had been in one place too long. Three days had turned into one week. It was time to move on.

*****

Rachel sat next to the window in a chair covered with crushed gold velvet and lined with gold painted wood. She rubbed her wrist, they still ached a bit from having to free herself from the rope he had used to bind her to the bed. This time she was stashed in an actual hotel, or was past as a hotel here in the underbelly of the earth. She crossed one leg over the other, and swung her bare foot as she contemplated ways to escape. She wore the only clothes she had left, a skirt and blouse borrowed from Tammy, who was probably no longer talking to her after what happened. Rachel felt so bad about using the girl, but she had to get away. If it hadn't been for the fat little Mexican guy she would've gotten away. She wanted

158

Forgive Me, My Love

to know if Tammy was okay. She reached up and touched a bright colored handkerchief that covered her hair, which was in bad need of a washing. She fumed as she thought of Nick. He had done it again. She hated waking up to find him gone, almost as much as she hated admitting it.

Just sixteen hours ago he had rescued her once again. The first time he'd been gone for three days and she would've paid any amount of money to know where he had gone. Then after he rescued her, he vanishes again. This time Paco was stationed outside her door, and the windows were bolted shut. One week of waking up in his arms was starting to get to her. She knew better than to let herself feel anything for the callus brute, but his presence comforted her in a strange way. She usually spent her day's playing cards with him or watching him sleep. His smile melted her heart, and his eyes warmed her soul. When he was at rest, or at ease he was such a pleasant man. She'd made sure she didn't not repeat the insanity of having sex with him again. That man was dangerous to her heart, and she had to remember that. Whenever his hand was on her she had to quickly knock it away, or fall prey to her own body's urges. She hated the fact that he'd had free roam of the whorehouse. Rachel told herself that she ouldn;t care, but she did. The only saving grace had been, he rarely left their room, he seemed content to spend his time with her. And as long as they didn't talk about why they were together, it wasn't to bad.

Her thoughts drifted back to just three days earlier. At the whorehouse she had to take their meager belongings downstairs to the basement laundry room to wash them. While she was down there two of the girls had approached her despite Paco, her ever-present bodyguard and prison keeper standing silently near.

Lonnie was short and round, she was so well endowed her shirt could barely hold her bosom in place. She had brittle blonde hair, and her skin was a dark brown and showed signs of age that was beyond her time. She had been leaning against a washer, puffing on a cigarette, her bright red lipstick was almost obscene in the bright light of day. While Tammy, the other girl was young, and attractive, she was like a little puppy, moving from one place to the next, unable it seemed to keep still. The moment Rachel walked in Tammy jumped up on a washer and started chatting to her like they were old friends.

"So I heard all kinds of things about you," she grinned at Rachel who was bent on ignoring her. "Some of the girls said Nick bought you right off a stage in Monterrey. But they say you're some kind of rich girl who was kidnapped and is now Nick's love slave. That he wouldn't let you go, and that you are about to be sold to us because he doesn't have the money to pay for his stay here."

At that Rachel turned to look at the girl. "None of that is true."

"Then why don't you tell us what is so special about you chica?" That came from the brassy blonde. "We not to talk to you, and Paco is guard of you night and day. If we tell you man you go out your room he will beat you."

"I'm Tammy," the younger one said. "That's Lonnie, she's always full of doom and gloom. She has the hot's for your man. He came down here last night and she almost had him but he pushed her away."

"Shutty you mouth up Tammy," Lonnie snarled. "You don't know what you talking about. I have him, and I can tell you that boy got what it takes. Did I say boy?"

She threw her head back and laughed, it turned Rachel's stomach. "That man, that stallion," she threw a nasty look at Rachel. "All he has to do is snap him fingers and I come a running. You been here long enough for us to know you don't keep him satisfied."

"And I suppose you do?" Rachel couldn't help saying.

"I do."

"You lie," Tammy yelled. "He don't want none of us."

"He want me." Lonnie's eyes narrowed. "You better shut up if you know what good fer you."

"I know what's good for me, you'd better stop lying before she grabs that knife you have tucked on the big leg of yours and cuts you."

"I said shut up skinny Bitch, you know nothing."

"He told us to stay away from his wife, you can't mess with her or Loretta is going to cut your pay. Now you shut up!"

Rachel felt light headed for a moment, suddenly her heart refused to beat. "What do you mean his wife? Is he married?" She cleared her throat to get rid of that terrible catch that made her words squeak.

Tammy laughed and jumped off the washer, she ruffled her colorful skirt and brushed by Rachel with a teasing grin. "We know you two were married, a week before you got here. That's the rumor I like to believe. We over heard him telling Loretta. Don't worry about it, we won't ruin your honeymoon. Its' just too bad you had such a run of bad luck and had to spend it here." She winked at Rachel.

"Are you wife, or no wife, anyway, either you work or you get out." Lonnie said, and then shrugged one

161

plump shoulder. "It no matter, if he want me, he get me." Lonnie tossed her brittle curls and waddled out of the room.

Tammy whispered close to Rachel's ear. "Don't worry Honey, we know he was your first so you have every right to be scared in bed. But don't fret you'll get over it. I'll let you have some of my things." Tammy patted Rachel's arm and was about to dance out of the room when Rachel caught her arm.

"What do you mean you know he was my first? How do you know that?"

Tammy giggled and shook lose of Rachel. "Loretta, she laughed about it but I think it's wonderful to be a virgin when you marry."

"How did Loretta know?" She couldn't keep the tremor of betrayal from her voice. *Had he told everyone?*

Tammy shrugged. "Is it true? I can tell by your flushed cheeks it must be true. Ahh, it's so romantic."

"I need to make a phone call," all of a sudden Rachel, her heart hammering hard in her chest, licked her lips. *I have to get away. That callus brute probably told the whole town how naïve I was.* It hurt to think that he would that. But this was a stroke of luck, she prayed Tammy was as naive as she appeared.

"Oh no, you can't do that. All our calls are monitored and we get charged for them. If you make a call it would have to be on one of our phones and I can't afford another bill."

Rachel's' heart sank, and tears came quickly to her eyes. "But I haven't told my mother I'm married. I have to let her know. She would be so hurt that I didn't wait until she could be there."

"Oh ssh," Tammy patted her shoulder. "I'll tell

you what." Hope stilled her breath as she waited. "I'll see if one of the girls can keep Paco company for a while then I'll take you to a phone booth. I'm sure your husband won't mind."

Rachel nearly jumped to the ceiling. "Thank you so much!" Then she sobered. "Oh, but I don't have any money."

"It's okay you can make a collect call."

Rachel's smile blossomed. "You're right, can we go now? I'm so excited." It wasn't a lie. This was her chance to get away from Nick, maybe she could find someone to help her.

Tammy was thoughtful for a moment. "Let me wake up Harriet, she is about the only one who can stand that ugly mug of Paco's. Besides his pecker is huge, and she loves that."

A few minutes later Tammy was back. She held her finger to her lips, and motioned Rachel to the side of the door. Rachel heard talking in the hallway, then soft laughter. As they snuck out the back door she felt a slight pang of uncertainty. She didn't know why, but the thought of never seeing Nick again distressed her. Tammy grabbed her skirt and started running down the street, and Rachel followed suit.

Five minutes later, they stopped at a phone booth. Rachel paused to catch her breath. "Why...wh...why running?" She shook her head confused.

"I'm not supposed to...be...on the streets. If the polica sees me they'll know who I am and Loretta will be fined. We are here, but we are supposed to be invisible."

Rachel was touched that Tammy would risk so much to help her. "Thank you Tammy, I don't know what to say."

163

"It's nothing, while you use the phone I need to get my fix from the drugstore."

Rachel froze. "What fix?"

"Chocolate, silly," Tammy laughed. "We aren't allowed to have any, so I sneak out and get some, this is as good a time as any. Hurry, make your call, then we have to get back."

Rachel nodded and Tammy took off. Rachel hurried into the phone booth, and picked up the receiver. She dialed the operator, and in perfect Spanish she said. "Collect call to Houston Texas please." She gave them the number and was immediately connected. Rachel worried the cord with her fingers as her eyes scanned the area. There were people on the street, and a little market selling fruit. Kids and dogs, people chatting it was the typical day only she was a hostage and she didn't know what day it was.

"Yes, I'll accept the charges." A female voice said.

"Mama!" Rachel yelled, as tears ran down her cheeks. "Mama, I love you! I'm so sacred."

"Rachel?" Pat said. "Oh Rachel my baby, stop crying tell me where you are. Your father is here." Rachel heard her mother shout and she heard the click of the other phone.

"Rachel," her eyes closed as that beloved voice filled her ears, she started crying again.

"Daddy," she said through her sobs, "how is everyone, was anyone hurt?"

"No darling everyone is fine..." John assured her.

"Did you get Bianca's body?" Rachel was anxious to know, "did you find her?"

"Yes sweetheart she's fine, she is recovering very

well…"

"You mean she's not dead?" Pat was saying.

"No she's fine, where are you? Tell me so we can go get you." John insisted.

"What about Simon, is he alright?"

"Yes, yes, where are you?"

"And Richard? He didn't get hurt did he?"

"Just tell me where are you?"

"Oh God," she exclaimed. "Don't tell me he's dead. Please…"

"Rachel, he isn't dead."

"Then what is it? He is alright isn't he?"

"He's fine, he's tucked neatly away in his office. Now tell me where you are?"

"You mean he didn't…"

"You were right, he isn't worth your time. Now darling tell me where you are."

"I don't know Daddy. I think I'm close to Henry's place. We were on horse back so no one could find us."

"Us? Are you still with that man?"

"I escaped him, but I'm scared daddy, I don't know which way to go."

"Ryan is around there somewhere, just tell me something so we can find the town."

"There is a church," she squinted into the distance. "It's called San Juan de Dios but that is all I can see." Rachel froze as the door was pushed open, she turned. "No, no por favor I'm…"

"I know who you are," the man said. "Do not scare your mother by screaming, just say good bye and put the phone down nice and slow."

Rachel stared at this new abductor, and weighed the odds. If not for the gun the man held she would've

165

taken the chance. She spoke into the receiver. "Mama, Daddy I love but I have to go it seems I am to be taken hostage again."

The man grabbed the phone from her and hung it up. He motioned her to follow him. "Move!"

She stiffened. "Which way?"

He chuckled. "You go that way until I tell you to stop."

She looked toward the end of town and she wondered what he had in store for her. "Look my husband will be here any moment he's big and he'll kill you. Just let me go."

"I said move."

Rachel could've cried, freedom had been within her grasp and now here she was a prisoner of some short fat Mexican who could barely spoke English. No doubt he would sell her to some whorehouse. It seemed like the thing to do around these parts. As she moved down the street she was amazed, no one cared that there was a gun in her back. It was broad daylight and not one person tried to stop them. At the end of town she could see nothing but green that turned into mountains. There were quite a few two-story houses around this side of town and she didn't want to guess what they were for.

"Get inside." The man had unlocked a door to what looked like an abandoned house. He pushed her from behind and she stumbled into the darkness. "Keep going, up there."

He pointed to the less than steady looking stairs. Rachel began to climb the stairs and for the first time she wished she was with Nick, and she prayed he would find her before it was too late.

Two days later, Rachel had been curled up in one

far corner. Fear made her shrink tight against the wall. One wrist was tied to what was left of the bed, there was a chamber pot in one corner and a candle that had burned itself out on the first night. And now this, booted feet dragged against the rough wood floor. She shivered, it couldn't be Nick, he didn't drag his feet, he always walked as if he could fly. This was more than one pair coming up the stairs. And before she could stop it she screamed loud and long. "Niiiick! Help meeee! Niiiick!"

Suddenly the door was thrown open and the hulking shape of a man stood over her. "Don't touch me! Get away!" She screamed as sobs made it difficult to do anything other than bury her face against the wall and cry.

"Hey, hey don't," Nick had said, and at the first sound of his voice she froze. Intense relief grabbed her and she flung herself at him. She stopped fighting and looked at him through her tears. Her instantaneous joy scared her. She threw her one free arm around his neck. "Oh thank God it's you, you found me."

"Did you think I wouldn't?" Even his cocky grin didn't irritate her, she buried her head in his shoulder and refused to let go. And now here she sat, waiting, afraid to move from this room. He had been gone another sixteen hours and she hated it.

*****

Pat ran down stairs as fast as her legs could carry her, only to be met half way by her husband. She grabbed his arms. "It was her!" She laughed with joy. "She alright my baby's alright." Suddenly she dissolved into tears and her head fell to his shoulder and his arms curled around her slight frame.

"I know," his body shook not only from her tears but his own. John put one hand in her hair and caressed her head as they shared a moment of release. When he could control his tears he looked up to see Bianca standing a few feet away. The story she told when she'd come home was enough to make his eyes mist over and his heart harden with hate. But he swallowed hard, and fought to clear his head, Pat needed him, he had to be strong for her.

His hand tightened around the back of her neck and he pulled back abit making her lift her head and stare into his eyes. "I'll find her, tell me where she is?"

"I don…'t know." She cried her hands tight on the sleeves of his shirt.

"It was a collect call," John insisted. "What did the operator say when you first picked up?"

"She called the town, hal…halistco, some thing like that. I don't know… Oh God, why can't I remember."

"Sssh, I'll find out. All I have to do is call the phone company, it may take a while but I'll get the name of that town but in the mean time I'll call Ryan and Tyrell tell them to look for that church."

That seemed to calm her. "She'll be home soon right John?"

"Honey I can't…"

She grabbed his shirt. "Tell me she'll be home soon, I need to know that she'll be home."

"Yes Darling, she'll be home soon. Now why don't you let Bianca take you back to your rooms, you may want to take a nap."

"I'm not an invalid John." She snapped.

"No you're not, but I don't want anything to

happen to you. I love you too much to lose you. Do this for me."

She nodded, and he felt the weight of the world on his shoulders. She gave him a light kiss and gently caressed his cheek before she turned and allowed Bianca to lead her back the way she had come.

John watched her go with a sinking heart. If he couldn't get Rachel back he would lose not only his daughter but he feared his wife as well.

*****

Nick was two miles from the hotel, but his thoughts flashed back to how Rachel had clung to him when he'd found her. He wondered at his reaction, and wondered if she caught the endearment that slipped so easily from his lips. He had just returned to town when he was informed that his wife was missing. Panic had hit him hard in the face. His first thought was of her being hurt. Had they killed her in his absence? Then one of the girls had taken pity on his sorrowful look and told him the truth. After what felt like a year of tearing the whole town apart he had run across Miguel.

He was on the street looking in every spot he could think of when he'd noticed a man standing in the shadows of a dark alley. Then the man hissed. "Nick!"

Nick squinted and turned at the sound of his name. He peered into the darkness, his hand automatically going to his gun. "Who's there?"

"Miguel, come here."

Nick hurried into the alley. "What are you doing here?"

"Keeping an eye on the girl."

Hope surged in Nick's battered heart, he caught

Miguel's arms in an unrelenting grip. "Have you seen her? Do you know where she is?"

"Si, si niño, calm down, she is safe."

Nick clenched his teeth, impatient but he let go of Miguel. "Where is she?" he asked in as calm a voice as he could muster.

"She was trying to get away, I was here to warn you of Henry's arrival but I saw her. Just in time, Henry and his men had just started ripping the town apart."

"Take me to her."

His heart had frozen at her first scream. He had known he had a limited amount of time to find her. If she spoke to her family that means they had probably tracked the call and were on their way here. And to make things worst Henry was already here for his money. He raced into the room and stopped in his tracks, the urge to kill was so strong he early chocked on it. She was sitting on the floor, her clothes dirty and her hair a mess, her feet were bare and she was chained to a bed. Her sobs touched him in a way nothing could. He hurried to her and unlocked the handcuff. "Darling, I'm here." He tried to pull her into his arms but she fought him like the hellcat she was. He held her arms and forced her to look at him. "It's me Rachel, look at me. It's Nick."

"Oh god," she sobbed and buried her face in his neck. "Oh thank God."

"I had to rip this town apart, but I found you Darling," he buried his face in her hair. He didn't care if she saw his happiness, he just wanted to hang onto her the rest of his life. But he didn't have to worry about her seeing his intense relief because her arms were wrapped so tight around his neck that he thought he might choke. He made a move to put her from him but she resisted. So he scooped her up in his arms and headed out the room, down the stairs and out the door. He got a room at the nearest hotel he could find, and then settled her into the bed. It pained him to do it but he had to bind her to the bed, it was for her own good. It had been so hard to leave her again but he needed to get their things from Loretta's and settle some things with Miguel. Primarily, why Miguel waited so long before telling him he had the girl? Why make her suffer like that? Nick tried to control the anger rolling through him but it was difficult when her imagine was in his head all day every day.

Hours later, Nick still couldn't shake her imagine from his mind. He admitted he was just worried about her, she was after all a pampered princess and she shouldn't have to go through that kind of abuse. He entered town and headed straight for the hotel. Still he felt bad about being gone so long, he'd only planned on an hour or so but it had turned out to be all day. Once at the hotel he paid Paco and relieved him of duty, then hurried into the room. Nick quickly closed the door after him, then leaned against it exhausted. He was only mildly surprised to find her in a chair instead of where he'd left her. The sight of her as always brought a smile to his face. She was proving to be very resourceful. Sleep was on his mind, but he had no time for that, he to get them on the road, so once again sleep would have to wait. He was dead tired, he had taken a full week to check out Blake's place. It was quiet, with very few guards, which he thought was odd given the type of work Blake did. But it looked peaceful enough to hide out for a spell, and get his legs under him. He felt as lost as a fish in a sand pit. Miguel had informed him that Henry and his men had gone to the next town. It was safe for a few more hours and Nick planned to let her have her bath, it was the last real one she would get until they made it to Blake's.

"Where have you been?" She snapped but he though he detected a bit of anxiety in her voice. "I've been in this room for heaven knows how long alone. I'm hungry and thirsty and I need a bath. I can't even go to a proper bathroom. And why did you tell those women at Loretta's we are married?"

"I take it you're no longer happy to see me."

"You're damned right I'm not. I don't like being tied up either. Why did you leave me again?"

"What is this, an angry wife syndrome?" Nick chuckled as he moved to the bed, on instinct she pulled away, with anger in her eyes. "Don't worry, when I decide to kill you, I'll let you know."

She turned away, her eyes hooded and her nose in the air. "You seem to do everything else behind my back, why not that? And no, it's the angry captive syndrome. Why?"

He shrugged, and sat down. "It was the easiest way to explain our presences. I couldn't tell them the truth."

"It seems you already did, lair!" She snapped. "According to those girls you told them the whole truth and nothing but to truth. Don't you think I've been humiliated enough without the whole whore house knowing how I lost my virginity? Have you been sleeping with any of those women?"

"And if I have?" He frowned, he hadn't told them anything. Then his forehead cleared, Miguel must have told Loretta. "Why do you care what I told them? You'll never see them again."

She turned and stuck her nose even higher in the

air. "It matters not to me. I would've thought you'd have more respect for a wife then to talk about intimate things with strangers."

"Would you believe me if I told you I didn't tell them anything?"

"No!"

"Exactly."

"Did you sleep with them?"

"Do you care?"

"If I'm supposed to be your new wife then wouldn't it be strange if you sought your pleasure elsewhere?"

"Not if you're frigid."

"Excuse me?" She lifted one brow at that and he smiled at her insulted tone.

"You know, cold, unable to perform in bed."

"I know what it means." She bit out. "Is that what you're telling them?"

"No, I'm not telling them anything. There is no need. Despite what you may think I can keep my pants on when women are around."

"Huh," she snorted, and looked away. "Did you bring some food?"

"Yes, little girl," he said, which is exactly what she looked like in the too tight clothes. He had bought the wrong size. He wanted to go out and pick up something else for her to ware but he was afraid it was too late for that. Food silenced her for a while but when she was done, she turned to the bath issue.

Nick didn't flinch at the sharp damning sound of anger coming from the girl. While she had been eating, he'd had the tub down the hallway ready, it was full of warm water and suds. He grabbed her arm and pulled her from the room.

"What are you doing? Let me go."

"That's all I seem to hear from you. If you can't say thank you, then shut up." Nick clenched his teeth as he propelled her down the hall towards the door at the very end.

"It's an honest question. And I have nothing to thank you for."

He opened the door and pushed her inside. He followed her in and closed the door. He turned, and lean one shoulder against the wall. He tried not to laugh as she squealed in delight. She raced to the claw foot tub that stood in the middle of the room. It had no shower curtain but it looked wonderfully inviting. She dipped her hand in the water, and then her eyes closed and she sighed with delight. The look on her face when she looked at him made him want to make her every wish come true, but only for a moment. He thought she might break and say thank you, but when she turned away his hopes were dashed.

Rachel wanted desperately to get into the bath she had been begging for, for the last three days. Showers just didn't cut it. The tub was deep, but not wide. A thin brown towel hung on a rack waiting to be used.

"Will you please turn around?" She asked, in her sweetest voice.

"Nope," he grinned and her face darkened.

"Look, I'm not going any where. All I want is a bath, I'm tired of being sticky and sweaty and dusty and anything else you can imagine. Please, just give me five minutes."

"I said no, either you do it with me standing here are you don't do it at all."

"Ooooh," she fumed. "I really hate you!" She stomped her foot, then headed for the door, behind him.

His hand snaked out, he grabbed her upper arm and dragged her to a halt. "Where do you think you're going?"

"I'm going to the room; at least there I don't have to look at you." She spat.

"I hate to tell you this," he leaned closer to her and inhaled deeply. "But you stink." She blanched and tried to pull away from him.

"I have never sank in my whole life. Let me go!" She clawed at his fingers. "Let me go I said."

"I heard you, but I am not sleeping next to a woman who reeks. Either you get in that tub on your own or I'll strip you and put you in it."

She froze and stared at him. "You wouldn't."

"Don't try me."

"You black-hearted bastard!"

"Be that as it may you will get a washing, one way or another."

"I don't want one."

"Liar," he snapped. "This will be the first time I've washed a little girl."

"Noooo!" She struggled, kicking and scratching at his hands, but he had the skirt ripped from her in no time. Then as she turned to run from him, he grabbed a handful of the shirt and ripped it from her body. She tried to cover herself with both hands frantically looking around for a towel. Then he was there, he picked her up and laid her in the tub.

"There now wash that sweet body of yours."

She flushed darkly and promptly sank under the subs.

Ten

NICK STOOD WITH HIS BACK AGAINST the door and watched as she fumed. He used supreme control to stamp down the desire that was running high through his veins. She was so lovely it took all of his will not to join her in that tub. "Go ahead, bathe. There isn't a part of you I haven't seen, and don't worry you're too skinny to be enticing."

"You bastard, you didn't say that the other night!"

"I was desperate," Nick wanted to put distance between them. Maybe if she continued to hate him, he could do what was right for both of them and let her go when the time came. As it was, he felt himself becoming too attached to her. "Tonight is a completely different issue. I don't go for young meat, especially not the type that hasn't been tenderized." As hard as it was to say, it would be even harder if he were to let himself fall in love with her.

"I hate you so much!" She sat there seething.

"Good little girl, now take your damned bath so we can go."

She stared at him, and Nick wondered if she'd kill him if she got the chance. It was a good thing, her anger, and he'd do everything in his power to keep those fires of anger burning. Her eyes never left his as she stood up and soaped her towel. Then she proceeded to wash herself, never once did she blink. Nick smiled, he couldn't help it, she was trying to follow his eyes to make sure he wasn't looking at anything important. It could've been erotic if not for her tight lips and the fire blazed in her lovely brown eyes.

"You could show some decorum and turn around or close your eyes or something."

"I could, if I wanted to die."

She huffed and sat back in the water. She sank beneath the water again and rewet her hair. After a brisk shampoo, she got out of the tub and wrapped a large towel around her body. "What am I going to ware? You tore my only set of clothes."

"I'm sure we can find something."

She ignored him and then reached for the plug.

"No, don't do that."

At her questioning look, he said. "It's my turn."

"What?" she screeched.

"Did you think you were the only one who needed to soak?"

She groaned and he thought she would sink into the floor. "Can't you let me go to the room? I promise I won't run away."

He laughed with very little humor. "Are you sure you won't run?" The hope in her eyes was a tragic thing to see.

"I promise, I swear."

He unbuckled his belt and slowly removed it, his eyes never leaving her frantic face. "I don't believe you."

"What are you doing?" She took one step back for every step he took forward. "Don't you touch me with that!" She waved a frantic finger at the belt but he continued. "Don't be a fool. My father would kill you if there's so much as a mark on my skin."

"From the looks of things I'm already dead."

She raised her hands as if to shield her face. "Please, don't do this to me."

Nick sighed hard and caught both her hands in his one. "Just to keep you still princess, I'll have to save the beating for a later date." He wrapped the belt around both her wrists then looked for a place to tie it off. "I'm sorry sister, but this shower pole is going to have to do. Be a good little girl and stay put. I wouldn't want to have to take one of my dirty socks and stick it in your mouth to keep you quiet."

She recoiled in revulsion. But her lips were sealed, not one word past through them.

Rachel glared at him. She had to keep her hands down in order to keep the towel from slipping from her body. She looked around the room, anywhere but at him as he started to undress. Her heartbeat went haywire and her breathing became hard to control. She closed her eyes and took a deep calming breath. It was good to know he wasn't attracted to her. It made her feel safer, at least where that was concerned. Rachel heard him getting into the tub and almost smiled when he sighed with pleasure. She could imagine him leaned back relaxing in the big tub.

She kept her mouth closed, when he had pulled off his belt she had thought he meant to beat her with it, and if he had it would've been the last thing he ever did because she would've killed him the instant she was free. She still might, but he was diligent about keeping her trussed up like a calf at a rodeo.

She wondered what he would do if she stared at his body the way he had done hers. It had been all she could do not to try to hide from his seeking gaze, she had watched as his gaze scored every inch of her body but he had shown no signs of being aroused, which is why she believed him. In a way it hurt to think this particular man wasn't attracted to her. She knew she wasn't a bad looking girl, not nearly as beautiful as Bianca but not horrible either. Boys had always wanted to date her. But then he was no boy.

Suddenly she heard the water being turned on and she felt his warmth next to her. She wanted to know what he was doing but she didn't want to open her eyes and find herself looking into his eyes. But soon she found herself unable to resist, slowly she opened her eyes. *What would he do if I stared at him the way he stared at me? I could show him I'm not afraid.* She found herself staring at his broad back. He stood under the showerhead letting the water cascade down his body and she bit her lip to keep from making any sound. She swallowed hard as her gaze followed the line of his muscle bound deeply tanned back. Her distressed gaze landed on his bottom, and what a nice bottom it was, it was lighter than his back. He had muscles even there, she wondered how they would feel cupped in her hands and she immediately flush.

"If you don't want to get an eye full I suggest you close your eyes, I'm turning around now."

She jumped at the sound of his voice. *How did he know?* She stiffened her back. "I'm not afraid of anything you are or have. And I'm not attracted to you either so what's the problem?"

He turned and she gasped her eyes immediately flew to his pelvic area. Her eyes snapped shut. It burned her pride that he didn't like her, especially since he was all she could think about. "I bet you wish that night that it was Bianca under you instead of me don't you?" She opened her eyes to stare at him, when he gave an exaggerated sigh.

"Did I look like I was in the mood for any kind of sex that night?"

She shrugged one shoulder and looked away from him. "It wouldn't have hurt you if it were her instead of me, I'm okay with that. All the guys liked her, she's very pretty, and she is white after all."

"Am I going to have to kiss you to make you shut up?"

Her eyes stretched wide and flew to his face. "That won't be necessary."

"If you'd like to see what you do to me all you have to do is look down." Her eyes snapped closed. "The problem little girl, is that you have never seen a naked man, it could come as something of a shock to your delicate little mind."

Her eyes snapped open, "I don't have a deli…" Whatever she was about to say was cut off by the sound of gunfire and running feet.

Nick pushed her to the ground and was out of the tub and plastered against the far wall. "Stay on the floor." She did.

He peeked out the window but he could see nothing. As quick as he could he threw on some clean jeans, grabbed his shirt and threw it on. Last he picked up his gun belt, slung it around his shoulders and tightened it across his chest.

"What's happening?" She cried and pulled at her bounds. "Its' my daddy!" She kicked and screamed at the top of her lungs. "Daddy! Daddy I'm in here!"

Nick cursed under his breath and grabbed a dry

wash cloth, wading it up, he hurried to her and shoved it in her mouth. "You don't know who the hell is out there! Shut up before you get us both killed!" She fought with the strength of four men rather than one small woman. He had to think. Everyone knew they were here. He looked at her and wondered if he should knock her out. It might be easier than having to drag her wrestling body everywhere. Then he thought better of it, she had already suffered too much trauma to her head and she didn't seem to have that thick a skull. She was after all the princess of the house, and her physical appearance echoed that. If he hadn't seen it for himself he'd sworn she was the fainting type, but this was no wilting violet, this was an ass kicking beauty with a tongue from hell. He was pretty damned sure her father didn't know that.

Nick peered out the window, suddenly he heard a dog barking. "Damn!" he had forgotten about Julie. She must've followed him. Thinking fast he hurried to Rachel, with any luck that wasn't his father's men or hers. Maybe it was just a bar fight.

"Come on out Nick." At the sound of Tony's voice Nicks' hopes crashed to the ground. It was worst then he'd thought. "If you weren't such a sap your dog wouldn't love you so much that she can't do without you." There was laughter and Nick tried to figure out how many were out there. "What kind of relationship do you two have anyway? Are dogs as good in bed as women? What about black girls? I spoke with Chuy before he died, he said she really put it on you. He said that girl was hot. I didn't take you for the desperate type. Or is it the Hero in you? I remember…"

He continued yelling, his voice drifting as if he were walking around looking for them. Nick tuned him out and looked at Rachel. she was busy trying to free herself. He moved to her. "That isn't your father." He whispered and her eyes widened, and she nodded. "They'll kill both of us, do you understand?"

Again, she nodded. "I'm going to take this towel out of your mouth, be a good little girl and don't scream."

She coughed when the rag was gone and wiped her mouth. "What are we going to do?"

"I'll get us out of here. Just don't fight me right now."

"Okay."

Nick unbuckled the belt that held her hands and released her hands.

"I need something to wear."

"Stay close." He moved to the door and slowly opened it. Peeping into the empty hallway he grabbed her hand. "Come on." They hurried down the hall and into their room. He dug around in his satchel and tossed a shirt and a pair of blue jean shorts at her. "Put those on. Tighten the shorts with the belt so they won't get in our way."

"I thought we were too far away." She said, as she got dressed. "How did they find us?"

He was busy tossing their things in his satchel and then he waited by the door for her. "Love, sometimes it can leave you cold and exposed, it can even get you killed."

She frowned. "What do you mean?" He held up his hand.

"Do you smell that?"

She sniffed the air and her eyes widened.

"Nick!" Tony shouted. "I gave you that chance, a blackened charred body is just as good as a live one in this case."

"Oh, my God," she whispered. "They're going to burn us alive."

"Not if I can help it, come on." Nick hurried out of the room and down the hall with Rachel close on his heels. "Can you jump?" He opened the window and looked around, seeing no one he gauged the distance between this and the next building.

"I was high jump champ in high school."

"Good, I want you to jump to the next building." He lifted her up and placed her on the ledge, she looked down and immediately clung to him.

"I can't do that, what if I fall. It's too far."

"Listen, we can't go downstairs the place is surrounded. They're looking for us to run out one of the two exits, maybe even a window down there. No one will be looking up. You have to do this."

"What if I make it and you don't, what will happen to me then? Where will I go? What if they catch me?"

He grabbed both her arms and shook her. "Get a hold of yourself. This is our only chance. Just think, if I don't make it you'd be free to go."

"Go where?"

"Will you just get your ass up and jump?"

"You go first."

"What and have you chicken out and stay here and burn to death? Not on your life, be a good girl and go."

"I'm not afraid, I...I...it's just...well that high jump thing was a long time ago."

"What, you want a kiss for good luck? Okay it's the lease I can..." he laughed when she jerked away from him and climbed out on the ledge. "What," he tried to appear wounded. "No kiss?"

She gave him a narrow look and took a deep breath, then pushed off the ledge. He would've liked to say he didn't care what happened to her, but he'd be lying to himself. He held his breath and clutched the ledge until her feet hit the roof of the next building. He released it and secured the satchel to his back then hoped over the ledge to join her on the other roof. He took her hand and keeping low they made their way across the building and into an open window.

"From here we should be able to get to the horses." They hurried to the ground floor and out the back door. Nick found the stables in record time and saddled their horses. He looked over and was pleased to see her saddling up a horse on her own.

"Nick?"

Nick turned as quick as lightening; his gun was in his hand.

"No, it is me."

"Miguel?"

"Si, Si...I waited for you."

"Here, take this, it's her necklace." Nick handed Miguel a necklace he'd taken from Rachel a few days ago. "It has a picture of her family inside. That should help with the proof."

"It's you!" She screeched, her eyes wide with fear. "Kill him Nick!"

Nick ignored her. "Can you keep Tony and his men here? Give us a chance to get away."

"Si...I can but this is not enough." Miguel took out a wicked looking knife and started towards Rachel. "I can give the patron a piece of her so he can send it to her father."

Nick grabbed his arm. "What are you doing, I won't let you hurt her."

"I need some of her hair and some skin. I found two bodies that fit your descriptions I had them tossed into the fire and it'll look like you burned. But I must hurry."

"How did you find them?"

"Let's just say, it's up my alley. This way any one who comes looking for you two will need proof that you are dead. If I have a body part I am sure it will be proof enough."

"What do you need?"

"No," she hissed backing towards her horse. "You're going to let him kill me? I knew I shouldn't have trusted you." She tried to jump on the horse but Nick caught her and swung her back down.

Holding her tight he said. "Take what you need."

"Aahh!" she screamed and he put his hand over her mouth.

"Shut up princess," he whispered, his lips close to her ear. Nick looked at Miguel and nodded. "As little as possible old friend."

Miguel lifted the knife and she screamed behind Nick's hand and then seeing that there was no escape she held still and waited. He grabbed a big fistful of her hair, at least eight inches and cut it off with one swipe of his knife. He stuck it in his shirt. Then he looked her over. "I'm very sorry chica but this will hurt." He grabbed her hand and wrestled to extend her pinky, once he had it straight out he lifted his knife. Nick shifted, effectively pulling her hand away.

"I can't let you do it."

"But it must be done Nick."

185

"Find another way."

"What about you? What will I give him?"

"Take my blood." Nick felt her stiffen, but he didn't release his hold. "Hurry, I can hear the party outside starting to break up."

"Give me your arm." Nick let go of her and held out his arm.

"No," she cried. "No, what are you doing?"

"Get on your horse." Nick order as he braced himself.

"Why are you doing this?" She flinched as the knife sliced across his skin, and bright red blood poured out, and she gasped.

"Give me the shirt." Miguel said.

Nick took off his shirt. Miguel wiped the blood all over the shirt. "I must do the same with her."

Nick shook his head. "No, leave her alone."

"But Nick…"

"I said no Miguel. Tell Blake I need to come by."

"It is done, I will make them believe."

"Thank you my friend. Here." Nick threw a bag full of money at Miguel. "You can leave him, start a new life."

Miguel gave a sad smile then turned and hurried from the stable. Nick turned to Rachel. "Get on your horse, we have to get out of here."

"What? You'll bleed to death. We have to get you to a doctor."

"No," he pushed her towards the horse she had saddled. "Get on."

She glared at him, but she did as she was instructed. Nick mounted his horse and look at her. "When we hit that door I want you to ride like the hounds of hell are after you."

"What about you?"

"I'll be right behind you."

"What if you fall, what if you can't keep up?"

"Get the hell out of here woman!" He slapped the rump of her horse and it took off at a hard gallop. He followed close on her heels.

Nick waited until they were free of the town then he gave a high-pitched whistle. Never breaking stride they rode into the night.

*****

Henry stood with his hands clasped behind him. He stared with narrow eyes out the window in the library. His home was no longer under siege. With everyone out looking for Nick and Rachel, it left him time to walk around his home at least in the daylight hours. Betrayal was always hard to take. A person who betrayed someone's trust had no self worth in Henry's book. The twisting knife always felt the same regardless who turned it. He wanted to believe Nick would come to his senses and bring the girl back. But he knew it was a foolish hope. He was too much his mother's child. She had believed in the righteousness of the Law too, until she had given in to the temptation of drugs. Then she had become useless to him. When he'd first seen her, he knew he had to have her. Her porcelain skin had been flawless, but for the roses in her girly cheeks. She had been fifteen and she sparkled with vibrant life. Her long hair was black as pitch and her lips as red as rose petals. He had even gone so far as to kill her parents so that she could be free to do as she pleased. And she chose to marry him. He made sure she never knew his line of work or anything about his lineage. Then they were run out of England and he had to tell her why. That was when the preaching started. She prayed everyday and threaten to leave him. By that time the only reason he kept her around was because she gave him sons. He would've had six if the other two hadn't died. So to keep her manageable, he started slipping cocaine in her morning drink. It made his life so much better. But within two years he realized his mistake.

He had needed a reliable woman to raise his boys and she didn't fit the description any more. That was why Nick defied him, it was because of his mother. If only Henry had had time to make Nick see the right of things, as it was she had been corrupting his youngest son from day one. Nick was the strongest of them all, he would've made what Henry had built into an empire. Henry was sure of that. If only he didn't feel so strongly about the right and wrong. And now it has come to this.

It left a bitter taste in his mouth to have to kill one of his sons' but it was for the greater good of the family. It was hard losing his oldest son, but even that paled when it came to losing Nick. Robert had been weak. He had let a woman take control of him and try to turn him away from his family. But Henry had shown them both who was the strongest, and Robert had returned home. Now to lose this second son, it was almost unbearable. But Nick was a serious liability, he had to be dealt with.

"Blake, Tony," he paused to catch his breath, and then turned to face them. "Miguel." His eyes clashed with Miguel's who stood in a far corner. His Stetson crushed in his tight grip. "Tell the boys what you told me."

"Si Jefe, si," Miguel swallowed hard, and then fought to calm his thundering heart. He turned towards

Blake and Tony. "I found two bodies, they were in that fire. Tony, you left before the blaze was done. Nick," he paused and lowered his head, and then sniffed. Actual tears squeezed from his closed eyelid, he reached up and wiped them away. "The night those men came here, both Nick and the girl must've been wounded in the gunfire. The bodies have bullet wounds. Tony, you knew they were in the building, I don't know why you burned them, but I buried them."

"What?" Tony screeched. "I saw that damned dog of his racing out of town... The only reason the dog would do that is if Nick called her, so we followed there was a trail, but it was so faint we lost it. You trying to tell me that by the time I got back to town you had those bodies buried." Tony shouted, his hands in fists at his sides. "You're lying, there are no bodies!"

"It is, I swear it is god's honest truth." Miguel turned to Henry. "I'd never lie to you. I can show you Jefe."

"You damned right you'll show us the bodies." Tony grumbled.

"Yet some one has been lying to me." Henry mused aloud.

Blake had been quiet the whole time, then he spoke to Henry. "Tony is sure he had them and that they got away some how. Miguel said they're dead. When do you want to go look at the bodies Dad?"

"You believe him?" Tony thundered, his eyes hot.

"Of course I believe him, why wouldn't I?" Blake yelled just as loud. "What does he have to gain by lying to us?"

"I don't know," Tony sneered. "But I smell a rat, maybe two."

"I say we let the tree decide if Miguel is telling the truth or not." Henry said without batting an eyelash.

"No!" Blake yelled, stepping forward. "You can't do that to him, he's been loyal to you for years why would you do that?"

But Miguel sighed and nodded. "It is okay Blake I will take the test."

"It's not a test Miguel," Blake growled. "It's out and out murder, he'll kill you. You know that's the hanging tree."

"If it is my time to go then so be it."

Tony stood grinning in one corner and Blake turned on him. "What the fuck are you laughing about idiot? Miguel and his whole family helped raise us. They taught us everything we know, don't you have any loyalty?"

"Question is where's your loyalty?" Tony sneered into Blake's face.

"I won't let him die." Blake said in as calm a voice as he could manage.

"If he's telling the truth he won't." Henry said.

"Dad, please," Blake shouted. "Lets go find the bodies, then we can have DNA tests done, we'll know for sure. He just said he was told it was them. Why are you being such an ass?"

Henry drew back one fist and plowed it into Blake's stomach, when he bent for the pain, Henry delivered another blow to the side of his head sending him to the floor groaning in pain. "You better pay attention to that pretty wife of yours," Henry hissed. "We wouldn't want her to have to go through one of our little tests now would we?" He bent down and kissed Blake's red cheek then helped him to his feet. "Now, let's get this over with." He turned to Tony. "Go get Maria and the kids."

They all met inside the courtyard. A hundred year old tree stood in the center, it's limbs spread wide and hung low. Many people had lost their lives to the tree of truth as Henry called it. Blake touched his swollen cheek. He stomach turned and tears rushed to his eyes. He hadn't missed the reference to his Sophia. As much as he loved Miguel and Maria he couldn't take the chance that Henry would do anything to his own family. This heartache will never end.

"Maria, give the children to Miguel."

"What?" Blake said what was written on everyone's faces. "Why?"

Henry shot him a look and Blake clenched his teeth.

"But why Jefe," Miguel said. "I will do this thing but please do not let them watch."

"Oh dear Miguel," Henry laughed. "You mean too much to me to lose right now. No, no friend, Maria will take the test for you." That comment met stunned silence.

"No," Miguel managed. "Please not her, she is my wife, the mother of my children, I can not live with out her."

"Then you choose which child do you want to take your place?"

"None," Miguel dropped to his knees. "Please none of them, please I'll do it, let me do it. They have nothing to do with this."

"Are you telling me that you are lying?" Henry asked. "Is my son dead or not?"

"He is I can show you. Please!"

"Get up and take the children or they will be

included in the test." Henry turned to Tony. "Set it up." Then he turned to Miguel. "If you are truthful it'll be known."

"Can I talk with my wife?"

"Yes, by all means do. You have until Tony is ready."

Miguel went to the shaking Maria. He took her into his arms and kissed her trembling cheek. "I can not do it Sweets. I can't let you die. I'll kill him myself right now. I want you to take the children and run from here."

"No," she sniffled. "No, he will kill us all." She cupped his cheek and then kissed his lips. "We knew this day would come. We knew we were not safe here and yet we stayed. I will do it. And I will see you all in Heaven."

"Oooh God," Miguel sobbed. "I can't let you!" His hands tightened on her arms. "I won't let you go."

"You will and then you will take the children out of here. Give then a chance to live a normal life, a happy life."

"Ready!" Tony yelled to Miguel. "If you're truthful everything will be fine."

"I can't live without you Maria."

"You must believe in God, he will protect us." She kissed him again then kissed each of the three crying kids then turned and walked to the tree.

"You know what to do Maria, so do it." Henry said.

She stepped up to the tree, one hand on the rough bark to steady herself, she climbed up on a chair then placed the noose around her neck.

"Tony wait for my signal." Henry's icy gaze took in the group. "Some one in this room is a trader. That person has given Nick refuge, given him personal information that he had no way of knowing on his own. He has wiped out a very important account of mine and taken money that doesn't belong to him. I have no doubt I am looking at that person. Is there anything any one wants to tell me?"

Silence. "Fine, Tony."

Tony kicked the chair out from under Maria and for a second Miguel couldn't breathe as she dangled, then through the grace of God the branch broke and she fell to the ground. Miguel hurried to her and gathered her in his arms sobbing his relief.

"We leave in the morning for the mountains west of San Julian I would see these bodies for myself." Henry said as he looked down on them. "Next time a bullet will tell me if you speak the truth."

Henry and Tony went into the house but Blake helped Miguel lift Maria and take her and the crying children into the little house out back. Blake knew he wouldn't have to do much talking to convince Miguel to take his family and move on.

Eleven

IT WAS DARK, BUT THE SILVER LIGHT from the moon lit the rocky path nicely. Rachel wondered why they were traveling night and day, but then she supposed it was to put as much distance between them and Henry's people as possible. After forty-eight hours in the saddle, Rachel slumped forward. Too weary to care what he thought any more. She felt she was only inches from death. If her horse stumbled one more time she was going to scream in agony. She was holding on by a tread, exhaustion was dragging her down. Every bone in her body hurt, and she was so stiff she knew if she moved pins and needles would shoot through her entire body. The sun was cresting over the horizon again, and she squinted into its brilliant rays. Even her eyes ached and she had to turn her gaze away. But she wouldn't complain, that was what he wanted, she was sure of it. See the city girl break down and beg him to stop. She'd just as soon die before she begged him for anything.

She glared at his straight back, he held onto the reins of her horse. She had long ago given up asking him anything. It didn't matter, she couldn't have escaped even if she had the strength. This rocky mountain landscape confused her. One pile of rocks looked just like the other, and every cactus was identical. Even the little streams of water they came upon were no help. So she closed her eyes and let him lead her where he would.

Her tired mind drifted to last evening. They had stopped beside a river, she had thought they were bedding down for the night, but boy was she wrong. He had jumped off the horse and looked at her. She had wondered what he was thinking, but she didn't have time to wonder.

"Come on, get down. We need to water the horses and wet them down. We don't want them dying on us."

She nodded and slid off the beast. "Come on Carlie lets get you something to drink."

"Not too much, it'll make her sick."

She nodded and watched him out of the corner of her eye. "So do you think we lost them?" Rachel was stiff and she leaned against the horse as it drank.

"Yep, I think so," he was busy washing down his horse, not once did he look at her.

"I didn't thank you for saving me."

"Which time, at last count I was up three to nothing."

Rachel gave a small laugh. "You're right, maybe one day I'll return the favor."

"I won't hold my breath."

"See that you don't." She had just started wetting Carlie down, when he started removing his clothes. "What are you doing?"

"I'm taking advantage of the water, we may not get the chance again. Julie is on guard she'll let us know if trouble comes."

Rachel shivered as his wet chest was illuminated by the bright moonlight. She remembered the last time they had had sex and her whole body went taunt. "You better do the same." She stared at him as his pants came off and he stepped into the water. He wasn't aroused which put her at ease. At least he wasn't going to jump her when she least expected it. Able to relax just a bit, she pulled off her shirt and then slid out of the new jeans he'd apparently bought for her. She had been astonished at the wonderful fit this time. There were two pairs of jeans, two shirts, some panties that were very lacy and even a bra. It was too small but at least he tried. He had even gotten her two pretty peach night gowns, hair ribbons and a comb, brush and mirror set.

She released the ribbon that held her hair in place and shook out the uneven mess. Then she unbuttoned her shirt, careful not to look at the tempting male not far from her. After taking them off, she headed for the water. Both horses stood quietly by and grazed on the rich green grass. Rachel eyes darted to him but his back was to her, and she had to admit she was highly disappointed that he hadn't witness her entrance into the water. She wanted to show him that she wasn't afraid of him. She shrugged and walked waist deep into the water. She sighed with pleasure as the warm water enveloped her pain racked body. She let herself fall backwards completely submerging her body. Then she floated for a moment, just staring at the stars overhead letting the calm water flow around her.

Suddenly, something brushed by her, she jumped and stumbled quickly to her feet only to find herself caught in strong warm arms. She looked up and there he was holding her arms helping her to stand up straight. "How did I get over here? I thought I was over there..."

He swooped down capturing her lips with his and he let go of her arms and buried his hands in her hair. Rachel was amazed at her response, she took a step closer until they had full body contact and moaned deeply as her body throbbed, her hands curled around his smooth waist then up his back pressing him closer. It was a kiss she didn't want to end, he felt wonderful and she found she wanted everything he had to give. He lifted his head then trailed kisses down her neck, and then he was on his knees in front of her. He caught her breasts in his hands and played along them with his lips and she buried her fingers in his soft hair holding tight. Then, just as sudden as it began, it was over. He untangled himself from her arms and swam away.

"What did I do?" She had asked, and thinking about it now, she could've kicked herself.

"Nothing," he had said. "It was me, for your own good I have to leave you alone."

She didn't argue. They had gotten dressed in silence, and saddled up but she went to him just as he was about to mount his horse. She caught his arm and looked into his eyes. "How's your arm?"

He shrugged. "It's fine."

"The bleeding stopped?"

"That same hour. It was only a small cut no big deal."

She looked at him forearm and nodded. It didn't look bad at all. She looked at him. "Can I ask a favor of you?"

He sighed and she watched his jaw flex as he looked away from her and then back. "What is it?"

She caught her hair in her hand and lifted what was left. "I can't go around like this. Will you make it even for me?"

"What do you mean? Cut it?"

"Yes."

He looked her over. "I could cut it, maybe cut

enough to make you look like a boy, just incase they papered the towns with flyers."

"No, just make it even, I think shoulder length is short enough."

"Sure what ever you say."

He pulled out his knife and at the sound of it leaving it's sheath she said. "Just be careful."

"You trust me?" He asked quietly.

"No," she said and turned her back to him. "Like I said, be careful."

"I'm nothing if not careful." She was gald to see him smile, it put her at ease. Then he lifted one section of her hair and sliced then did the same with the others. Soon she stood in a puddle of hair, she felt light headed, with all that weigh gone.

"All done," he announced, and put the knife back where he'd gotten it.

She shook her head and turned to him with a grin. "How do I look?"

"Like I could eat you up," he said and her smile dropped. She stepped away.

"That's not funny. Just say it looks awful and be done with it."

He grabbed her arm and swung her back around to face him, then lifted his hand to her cheek in a gentle caress. "It becomes you."

Rachel wanted to look away from the intense heat of his blue gaze, but her fluttering heart wouldn't let her. She waited, wondering if he would kiss her, and if he did would she push him away? Then her hand went to what was left of her hair and she looked away, wondering what she must really look like. "Thank you, now I don't feel like a lost soul."

"Come on, we've got to go." He released her and picked up the fallen hair, looped a rubber band around it and then stuffed it in his duffle bag.

"Why are you keeping that?"

"It may come in handy one day." Was all he said.

They took off, once again on the trail Rachel still wondered what he meant by that, but he didn't seem to be in the sharing mood. She became lost in the moment just past, and the thought that she would've let him kiss her had he tried.

Nick looked behind him. She was bouncing along atop her horse totally exhausted. Her hair did look better. It had dried in soft curl that framed her pretty face. But the ride was rough on her. The rocky terrain was great for hiding their trail, but the heat of the sun reflected from the bare rocks was enough to zap anyone strength let a lone this small woman. He wanted to stop but they were too close yet, last nights break had almost been a disaster. He could've kicked himself for being so stupid. *Why did I touch her?* His body was still hard and aching with the need to posses her sweetness. It made for hard, painful riding, either he would have to stop soon and relieve himself or he would have to suffer. Last night as he had been on his knees in front of her, with her hips in his hands and his lips on her belly, the reality of it all hit him hard in the gut. He had leaned back and stared at her belly, fear so deep it was almost crippling had froze his whole body. The only thought running through his head was; *What if she is carrying my child?* The thought brought such joy his eyes teared up. Then the fear started, out here alone, there was no way she could have his child. She hated him, her whole family and most of his hated him. Odds were good that he would be dead by the time

199

this was over. Could he leave her pregnant and alone, could he leave his child to face hatred and possible abandonment?

Suddenly he heard a rustling noise and Julie jumped out of the bushes to run along side of him. That gave him renewed vigor and he pushed on harder.

After a full two and a half days in the saddle, he pulled to a halt. He took in the horizon, if someone found them here it would be because that person was psychic. Large boulders loomed overhead nearly blocking out the sun. He hadn't stuck to any particular path, but had chosen to zigzag. It took more time but it would secure their route for a while.

Nick caught a glimpse of her out the corner of his eyes. She had lifted her hand to her face three times already. *Does she think she's fooling me?* She was crying it had to be from being in the saddle so long. He felt a pang of conscience, he shouldn't have pushed her so hard, but he didn't trust himself, if they stopped he would probably taste her sweet charms again. And that couldn't happen. Right now he needed to check her legs to see if she had any bruising but as tired as he was, he had forgotten. Now was as good a time as any. He sighed, not relishing the fight to come.

Rachel had tried to keep her dignity by sitting as straight as her back would let her in the saddle, but that only held out for the first day. Every hour after that had been hell, each step the horse made sent waves of pain through her entire body. She glared at his stiff back as he road slightly ahead of her. She was past asking him to stop, anyway, if they stopped it would be that much harder trying to get back on the horse. So, she suffered in silence.

Forgive Me, My Love

He pulled the horses to a halt next to the only tree in the area. He eased off his horse, and shook himself. It had been a long time since he had been on a horse and he was sure if he felt this bad she must be raw. Nick looked at Julie. "Go check it out girl." The dog took off running into the brush. A few minutes later she came back wagging her tail, she sat next to a rock and waited for new orders. Nick reached for Rachel, slowly he pulled her from her perch and she groaned, her arms coming up to encircle his neck and her face buried in his shoulder. He felt wetness on his neck and shoulders he cringed.

"Ouch," she cried and clung to him. "I can't breathe it hurts so bad."

"Ssh, I have some aspirin, I'll give you some in a moment." He walked the lone tree and as gently as possible he laid her on the sandy earth. She curled up on her side and rocked herself, her face buried in her shoulders.

"Why are we stopping?" He steeled himself against the wavering of her voice. Nick tied the horses to a big bolder.

"Aren't you going to answer me?"

"No."

"Fine." She sounded like an angry child, he almost laughed. "What…what…" She said confused as he came towards her.

"Just shut-up." He said as he lifted her in his arms once again and moved her to a soft patch of grass near a large rock, then set her on her feet.

"Ooooooh, ow…ow…owww…" she cried and tears raced down her cheeks, and she nearly fell. "That hurt so bad. Oh God that hurt."

"I know," Nick went to his saddle and took out

some rope. Then he went back to her and looped it around both her wrist. She hurt so bad she ignored him and for that he was grateful. "Sit." He said and she did more then that, she lay down and cried, soft sobs coming from her clenched teeth. A piece of the shirt she wore was caught between her teeth. She didn't seem to care what he did, until he placed the gag in her mouth. She frantically shook her head.

"It's necessary," he ignored her frantic attempts to take off the gag and held her hands over her head. "Listen to me. You are hurting. I have to do it this way because you won't let me do it any other way."

She glared at him with hostile eyes.

He turned to the dog. "Julie, intruders."

The dog took off. He turned to her. "Don't fight me, I'm just trying to help you."

She threw up her chin and muttered something at him. He laughed. "You're welcome I knew you'd understand. Now be a good little girl and let me take care of you." He caught her tied hands and tied off the end of the rope to a small stump. He talked to her as he went about getting the things he needed. "Now some would say, why not just hold her down and do what you need to do? My answer to that question is, I want to get you out of pain as soon as possible, so that we can continue on our way at a faster pace. You'll have to forgive me Princess, but I am a man who doesn't like to be slowed down. And you my dear are slowing me down."

Once he had what he needed he went to her. Without preamble he caught the jeans on either side of her hips and yanked them down her legs. He was glad he had thought to put the gag on her; she was screaming bloody murder behind that gag. It could be from pain or from the fact that she wore no underwear, he didn't know and didn't care. He straddled her body and stared into her blazing eyes. "Now you have a choice, you can keep on acting like some scared virgin in which case I'll have to tie you spread eagle out here or you can keep still and let me help you."

Looking into her anger glazed eyes was difficult, hurting her was the last thing he wanted to do. He was relieved when she nodded and turned her face away. Nick moved down her heaving body and Finished removing the jeans. He tried to keep his eyes from her carefully groom little patch. *Rich people.* He shook his head and gave a snort. It just so happened he preferred his women with little or no hair. But with her everything was groomed. From her cute little head to her sweet little toes. She had been well taken care of, her parents had taught her well.

"Open your legs for me?" She made a strangled sound and shook her head no. "You said you wouldn't make me tie you down."

Slowly her beautiful legs parted, he pulled the tails of her shirt down a bit to give her some dignity and save him from temptation. He moved between her, the closer he got the more he cringed. The delicate skin of her inner thigh was flaming red and raw, it looked on the verge of bleeding. The only thing that saved her was the jeans she had been wearing. The underside of her buttocks was just as bad. The only thing he had was a generic antibiotic cream, hopefully that would work until he could get her to Blake's. Nick squirted some in both hands and rubbed his hands together. "This may hurt a bit, but it'll help you heal." In slow gentle circles he applied the ointment to her bruised parts.

Rachel didn't want to think kind thoughts of him.

He was a monster, a monster that wanted to help her. His hands were so gentle she almost forgot about the pain as his fingers massaged her inner thighs, then her outer thighs, but when his fingers touched her bottom, she jumped. It was a totally different sensation, she tingled from head to toe and her body tightened in a strange way. She wanted him to keep going, but when he stopped she was unreasonably disappointed.

"There, that should hold you."

He shook his head and stood up, she closed her legs. "Don't close them yet, I have to put your jeans back on." She nodded and a sniffle came from her. "You may not like this, but I'm going to have you ware a pair of my underwear." She flinched at that, and started shaking her head. "They're new. I haven't worn them yet so calm yourself." She lay glaring at him. "The only reason is because they're big, they won't cling to you and will give that area a chance to breathe, giving you a chance to heal." After he had the underwear and a pair of his shorts on her, he cut the bindings and helped her sit up.

"Why didn't you just tell me what you wanted to do? I would've let you." She said, now lying on her stomach.

"I don't believe you."

"You're right, I would've fought you."

He smiled as she admitted that. "You should start to feel better soon."

"What about you?" She asked, and he was touched, did she really care? "Aren't you hurting, I noticed you were walking kinda slow earlier."

"Do you care?" He had to ask.

She shrugged. "Well I could say no, but the fact is, I'm too soft hearted to be so mean. You've helped me and

I wouldn't like to think of you hurting."

"Well," he grinned. "Maybe you're not as spoiled as I thought."

"Oh, I'm spoiled alright, very spoiled, so spoiled that I know my parents are the only ones who will give me anything I want. Which means I have to get back to them."

"What about your Richard, surely in your world of the rich and famous, he'd bend over backwards for you."

She became quiet, then rolled to her back. Nick sat down beside her, and propped himself up on the rock. "Richard is everything I thought he was, he turned out to be exactly what I thought."

Nick found that a bitter pill to swallow. He hated this Richard, and he didn't even know him. "I'm sure Dick will be waiting for you with open arms." He couldn't keep the snarl from his voice.

"Yes, he will, but he'll be there with a fake smile on his pretty lips, and one hand inside my daddy's pocket, and very possibly some other woman in his bed."

Nick frowned, but his heart took a leap of joy. "What does that mean?"

"You're going to be mad, but," she swallowed, then cast those molten brown eyes on him, and he felt himself drowning in them. "I called my parents in that town. Richard isn't here, he refused to help them look for me." She sounded so sad he wanted to pull her close, and comfort her, yet at the same time he thanked his lucky stars he'd been right.

"Are you terribly upset by that?" He asked, really wanting to know.

She shrugged, and gave a cute little pout. "Only because it means you were right." He laughed and she let loose a small giggle. "I told my dad all along that Richard wasn't the man he thought he was. I told him I didn't want to marry Richard."

"And he said?"

"It's okay darling, most people have to get to know each other after they get married. I believe Richard is perfect for you." She mimicked her father's voice. "I told him that just because Richard's dad is a wonderful guy who has been his friend for years and seems to be a loving husband, doesn't mean Richard will be. The son is almost never like the father."

"Amen to that." Nick said, with true conviction. He hoped when the day came, she'd remember those words and not judge him too harshly. In that moment he realized, her opinion mattered to him.

"Anyway," she was saying. "He's handsome, but not as tall as you, he has big brown eyes that could melt any girl's heart. Only he doesn't have a faithful bone in his body."

"How do you know that?" He said in as pleasant a tone as he could manage.

"I walked in on him and some girl all hot and heavy at a party, at that time we weren't engaged, but in our circle of friends we were considered an item. He said he was sorry and that I would understand that kind of base need once I became active." She was staring at the clouds over head, but her cheeks had darkened.

"Active in what?" Nick had to ask just to see her charming blush.

"You know, sex and all."

"So now that you are active, do you understand?"

"It's not at all the same thing!" She snapped, and flashed him a quick look. "We don't love each other, we did that because we had to."

"Do you think he loved that girl?"

She frowned and became thoughtful, then as if mentally dismissing it she said. "It's supposed to be only when you love someone. I don't know about strangers, I don't think they count."

"What about at Loretta's?"

She turned her back to him. "I don't know what you're talking about."

Nick grinned, he wouldn't push the issue, he didn't need to, they both knew what he was talking about. Gingerly, he eased down beside her and lay on his back. "We'll have to leave in an hour or so."

"I know, but if I get back on that horse it'll only get worst."

"I'll figure something out." Nick whispered.

"Those men in that town seem to know you," Rachel said as she turned to find him stretched out way to close to her, but knew she had hit a nerve when his shoulders tensed. "Who are they? And who are you? And why did you take us to Henry's hacienda? Why won't you let me go?"

"I told you I don't answer questions." His tone was low as if warning her to leave it alone. But she had to know. There was no doubt in her mind that she was falling in love with him. She was already trying to figure out away to get him out of this mess. First she would have to keep her family from killing him. As for Henry, Nick may have evidence against Henry that could be used to free himself.

She sighed, his tender moment was gone. He stood up and walked away and never once looked back at her. He stood with his back facing her, apparently staring out at nothing. "Don't you think I deserve an answer?"

Then he turned those azure eyes on her, and she almost melted, until he spoke. "You are a casualty of war."

She frowned, and sat up. "What the hell does that mean?"

"Stop cussin' little girl, it doesn't fit you."

"I'll stop when you stop calling me little girl."

"That proves how young you are."

"Just tell me what you mean by casualty of war."

"It means my sweet little girl, that you have no rights. You are at my mercy and will be until I say otherwise."

"But I don't understand," she whispered, genuinely confused. "Are you at angry with my father, or Henry? Certainly not Henry, or you wouldn't have taken us back to him. So, it's my father you're after?" When he didn't answer, she laughed and jumped to her own conclusions. "You might as well pick out your grave marker son, because my father won't rest until I'm home, whether I'm dead or alive, he'll find me, and when he does, it'll be all over for you."

"You think so?"

She didn't like the way he said that. "I know so, my brother Simon the one you knifed with that bullshit move you pulled, was a Navy Seal, he knows how to track his prey, he'll find us and when he does you'll wish…"

"I wish you'd shut up," he snapped. "The more you talk the more of a little girl I see. Just shut-up for a while."

"What, you getting scared?" She taunted. "You better be because…"

Forgive Me, My Love

"I know because my big bad brother will make you rue the day you were born." Nick mimicked her, he stood a few feet from her, leaning against the tree. Anything was better then being close to her, he didn't know if he could trust himself not to tackle her to the ground and make sweet tender love to her. The way his body was feeling, it was better if he kept his distance. "Give it a rest. If your brother or father comes after me, they'll die, end of story. I'll make it quick for them, but rest assured they will die."

That shut her up. Nick scanned her pale face and fought the urge to tell her the truth. Maybe she could handle it, maybe she was adult enough to see that he was trying to protect her. But something inside him froze, to tell her would mean telling her everything. Right down to the last dirty details of his family, and she would hate him. She'd look down that pristine, honorable little nose of hers and spit in his tainted face. Why he even cared what a child thought was beyond him, but he did. He wanted her safe and that was all he really cared about.

"What are you looking at?" She snapped.

He refused to look away. "All two hundred fifty thousand dollars of you, mine to do what I want with." He smacked his lips and nearly laughed as the color in her cheeks darkened.

"That's it, you want your money back! Well I have news for you Mr.! If I can't get my virginity back, then you can't have your money back."

"Well since we're both shit-out-of-luck, why don't we compromise?"

Her eyes narrowed. "How?"

"You keep me all cozy and warm anytime I ask for it, and I won't kill your father when he comes looking for you."

She gasped, and her hand flew to her mouth. "What!" She screeched, but he kept a straight face.

"You heard me."

"Do you mean to trade my father's life for sex?"

He shrugged, "If you want to look at it that way."

"What other way is there for me to look at it?"

"I said cozy and warm, you said sex."

She paused, and he could almost see her brain working. "You're right I did say that. So all you want is cozy and warm?"

"Nope, now that you mentioned it sex is better. I mean, I know you have no idea how to please a man, but a warm soft body is better than nothing. I could teach you a few things."

"Ooh!" she huffed and he thought she would explode. "I will not be your...your... sex toy!"

"Hey, you're the one who brought it up, and as your captor I think it's a wonderful idea."

"It's not a wonderful idea!" She snarled. "I'd think you had enough at Loretta's." She huffed and crossed her arms in front of her.

He paused and looked at her, she looked so injured he went to her and sat as close as he dared. "What does that mean?"

"It means you were gone long enough to sleep with every one of those loose girls." She yelled. "Why didn't you? Then you could just leave me alone."

"How do you know I didn't?" He raised a brow at her and her face flamed, then her eyes narrowed.

"You left me in that room all alone so you could make love to those women?" He wanted to laugh at her astounded look. But when he didn't answer some of the light left her eyes and she looked incredibly hurt. For no reason at all he wanted to reassure her.

"I didn't sleep or have sex with any of those women. I had other business to take care of. Besides I've got one Hellcat on my hands, why would I need any others?" He was relieved to see some of the spark return to her eyes.

"Are you saying you never made love to Lonnie, or Colette or Maria?"

"First of all I don't make love, I have sex, pure and simple. Why do women always call it that? And why are you asking me this? Didn't I look dead on my feet and smell of horse when I came into the room?"

"No," she snapped with fire in her eyes. "You were clean and you smelled of cheap perfume."

"Oh," he grinned. "That's right, I took a bath I didn't want to sully someone as sweet as yourself."

"Yeah right, I don't believe you. I think you had sex with all of them."

"Is that a compliment?" he laughed.

She kicked at him. "Get away from me!"

"Again, why are you asking me this?"

"They each, one at a time came into my room and told me what a good lover you were and how you didn't need me any more. They said I could stay there and work with them to earn money to get home."

"And did you think about it?" He tried to keep the anger out of his voice, and she laughed. There was nothing funny.

"What do you think?"

He leaned in and kissed her softly, then leaned back and stared at her. She hadn't moved away. "I think you'd never lower yourself to do that."

211

"You're right. But I seem to be lowering myself to do what you want, now don't I?" He grinned and she flushed.

"This is how it'll work." He stated, and she stared. "I'll come to you anytime I'm in need of a quick release and you shell willingly provide it. Now, for my part I won't kill your father or your brother when they come looking for you."

She sat dumbfounded, staring at him, and he didn't crack a smile.

"You want me to whore for you to save the life of my family members when surely they would kill you first."

"Do I look like a man that would be easy to kill?"

Her eyes ran the length of him, she had to say he didn't.

"What's it going to be?"

"Okay," she murmured.

"What, I didn't catch that."

"I said fine, I'll do whatever you want."

"That remains to be seen," he got up and headed towards the horses. "Come on, we have to go." She followed him slowly. He tied her horse's reins to his saddle, then grabbed the reins of his horse, and walked to where she was trying to get on hers. "Hold still for a moment." He caught her hand and walked to his horse, then he jumped into his saddle, and then pulled her up until she was settled across his lap.

"Can he hold both of us?" She asked trying to ignore the feel of his arms around her.

"He had better, if not we're damned out of luck." Nick looked into her eyes and his stomach tightened. "We still have hours to go yet, you should get as comfortable as possible and try to keep your mouth shut."

She glared at him and turned to stare at the passing scenery or lack of. "I think I can ride my own horse." She said in an injured little tone. He nodded, but didn't let her go. He would be grateful to be away from her closeness if she rode her own horse, but he needed her healthy, times to come maybe a little rough. He wondered if she could feel the effect she was having on him.

"You aren't healed yet but most of the redness should be gone. Still, I don't think five minutes is enough time to heal completely, so sit here and shut up."

"Why can't we find a car or an all terrain vehicle?"

"Because I want to live a while longer. To get one I'd have to steal it, and I don't want the cops to have a legitimate reason to come after us."

"They don't have a reason now? We did kill people and burn down a place."

"We didn't burn down any place. They burned it down."

"But we did kill people."

"Yes, I did but only in self-defense. You didn't kill anyone."

"I could tell them I did." She said quietly and he wondered at that.

"Why?"

"So you don't go to jail."

"I've been there before, but I don't think that's where I'll be going."

"Why?" She turned those eager eyes on him. "Do you have a plan?"

"Not yet, but I'm working on one." He looked into her eyes. "Don't ever tell any one that you killed any one.

It's not true, and I won't have you lying for me."

"But I could help…"

"You didn't kill anyone."

"Will that save us?"

"It depends on who finds us."

"Ooh," she fell quiet.

Hours later, Nick reluctantly pulled the horses to a stop and she stiffened.

"Surely you don't mean to have me here and now?" She stuttered.

"Is that what's been on your mind? I was wondering why you haven't been talking my ear off. To answer your question, I wasn't planning on it, but I can accommodate you if you like."

"No way," she frowned, and pushed against his chest. "I just don't want to be surprised."

"Don't worry darlin you'll see it coming, now give me your hands."

She did and gasped with outrage when he tied them to the pommel of the saddle. "What are you doing?"

"We're almost to our destination and I don't want you getting any ideas."

"How do you know where we are, its so dark out here I can't see a thing." He walked, leading both horses for a good ten minutes without saying a word. And she was too busy trying to make out where they were to care.

Soon he untied her hands, and pulled her from the horse. "Aren't you going to answer me?"

"Why, you have all the answers don't you?"

"Stop being a bastard and answer me."

He tied her hands and feet then pushed her to the ground. She gave a small yelp and lay glaring at him.

"You wait until I get a weapon, what ever kind it

is you'll be so sorry…"

"Yeah, yeah save it." There was a small indent in one of the rocks, with a small overhang. He had found it when he'd staked out Blake's house last week. It didn't conceal much but it would act as shelter for her until he got back. "Julie stay." He was satisfied when the dog took her place in front of Rachel. Nick left them like that, he had to tend the horses and get something for them to eat. There was enough room to hide the horses beside this outcropping of rocks with them. Once that was done, he stripped them of all their gear and gave them a quick rub down.

He turned to find her struggling to get to her feet. "Stay put, I'll be back."

"I don't want to stay put, take me with you."

"No," he was about to leave, then he turned back. "Julie, you stay with her. Don't let anything happen to her." Nick motioned for the dog to stay and she lay down with her head on her paws, looking almost defeated. "I know girl," Nick said to the dog. "Sometimes I don't like her company either. I'll bring you something special back." She nodded as if she understood and seem to smile at him.

"Don't worry, by the time you come back she'll like me better than you. And I'll have her rip your throat out."

The last thing she heard was his laughter as he disappeared into the darkness.

Tweleve

WHEN NICK RETURNED HE STOOD over her staring. He had gotten back to her as fast as he could, but half the night alone must've been rough on such a delicate woman. He looked around it was dank, musky, and dark. But it was the safest place for her right now. His eyes fell to her again, she was laying on her side on the blanket. She was cold, he could tell by the slight shiver passing through her slim body. He went down on one knee, one hand propped on his bent leg as he came closer. She was beautiful. Even in sleep there was no denying it. It saddened him that her first experience with a man had to be with someone like him. She was as close to being a child as anyone he had ever met, no doubt she believed in love and fairy tales.

Her soft cheek lay cradled in her butter soft tightly bound hands and what was left of her hair lay in waves about her small head. He took out a thin rope and lay down beside her, after tying one ankle to hers, he tucked her neatly into his arms and with Julie guarding them, and an escape route firmly in mind, he allowed himself to get some sleep.

Rachel moaned, her bed was hard, but she felt so comfortable. She nestled deeper into the strong arms that held her and sighed. Suddenly she felt something sharp digging into her hip. She frowned and opened her eyes, a strange silver light filled her room. She gasped and looked around, and then she fought the tears that came to her eyes as she remembered the whole mess. She moved her legs and gasped in pain, she looked down at the hand covering her abdomen and remembered him. She lifted his hand and looked at his cut. Again, she wondered why he had done it.

She lay on her back, half tempted to knock his hand off her stomach. She turned her head to her left and found her face barely an inch from his. Instead of turning away, she let her eyes roam his face. He had days worth of black stubble, his hair was mused and a curly mess falling into his face. He looked tired, his sometimes harsh lips were softened as he slept. He looked haggard and if she didn't know what a tyrant he was, she would've felt sorry for him. Her thoughts jumped back to her fleeting image his manly attribute in the shower as well as at the river and she felt her temperature jump up a degree. He was by far the sexiest man she had ever seen. Her body tingled with every touch of his hand. And yet she didn't want to be attracted to him. He was a scoundrel, a liar, and a kidnapping, murdering, thief. He took what he wanted without so much as a by your leave. She was too much of a lady to even give his type the time of day. Still, these were desperate times, and she needed his body heat. She wiggled closer and drifted back to sleep.

Nick woke to fine hairs brushing his face. When he realized what he had done he jerked awake. Sitting up he surveyed his surroundings. Julie lay next to them, a half eating rabbit tucked in front of her, at his movement her ever alert eyes focused on him. It was still dark, the moon caste its glow on the ground around them. He felt her move and realized he was wrapped in her legs and her hand lay on his stomach. He shook his head, at a time like this he had let himself become distracted, they could be dead right now or wishing they were. They had to get back on the road. He pulled the knife from his boot and cut the zip-tie that bound him to the girl. He untangled himself and gathered the horses.

From here on out they would have to move faster. He had seen tracks in the dirt, and they hadn't belonged to them. Someone was close on their trail, whoever it was had to be very determined. He needed to see Blake, from there, there was an abandoned adobe house a few days away, if it was still standing it would make a great place to hide out for a while. The horses were readied for travel.

Once that was done he walked back to the girl and watched her breathe. "Damn what a mess!" He didn't take the time to wonder how he had gotten in the middle of his fathers feud, but he did know this time he would win. He was no longer the ten year old who trusted, and loved so freely. That had changed with his mothers last breath. He lifted his hand and delivered a light blow to her backside. She jumped up with a squeal and rolled as fast as she could away from him. Nick laughed at the look on her face.

"You!" she spat, like he was the last person she wanted to see. "Where the hell have you been? I could've died out here. I could've been eaten by something, and no one would've known. I'm tired of you leaving me alone!"

"You're right," he gave a careless shrug. "But we all have to go sometime."

"Ooooh," she said from between clenched teeth. And he waited, wondering if her hair would stand on end. "That doesn't mean I want to go now!"

"I left Julie here to guard you, she'd die before she

let anything happen to you."

She had gotten to her knees and was now struggling to get to her feet. "Julie. That's a stupid name for a dog."

"I named her after an ex-girlfriend. She was a real bitch, it seemed appropriate."

She held her hands out to him. "Take this off."

He lifted a brow at the demand in her tone. "Orders? Or we giving orders now?"

"Take them off, I can't run away I don't even know where I am. I can't kill you, I'd die out here all alone."

"Do you expect me to believe you?"

"Of course, it's the truth."

"Maybe in your mind it's the truth, but in my mind it's a stinking lie. You'd forget about being helpless the minute an opportunity to slit my throat arose."

"I would not!"

"I would if I were you."

"Please, they hurt; they're cutting into my skin."

"Keep the cute kitten eyes to yourself, or try it on someone who cares. Get on that horse."

He had to give her credit; she knew when to shut-up.

They left the shelter and headed deeper into the mountains. It was finally getting dark, and it was warm and dry. That night they pulled to a stop. "Why are we stopping?" She was so tired she couldn't keep the exhaustion from her tone.

He jumped off his horse and tied the reins to a small branch. "I think it's safe enough for us to take a break." He looked at the dog and said. "Get food." The dog took off like an arrow. Rachel didn't want to be, but she was impressed at how well behaved the dog was.

"From now on we travel only at night."

"Why?"

"We don't want any helicopters or airplanes spotting us."

"Speak for yourself, I wouldn't mind being spotted."

"Even if it's by the people who want you dead?"

"I thought you were one of those people, aren't you working for Henry?"

"Do you think you'd still be alive if I were?"

She shrugged. "I don't know what the plan is, maybe once you've gotten the money from my father you'll kill me. Why else would you keep me alive and refuse to let me go?"

"Did I ever tell you, you talk too much?"

"No, but as a future Lawyer I'll get paid to figure things out. Oh wait," she said. "At the moment I don't have a future do I?"

"Don't make me tell you to shut-up again." She watched as he walked around the area to make sure all was safe.

"Why should I listen to you?" Rachel snapped, she wanted more from him than a flippant attitude and a caviler answer. She needed him to feel something for her, anything, even hate was preferable to this icy distain she felt coming from him. "I know now that you can't kill me yet. I might as well make you miserable then when it's time to kill me you can look into my eyes and do it just to get some relief."

"Maybe I should kill you right now and end this for both of us."

"If you did I'd have more respect for you. I would

know that you aren't just some lowlife patsy who is risking his life for some scum of the earth insane criminal."

He dropped what he was doing and hurried to her. Her eyes widened as he grabbed her arm. She gave a startled shriek and tried to cling to the saddle horn, but she found herself falling from the horse to land in a painful heap on the ground. She rubbed her sore rump and glared at him.

"You want to die? You want me to end this right now?" He stormed, and she inched away from the rage in his voice. "This isn't just about you! Because of you, I'm a wanted man, not only by your family and the Mexican authorities, but by Henry's people too. In helping you I've slit my own throat. So don't sit there as pretty as you please and tell me you have no respect for me. It's you I have no respect for, if it weren't for me you'd be dead right now!" He loomed over her, his eyes blazing. "Get back on that horse and keep your mouth shut before I do it for you." He stomped off, and jumped back on his horse. "Spoiled little Bitch!" He muttered.

"I resent that you rotten bastard!" She yelled, Rachel dusted herself off and slowly pulled herself back up on the horse. "I thought we were taking a break!" She screamed.

"You ruined it!" he yelled back. "Now get your ass on that horse!"

Rachel glared at his back, she vowed she would find a way to leave him. She clenched her teeth, and with firm resolve she kicked her horse into a trot.

As luck would have it her chance came sooner than she could've hoped. Her horse developed a noticeable limp. Try as she might she couldn't ignore it.

Her lips tightened, as much as she hated speaking to the big ape, she had to tend her horse. She cleared her throat. "My horse is limping." She said loud and clear. Anger rolled through her at his reaction. His shoulders heaved, and he shook his dark head as if she were the biggest pain in the butt he had ever come across.

But to her relief, he pulled his horse up, and slid off. She followed suit. Rachel caressed the sweaty mane and whispered to the animal. "It's okay darling, I'll fix you up." To him she shot a hard look. "Give me something to get this out with."

"Get out of the way," he yelled as he came up behind her. "Julie," he barked. "Stay." The dog took a seat on the ground and watched the activity.

"I need some water." Without waiting for his reply, she headed off in the distance towards a small river they had been following. The terrain was rocky, it made walking hard and riding even harder.

"Stay where I can see you." He shouted, his head bent over the horses hoof.

Rachel stopped, she looked around and her heart took flight. This was her chance, she was level with his horse and her horse was out of commission. Without another thought she hurried towards his horse and jumped on it. Loosening the reins she yelled and slapped the horse's rump, it took off like an arrow. All she could hear was Nick shouting at her to stop. She smiled from ear to ear, she was free! Rachel tucked herself low in the saddle and raced the through the wind. Now all she had to do was back track and she'd be home free.

She kept looking behind her terrified that he would be on her trail in no time. But after she had gone a pretty good ways and there was no sign of him, she started to relax. Then she heard a bark and a piercing whistle, and she pushed her knees deeper into the horse's sides. But to her dismay the horse was turning. "No," she cried and pulled on the reigns. "No, what are you doing?" But Rachel found herself charging headfirst back the way she had come. The only way she could fix it was to let go. She tossed up a quick prayer and threw one leg over the saddle, then untangled her foot from the stirrup, with her eyes closed, she jumped from the saddle and landed hard, pain shot through her entire body as she let her body roll. Then as she lay still, she pulled in a breath and saw stars as agony ripped through her. She lay as still as possible, and tried to control her breathing. Rachel couldn't help the tears when they came, but she knew she couldn't stay out in the open, he would find her, and then all would be lost.

She pulled herself to her feet, and looked around. She couldn't see much through the tears, but she did see what looked like big boulders. Hope surged again and she stumbled towards it. She was pretty sure nothing was broken, but she hurt like hell. She knew after a restful night she would be right as rain and ready to start out again. Just the thought of freedom made her feel better.

"Julie, go get her!" Nick cursed long and loud, he hurried to dig the rock out of the mares hoof, but it was deep and she wouldn't keep still. At that moment he cursed all females to hell. Every second seemed like an eternity, then finally he removed the stone. "Sorry girl, but I can't wait for you to feel better. There is another one of your kind who needs a lesson in loyalty."

Nick jumped on the mares back and took off in the direction Rachel had gone. After an hour, he was starting to get anxious, the trail was so erratic he had to walk the horse in order to keep on the trail. Then he whistled loud and waited. For a nervous moment there was nothing. Then from the distance he heard a faint bark, and then he smiled. Nick put two fingers to his lips and let loose a long low whistle. Hopefully the horses from Henry's ranch were just as well trained as when he was a boy. With any luck she would be back in his arms a matter of minutes. Nick kicked the horse into a trot and hurried out to meet his hissing Tigress.

The closer Nick came to the horse the more he frowned. The saddle was empty. "Damn that girl!" Nick gathered the reins, and refused to give in to the knot of fear curling in his stomach. How long had she been off the horse? Had she fallen and hurt herself? Had she broken her damned fool neck? He kicked his horse to urge her faster. He scanned the area and froze, a few yards ahead of him was a dark stain. Nick jumped from his horse and hurried to the area. It looked bad, he knelt beside the puddle and lifted the dirt filled liquid to his nose. It was blood, and it was fresh. He looked around, there was a line of blood leading into the rocks. Suddenly there was a piercing scream and the furious growls of dogs.

Instantly, he was ten years old and everything was happening again. His knees trembled as if ready to buckle, he didn't want to look over the rocks, heart pounding fear, paralyzed him. Then he heard screaming again and the pained shriek of a dog. Nick shook aside the old fears and jumped on his horse, in the process he pulled out both guns as the horse took a leap over the rocks. It was worst then he feared, Nick took aim into the pack of wolves, he shot as many as he could. But in the end he was seeing the same scene.

Forgive Me, My Love

Julie was dead, he could tell by just looking at her. But it looked like she had taken many of them with her. Nick felt his heart turning to stone. He had to think past it, he needed to find Rachel, but fear made it hard to look for her. The pre-dawn light showed him more than he cared to see. Nick closed his eyes for a second but even with them closed he saw the scene in vivid color. Blood, like black ink covered the area, dead wolves littered the ground. Julie had done well. His anxious eyes searched for Rachel. There was a slight movement to his left beside a rock, and he lifted his gun, ready for anything. As he turned the corner, there she was, curled in a tight ball with a rock clutched in each fist. Her eyes were closed tight and her shirt in tatters, blood covered the sleeve of one arm and her chest. She had her head buried in her arms.

Nick fell to his knees beside her. "Look at me." He murmured.

Slowly she did. Her eyes were red rimmed and her whole body was covered in blood. Nick was afraid to touch her. "Where are you hurt?" he didn't recognize his own voice, it was so deep with emotion.

She shook her head, and to her credit she wasn't crying.

"Tell me where you're hurt Rachel." He asked again.

"I...I..." she took a shuttering breath, and wiped her eyes. "I thought I was dead..." she whispered as if she was explaining something. "They came out of no where..."

"Just answer my question."

"I hurt everywhere," she gave a guttural laugh that bordered on hysteria. "I'm hurt so deep I think my soul is scarred. I don't think I can make it through another day, that's how bad I hurt."

Nick nodded and stood up, he had to get away from her. His relief had been so severe it had brought tears to his eyes and he couldn't chance her seeing them. "I have to see to Julie, you stay put." As he walked away he ran the sleeve of his shirt over his face and went to bury his best friend.

After saying a few words over Julie, Nick turned to see Rachel sitting on her horse. Her head down and her eyes closed. He walked to his horse and pulled himself up on it. Slowly, so as not to jar her, he headed back the way they had come.

The sun had risen when they found the cave again, but he bypassed it and headed straight for the river. He had to see her wounds soon. Nick scanned the sky for any sign of air surveillance. There was none. Finally, back at the river he led them under an outcropping of trees, he slid off his horse. He couldn't look at her, if he did he knew he would do something they would both regret. He was angry, hurt and relieved. Each emotion was so intense he didn't trust any of them. He went to her horse and caught her around her waist. Then he swung her to the ground. "Let's get you cleaned up."

Rachel was grief stricken, she wanted to ask his forgiveness. That dog had been his world, she knew it without being told. Her brothers had had dogs, and every time one of their pets died, they would go some place and cry their eyes out. They'd cry for weeks. She looked at Nick's broad back as he bent at the waters edge, even now, after all she had done he was making sure it was safe for her to get in. She looked down at her arms and cringed. The blood had dried, but there was a hole in her upper shoulder where the blood bubbled and oozed. It dripped down her arm and she shivered as she remembered. The biggest wolf she had ever seen had just clamped his jaw on her shoulder when Julie had jumped on him, and he had released her to face Julie. That dog had fought so hard to protect her. Rachel looked up to find him standing in front of her.

"The water will wash away the dirt, and then I can see how bad you're wounds are."

She reached out to him. "Nick I..." But he flinched away from her, and she wanted to cry it hurt so badly.

"Don't talk right now," he said and her heart crumbled at his raspy tone. She was right, he was hurting and it was her fault. He put his hat on and walked away.

Rachel clenched her jaw as she stared after him. There was no way to make it up to him, she would just have to live with what she had done.

Once she had finished washing away the blood and dirt, she put a rag over her wound and held it for a moment then pulled on a shirt, and a pair of shorts. On bare feet she walked to where he had already tied the horses. She went to Carlie and rubbed her velvet nose. "It's a good thing you weren't with me. I might've gotten you killed too." Rachel sniffled, then she let the tears she had been trying so hard to hold in, flow against the horses neck. "I'm sorry Julie, I'm so sorry."

"Come over here and let me look at your wounds." Rachel's head snapped around at the first sound of his voice. He was standing directly behind her, but his face was still tight and she was afraid he would really hate her now. She swallowed, and wiped her eyes, then wiped her wet hands on her shorts.

"Sit here." His voice sounded wooden as if he

only spoke to her because he had to.

She sat on the flat surface of the rock and watched him move around the small fire he had built. Then he went to his bag and fished around for something. She looked at the small puncture in her arm, the bleeding was now just a slow trickle, the rag she had pressed against it helped. She tensed as he came to her with a hand full of things. "What's that?"

"I'm going to clean up the bites." He was straight forward, but his eyes never met hers.

Rachel couldn't take it. "Can I say…"

"No, you can't!" He snapped. "When I finish I want you in that cave. Don't speak to me until I ask you something."

Rachel clamped her lips tight, and nodded.

"I'm going to remove the rag on your wound, I want you to take off the shirt you are wearing, then I'll see if you have any other wounds." She did as directed, and soon she was sitting in just her shorts and bra.

Nick stood in front of her and cringed at the big purple bruises; she had one on her knee, and one on her ribcage and another one on her forehead that looked like a blood blister. The only one that worried him was the hole. It looked awful, it had to be the size of a dime, but the worst part was he would have to explore it to see how deep it was and make sure there was nothing inside it.

He opened the first aid kit and ripped opened an alcohol pad. "This is going to sting."

She closed her eyes and bit her lip. It took five two by twos but he had finally disinfected her wounds, none were deep, then he turned his attention to the hole. "Rachel?" Her eyes flew open, and she stared at him. "I'm going to have to explore this hole on your shoulder.

It's going to hurt so hang on to my leg." She nodded and grabbed his leg with both hands. "Now, after I'm done I'm going to put at least two stitches in it." Again she nodded. "Here we go, don't scream."

Nick examined the wound with his pinky finger and felt around it, it was bloody, but it wasn't as wide as it looked. He closed his eyes and put a finger inside. She gave a small yelp and her fingers dug into his thigh. "Okay it's clean," he said and resisted the urge to wipe at the sweat on his brow. "Now for the stitch, just one it's with gut so we don't have to remove it."

"Just do it." She panted.

Nick put the needle to her skin and she growled something between her teeth then she was shaking, by the time he finished she was covered in sweat. And so was he, Nick wiped his brow and looked down at her. She had fallen forward, and now her head lay on his stomach. She had fainted. "Come on," he said just incase she could hear him. "Let's get you to bed."

He reached down and turned her so that her injury was away from him and picked her up in his arms. He hadn't meant to, but he dropped a kiss on her forehead, and savored her closeness.

Much later Nick built a small fire in the center of the cave, there was a gaping hole in the ceiling and the type of wood he used left only a small puff of white smoke that blended well with the night sky. He put a small metal pot on the hot rocks, filled it with water and threw in a few pieces of beef jerky. While that cooked he went to the caves entrance and stared out. He was in the middle of a no win situation. He knew that. It had been three weeks since this thing started. He had a good idea how it would end. He looked over his shoulder at the

229

sleeping girl. She had no business being in this kind of situation. She shouldn't be with someone like him.

His thoughts went to Julie, and as much as he hated it tears came swiftly to his eyes. He had had her since she was weaned from her mother. He had taught her to be loyal, faithful, to follow his every command, and she had loved him. It had been the only true and pure love he had ever known. Women were jaded and temperamental. The ones who claimed to love him had all betrayed him in one way or another. With Julie he had always felt like a proud papa. And now she was gone. She died doing his bidding. His gaze swung from Rachel and he wondered if he should just let her walk away, let her family protect her. He didn't want to look deeper into why he hadn't let her go. He didn't know her, and she didn't know him. She hated him, she had every right to. But would she be able to survive without his help?

Rachel opened her eyes, she knew where she was. Without his warmth she was well aware of the circumstances surrounding her. She saw Nick standing at the entrance of the cave, his shoulders were slumped and his hands covered his face. Red rocks glowed in front of her, and on them was a small pot of boiling water. She sat up and looked from him to the pot. Slowly she got up, then on silent feet she took the pot off the rocks.

Nick tensed as he heard footsteps behind him, but he wouldn't turn around. He waited to see what she would do. He knew he was in danger, she could do real damage to him with the water he had left boiling, or the knife he'd left beside the pot.

He held still as she came closer, then he sighed as her arms came around his waist, and she lay her head on his back. His relief was so intense his throat squeezed.

Forgive Me, My Love

She tightened her arms around him, and he let his hands cover hers. If he didn't know better he'd think she had just dropped a kiss on his back, but then his shirt was getting wet. He frowned and turned her in his arms.

"No grita el dulce." He said in Spanish and she looked up at him

"What does that mean?" she asked. He told her.

"I'm not sweet, I'm anything but sweet."

"To me you are sweet," he wiped her tears. "Don't cry."

"But that's all I feel like doing. I hurt you so bad, and I'm so sorry. She was wonderful, you trained her so well and anyone can see she…she lov…ed you as much as you lov…ed her."

"Stop crying it wasn't your fault." They both knew it was her fault, but he couldn't think of anything else to say. Nick kissed her tear stained cheeks, but resisted lifting her chin to kiss her lips, no matter how bad he wanted to.

She surprised him, and ran her hands up his chest and rocked them around his neck. His eyes clashed with her. "What are you doing?"

"I want to be in your arms."

"Why?"

"Because, I need you," she pulled his head down to hers and nibbled at his lips, when he parted his lips, she deepened the kiss. Then he wrapped her in his arms, and cradled her body close to his.

Nick accepted what she offered. He plundered her willing lips one hand traveled up her back until he cupped her head and held her still as he drank freely of her. Then he released her head, and ran his hands down her back and cupped her bottom. He pulled her tight against his raging need, and she answered his need by pushing against him, she wrapped one leg around his and moved against the heat of him while her mouth did wonderful things to his. Nick groaned deeply, his heart was nearly beating him to death. He lifted her in his arms and took her into the cave. He set her on her feet and took off his shirt. In the moonlit night they could see very well, and he was surprised when she took off her shirt. So he unbuttoned his jeans and let them fall to the floor. He stood in only his boxers.

She unbuttoned the shorts she wore and let them fall to the ground, then she kicked them off and straight into his arms. She giggled and it was the sweetest sound he had ever heard. He dropped the shorts, her giggles had stopped and she stood with her fingers wrapped in the band of his boxers. He was standing in front of her, and he lifted her chin and brought her lips to his. It was a kiss full of sweet meaning and endless promise.

Rachel couldn't help what she was feeling. He was so different from anyone she had ever known. There was a connection here. She knew it, and she wanted him to know it. She let her hand rest on the warm muscles of his sculpted chest and jumped as those muscles flexed under her hand. She lifted her hands and traced the contours of his body praying that she never wake up from this wonderful dream. Here was a man, red blooded handsome man. Who sought to protect her from all evil, and he wanted her. Lil' ol skinny Rachel, how had that happened. She had always thought of herself as young, still a child. But in these last few weeks she had had to grow up, and here she stood in the arms of a real man. She swallowed hard as she remembered that morning at Loretta's. She wanted what he made her feel.

Forgive Me, My Love

She ran her hands down his chest, and to the front of his boxers and gasped, he did want her. Then she smiled as he trembled. Then her smile dropped when he hooked his fingers in the panties she wore and pushed them down, his lips were on her neck and she shivered, he had such great lips. She captured them again with hers and suckled his lower lip between hers, them she hooked her fingers in his boxers and pushed them to the ground. He sprang free and his hardness thrilled her, it lay pressed against her belly and she wrapped one leg around him pressing her center against his straining shaft, but he lifted her without breaking the kiss and she wrapped both her legs around his hips. For a few delicious moments she pushed against his throbbing manhood that was trapped between where she was so open and his stomach, she moved her hips against him and he threw his head back and growled in his throat.

Rachel kept grinding on that wonderful tool until her whole body was quaking, and she found herself nipping at his shoulder, then just as it started to ebb he lifted her higher, and lowered her wetness onto his member. He shivered and she shook, her legs tightened and then she caught his soft curls in her fists and let him control their movements. He was slow and for a moment she thought he was teasing her. And she began to wiggle, then out of no where he gave a mighty lunge and she thrilled at the chills that ran through her body at how great that felt. She pulled his head back down to hers and wrapped him in her arms, his hands on either sides of her bottom, he helped her raise and fall against him. The sounds a labored breathing and sweat slicked bodies that filled the area excited Rachel to no end.

"Put me down Nick," she panted. And he caught

her waist holding her close, he buried his head in her neck as his body slowed its movements. He detached her and she lay on the blanket looking up at him. Her heart in her throat she let her eyes travel the length of him then looked into his eyes. "I want all you have to give." She whispered, and he came to her.

"That's a lot, are you sure your're ready?"

She nodded and licked her lips, she opened her legs to him and he went to his knees. She reclined on her elbows as he lowered himself over her, and took her lips in a soft kiss as he fitted their body's back together. Her head fell back as he made them one, and she screamed as he did a fast pumping movement with his hips, and she saw stars. Her body tense and she clutched him to her. "Oh, please don't stop! Oh god yes!" She screamed, and her legs came up around his waist.

Nick tingled from head to toe, he slowed down and focused on something other then her delicious body moving so sweetly under his, then her soft lips were on his chest and her fingers were cupping his bottom and Nick struggled to fight the feeling, but it was there, then she was screaming her pleasure and he joined her. He cupped her bottom and hiked her up then he was on his knees pumping and grinding and she was begging him not to stop. Nick wished he could oblige her, but his body was about to burst, and he could wait no longer. He let go of her and pulled out, and his seed sprayed on her soft belly. Once it was over they both looked at the puddle on her stomach and the streaks on her chest. He ignored the question in her eyes. "Let's get washed up."

At the river she kept looking at him, they stood as naked as Adam and Eve, but she wouldn't take her eyes from him. Nick went back to the cave and dried off, then dressed. She followed. Looking incredibly hurt.

"What?" Nick snapped, and was immediately sorry.

"Nothing." She turned away. Once they were cleaned and changed Nick looked at her wound, it had started to leak. "Let me change that dressing for you."

"No," she said with that stubborn fire in her voice. "Don't touch me, I'll do it myself."

"Fine!" He kicked over the pot, and it bounced off the rock wall.

"What was that for?" She yelled.

"Why are you looking at me like that?" He growled, he knew she was hurt, but so was he. He'd only done what needed to be done.

"If you don't know then I won't tell you."

"You know what? I could care less." He started throwing things in his bag.

"What're you doing?"

"We're leaving."

"Fine."

Nick watched her struggle with placing the bandage, and he had to stop himself from helping her. He felt like a heel for pulling away from her at the worst possible moment, and denying them both such great pleasure, but he was looking out for her. *Didn't she know that?* Nick pulled two scarves out of his pocket, one he wrapped around her eyes. "Open your mouth."

She did but he knew it was to complain rather than obey, so he took advantage and quickly tied it around the back of her head. He leaned over and kissed her ridgid cheek, then he whispered. "Until tonight chica," he snorted at her muffled protests. That would give her something to think on while he found a way into Blake's home undetected.

*****

Blake stood at his bedroom window staring at nothing but seeing everything. Anything that moved was a potential threat to his family. Under his shirt was a gun big enough to put a hole in the side of a tank. But it was as silent as it was deadly. He looked over his shoulder and some of his anxiety left. A smooth warm feeling flooded his soul. Sophia sat with both children nestled against her. Her arms were around them as she read to them. It was the most beautiful sight he had ever witnessed. And because of loyalty they're lives were in danger.

Blake clenched his teeth, and turned back to the window. He had been jumping at shadows ever since he had helped Miguel's children escape. It had been difficult, he had wanted the whole family to run, but Miguel wouldn't go. He had some kind of misguided idea that if he stayed, Henry wouldn't try to find Maria and the kids and kill them. Then Maria wouldn't leave without Miguel, so the plan had changed. Their daughter Cynthia had taken the three younger children, and the money Miguel had gotten from Nick, and fled the country. Henry had been incensed, he felt he no longer had leverage over Miguel, but it was Miguel who tried to calm Henry. And now Henry wouldn't let Miguel out of his site.

Blake shook his head. It had been terrifying, but it was something that had to be done. Getting the children away had been as bad as an actual kidnapping. Cynthia had taken the kids to the market, Blake cringed even now as he remember how terrified the children had been. Even Cynthia had, had no idea what was going on. All they had were the clothes on their back and a suitcase of money. Blake had made arrangements for them to go to Sophia's parents in Spain. How they had cried for their parents. But once they were at a safe house, Blake had explained to Cynthia what was happening, and at eighteen years old, she cooperated fully.

But Blake felt Henry suspected him of helping. He couldn't shake the thought. If Henry thought he had anything to do with the missing children he had just signed a death warrant for his family. Blake swallowed hard, fear clogged his throat. He swore he'd kill them himself rather than let Henry have his family. He needed Nick to get here and get here fast. He couldn't go out and look for him. There were already too many people looking now. This was turning into a royal circus. The girl's father and brothers had already terrorized three towns. They had no regard for the law.

Bodies were turning up every where, until they'd found the girl's body. He doubted they believed the girl was dead. They had to have done the same thing Henry had done with Nick's remains. The DNA tests had proved they were dead, but still Tony searched. It was getting ridiculous.

The instant Nick showed up they would form a plan then maybe they could all be free of Henry, once and for all. He didn't know how he felt about possibly having to kill his father. But he did know, if it came down to it, he wouldn't hesitate to put a bullet right between Henry's eyes. Blake wondered if he were being overly optimistic. Miguel said Nick had grown into a fine man, trustworthy, honorable. *But what if it wasn't true? If Nick... No I won't think about it. I'm sure I can trust Nick. He was after all a police officer.* Blake couldn't help, but think of how betrayed he felt when Nick had left home. They were only a few years apart in age, and Nick had been his best friend. His only friend. Then he left, Blake had felt abandoned and his resentment had grown. But when he'd met Sophia, her soft forgiving ways had rubbed off on him. Blake just hope Nick had picked the right side and he wasn't being a soft hearted fool.

Thirteen

THEY RODE THROUGH THE FOREST A WHILE longer. Then as they drew closer, Nick pulled the horse to a stop, then he surveyed the area. He shook his head in amazement. *Blake can't be this careless.* He could see the house, which sat some three hundred feet away from where they were.

Nick tugged on the reins of her horse to urge the beast forward. When they reached a crop of trees on the west side of the property he brought both horses to a halt and tied them to a sturdy tree. "That should keep you two until I can make sure we are welcome here."

Hearing muffled sounds, he turned to find her slumped over the saddle. He sighed and went to her, reaching up he caught her slim waist and swung her to the ground. He made sure he kept an arm around her and sure enough her legs buckled. He lifted her in his arms, and carried her to the tree. "Sit here," he said. "I need to take care of the horses."

After he had the horses brushed down and their saddles tightened just in case they needed a quick escape, he went back to her. The choice was clear, leave her here for someone to stumble across, or take her with him and risk them both getting caught.

"Come on Princess if we have to die, then we die

together." Her eyes widened, and she growled something at him. He ignored her and bent down, then swung her over his shoulder and started towards the lights in the distance.

Nick held her legs close to his chest and hurried through the back gate. The house was large, it was almost a replica of Henry's, only the landscape marked it as a home. He peered into one of the back rooms. All was dark but he could see it was the kitchen.

Click. Nick froze; he knew the sound of a gun being cocked. He swallowed and held up one hand. "I'm here to see Blake Dennison."

"And just who is calling at this time of night." Nick squinted at that voice, it was familiar but it had an edge to it he didn't recognize.

"Nick."

The man stepped around him and grabbed the handle of the door and pushed him inside. "Keep her quiet and follow me."

Nick was relieved when he recognized Blake. Maybe his luck was changing. Nick followed him through the kitchen and up the back stairs, then down a dark narrow hall and stopped. "She'll be safe in here."

Blake opened the door and Nick hurried in, he went to the bed, and flipped Rachel from his shoulders to lay on the bed, then he leaned forward and stared into her blazing eyes. "See you in a minute love." He whispered, then kissed her cheek and walked away.

He mentally closed his ears to her muffled screams. They left the room and Nick looked at Blake. "I don't know where you stand on this but…"

"Wait, let's go to the study and be quiet."

Nick nodded, and followed him down what looked

like a staircase built into the wall, and it opened into a large library. He noticed Blake didn't turn on any lights. "Stay close to the wall." Blake hissed, and Nick nodded. They headed to the back of the room and Blake put his arm into one of the towering bookshelves, and it moved easily, revealing hidden stairs. "This way."

Nick followed him, and just as Blake flicked on a flashlight the bookcase shifted back into place.

"Where are we?"

"Come." With a flashlight firmly in hand Blake led the way, after a short distance they came to a door, he pushed it open and waved Nick inside. He closed the door and flicked on a light. Nick shielded his eyes for a moment then looked at Blake.

"What is this?"

"It's the only place we can be safe. Have a seat."

Nick looked around. The room was big and deep, it was filled with all kinds of supplies and cases of water.

"Father thinks you're dead." Blake said from his seat across from Nick.

"I had hoped so. What happened?"

"In that little town they found two bodies. They were burned to a crisp, but they took pieces of each and they matched you. As for the girl I don't know, but they maybe still working on it."

Nick shook his head and clasped his hands in front of him. "So Henry hasn't given up?"

"You know Father he wants what he wants. He's slowly slipping into madness, and he is determined to take us with him."

"Why are you helping me?" Nick wanted to know.

Blake looked him in the eyes. "I'm a prisoner here. My family isn't safe. If I leave him, he'll kill my children and sell my wife into prostitution."

"Jesus Christ!" Nick brushed his hands through his hair and stood up. "He can't do that! Why are you letting him do this to you?"

"I have no choice, Tony is his right hand, and if I didn't fear Father then there is Tony to recon with. I can't go round killing my brother and my father."

"Why not? Do you love them more then you do your family? Are they worthy of your loyalty?"

Blake stood up and glared at Nick. "Sophia is the best thing that has ever happened to me. Without her I'd be as dead as driftwood. I can't live without her and I can't let them hurt her. But I helped Miguel get his family out and now I'm afraid Henry will send me a lesson, as he calls it."

"Look, on the horse I have some money. I'll give it to…"

"What the fuck are you talking about? It's not about that! It's about getting away and feeling safe, we can't do either. It's about living in peace and knowing you can plan a future without fear that it'll be taken from you. Money has nothing to do with that."

"Blake there's a war going on. They will never be safe. You can't protect them by yourself. If you thought this would blow over you're wrong. Get them out of here now."

"How? Don't you think I thought of everything. Any and every thought comes back to one thing. He'll know, he'll go after them."

Nick nodded, he paced the room with slow deliberate movements, then he looked at Blake. "I'll give you the name of a friend of mine. He's a bounty hunter, but he's also married and can be trusted. You can either put them on a plane to Spain and hope her family can protect them, or have my friend meet them at the airport and then smuggle them into Texas, he can put them into hiding and when this is over you can go to them."

"You're asking me to put my very soul into the hands of a man I know nothing of."

"I'm asking you to trust me. I'll see them safe, and then we can fight the battle to come."

"Why don't you just stay hidden for a while?" Blake asked with desperation in his voice. "Can you give me time to get things together? I'll have to talk her into it. I have to prepare the kids."

"Don't tell them anything, that way nothing slips, just put a note in her bag, when she finds it, she'll be upset but she'll understand, and they will be safe."

"That's what we did with Cynthia and the other children. You should've seen how hard that was on them."

"Would it be any harder then watching them die, or having to kill your father?"

"Why are you here Nick? Miguel told me about the account, why don't you take that money and leave? Give the girl back to Henry or her father then leave. Everything will go back to normal."

"What's normal? Being afraid to live isn't normal."

"God damn it Nick," Blake growled. "It's not that easy for us. You can just pick up and walk away. I can't!"

"You can!"

"Why did you come here? Why not keep moving?"

"I couldn't leave knowing you needed me. I want to help you get out of this."

"The only way to help is for you to run, forget you ever knew us."

"I can't forget," Nick said quietly.

Blake ignored that, and went to the dresser that stood in the far corner. "Tony was hurt in the first gun battle, and I was shot in the leg. Robert was killed."

Nick closed his eyes against the pain. "How did it end?"

"After you got away, the shooting stopped. I think they went after you. I wanted so bad to get to you and help you, but I couldn't, not with him watching my every move."

"What about Father, was he hurt?" Nick hated himself for asking, but he needed to know.

"That bastard will never get hurt. He'll see us all dead."

"I don't understand, why he would involve us?"

"He's losing money, Tony is stealing it, but Henry won't hear that. He thinks Tony is the only one he can trust."

Nick snorted. "Yeah, they were cut from the same stone."

"The girl will die Nick," Blake said in soft tones.

Nick stiffened, and his eyes narrowed. "What do you mean?"

"Father says if she is still alive he'll find her and avenge his son. He says she has to die and he blames this whole mess on her. He said she hoodwinked you, and turned you against us."

"That's not true. I didn't even know her, and she didn't know me. She is as clueless as I was about this whole mess."

"I know, but he says someone has to pay."

244

Forgive Me, My Love

"Someone will pay, but it won't be an innocent woman."

"What, do you have a plan?"

"Not yet, I thought I'd let the two sides hash it out, and see where the pieces fall. Then when the coast was clear I'd take her home and be done with it all. But now, I just don't know, looks like I may have to join the fight."

"I'll tell you what, you send for this friend of yours. Then we'll send the girl, Sophia and the kids with him, and we'll fight this battle together."

Nick was already shaking his head. "I don't know about Sophia, but this girl is a fighter. She will do just what I tell her not to do and get herself killed in the process."

"What if you tell her it was just to protect the children?"

"She'll do it until they reach Texas, then all hell will break lose, she'll probably call in the Calvary and try to save the day, and end up getting everyone including herself killed."

"Are you so sure?"

"Yes, this girl is safer at my side, where I can keep an eye on her." Nick didn't add he couldn't sleep if she were not by his side. That was a habit he knew he'd have to break.

"I think it's the same with Sophia, she's a wildcat and she'll be spitting nails."

"Will she go without you?"

"No, not if she knows why she's going. It's better to lie to her. Your idea about the note is a good one."

Nick stood up, and approached Blake. Blake straightened and they stared at each other. Nick was first to speak. "I missed you little brother."

245

Blake's eyes flooded as forgotten fears came rushing back. "You don't know how often I wished you had taken me with you. I wanted so bad to be gone from here. After mother…"

"Don't," Nick grabbed him and pulled him into his embrace. "Don't ever speak of that."

"We thought you were dead. When you went after her and didn't return I got on my pony, and I started after you but Tony knocked me off and kicked me in the ribs. 'He said be a man! Father did what had to be done, one pussy in the family is enough.'" Blake sniffled and his arms tightened around Nick for brief instant. "When I heard you were alive I was angry. Angry because you had gotten away and you were happy. Angry because you had forgotten about me."

Nick felt his eyes start to burn. "I never forgot you little brother. I thought of you often, more times then I care to admit. I love you, Blake, you were my buddy, my friend and secret keeper and then…" his voice caught and a sob. "Then I thought you had all abandoned me. I searched for her, but I was afraid, it was dark and for the first time in my life I was alone. When I found her, she… she was dead. The wolves were at her and I shot as many as I could, with that huge old gun I'd gotten from Henry's gun case, the rest ran away. I buried her."

"When this is over, will you show me her grave?" Blake pulled away from him, and dried his eyes.

"Yes, let's just hope we get out of this alive." Nick wiped his face with the tails of his shirt and cleared his throat. "This girl has to be protected, I can't let anything happen to her." He said quietly.

"I know," Blake nodded. "But if you gave her to Henry it would show him that you are on his side. He might leave us all alone."

"Are you kidding me?" Nick frowned in annoyance. "He'd kill me and never think twice about it."

"But he loves you Nick, in his own way he loves you more than any of us."

"I doubt that."

"No, he does, maybe it was because you got away. Maybe because you showed him how strong you are, that you aren't afraid of him. He always did like courage."

"It doesn't matter now, in his book betrayal out weight courage. Besides I can't hand her over."

"Why not, she's just a pawn, he'll continue to try and bargain for what he wants. When he gets it he may give her back and we can all go back to our lives."

"Do you hear yourself Blake?" Nick growled. "Do you really believe what you're saying? No, this won't end by simply giving her back. You said yourself that she'd be killed because of Robert. I can't let that happen."

"I know," Blake dropped into a chair, his head hanging. "It was just a thought."

They were quiet for a few minutes when Nick said. "Why were you outside? Where are your guards?"

"I let them go. I knew you were coming, and I didn't think I could trust them not to tell Henry you were here, so I had to let them go. I've been waiting for you for weeks. Besides, I'm afraid they would turn on me at any second if Henry told them to. Things still haven't settled with the missing children and how it happened."

"He thinks you had a hand in it?"

Blake shrugged. "Can't say if he does, but it's best to keep his men as far from us as possible."

"You're not worried about your family's safety."

"No, we live to far from town for any random act

of violence, besides everyone knows who my father is. They don't dare harm a hair on our heads. Henry is all we have to fear."

"I guess that's one thing to be said for him."

"I want you to stay the night, then I have a small cabin north of here, you can stay there until…"

"No, I won't put you in that situation. I'll leave, but I won't tell you where I'll be. When I get in touch with my friend I'll send you a message."

"Don't call, all my lines are tapped."

"Fine, I'll find a way to get you the message."

"Let's go get your horses."

"Can we get some real food? It's been awhile on dried beef and Nopales. I'll never look at cactus again without cringing."

"Of course, I'll go back upstairs before the missus wakes up."

"I'll grab the girl and come back down here."

"Sure there's a bed in the next room."

"Okay, she could use a good night's sleep and a hot bath."

"Let me show you around," Blake walked into the next room and went straight to a blue brocade curtain with dark print. He pulled it back and revealed six nineteen inch monitors. At a closer look Nick saw that every section surrounding the house was covered.

"Very nice."

Blake looked at him over his shoulder. "You like?"

"I do indeed. Clever, how many people know about this place?"

"Henry helped me build it, then he killed everyone who knew of it, so only he and I, and now you know it exists."

"So you can't use it to hide your family?"

"No, it would've been great."

"Do you know if Henry bugged your stairwell, or maybe that room where we put the girl?"

"He hasn't. I went over the place with a fine tooth comb, it's clean." Blake gave a humorless chuckle. "I wouldn't have brought you here if I thought other wise."

"What about the house?"

"The second floor is pretty much clean, there are a few monitors that are linked to his place which is why I want you to keep the girl quiet. If he sees her it would be over for us all."

"So do you have a bath and bed down here?"

"Yes, I'll get the water turned on for you. The sheets are in the next room. You can get a set and fluff them out."

"Fine," Nick nodded. "I'll go get her."

"No, I'll get her," Blake grabbed his arm. "If Sophia sees you she'd be scared to death. I'll go."

Nick nodded.

"There's a door on the far side of the room, open it and you can start airing the place out. When you turn on the water in the bathroom, just let it run until it gets clear."

"Will do." Nick said, already opening the door that led to another room.

"I'll be right back with your girl." Blake turned and hurried down the hall and out of sight.

Rachel had just about fallen asleep. She was jerked awake as the door opened, and a light poured into the room. She prayed it was Nick, but some how she knew it wasn't. His presence always made her feel safe and right now she didn't feel safe. The man walked closer to the bed and she knew from his outline that it wasn't Nick. When he was close enough she lashed out with her bound feet catching him in the chest. He let out a sharp cry, and fell to the floor. She wiggled until she was off the bed and landed hard to the floor straight on her chest, she cringed from the pain, then opened her eyes and saw male shoes standing beside her. She screamed behind her gag and kicked.

"I'm not going to hurt you." The man said as he reached for her.

She wanted to scream. *Where's Nick?* But through her gag only muffled sounds came out.

The man caught her chin between his fingers and held her still. "Listen to me!" he snapped. "If you want to live you will keep still."

She froze and stared.

"That's good, do as I say and no one will get hurt." He threatened and she nodded. "Now I'm going to but this blindfold on you." She franticly shook her head. "Either you let me put it on you or I'll have to knock you out, what's it going to be?" She nodded, and trembled with fear. A horrible ache started in her heart and worked it's way down her entire body. Once the blindfold was in place the man threw her over his shoulder and started out of the room. Rachel was at a loss, all she could think of was Nick. What would she do if he were dead? How would she survive? Would they kill her too? *Why do I feel so cold and empty without him?*

Soon she felt herself being lowered. "You'll stay here for at least the night, then when we're finished we'll figure out what's to be done." She heard a door being closed, and she raised her hands to pull off the blindfold but before she could get there other hands were on her, they untied the blindfold from the back and were working to release her hand from the zip-ties. She was afraid to look behind her, afraid to see who it was.

"What? No screaming…" he never finished, she turned and jumped into his arms squealing with relief.

"I thought they had killed you. Where were you? Who was that man?"

Nick laughed extremely amused by her reaction. "I take it you're happy to see me?"

She jerked away and glared at him. "Where were you?" She took one step and fell forward, having forgotten her feet were bound. He caught her easily, but she pushed away from him. "No, I'm not happy to see you," she said in a surly voice. "I'm just glad I don't have to learn how to get over on new captors."

"Oh, is that what I am, a captor?"

"You know exact what you are." She took a moment to look around the room. "What is this place?"

"Hold still and let me take the ropes off your feet." She did, but he didn't make a move to remove the ties. "This is our room for the night."

The room was large, it looked like a master bedroom suite in a Hotel. It was very pleasing to the eye, even elegant. "Where are we?" She turned to stare at him. "Last I looked we were in no man's land, and now we sit in the lap of luxury?"

"If I told you I'd have to kill you." He said slowly, and walked away from her.

"That's lame, try again." She yelled, and then said. "Take these things off my feet."

"No, stay where you are, I'll be back for you in a minute."

"Buy I want to sit down."

"I said no, you are as dirty as I am and we are not sitting on any of this until we're clean."

"And when will that be?" He came back into the room and picked her up. "I do know how to walk you know."

"This is faster, I want to get clean and then get to sleep, we have a long day tomorrow."

He pushed opened the door and her mouth fell open. "Oh my God!" She gasped. "This is wonderful, look at that tub it's big enough for ten people. And the pink marble counter tops and double sinks. And look at the crystal faucets. What kind of place is this?"

Nick set her on her feet, then grabbed his knife and sliced through the bounds that held her feet. She stopped rambling and stared into his eyes. He lifted his hands and started unbuttoning her shirt, one slow button at a time, his eyes never leaving her.

Rachel wanted to brush his hands away, she wanted to tell him never touch her again. But she knew to be without his touch would be like having no sun to warm her skin. She needed to feel his hands on her skin, and while she would never let him know it, she could never push him away.

Nick tried to keep his heart under control, as her small hands came up and started to unbutton his shirt. It gave him great promise, that she didn't push him away, and she actually seemed to respond to his touch. Once her shirt was undone, he gently pushed it from her shoulders leaving her bare from her neck to her waist, then his hands went to her belt that was holding up the shorts she wore. With a single tug they were free and falling to the floor to join the shirt.

Forgive Me, My Love

Rachel knew she should feel embarrassed to be naked in front of a man, but she wasn't. With this man she felt free even though there was no love between them she felt a strange sense of respect for him and his opinion, it was obvious he didn't feel the same for her. But then that would make it just that much easier to leave him when this was all over, but for now there was nothing that said she couldn't take advantage of what he offered.

With a small smile she slid his shirt from his broad shoulders and placed small kisses along his ribcage. She smiled wider when he stiffened and sucked in his breath. Her fingers worked at his belt while her lips teased the salty skin of his well muscled chest, she shivered as his hands ran over the plains of her back and brought her nearer so that the tips of her breast were against his chest. She almost cried out at the electricity of his touch. Then his jeans were falling to the floor and all she could do was stare. Her stomach did flips and her whole body throbbed for no reason at all.

There was no denying his desire, he wanted her and he wanted her to know it. Nick look down at her head as she stared at his manhood, standing straight and proud, ready to make her his once again. Then her flushed face turned to look at his and he almost lost it. His knees weakened and his heart pounded with fierce desire. He placed his hands in her hair and pulled her close, his lips seal hers and she moaned, and his stomach tightened. Her leg came up to curl around his and she deepened the kiss, her tongue doing things to his, that he had never felt before, things that made him want to drop them both to the floor and take her without thought, without reason, just pure blind lust. But she deserved better than that. She was new to this and had no idea what a tender lover he could be; so far she had only seen his greedy side. It was time to show her how good this was.

Nick hooked his arm under her legs and lifted her, not once did he end the kiss. He stepped into the sunken tub and maneuvered them down the three steps. Once he was seated he broke the kiss and let her go, she promptly sank under the water.

She rose with a squeal and tossed a handful of water at him. At least he knew she had a sense of humor. They splashed around the tub alternating in games of chase where the loser had to kiss the winner. They stopped long enough to wash each other, the soft sensual feel of soapy hands gliding over naked flesh was too much for Rachel. She rinsed all the soap off him and said. "I lost our last game, I guess I get to kiss you." He shrugged and reached for her, but she dodged him. "I can pick where I want to kiss you?"

Her question fired his blood and his imagination. With a slight suspicious look he said. "It's your choice kiss what ever part of me you like."

"Close your eyes," she said, and he smiled.

"Why?"

"Because I want you to." When she licked her lips he tensed, then her look became sly and he waited, wondering. He closed his eyes and didn't have to wonder long. He gasped and his entire body stiffened as the tip of her sweet tongue traced the contours of his shaft. His hands rose ready to pull her away but then her lips was around him and she moaned on him sending vibration through his body. His eyes closed of their own volition and he clenched his teeth against the wonderful feel of her hot mouth. That she was a novice was obvious, he wanted to put his hands on her head and show her how it was done but he just couldn't move.

Rachel loved the power she had over him. He was like putty in her hands and she relished it. She licked him like a cherry lollipop and marveled at the taste of him. This wasn't something she had ever thought to do, had indeed never even imagined it, but when she had seen his shaft standing out like that all she wanted to do was get it back in that position. And now here it was, standing out of the water proud and pulsing in her hands. He was well endowed from what she had heard from Bianca. She tried the measurements and found him more than exceeded what Bianca tests said. *That had to be good.* Smiling she kissed the tip once again and engulfed the top of it in her mouth then trailed kisses up his stomach to his lips. Once there she opened his lips with her tongue and kissed him deeply.

Nick wanted to return the favor but she was straddling his legs, her lower regions nestled against his raging need and her little tongue worked his, until he found himself lifting her onto him, he found her orifice with the tip of his shaft and pushed. She froze and her eyes popped open. But he wrapped his arms around her and plundered her sweet lips until her arms were around him and her body begged him to take her. Her small bottom wiggled, until he pushed more of himself into her, she nipped at his lips, then bit his earlobe and her legs wrapped around his hips as he worked to get them fully ensconced. She threw her head back and gave a huge moan as he penetrated her. "Oh God!" She groaned. "Oh Godddd!"

He stopped once she was full seated on his lap and buried his head between her breasts; he turned his head and took one nipple between his lips and her body jerked hard against him. He turned and got to his knees, so that she was sitting on the step, his mouth and tongue moved up to her sweet mouth and captured her lips, and he deepened the kiss until she was pulling at his arms, her hands buried in his hair, as she greedily took everything he had to give. Then he was moving, his knees on the floor of the tub, he anchored her bottom in his hands and held her tight and he thrust in and out, never once breaking contact with her lips. He strained to keep his rhythm gentle and steady and he rocked against her, but she became wild in his arm her mouth left his and trailed kissed over his chest and she captured his nipples between her small teeth and gently worried the tips, he increased his rhythm, water sloshed all around them but they neither noticed or cared. She wrapped her legs around his flanks and her arms around his waist and held on, her lips driving him crazy his mind forgot she was new to this, he forgot she was delicate and she couldn't take everything he had to give. "Don't pull away from me Nick."

"Never," he shook his head and said. "Never again." Then his mind went void and then filled with nothing but her, and what she had done to him earlier. And he trembled with thrust after mighty thrust and she yelled her release against his hot skin, he shuddered hard and gave one last thrust before he erupted into her and sent then both into the stars above.

After they were able to catch their breath, he removed himself from her, still on his knees in the water and he held out his hand. She took it, going to her knees in front of him she looked up into his eyes, and what he felt at that moment made his heart ache with the need to tell her everything in his heart. But the words wouldn't flow past his lips. All he could do was smile. She returned his smile and lifted her hands to his hair; she buried her fingers in it, and pulled him close for a kiss that had him tingling to have her again. But then she eased back and grabbed the soap and a sponge. He took her queue and grabbed one himself.

Rachel was so full of longing, loving this man hadn't been in the plan. He knelt in front of her as magnificent as a sculpture, beautiful, bronze, his sapphire eyes were dark and daring. Daring her to love him, daring her to take what he offered. Now she would do her own daring, she would dare him to love her, not just her body, but also her mind, her heart and her soul. But she couldn't say that to him, not now, not after they had just started to find their path. So she kept quiet, she kissed him with all the love in her heart, and hoped he saw it for what it was. It was an impossible situation, she knew it and so did her heart. They were in deaths path, a path she wasn't ready to take, yet she wasn't willing to give him up. She moved around the back of him and slid the sponge over his broad back. She allowed tears to slide down her cheeks, but quickly wiped them away as he turned and began to wash her.

Once they were in bed and he had her safely tucked in his arms, Nick brushed her hair with his hand, as he thought about what had just happened. It was mind blowing and exciting and so tender. Had he given her some part of his heart without knowing it? It felt like it, but how? He frowned in the darkest, and his hand tightened on her shoulder.

"Why did you do that thing to me?" he asked trying to get his mind on other things, things that couldn't rip his heart out.

"What thing?" she asked quietly.

"When you took me in your mouth," he didn't want to sound jealous, but it was hard to think she had been experimenting with other guys. "Have you done that before?"

"Would it upset you if I said I have?"

He jerked his arm from around her and sat up. "No," he said, but his voice was sharp. "I don't give a damn what you did before."

"That's good," she sighed pretending his reaction didn't affect her. "You're the first guy I've ever done that to…"

He was on her in half a second, his hands on her arms and his lips on hers in a hard kiss that had her purring and moving against him. He broke the kiss and stared at her, his nostrils flaring and his eyes burning. "Why did you do it!" he growled.

"Stop being stupid Nick!" Rachel yelled. "I did it because I wanted to taste you. Bianca said men liked." She whispered her eyes on his lips. Nick kissed her again, his relief astounding. He felt it all the way down to his toes.

"You're a quick learner." He said and rolled off her.

"I know," she said. "If I want something bad enough I know how to get it."

"I bet you do." He got back under the sheets and she curled up against him. "Don't lie to me Rachel, don't ever lie to me."

She shivered at the use of her name, it was the first time he had used it, and she found she liked the way he said it. She nodded and kissed his forearm where it curled around her neck, her head lay cushioned there and it was the best pillow she had ever had.

"What do you want to be when you grow up?" Nick asked her.

"What do you mean when I grow up?" She snapped.

"You know what I mean Tigress. Stop getting so ruffled." He kissed her earlobe and smiled when he felt her relax. "I just meant what are you going to school for? At the gas station I saw all the Texas A&M stickers on your car and I overheard something about school. What are you majoring in?"

"I'm an intern with a law firm in College Station. I'm in my last year of actual class. I'm going to start with a firm in Houston after I pass the bar."

"What kind of law?" he twirled a piece of her hair around his fingers as they talked.

"Criminal law," she said quietly, and he stiffened. "We could get through this together Nick." She whispered and entwined her fingers with his. "I know ways to get you out of this. I'll tell them it wasn't your fault that…"

He turned her towards him and kissed her into silence. The hope in her voice mirrored his own and he had to stop her before she made him believe in the impossible. He released her lips from his, and sighed, his forehead against hers. "It's too late for me. Too late for us, there's nothing but ashes between us now. Don't ever think there could be anything else." He shut his eyes as her body jerked, and knew she was crying, even though she never made a sound, he knew. "Estoy enamorado de ti, mi corazón, mi alma, mi para siempre, mi amor." He whispered in her ear and kissed her softly. For a brief second he wondered if he'd made a mistake telling her he loved her, but she didn't speak Spanish so she'd never know what he said.

259

Fourteen

SIMON SAT IN THE AIRPLANE beside his father. His pain filled eyes fell to the open briefcase and the vacuumed packed bag that lay in the bottom of it. His stomach tightened and tears came to his eyes. Twenty-eight days after she had gone missing the contents of that bag was all that was left of her. He crashed his open palm into the thick glass of the window beside him.

John reached over and pulled him into his arms, but Simon resisted, then finally the fight was out of him and all he could do was cry on his fathers shoulder.

"Why?"

"I don't know son," came the watery reply. "I'd give anything to know why this happened."

The rest of the trip was done in pained silence. Simon could only think of Bianca and his mother. They had counted on him. His whole family had counted on him to find her alive. To bring her back to them and he had let them down. He had let her down. He clenched his fists, and brought one to his aching eyes and pushed hard, he needed the pain to go away. He tore off his seat belt, and hurried from the seat and into the restroom. He slammed the door shut and fell to his knees, gut wrenching sobs tore from his throat, and he didn't know if it would ever stop. His mind went over what he'd been told.

Forgive Me, My Love

Some old Mexican name Miguel had sought him out having heard he was looking for a young black girl. An American. After making sure he had the money, Miguel began to tell them of the rape, that she had screamed and it had taken days for her to die. Many men had used her badly. She had screamed for her Daddy and someone named Simon. She had said he would find her. In the end some man named Juan had broken her neck.

Simon vomited in the small steel sink. He clutched his side, it hadn't healed completely and with every movement it hurt. Sweat made his clothes stick to his body, as he remembered. He had picked his father up off the ground where he had fallen and demanded the man show them her grave. It was a little patch of land near the town; the only marker was a small white cross-inscribed Las Americana. After digging for a short while they came to a box. It wasn't a very big box and Simon frowned, he looked at Miguel. "What the hell is this? That box isn't big enough for her. Are you lying to me?" Hope nearly floored him.

"No, no Senor, is her, I see they burn her up so nobody will know."

Simon nearly doubled over, he closed his eyes and gathered his strength, he looked at John and they drew strength from each other. "Open the box."

When it was finally opened all they could make out was a pile of blacken bones. Simon pushed the lid higher until it was out of the grave. He took a closer look, then the suns rays hit something and it blinded him for a moment. He reached in and pulled out a tarnished gold necklace. With trembling, dirty fingers he looked at it hard, it was a locket. He flicked it open and cried. He handed it to his father, he sat with his head clasped in his hands. An unreal quality taking hold of them all.

"That's her, that's our Rachel," John sobbed above him.

Simon said. "Give me that briefcase." Miguel handed it to him. He pulled a handful of hair from the corpse and sealed it in the bag. "We'll see who this really is." He wasn't willing to believe she was dead. It could've been anyone. "Have your Police box up this body, we're taking it with us."

"But Senor it is not good to disturb the dead."

"I assure you I don't care. I'll be sending at least two more to join her in the afterlife."

Simon sighed and turned on the cold water and washed his face. No more of that. He was done crying. Now he would make sure someone else did the crying. The only good thing to come out of this was the Mexican described Henry and told them where he could be found. He dried his hands and left the restroom. He made his way back to his seat.

"This is going to rip your mother apart," John said.

"I know, all we can do is hope it isn't Rachel."

"What if it is? She died because of me," John thumped his chest. "I don't know what I'll do, I can't cope with this, I'm lost, what do I do. How can I help Pat when I can't help myself?"

"Dad, you have three sons who love you. Bianca is here. Don't forget about her, she'll need us also. Rachel was like a sister to her. She'll be devastated. Maybe Mom and Bianca can comfort each other."

"Yes," John sighed hard. "Bianca has been a Godsend."

"I won't let this go." Simon muttered. "As soon as

we know for sure, I'm coming back. I'll find that Bastard and I kill him the worst way humanly possible. He'll suffer the way she suffered. He's going to beg me for death."

"Miguel said the man she was with was killed. That had to be one of Henry's sons. He had four, now he has two. One of them had Rachel, but with him dead who do we look for?"

"One of Henry's sons is married, the other is his henchman. As far as I'm concerned they are all as good as dead."

They fell silent, neither spoke the rest of the flight. As soon as they arrived at the airport they dropped the body at the coroner's office. Then they hurried to get the information to their family Doctor. He ran the tests on the strand of hair and it was an identical match.

Going home was hard, almost impossible. They had barely walked through the door when the women were on them.

"Where is she, you said you have her," Pat cried as she looked from her husband to her son.

Bianca was standing a few feet behind her staring at Simon, and it was all he could do not to look away.

"We need to go into the living room."

"Why?" Pat cried. "Where is she John? Tell me."

Simon nodded at Bianca. "Is Tyrell and Ryan here?"

She nodded, her arms crossed in front of her and one fingernail caught between her teeth. "Can you go get them?"

She hurried off. Simon watched her go with a heavy heart. She had told them everything Henry had done to them. It wasn't hard to believe that they would use Rachel so badly then kill her. It was so hard not to go down there and kill every one of them.

"What is it?" Tyrell came into the room with Bianca trailing at a slower pace. "She's crying her eyes out." He pointed to Bianca. "Why?" He demanded.

"What's going on?" Ryan demanded his young face a mass of confusion and dread.

"Have a seat Bea."

"No," she cried. "I don't want to sit."

John nodded. He held Pat's shaking hands in one of his and dug into his pocket with the other. He produced the locket they had given Rachel for her sixteenth birthday. Pat stared at it and shook her head. She pulled her hands away from his and got up. "No," she whispered. "Why do you have it? Where is she?"

"Darling," John paused, the words wouldn't come. "Darling please, come back. Sit down next to me."

Her eyes were stretched wide as she waited. Her breath caught in her throat as she struggled to breathe. "Say it!" she screamed.

"She's dead," John said and the whole room went silent.

Pat stood frozen, tears running down her cheeks. She stared at him as if he had lost his mind. Then she started to speak. "She's not dead."

But John nodded. "Yes, dear she is."

"No," she cried. "If she were, I'd know. I would feel it. She's alive some where. You have to go back." John went to her and took her into his arms but she beat at his chest and cried. "You can't leave her there, you have to go back for my baby."

"We brought her body back," Simon said softly. "We took samples of her hair, and had it tested. It was a match."

"I don't care what you did!" She snarled. "That was a stranger's body, it wasn't your sister. She is alive I'm telling you."

"Mom," Tyrell tried. "Mama please, she's gone, you have to let her go."

Pat pulled away from them all, and her hand flew to her chest. "I won't listen to this. There is no hole in my heart!" She turned to Simon. "Darling, go find your sister for me. Find my baby." She went to Bianca and pulled her hands from her face. "You stop this right now." She scolded her. "What would Rachel say if she knew you had given up on her?"

"But Mom they said..."

"I could careless what they said. Don't you know your sister? Rachel would never let them kill her. She's a fighter, don't give up on her." Pat wiped Bianca's eyes and led her out of the room. "Remember when we would all make cookies in the kitchen after school?"

Bianca nodded tearfully, and looked behind her as she was led out of the room, all four of the men stood staring.

Simon turned to his father. "What are we going to do with her?"

"What do you mean?"

"Mama has lost her mind. She refuses to accept this."

"She'll have to when she goes to the funeral." Tyrell said.

"What if she doesn't?" Ryan yelled. "What if we've lost our mother as well?"

"We'll deal with that when the time comes." Tyrell said. "For now let Bianca stay with her."

Later that night Simon knocked on Bianca's door.

"Come in." He turned the knob, and walked into the room Bianca had had since she was ten. She still lived with her Mother but this was her room when ever she was here, which was a lot. But these days she never went home.

"I can't believe she's dead." Bea shook her head, and wiped her nose, she was sitting on her bed with a napkin clenched in her fists. Simon went and sat beside her. "Are you sure Simon? Could it have been someone else you saw? Mom's right I don't feel empty. I feel like she could walk through that door any minute."

"There were witnesses who said it was her. They knew from the photo I showed them. It was the first break I'd had since that bastard took her."

Simon stood up and went to the dresser. Bea had been a constant since she had returned from Mexico. His mother wouldn't let Bea out of her sight, it was as if she were closer to Rachel with Bea around.

He had wasted precious time on his back recovering from the wound that had started festering in the wilds of Mexico. Simon slammed his fist into a near by wall, hatred such as he had never experienced rushed through him. If the man who had taken Rachel wasn't already dead Simon would've gladly killed him with his own hands.

"Simon please," Bianca called from her bed. It had been six weeks since her brush with death and she was still healing. He knew why and he wondered when she would ever trust him enough to tell him.

Simon went back to her and sat beside her as she reclined on her bed. "How are you feeling?" he asked softly, he had been worried about the broken ribs and she had fine cuts along her stomach, which she refused to tell anyone how they got there. That coupled with bruises on her neck, arms and back had him worried to know end. She hadn't stopped crying since they had been back and she spent most of her time in Rachel's room.

"I'm healing well the Doctor says."

"Healing on the outside, what about the inside?"

She gave a watery laugh and looked away from him. "I used to wish I was Rachel you know. Whenever I had to go home I would cry and cry. I love your family. Then after a while I got to where I no longer wanted to be her, I was just happy to be around you all. To me, you were a happy family, you have a sweet understanding Mother, a tender loving Father, then you have the possessive, strong and protective older brothers, the headstrong angry younger brother and last, the little Princess who was just as headstrong and determined as her brothers."

"You're just as much our sister Bea…"

"I know, I felt that and it made me feel so special," her voice caught on a sob. "What will I do without her?" Watery green eyes focused on him. "I don't want to be her; I want her here with you all. If I have to leave to make that happen then I will, I'll leave and never come back just please God bring her back!"

Simon couldn't stand her tears. He pulled her trembling body into his arms and caressed her back until some of the shaking stopped. He lifted her chin and made her look at him, then with slow deliberate movements he brought his lips to hers, as soft as velvet he kissed her. He broke the kiss and looked into her eyes. "You know I've always…"

Bianca held her breath; her hand flew to his lips,

she couldn't let him finish. Every thought, every dream about Simon came rushing forward. It hurt too much. He was her dream lover, the man she wanted to spend the rest of her life with, when she was ten she had started having thoughts of having his children, of being married to him and now here she was in his strong arms, his beautiful lips tasting hers and if she gave in to him, he would die. She pulled back sharply and turned from him.

"I'm sorry Simon, but I can't," her voice shook from the fierce need to be held by him. "Please leave," she couldn't trust herself and the only way to protect him was to force him away.

He held onto her hands. "Bea, I'm sorry Darling, I didn't mean to frighten you. I know you've been through a lot." She hardened her heart against his soft caring words.

Bianca looked at him; she forced her voice to be hard and her lips to say the words that would push him away forever. "Look Simon, you're nice, but I'm not into the black thing. You probably think all white girls just lust after black dudes, well I'm sorry to break it to you but I'm not. I love you, but like a brother, nothing more." Her heart crumbled at the look on his face. She winced as his hands crushed hers, then he flung her hands away from him and stood up. She wanted to hide from his rage, and from her own cruelty, but it was either hurt him now or bury him later. His lips worked as he fought to say something and she waited with building dread yet he never uttered a word, his eyes raked her and then he stormed from the room, slamming the door behind him.

She grabbed a pillow and lay on her side staring into space, tears slipped unnoticed down her cheeks. "I love you Simon," she whispered. "I do I do, I do, please you have to hate me. Don't give me a chance to kill us both." Turning her face into the pillow, she cried for so many different reasons, to many to count.

*****

Rachel was angry, angrier then she had ever been. He had done it again. He had left while she was sleeping. They had just shared a wonderful twenty-four hours, nothing but good food, wine and candlelight. He had been sweet and tender, loving every inch of her until she screamed, and now this. *Where is the trust?* She'd been okay for the first day, and then irritated the second, then the third she had been afraid, now she was just angry. Four days, and she had had enough. She rummaged through a closet and found all kinds of beautiful things to wear. Practical things and seductive things, she found a blue and gold backpack and picked out two outfits. She grabbed a brown shirt and a pair of jeans. She dressed in a green shirt and a pair of blue jeans. Last she took a white hat and a flashlight. She grabbed a bottle of water and then packed it all in the bag. She didn't know where she was going but she knew she was getting out of here.

Rachel opened the door and peeked out. The hallway was made of dirt, when she had first seen it she had been afraid. But now she just wanted out. She walked down the hall not knowing which way was the exit, there were no other doors just one long tunnel. The more she walked the deeper she went and as she flashed the light on the walls she realized there was water on the floor. She had been going down a gradual slope, she flashed the light and gasped at the pool of water in front of her. She looked back at the way she had come, then again at the water. If she went back she might never get back to her family, but if she went into the water, who knew what might await her.

She dropped her backpack and decided to try it, she would come back for the backpack. She tied her hair back then looked at the water, then the pack and decided to take the pack with her, just in case there was no coming back. With the backpack firmly tied to her waist, she carefully walked into the cold water. She tasted it. It was fresh water, which meant it was spring fed, the question was how far did it go. She sent a silent prayer to God that her journey would be swift and sure. Taking a deep breath she dove into the water.

Nick couldn't wait to see her, it had been hard waiting for the sun to go down so that he could sneak onto Blake's land. But wait he did, and now it was time. He knew she would be mad, but she never stayed mad long and he had just the cure to wipe the frown off her lovely face.

Blake met him at the back door. "She's gone."

Nick froze, he grabbed Blake by his collar. "What did you say?"

"Let me go. I was just about to go out and look for her."

"What do you mean she's gone?" Nick thundered. "Where could she have gone?"

Blake cleared his throat. "The bottom of the hallway is filled with water, it's where we get all our fresh water. That's the only way she could've gotten out."

Nick didn't want to ask, but he did. "How deep is the well?"

"From the surface to the bottom is about two hundred forty feet."

"Where does the water go? I mean is there a pond it's attached to?"

"Yes, but it's too far from the house for anyone to swim to it, especially in the dark."

"You mean swim and live?"

"I'm sorry Nick, I just don't know."

"Do you have any idea how long it would take her to get through the water?"

"I don't, when we built the room we stopped when we hit water. I have no idea how far it goes."

"Show me the well?"

They headed off into the darkness. When they got to it Nick's guts were tied in a knot. He looked down and there was an endless nothingness. "Rachel!" he yelled and received an echo. He looked at Blake and said what they were both thinking. "She couldn't have survived this."

"Wait," Blake said. "There's another opening, about twenty yards from here. Come on," they turned and hurried down the slope. There was a pool of water, but nothing seemed out of place.

Then Blake saw the backpack. He picked it up and examined it. "She must've made it, this is Sophia's. It was in that room with you two."

Nick wanted to kiss the sky, but he had to find her first. "Look, are those hoof prints?" Just as Blake was about to answer a flash of light came from the house. They dropped everything and ran as fast as they could. Then screams and male laughter filled the night. They arrived in time to see Sophia screaming and beating on the back of the man that held her. The children were thrown over the back of another horse. Blake started to charge, but Nick held him back. "Let's see how many of them there are, I don't see Rachel."

Blake nodded his cheeks flushed with rage as he tried to collect himself. "Let's get some horses, we'll follow them."

"Do you have any guns?"

"What kind of question is that? I'm a criminal, wouldn't I be stupid not to be prepared?"

"Go on little brother, lead the way." They hurried to the barn. Nick was so worried again about Rachel, he almost couldn't think straight. Once inside the barn Nick grabbed some horses and saddled them while Blake went in search of weapons. He returned with what looked like a large suitcase. He flipped it open and tossed Nick a pistol and some ammunition. Then he handed Nick a knife. "Very nice, I lost mine weeks ago." He looked at Blake. "You ready?" Blake nodded. "We don't kill them until we know where Rachel is."

"I'll try to wait, but I can't promise you anything. You know Henry is behind this."

"How do you know?"

"No one would be stupid enough to touch us. Henry set them on me, probably to kill my wife like he did Robert's."

"What?"

"I'll explain later."

"Just promise me one, the rest you can kill, just leave me one."

"Done."

They followed behind the group; close enough to hear what they were saying. The men were Mexican bandits. They knew whose wife and children they had just stolen. They argued amongst themselves about this potential problem. If the boss changed his mind later, would they suffer for what they were asked to do tonight?

Forgive Me, My Love

One said it would be better to get rid of the whole lot.

Nick breathe a sigh of relief when he saw Rachel sitting atop a horse, her hands tied in front of her and her mouth tapped shut. She was dripping wet. He knew she had to be spitting mad, and he would welcome her anger. He saw her stiffen at the talk of killing the children, and he wondered with no little trepidation if she did understand Spanish.

They rode hard, and it seemed the children were slowing them down. It was agreed that they would get rid of the kids but they had to get further away before they could do it. Nick knew it had to be hard on Blake hearing that and holding steady, but he prayed Blake would give him the time he needed to get everyone out unharmed.

One man dropped back to where Rachel rode next to the children. The man pulled his gun as he skirted around her. Nick's heart jumped as she lashed out with her foot and kicked the man in his chest, almost unseating herself in the process. The man yelped at the unexpected attack and fell from his horse. It reared, it's legs flaying in the air. Rachel rammed her knees into her horses sides and yell through her gag sending the thing at a dead run straight through the reins that held the kids to their mother. And Nick wanted to strangle her. *What does she think she's doing? She's about to get herself kill.* The children's horse free, she kicked its romp and sent it running into the night. Screams of terror erupted from Sophia as her children disappeared from sight.

Blake took off after his children while Nick drew his gun and watched as Rachel was knocked from her horse by a backhand across her face. She fell into the dirt and lay there choking as she tried to cough. Five men surrounded her, while Sophia screamed in the highest pitch humanly possible. Nick took aim, ready to kill the bastard that touched Rachel. One man reached up and dragged Sophia from her perch. She landed beside Rachel, who already had the tape pulled from her mouth, and was now yelling in perfect Spanish at the bandits. Nick didn't have time to be shocked, but he tucked this piece of knowledge away for later use. She told them they were lower then dirt and they weren't worthy enough to touch her foot let alone look at her. She screamed, that they were afraid of her, which was why they tied her up, there wasn't a man among them that could handle her.

They laughed and Sophia hid behind Rachel as she stood and dared them to touch her. By the time Nick a had clear aim, she was spitting blood at them. Them someone cut her bound hands and she was free, for all the good it did her, she had no weapon.

Nick was impatiently waiting for a moment when neither of the ladies were in harms way. But from the looks of it Rachel would be dead before that chance came. Suddenly all the men froze. Nick couldn't see why, he moved closer, just in time to hear Rachel say.

"Which one of you sons of bitches wants to die first?"

Shocked, he noticed she held a small gun in her palm. One man took a step towards her and she fired. Nick cursed her reckless disregard for not only her life but Sophia's as well. But he fired too, he rode his horse into the group at top speed scattering everyone. He jumped off his horse onto one of the men and snapped his neck. Then he heard shots and turned to see the women running into the wooded area, he ducked behind a pile of rocks and exchanged fire with the remaining men. Before to long he made his way deeper into the woods and all the firing had stopped.

"Rachel!"

"Nick!" He tensed it was Blake. "Nick, we're over here."

Nick hurried into a clearing and saw Sophia's platinum head bent crying over her children and they were hugging her. Blake sat next to Rachel on the ground they were talking about something.

"What the hell did you think you were doing Rachel?" Nick said as he walked closer. "You had one gun, they had at least ten!" he shouted, then he saw a dark stain on her shirt and she was holding her side. "Oh God you were shot."

She gave a weak laugh and nodded. "It's what I get. I should've kept my mouth shut and…oww…oww." She winced when Nick touched the area.

"I think the bullet is still inside Nick."

"She needs a doctor. I'll take her to town."

"Think Nick," Blake growled. "You can't do that they're looking for you."

"She needs a doctor, I won't let her die out here."

"She's not going to die. We'll take her back to my house and Sophia will take a look at her."

"Fine, let's get out of here." Nick picked Rachel up and couldn't stop himself from kissing her cold lips. She looked up at him.

"What was that for?" she asked.

"For being brave and stupid," he said, and she tucked her head in the crock of his neck as he headed for his horse.

Once they were close to the house Sophia turned to Blake. "Let me go first, I'll turn off the system." He nodded and she rode ahead.

Dean King

"Daddy…"

"Ssh, not now Dom, we'll talk later." The boy fell silent and Nick looked at Blake, they exchanged a smile. When the lights went out Blake said. "We have to hurry, they'll only stay off for five minutes then the generator kicks in." They raced across the lawn, horses kicking up clumps of dirt in their haste.

Nick only had time to make it to the first
bedroom Blake had shown him earlier, before the cameras
came back on.

The phone rang. Blake hurried down the hall and
answered it. "Hello?"

"Hello son, is everything alright. I was told your
alarm went off and we lost you for a while."

"No, Dad we're fine. It was just an accident… We
lost power for a while. Everything's okay now."

"How is Sophia, and the kids? It's been a while
since I've seen them. Are they doing well?"

"They're fine, never been better," Blake clenched
his teeth against the words he wanted to say. "They'll be
leaving in a few days to visit her mother, but I'll be sure
to bring them by when they get back."

"Fine, but you know we're still in hiding. Those
rotten bastards burned down the hacienda. They seem to
know every move I make. You'd have thought with the
girl dead they would go away. But they're hanging on like
ticks. That damned McKinney is insane."

"Okay Dad, we'll see you later."

Blake hung up as quickly as he could and walked
with patience he didn't feel towards the second floor, then
to the room at the back. He opened the door and was glad

to see Sophia sitting on the bed looking at Rachel's wounds.

"I'll need to take the bullet out and close the wound. I have an emergency kit in the kitchen, I'll go get it." She stood up and when she past Blake she leaned in and kissed his cheek, and held onto him for a moment before she left the room.

Nick brushed Rachel's hair back from her face and stared as her eyes drifted closed, the Valium Sophia had given her was starting to take effect.

"Why did you leave me?" she sighed.

He leaned forward and brushed her lips with his. "I had to get help for Blake and his family. They were supposed to keep you safe."

"They couldn't keep me safe from myself," she giggled and he leaned closer. "Thank the lady for the gun, for me will you."

"You'll have to tell me how you got out of that room." He squinted at her but she was already asleep. His eyes caressed her sleeping face and he kissed her cheek, he refused to let go of her hand. He looked down at the packing on her side and saw it was leaking again.

"You know how this has to end don't you?" Blake asked from the corner where he stood.

Nick nodded. "I know."

"You're going to have to make a choice, if you feel for her what I feel for my Sophia, then I'm sorry for you both. You're in for a life of hell."

"I know."

"He'll kill her, or you will have to kill him."

"I said I know, drop it."

"I don't want any more dying in my family. You have got to get her away."

"Don't you think I feel the same way?" Nick growled. "I didn't ask for any of this. He brought me into it. He threw her in my lap. What am I supposed to do now?"

"You're not supposed to fall in love with her."

Nick clenched his teeth, and looked away from her. Then his eyes shot to Blake. "I couldn't help it."

"I understand," Blake nodded. "She's one hell of a woman from what I've seen."

Nick smiled, and nodded. "Yes she is, and I can't let her go."

"Her family thinks she's dead. They took that body Miguel buried." Nick nodded. "Her people burned the Hacienda to the ground."

"Wonderful." Nick couldn't keep the sensure from his voice.

"Now what? What will you do, where will you go?"

"We'll go into hiding just as I planned. Then in a month or two I'll figure something out."

"If you come back from the dead this thing will start up again."

"I know that."

"Then what?"

"I don't know."

"What's going on?" Sophia asked as she walked into the room with her arms full of medical supplies.

Blake spoke first. "This is Nick, he's a friend of mine from a long time ago and that woman is his wife. Her name is Rachel."

"Hello Nick," she held out her long slim hand. "It's nice to meet you."

"Likewise," Nick said, and shook her hand, and

279

then shot Blake a questioning look.

"Your wife is going to be fine." She said in soft tones. "I'm going to remove the bullet, and sew up the wound. I don't know how deep the bullet is in there but let us hope it's close to the surface." Nick nodded. "I'll need you to hold her down for me."

"What?" Nick flinched, thinking of her in that kind of pain was hard to take. "You don't think the Valium is enough to take away all the pain?"

"No, it wasn't enough to knock her totally out, just make her very sleepy. This will hurt her and she will try to move away from the pain. If you hold her she may recognize your voice and feel safe in your arms. It will comfort her." Nick very much doubted that, but he was willing to try it, anything to spare her. He sat on the edge of the bed beside Rachel's hip and lifted her into his arms. He made sure he had a good hold on her, then nodded to Sophia.

She opened the jagged flesh and began to feel around with two fingers. Sure enough Rachel started moving, she murmured things that were incoherent and she fought against him. Then he whispered in her ear and she calmed, she relaxed against him, but he could tell she wanted to run from this. He continued to whisper in her ear and comb her hair back with his fingers and she quieted.

"I got it." Sophia said. "Now, I need to pull it out."

Nick flinched when she picked up the biggest pair of scissors he had ever seen, and stuck it inside the wound. She dug abit, after what seemed like an eternity she pulled it out. Clamped in the scissors was crushed metal.

Forgive Me, My Love

"Now, I will sew her back together." By the time she was done Nick felt as if he'd been the one being treated. His whole body was wet with sweat.

"I'll bring you dry clothes for her, and some towels you may want to bathe her." Sophia was saying.

Nick looked down at Rachel and for the first time he noticed how wet and muddy she was. "Thank you Sophia."

"No, thank you and your wife. At first I did not understand what she was doing. I thought she would get my children killed. Then I understood, she saved my children and myself. We owe you more then mere words can ever repay."

In tears Sophia ducked out of the room. Blake walked to Nick. "Like I said, she is one hell of a woman. If I hadn't seen it with my own eyes I would've never believed it. Sophia is right, I owe you."

"You don't owe me a thing, let's talk tomorrow I need to tend to her."

"Just take the clothes into the room next door and leave them in the bathroom."

"Good night little brother."

"Good night Big Brother.

Nick spent that night taking care of Rachel and trying to come up with a plan that could save them all. But all he managed to do was stare into her sleeping face all night long. He wondered what she would say if she had heard what he whispered in her ear. He gave a silent chuckle, and traced her ear. She'd probably laugh in his face, Nick knew in different circumstances he wouldn't have been allowed to touch her hand. But here, now, under these circumstances he had been allowed to fall in love with a woman he could never have. The up side, he'd be dead by the end of all this. By all rights, he should love her as much as he could right now. But he would keep the words locked away. She didn't need to know how he felt. *Why burden her more than she'd already been?* Nick's heart squeezed tight with an agony he refused to acknowledge. If he could help it, she would go on, she would live a full life. And he would be happy for her. He drifted into an uneasy sleep, with thoughts of losing Rachel, and his life in one single instant.

The next morning Nick woke first. He stretched and dropped a kiss on Rachel's cool brow, then sat up. He went into the bedroom and bent over the sink, he turned on the water and splashed his face. He stiffened as soft arms wrapped around his waist and a warm cheek was pressed against his back. He turned quickly, and picked her up in his arms.

"What are you doing?" She asked, her voice a dry croak.

"What are *you* doing?" He countered. "You shouldn't be out of bed."

"I just wanted a morning kiss from my knight in shining armor." She giggled at his look and Nick's franticly beating heart softened.

"There's no knight here woman. I'm putting you back to bed."

"Can you give me a kiss first?"

Nick settled her in bed, and tucked the sheets around her. He couldn't stop himself, he sat next to her and caught her face between his hands, and kissed her sweet lips as if he had no intentions of stopping. The second she started to purr, he pulled away.

"Hey," she murmured. "Why did you stop?"

Suddenly there was a knock on the door. Instead

of answering her Nick chose to answer the door, he put a finger to her lips. "Hold on a moment." She pouted and he laughed ads he hurried to the door.

"Good morning," he was surprised to see Sophia.

She ducked into the room with a tray of food in her hands. "I can't stay, but here is something to eat." She put the tray on the table and hurried back the way she'd come. "Rachel, I'll be back to check your wound later, my husband say's I am to be quick in and quick out."

"Good morning," Rachel called but Sophia was already leaving, she gave a quick wave and closed the door behind her.

"That was odd," Rachel said, and then looked at Nick. "What..."

"Come on let's eat," Nick sat beside Rachel and helped her eat the broth Sophia had brought in. A few minutes later Sophia hurried back in.

"I'm sorry, I promise I'm not a crazy person. There were some things I needed to do. Now I can come and talk. May I sit?"

Rachel nodded, she looked at Nick. His face seemed to have closed, and she wondered about that.

"You were so strong and brave last night," Sophia gushed, she sat perched in a wicker chair a few feet from them. Her Spanish accent was chaming. "Your husband must be so proud."

At Rachel's surprised look Nick took her hand in his and said. "I am, I always knew she was a wild one, but I just didn't know how wild."

"How long have you two been married, and what are you doing here?" She asked her big indigo eyes wide and expectant. "I didn't know we had guest, I would've..."

"Wow, hold on a second, catch your breath. We've been married two months," Nick said, and Sophia clapped her hands.

"Aaah newlyweds," she sighed obviously happy for them. "Are you still on your honeymoon? Were you just getting here when the bandits came?"

"Yes." Nick said.

"Oh I'm so sorry, this place is a bit untamed. I hate it that you had to go through that."

"It wasn't your fault, we just came at the wrong time."

"What made you decide to come to this part of Mexico? It isn't overly beautiful, and it's so rainy, and cold, this time of year."

Rachel smiled at that. "It wasn't a decision I had a lot of say in. Let's just say I was kidnapped."

Sophia's skin paled, but Nick laughed. "Yes, I just grabbed her and ran for the nearest exit."

"Oooh, how sweet," Sophia looked splendid in her white flowing skirt and white breezy shirt, her sandals matched as well, even her hair looked perfect, and it left Rachel feeling like a dark stain. She wanted to cry, she'd never felt ugly before, but now as she lay on white sheets, her skin was dark, darker then she could ever remember it being. The Mexican sun had turned her into a burnt potato. She looked at Nick, he was equally dark, but he looked great, he was a beautiful man and anything looked good on him. She watched as he spoke with Sophia. And wondered what he was thinking. He was charming and polite, he even stood when she left the room, and opened the door for her. Rachel's heart ached. *Why doesn't he treat me that way? I wonder if he's attracted to this artic looking beauty?* Rachel couldn't help the tears that seeped from her closed eye lids.

"What are you thinking?" He came back to her side and sat next to her. But she looked away from him, even his voice was soft. He never spoke to her in that soft sweet voice. "Tell me what has you frowning so fiercely." He caught one of her hands in his, and held it. She looked at the color difference and wondered what he saw when he looked at her. She remembered her hair, and it had been years since she'd been able to lotion her skin or apply perfume to any part of her body. Her lower lip started to tremble, and she bit it, she couldn't break down in front of him. It would give him one more reason to think her weak and add to her list of ugly.

"I don't like the pout coming to your pretty lips or the way you're frowning at me." He said. "Tell me what's on that mind of yours."

"She is pretty isn't she?" Was all she could get out.

He shrugged, and looked towards the door. "Yes, she's very pretty."

Rachel pulled her hand away and laid them on the white sheets. "She did great having that gun last night, she's very brave. The kind of woman any man would want."

"I'm sure she'd love to hear you say that. But it was you who actually used the gun. I'd say you were very brave."

Rachel looked into his eyes, and couldn't stop her tears even if she tried. "She looks like an angel doesn't she?"

"Well," he sighed, and he pulled her into his arms. "I don't know about that, maybe to Blake she is an angel. My vision of an angel would be…" He paused and she looked up, he brushed away her tears with the pad of his thumb and kissed her cheek. "Why, I believe I'm looking at one right now. What a vision," he caressed her cheek and said. "You must have the ear of God himself to be as lovely as you are. You are everything I envision an angel to be." He leaned forward, and gently kissed her lips, and her heart swelled with love for him. He leaned back and lifted her hand, and then kissed the back of it. "You lay back and get some sleep, we're leaving tonight."

Rachel gave in with a blinding smile. "Will you lay down with me?"

"Only if you promise to behave yourself."

She winked and laid back, her arms out stretched. "I promise."

He grinned and gladly went into her arms.

Later while she slept Nick went to the room next door and met with Blake.

"What happened last night?"

"Dad's henchmen, he's still in hiding, even I don't know where he is. But once I find out, I'm going to slit his gut open and watch him die."

"You don't mean that Blake."

"The hell I don't. I won't give him the chance to ruin my life again. I'm tired of it."

"Don't talk like that, that kind of thing isn't in you."

"What would you do if Rachel were your wife? If you two had kids? Would you let him have his way, let him do as he pleased? Hell no, you'd have killed him by now! I've been too afraid, I'm ashamed of that, but I can't hide any more. They need me to be strong. You're not going to face this alone. This is a fight we have to win."

Nick sighed, he caught Blake's arm and pulled

him close for a brief hug. "You're not going to like this, but once we get your family to safety I want you to stay put."

"I can't, I won't let him do this to me again!" Blake pulled away from him. "When Sophia is safe, I'll find you, and then we'll end this together."

Nick stared at him, but Blake turned away. "Tell me?"

"There's nothing to tell."

"Out with it Blake," Nick said with as much force as he dared. "This is more than just Sophia."

Blake's shoulders heaved, and he turned moist eyes on Nick. "I was in love before. You remember Cara?" Nick nodded and Blake continued. "We were fifteen when we fell for each other. It was the happiest time in my life. She was beautiful Nick. Long flowing black hair, ruby red lips and eyes of the finest chocolate. She had a temper, we fought all the time, but when we made up it was magic. We told our parents that we wanted to get married. Henry didn't argue, he just smiled and walked away. Two nights later Henry gave what we thought was a dinner to celebrate our plans. Miguel and Maria were there as well as Tony and Robert. We were so happy, and then Henry stood up. He said he loved me and Miguel. He said he wouldn't let this girl ruin our lives. Because she was Miguel's daughter, he couldn't kill her but he would make sure she never had the chance to break up his family again. I jumped out of my chair and raced towards Cara, but she was already in the arms of Dad's men, how she fought and screamed for me to help her. I tried to get to her, but Tony held me back. Then Henry pulled his gun. He pointed at her and said. I was to forget she ever lived. If I loved Miguel and Maria, I was to pretend this girl was never born, that was the only way they would ever get to see their child again. From then on she was gone. She was only allowed to visit once a year."

"I don't know what to say. I didn't know."

"There's a lot you don't know."

"Fill me in."

"What's the point?" Blake yelled, agony in every word. "You couldn't stop it! As it was it's probably better that you weren't here. You might be dead by now if you were."

"I want to know." Nick insisted, hurting with him. "Your pain is my pain little brother. I want to know that when I kill Henry, he deserved to die…"

"I'm going to kill Henry. Besides, you have your own problems now."

"Tell me what happened to Robert's wife."

Blake shrugged and shoved his hands in his pockets. "To make a long story short, Robert ran away when he was twenty one. He fell in love with a lady named Irene. Henry of course blamed her for Robert's desertion as he put it. Robert didn't even meet her until he was twenty three. Dad and Tony visited them. Tony and Robert fought, and Henry raped Irene. Then they left and Robert couldn't forgive himself for dragging her into our family. Two days after it happened, she shot herself in the head. Robert came home."

Nick's stomach turned. "Knowing this you got married anyway?"

"I didn't know any of this until after I was married. Tony thought it would be a nice wedding present to show me what happens when one of us lets a woman come between family."

"I knew they were sick, but I had no idea how

288

sick."

"I saw Robert leaving the hospital right after he was pronounced dead after that fire fight over Rachel."

Nick froze and stared at Blake. "You saw them take his body out?" Nick asked his frown deepened.

"No, I'm pretty sure I saw him, alive and well walking out the back door dressed as a doctor."

"Did you say anything to anyone?"

"As far as I'm concern, if he wants to be dead, then let him. I love him, but he's been through enough." Blake said.

"Look, if you don't stay put Henry will know something's wrong." Nick entreated. "When he starts looking into things he could find them, then we'll be in a deeper mess. I spoke with the bounty hunter I told you about. His name is Jackson Caldwell but his nickname is Beast. I'll give you a description and his numbers. He's on a case right now, but will be here in about three weeks. Let him do his thing, and then we'll go from there."

"Are you sure I can trust him? This is my family we're talking about."

"I know, you have to trust me, I've known him for years, he's hard, but he's fair and honest."

"What are you going to do now, where are you going?"

"To lay low, it's the only thing I can do until I figure this out."

"Figure what out? Henry has to die, which means so does Tony."

"I know, but I'm talking about the girl. What do I do with her?"

"Well, I tell you what I'm going to do; I'm going to liquidate as many of our assets as I can. Then hopefully

I can get everything done before he finds out."

"I wish you luck. As for myself any way I go, I lose."

"I'm sorry it came to this Nick, but I'll be by your side."

"Thanks," Nick embraced Blake and slapped him on the back. "If I don't see you, enjoy your life and take care of those beautiful children."

"I will, and you take care of yourself."

*****

Nick rode with Rachel tucked securely in his arms. The soft gait of the horse had lulled her to sleep hours ago. Her soft curls tickled his chin and his mind went to all that Blake had told him. Yes, he would kill to protect this woman in his arms. They had a full two more days traveling time, it was all to confuse her and make her think they were further from town then they were. The cabin he was looking for was really no more then a shack, but it would do for now. He would stash her in the shack, then run to town while she slept, he would be back before she even knew he was gone.

Finally they reached the shack. It was close to afternoon, the sun was high. Her side was still oozing blood through the white gauze. The ride had been rough on her. The tattered remains of what used to be pretty curtains hung menacing in the two windows.

"You're not serious about staying here?" She asked, and he could hear the horror in her voice.

Nick felt her cringe and forced a laugh. "It's okay honey, you can make it look like home just by standing in the doorway."

She turned sharp eyes on him. "Is that supposed to be funny?"

"No," he said quietly. "Any where you are is home to me, how's that?"

"I say you're full of it." She slid off the horse, then brushed off her pants. She looked up at him. "Are you coming?"

"No, but I'd like to."

"Nick!" Her eyes grew wide, he laughed and was relieved when she giggled with him. "You are horrible."

"Don't go in there, until I can check it out." He called as she walked towards the abandoned hut.

"Don't you worry, I'm not going anywhere without you." She gave him a small salute. "I've learned my lesson."

"If only that were true," he murmured and slid off the horse, he watched as she went to her horse. It warmed his heart that she would take the time to see to the horses needs.

"Come on girl," she said, "let's get you comfortable."

Once they were done, Nick went to Rachel and took her in his arms. "I'm going to jump in the river in a minute, want to join me?"

"Sure," she reached up and kissed his chin. "Let's eat first, I'm starved."

Nick released her and headed for the broken stairs of the cabin. He took out a flashlight he'd gotten from Blake, and walked through the door. There was a small scurrying sound and a squeak here or there, but for the most part it was safe. "You can come in Rachel."

Rachel ducked her head through the opening, and wrinkled her nose. Nick had lit a few candles he'd pulled from his bag, and was setting them around the room adding an unearthly glow to the ugly place. She looked at him. "Hummm," she placed her finger on her chin and said. "I think you're right, any place you're in is home to me."

She smiled as he turned. The look on his face was definately lustful and she shivered. "I'll get our bags and meet you at the river." His voice had a husky tint to it, and then his warm breath was on her neck as he brushed past and she shivered again.

Fifteen days later, Rachel sat on a big warm rock. It was starting to rain. This was the time of the season when it rained everyday. She was starting to get sick of it. Mud was every where. But on this rock it was dry, it hadn't rained yet today. Nick was in the river below her, trying to catch their dinner. He looked great, every time she thought of him her body tightened. He was a wonderful man. He'd thought of her every need.

She was sure he loved her. And just as sure she loved him. But she wasn't stupid. He thought that at the end of this he'd be dead a buried. She also knew she would rather die with him than lose him. She looked down at her belly, careful not to lay her hand on her sweet little bundle, proof of their love for each other. She didn't know how to break it to him. Last night after dinner, she had been washing the plates when her stomach had heaved, losing all it's contents, then again today after breakfast. She knew the signs, but she wasn't sure if he knew them. It wasn't until this started that she realized why he had pulled away from her that time during their love making. She didn't know if she felt bad about forcing him not to pull out, but she did know she was the happiest woman on earth. She was carrying her man's baby. *But would he be happy?* That thought halted her happy ramblings.

"What do you think of having a family one day?" She heard herself blurt out before she could stop the words. She saw his shoulders stiffen.

He didn't look up. "Never thought about it."

"If you had to think about it, how would you feel? Most men want little replicas of themselves running around."

Then he looked up, and she wanted to turn away from the fire in his eyes. "I have no children, I don't want any children. As for a wife, it'll never happen. So to answer your question, the thought scares the hell out of me. I don't need that kind of trouble."

Rachel stiffened, she tried not to be hurt but it was hard. "What do you mean trouble?"

"I don't want to be trapped into getting married. If some woman thinks she can get me to the alter by telling me she's pregnant she might as well save her breath, it'll never work."

You're right, it's nothing but trouble." That was all she could bring herself to say. And he went back to fishing. "I couldn't possibly do that to any man."

Later that day, she sat on the floor, her metal plate in her hand. She refused to look at him, her monthly hadn't come and it confirmed what she already knew. She was three weeks late. She sat near the small fire that had been lit in the middle of the dirt floor inside the cabin. The rabbit on the spit smelled like heaven, and yet looking at the grease dripping from it turned her stomach. After her impromptu question this afternoon, he had lost the urge to fish, and had gone hunting instead. She had decided it was time to try to get home. Her mother would know what to do. "I still don't understand why I can't go home."

Nick sighed; he wasn't in a particularly good mood. "I explained that to you. Henry won't rest until he gets what he wants."

"And what's that?"

"That would be you! Rachel we have talked about this. We have to keep going."

"But I'm dying Nick, I feel so sick all the time." She couldn't tell him about the baby, but there was no way to hide her sickness.

He went to her, and sat on the ground beside her, he pulled her into his arms, and she laid her head on his chest and then he gave her a small squeeze, and she wanted to cry again. "Don't worry, I'll find something that will make you feel better in no time at all."

She lifted her head to stare at him, and his eyes dropped away from her. "Really," she doubted that he could, but she played along. "What is it?"

"An old Indian recipe, that'll fix anything that ales you."

Her heart in her throat, she said. "So you know what's wrong with me?" He reached up and tweaked her nose.

"You dear heart are about to get a cold. Let's just hope we caught it before it turned really ugly on you."

She sighed, and pretended to be relieved, and then leaned forward and kissed his lips, she looked into his eyes. "You're really charming sometimes."

He laughed. "Only sometimes,"

"Yes, if you'd let me go home I would proclaim you my rescuer and everyone would thank you."

"I'm sorry but that won't be enough."

Forgive Me, My Love

"What do you mean?"

"I mean we're moving. Tomorrow we go deeper in the mountains."

"Nick it's been months already can we at least go into town and get some more supplies? It'll be Christmas soon and I'd love to be a part of the celebration. It has to be a grand one here in the heart of Mexico."

Nick stood up and walked away from her, he prowled their little house. He had taken big palm leaves and made them a nice somewhat comfortable bed, but she deserved so much more. He decided that he would take her back to the States, but he'd still make sure she didn't know where they were. That way he could give her so much better than this and still keep her in his arms and out of harms way. He walked up behind her and sat down and then wrapped his arms around her.

"If you want to go to town, I'll take you." She jumped, and squealed in delight, and then she turned and kissed him.

"Wonderful! Great, we're going to have so much fun. I'll buy a new dress and we can stay in a hotel and…" He silenced her with a kiss of his own. Then she said. "And we'll get in the tub together rather then some cold river."

"I like the cold river," he murmured. "It's so much fun getting warm again." He bent to kiss her, but she turned and raced outside. His eyes closed as she threw up everything she'd eaten today. She came back inside with a sheepish look on her lovely face.

"I'm not feeling very well lately."

"I know."

"Maybe I should stay away from the cold water."

"No Darling," he whispered. "Maybe I should've

stayed in it."

She laughed and frowned at him. "What are you talking about?"

"Nothing," he said. "Just let me hold you."

She burrowed into his arms. "Anytime and where."

Nick squeezed her close and prayed like he had never prayed before.

On the day of they entered town there was a carnival in progress and Rachel was in high sprits. Arm and arm they walked from vendor to vendor picking up scarves and skirts and new boots for the both of them, and a new hat for him. He bought a pair of blue jeans for her, as well as a hat to match his.

It was fun to watch her enjoy herself. Nick was careful not to let her have the margarita she so dearly craved. Instead he ordered her a virgin margarita, and was relieved that she didn't seem to notice the difference, and enjoyed it just as much.

He couldn't get over a very damning fact, she was probably pregnant and he needed to get rid of the baby without her knowing that there had ever been one.

"Oh, look," she cried, and took his hand pulling him towards the open area. "It's live music."

"You like the Mariachi?" Nick scanned the crowd, but no one seemed to be interested in them, so he allowed her to pull him where she wanted. She stopped in front of the group and began clapping her hands to the beat and tapping her toe. The smile on her face could've lit the darkest canyon. And Nick stepped back, thrilled just to watch her. Then she started to sing. He frowned. "Do you know this song?"

She through him a look over her shoulder that

said, 'Why don't you?' But her lips said. "Of course, I live in Texas, who doesn't know at least some Mexican music?"

"I've heard some, but I don't know the words."

"I love music," She winked at him, then through him a look that made his body tighten. The lively song changed, now they played a sensual ballad, and again she sang along with them. But she separated her self from the crowd and started to sway, her eyes on Nick and he couldn't look away. She sang in perfect Spanish and her eyes beckoned him.

Nick found himself following her into the ring, one of her hands went to his waist and and the other caressed his cheeks. Nick found his hand on her waist as she moved around him. He moved slowly to the rythme, never loosing eye contact with her. Then her gaze wandered up and down his body, and the only thing he could think of was the promise in her dusky eyes. Too soon the music died down, and Nick grabbed her in his arms and pulled her tight to his chest, then turned and dipped her, and the crowd cheered loud. He dropped a kiss on her smiling lips and then whispered. "I thought you couldn't speak Spainish?"

She gave a cheeky grin then kissed him back. She broke the kiss and said. "There's a lot you don't know about me."

"When can I start to learn more about you?" He asked.

"How about tonight?" She grinned.

"I look forward to it." Nick let her up and grabbed her hand. "Come on, let's go."

Later that night while Rachel was in the tub Nick got dressed and ducked his head in the bathroom. He smiled then she just looked at him and smiled. "I need to go out for a moment, be a good girl and stay put. I'll be back in no time flat."

"Don't take too long." She blew him a kiss and he closed the door.

Nick walked down the street, he felt a sick churning in his stomach; he prayed his suspicions weren't true. But from the look of Rachel, he knew in his heart it was. They couldn't stay in the shack any longer then they had. They had been traveling for over two months trying to lose any and all trails and now this. Nick ducked into the back of Loretta's and waited. It was early the crowd was just starting to pick up. He didn't have long to wait.

"There you are my big stud," Loretta sashayed her big hips towards him and caught his body in her fleshy arms. He didn't resist when she planted a wet sloppy kiss on his neck, neither did his arms curl around her. She stepped back and grinned.

"Did Paco tell you what I need?" he asked, and he could shake the pain that was fast weaknening his resolve.

"Yes, and you have what I need," she licked her plump lips and placed her fleshy hand over his crotch. "This is the only payment I need."

He grinned, even though he felt like throwing up. "And that is the only payment I can't give."

"You got cash?"

"Plenty."

"Fine," she dropped the vial into the cleavage of her ample bosom and it slid out of sight. "Put the cash on the table but if you want this you'll have to get it with your teeth." She gave a wicked laugh and he chuckled with very little humor. While he had his face buried between her massive bosoms she told him how to administer the stuff. "It works fast Dove. If this girl is pregnant, and you give it to her tonight, tomorrow when she wakes she will no longer be with child. And you my little Dove will be free to try again." She giggled and held his head tight against her. "All it takes is one drop, but be careful how you use it. It can kill the mother as well as the child. It's very powerful. And there will be much pain, and she will bleed." She laughed as he lifted his head with the bottle between his teeth. "Bravo!" She cheered. "Well done."

"Thanks," Nick winked at her and left with the bottle clutched in his fists. His stomach was sick, he tried not to think about his child.

Rachel's child, he didn't want to believe it was real. But for the life of him he kept seeing a little girl with long black pigtails and his blue eyes. Her skin was an olive color and she looked just like her Mama. The girl would smile at him and throw her small arms around his neck, she would kiss his cheek and wink at him just like her Mama. And he would laugh and squeeze her until she squealed with delight. Sadness erupted through his entire being, and his eyes clouded. Right now was the worst time for a child. All of their lives were at stake, to bring a child into this would be sheer madness. Besides, Rachel would never be happy with him, she was the heart of her family and she would never choose him over them. Added to the fact it was his father who'd kidnapped, her and sold her into prostitution, that wouldn't go over very well either.

He made it back to the hotel, with a heavy heart. He unlocked the door and froze, his battered heart did summersaults. She stood in a flowing sheer pink teddy. On her feet was a pair of fuzzy pink slippers. She raised her arms and turned.

Then she stopped, and stuck her bottom out at him, then winked. "What do you think? I had a hard time trying to buy it with you right next to me, but I did it." The look on her face captivated him; he dropped the vial in his pocket and closed the door. He leaned against it and she walked to his. She reached up and leaned in to seal his lips with a kiss, and then she frowned, and pulled away.

"What?" He frowned, she pulled back her hand and delivered a stinging slap to his face.

"How dare you!" She screeched, and turned on her heels. He caught her arm, and spun her around to face him.

"What did I do?"

"You rotten son of a Bitch!" She yanked her arm free and went into the bathroom and slammed the door shut. When she came out she was fully dress and was putting on her shoes.

"What are you doing?" He grabbed her boots and tossed them across the room. "You're not going anywhere. Tell me what's wrong?" He was struck when she looked at him through tear filled eyes.

"How could you Nick?" Then she was crying, he moved to take her into his arms, but again she pushed him away.

"Tell me."

"Am I not good enough for you? Do you have to have a wide variety of women?" She laughed through her tears. "How could I be so stupid? Why are you with me Nick? Why am I still here? Let me go, just to get rid of me, let me go home, or kill me. Just end this now!"

"I don't know what you're talking about. I haven't been with any other woman since well before I met you."

Forgive Me, My Love

"You liar, it's all over you! You reek of sweat, sex and stale perfume. You smell just like Lorett..." Her eyes cleared and his heart dropped. "Is that where you had to go all of a sudden? You needed to get laid by a professional?"

"No Rachel it wasn't like that I did go there, but it was just to..." he was at a loss, he didn't have a good reason to be at such a place.

"To what?" The hope shining in her eyes was hard for him to turn away from. But he did, this would be his excuse, his way out. It would hurt her, but there was no other way, then she'd be free of him and his child. He needed a wedge and this was as good as any, no matter how it broke his heart.

"Okay," he threw his hands up, and pretended to confess. "The only reason I brought you here was so I could go there. I needed some one who knew what they were doing. There, are you satisfied?"

"You Bastard!"

"Yeah, well you asked."

She sat on the bed and cried as though her heart was broken, and all he could do was watch. "I'll be back when you can get that shit under control." He slammed out of the room. He couldn't go far, leaving her had been hard enough, so he pulled up a chair, and sat beside the door. He hid his face with his forearm as he listened to her sobs, and wiped at his own tears. What seemed like hours later, he went back into the room. It was quiet, he could hear her sniffling, but other than that she was probably asleep. He went into the bathroom and took a quick shower, then slipped on a pair of clean jeans and a shirt. The bed looked too good for him to ignore, so he crawled in behind her and she immediately curled against

301

him and nestled into his arms. He sighed, she had to be asleep, if she wasn't she'd have bitten his hand rather then snuggle with him. He nestled his nose in her sweet smelling hair, for what he was sure was the last time, and let sleep claim him.

The day dawned, and Nick could tell it was going to be a beauty, his back stiffen at the sounds of her suffering in the bathroom, she was sick. Reminding him of why he had come to town in the first place. When she came out of the bathroom she wouldn't look at him, he knew if she did he would pull her into his arms and all would be lost. But she dressed slowly, and put her hair in a pony-tail, then sat on the edge of the bed staring at nothing.

"So this is how it's going to be?" he asked, his voice gruff despite his attempt to stay firm. "You gonna give me the silent treatment?"

"I don't mean anything to you," she said in a tone that wanted to weaken his knees. "I'd rather not waste your time."

"Thank you." Was all he said.

"Don't mention it, as long as you insist I be your captive, I think we should at least be civil."

"You're right."

"I don't want to go back to the cabin," she said quietly. "It made things seem different between us, and I don't want to be fooled again."

"You have no choice."

She turned those golden eyes on him and he flinched. "I said I won't go back! You have every thing you need here. I wouldn't want you to get desperate and have to lower yourself and sleep with me again."

"You weren't that bad."

Forgive Me, My Love

"Still," she said in that sad little tone that ate at him. "I believe I can find better and it's obvious you think you can." He wanted to make her be quiet, just the thought of her in the arms of some man made his blood boil.

"Yes, well we all do what we must." Was all he said, before he walked out of the room.

Rachel cried again. She didn't know how to stop it. Every time she thought of him in the arms of some other woman she just fell to pieces. Her heart was far too gone to ever love anyone else, and yet he didn't love her. *Is this how Richard felt when I wouldn't have sex with him? Does he love me so much that he would take me back after all this?* Rachel shook her head. What was she thinking? She could never go back to Richard not after this, it wouldn't be fair to either of them. Besides, he didn't love her either, she must be losing her mind to even think of going to a man who didn't love her. *Maybe I'm desperate, I need a father for this baby.* Then she froze. *Can I do this all by myself? What am I thinking? I'm a grown woman and I'm almost done with school. Once I find out if I past the bar I'll be self-sufficient.* Feeling only marginally better she sat up straighter. She would finish her internship then get that job in Houston and forget all about Nick and his smoky blue eyes.

That decision made she wondered why her heart still ached? *Mama!* The word seared through her brain. She needed to talk to her Mama. Simon had to still be down here looking for her. Rachel got up and walked to the door. She peeked out and was relieved to see Nick wasn't there. She hurried down the hall and out the door. Then jumped into the nearest phone booth she could find. She picked up the receiver and dialed the operator. "Hola

Señora collect call to Houston Texas." After giving the woman the number she told her who she was. The call was accepted.

"Hello?"

"Mama, I'm so glad you're home. I need…" Rachel found herself pulled out of the booth, she screamed bloody murder as she was hauled back into the hotel.

"What the hell do you think you're doing?" Nick yelled at her. She turned away from him and crossed her arms over her chest.

"I needed to talk to someone who loves me." Nick lifted his arms ready to pull her into his embrace, he wanted to tell her he loved her, and that he'd take care of her. But her shoulders were shaking.

"We're leaving, go get your stuff."

Sixteen

PAT RACED DOWN THE STAIRS, her gown clutched in her hand. "Simon!" She screamed. "Simon, John, Bea!" The halls erupted with the sound of running feet.

"What is it?" John huffed.

"What happened?" Ryan asked.

She held up her hand, and waved them silent while she caught her breath. "I spoke with Rachel, she just called," her words were met with silence. "Listen to me, did you hear what I said. She just called me collect from Mexico. She said Mama I need and then she was screaming and I didn't get the chance to tell her anything." Pat burst into tears, and John took her into his arms.

"It's okay Darling, let's just get you back in bed."

"No, it was her, I swear it was. You have to help her. If you don't help her then I will! I'll get my things, and go down there and find my baby!"

John led her away and they all stood staring at each other. "Do you think it's true?" Ryan asked.

"No," said Tyrell. "She wants so badly for Rachel to be alive that she wouldn't even go to the funeral. She has convinced herself that Rachel is still with us."

"If it was a collect call all I have to do is call and

find out where it was placed," Simon growled. "Then I'll go there myself and God help the person who placed it."

*****

Nick pulled up to the hut, with dread. Sighing hard he slid off the horse and turned to help her off hers, but she'd already gotten down. He nodded and tied both horses to a near-by tree. As soon as he walked inside he saw her sitting on one of the chairs staring at nothing.

"Give me your wrists," her red rimmed eyes shot to his.

"Why?" Already she was easing away from him.

"Because I said so, now give them to me."

Reluctantly she held out her hands. "I thought we were past this." She whispered, and her eyes started to get glassy.

"You can't be trusted. Didn't you just prove that?"

She gasped when he cut the bounds and rubbed her wrists. "What do you mean I can't be trusted? You're the one holding me against my will."

"Like I said, you can't be trusted."

"You're the one who can't be trusted, you black hearted..."

"Okay! Enough, if you don't want to spend the rest of your stay bound, then I suggest you shut that mouth of yours."

She did, she sat in one of the same chairs she'd been so proud of when he'd made them, and glared out the window. She was still pissed, but as he looked around the room he was amazed at what a woman's touch could do. She had taken a white skirt from her bag and made pretty lacy curtain's for the two windows, then tacked them up with the thorns from a cactus. Then she'd cleaned the whole place, just simple sweeping with a broom he'd made of palm branches. There were candles on the rickety table and little lace dollies under the candle holders.

"I'm going to sleep." She announced. Then she stood up and removed her skirt, leaving her shirt to hang, covering her from his exploring eyes, then neatly folded the shirt across the back of the chair. Still she refused to look at him. She went to the makeshift bed and lay down, after pulling the blanket up over her shoulders she said. "Find somewhere else to sleep would you?"

Nick snorted, and picked up his hat. This would be a good time to see how cold the night could really get. Besides, after he got rid of the child she carried, he had to think about how he was going to get her back to her family. That was where she needed to be, he could no longer justify keeping her with him.

Rachel didn't know what had awakened her, she lay still for a moment, but when all remained quiet she ventured a look around. Nothing looked out of place, except the space next to her was empty. Her heart seemed equally empty. She yawned and sat up. It was dark outside, and a small piece of the candle on the table was still burning. She looked at his empty spot, and her heart squeezed, it was and unfamiliar feeling not to be in Nick's arms. She vowed to find him, and make their days together worth something. Even if he didn't want her or their child, she still loved him. There was no denying that. And as long as he was available it was her right to take advantage of it. She threw off the blanket and stood up, she tossed her skirt back on and slipped on a light jacket. It was cold in the mountains at night and starting to get warm during the day.

She stepped outside, there was a small fire burning but Nick was no where to be seen. She looked around, *surely he wasn't fool enough to get in that frigid lake.* She thought as she made her way towards the river.

"What's this?" Rachel froze at the unfamiliar voice.

"It's what I been wishin' for since we started this fool mission." Another man growled.

She turned and a gasp jumped from her lips. She was surrounded. Three men stood staring at her as if she were their first and last supper.

"This can't be the girl. She had longer hair. This one looks like a boy."

"What's yo name sugar?"

They spoke English. *Maybe American.* Her mind whirled. Was this her chance? Could they help her?

"Speak up damn you!"

She jumped back and shook her head. Her hand flew to her belly, and she turned to run. But one of them caught her arm and spun her around so hard she fell face first on the rock filtered ground. Pain shot through her jaw, but she scrambled to her knees and tried to crawl away.

"She's getting' away," One man grabbed the back of her skirt and halted her bid for freedom. They spoke as if she were just a means to an end for them. They didn't care if she lived or died.

"As I see it we got two choices. There are two posters. The one that says she's to be returned unharmed is offering more money."

"But the other one is closer and is offering almost as much."

Forgive Me, My Love

The tallest of the men hit the littlest one. "Damn Skeet, you ain't never been smart. Twenty-five thousand ain't no where near two million."

"What do you think Gus? Think they just gonna have that kinda money laying around. Look at her, if she knew people with that kinda money do you think she'd be lookin' like this? I say we go for the closest, the sure money. I think twenty-five thousand would be easier to pay."

"You makin' all kinds of sense. But them millions will last us forever."

"Stupid, I'm sayin' no body would give us two million for this scrawny thing."

"My father would," she stopped fighting and now sat on the ground listening to them. "My father is rich, he'll pay more then that if you take me home."

"If that's true what you doing down here?"

"I was kidnapped."

"Happens all the time." The one named Skeet said.

But Gus didn't look convinced. "What'd you think Cane?"

"I say take the sure money." Cane said, his voice low, it held a menacing quality that told her he was the leader of these lowlifes. "That one don't care if she's dead or alive. I don't have time to baby-sit. If she dies in the transport, it's winter, the carcass won't stink."

"No," Rachel cried, directing her plea to Crane. "Listen, my father will pay you. If you take me to Henry he'll kill you all rather than pay you."

"Henry Dennison?" Skeet asked, and his voice croaked.

"Yes," Rachel seized on his anxiety. "Dennison,

he has a heart of the foulest black. He'd kill you the second he laid eyes on you. Please, you want to be rich don't you? Two million would do that."

"Skeet," Gus said. "Tape her mouth and tie her hands. What ever we do we need to do it and get the hell outa here. She had to be with that fool you knocked out at the river, and I doubt if he'd take kindly to us stealing his fare."

"Hey, how about I go over there and kill him. Then we don't have to worry about nothin'."

"No!" Rachel screamed, as what they said sank in. "Nooooo!" She lashed out with her foot and someone screamed, and then she bared her nails as they came closer. "Don't touch me!"

Gus snarled something, she didn't know what he said, her head was to busy ringing from the massive slap she'd just received. He picked her up and slung her over his shoulder and all she could do was cry. They were going to kill her child, and she couldn't say anything to protect it. "Nick!" she screamed through her tears as the cabin became smaller and smaller.

Nick shook his head to clear it, and the world slowly came back into focus. The last thing he remembered was the need to get away. All he'd been able to see was her, her smile, her tears stained face, her walk, her voice. And he couldn't keep his eyes from her belly, he wanted that child she carried beneath her breasts more than he had ever wanted anything. Most of all he wanted her, in his arms forever. She had a quick wit that made him smile every time they spoke. Her mind was incredible, and her body had to be shaped by God himself and she fit in his arms perfectly. He had lit the campfire to keep the animals away, then picked up the gun he'd just bought to replace the one he'd lost days ago, and walked towards the river then all had gone black. Suddenly he jumped up, it was morning, and the rain had started. His first conscious thought was Rachel!

He ran to the cabin, as soon as he entered the clearing he knew it was empty. Her presence was gone, everything that made him feel alive was gone with her. The horses were gone, even though he knew all his things were gone, he had to check. He walked into the cabin and his heart shuddered in his chest. Signs of the fight she must've given them was everywhere. The room was a mess, the makeshift bed was in shambles. Nick righted a chair and sat for a second. He had to think, he needed to get passed the blind rage the shook him. He closed his eyes and swallowed hard. But all he could see was her tear stained face. *Does she think I abandoned her?* The thought cut him to the core. Nick wiped his eyes and focused on the cabinet, there was a pool of blood on the counter, his eyes traveled down the trail of blood and his heart leapt, there was one of his knives. He picked it up, there was blood on the blade. He prayed it belonged to the person who took her.

Nick hurried out of the cabin. He let loose a loud whistle, but there was no response. He scoured the ground around the cabin until finally he picked up the tracks. Looked like five horses, so there were three men. One girl against three men, the odds didn't look good. The good thing was they didn't seem to be in any hurry. Nick smiled, if Rachel could slow them down, it would give him a chance to catch up. *Then God help the sorry bastards.*

Rachel needed to rest, she had been in the saddle for hours, if she didn't get some rest soon she would fall from the saddle. The rain was falling heavier by the minute and she was afraid it would wash away their tracks. She slumped over and groaned into the tape.

"What's wrong with her?" Skeet asked, he seemed frightened, and Rachel wanted to smile. He wanted the two million, he was probably willing to do anything to get it, including kiss her feet.

"What am I," Gus said sarcastically. "Psychic? Ask her you dumb ass."

"Stay away from her," growled Cane, but his voice was sluggish. "That Bitch can rot for all I care." He was still nursing the stab wound Rachel had inflicted on his arm. It was deep, he'd lost a lot of blood. It looked as if it would need stitches. He was already looking green. Rachel didn't like the way he was glowering at her. If it wasn't for the other two she'd be dead right now. Cane had gone for her throat, she still felt his beefy fingers around her neck cutting off her air.

"If we want the two mil we have to look after her. If she needs something we have to get it." Skeet said.

"Pussy!" Cane yelled. "She don't need nothin'!"

They all fell silent, and Rachel kept her horse at as slow a pace as she dared. Suddenly Cane fell from his horse and landed face first on the ground. That stopped them.

"Shit!" Gus cussed.

"What do we do?" Skeet said. "We have to take him to the Doctor."

Blood coated the shirt that was wrapped around his arm and the rain was turning it pink. She grabbed her saddle horn and slid down, the minute her feet hit the ground her legs buckled. She fell to the muddy ground and stayed there. Then she started to shiver as she realized how cold it was, but still she couldn't move. All she could do was listen.

"I say we take him to the hospital in town."

"But what if we're recognized? We have wanted posters in every town down here."

"But remember, if we weren't checking out our posters we'd have never come across that fat purse over there." Skeet pointed in Rachel's direction.

"What the fuck does that have to do with anything?" Gus snapped as they stood over the rapidly paling Cane.

"That means," Skeet explained. "I want that two million. Without Cane, we get one mil each. The way that girl talks I believe her, I think she can get us that money and our lives."

"You stupid?" Gus hit him behind his head. "When have you ever known a black to have that kinda money?"

"There are some," Skeet insisted. "I ain't always been stupid, I lived in Texas. In Texas it's a free for all. Anyone smart enough can get all the money they want. That's all I'm saying."

"Come on," Gus said and Rachel tensed as their slushy footsteps halted in front of her. She rolled to her back and stared up at them. She was no more concerned about the rain now then when she had been a girl, and used to lay out in the grass during thunderstorms. It pelted her face, and she shelted her eyes as she returned their stare.

"Are you rich?" Gus asked.

"Yes," Rachel said. "I was kidnapped." She said again just incase they had forgotten.

"Your daddy will pay us?" She tried to still the

crazy hope that was about to kill her.

"Yes." She said in a voice full of as much culture as she could manage.

They stood over her, but for the most part ignored her. "So, what say you?" Gus asked.

"I say we kill Cane, he's half gone already, we'd be doing him a mercy."

"Mercy killing?" Gus thought it over. "Never done that before," he smiled. "Makes me feel honorable."

Skeet looked at Rachel. "If you lying, you and yo daddy are as good as dead. You lucky we need that money."

Rachel turned her head away at the sound of the gun shot. And her empty stomach heaved, foul bile burned her throat making her want to throw up until not even bile was left.

Nick heard the gun shot. He couldn't believe he was that close. At least he prayed it was them. The rain wasn't letting up. It was getting worst, he wondered what she was wearing, was she warm enough? She would get sick in this cold wet mess, and it was all his fault. He promised if he could save her, he'd take her home, right where he should've taken her from the start. He wiped the water from his eyes as he came to a boulder. Nick crouched low and peered around the edge. For a second he closed his eyes. She lay on the ground, on her back next to the horse with the rain beating down on her. If the horse took a side step he'd crush her. Her hands were tied in front of her and her lips were still. Nick didn't want to think it but what else could it be? No one would lay in the rain like that. She had to be dead. His burning eyes went to the men who were kicking the body of a dead man, and then going through the fallen man's pockets. Nick's heart jumped when her hand came up and wiped at her face.

"But why is she laying there like that?" He wondered out loud. He moved, and made his way as quiet as he could to a pile of rocks close to where she lay. When he was near her, he made sure the horse stood between them and her captors. Nick said as softly as he could. "Are you hurt?"

She stiffened, and slowly her head turned towards him, the instant joy on her face filled his heart. Then her lips started to tremble and she nodded. "Just stay calm, I'll get you."

Rachel was in an awkward place. Should she allow the man she loved to rescue her, or let these money hungry men take her home? She needed to get home, if her child was still alive then she wanted to get home now, so it can be born in safety and with people who loved her. But if she told them that Nick was here they would have the upper hand and they would kill him. She couldn't let that happen. There was no way out. So, she laid on the ground and cried for another missed opportunity. She had no doubt Nick would save her. He would kill anything that stood in his way, but he would save her. Maybe in his own way he did love her, he just didn't know it.

She pushed herself into a sitting position, and wiped her face. For all the good it did her. "Grab my bag and come here." Nick whispered.

Rachel nodded. She got to her feet and trudged to Nick's horse. She untangled the reins from her horse and slapped it's rump sending it speeding out at full gallop. She screamed as if something was wrong and threw herself to the ground.

"What the hell happened?" Gus yelled.

"You stupid bitch!" Skeet surprised her, and

grabbed her blouse and pulled her to her feet, then backhanded her and tossed her back to the ground. "Look what you did! We was gonna git good money for that horse."

Gus grabbed his arm as he was about to deliver another blow. "What's wrong with you? The poster said unharmed. If you gonna hit her make sure it don't show."

"Forget that," Skeet said. "She gonna tell her daddy anyway."

"Not if she can't talk."

"You want to cut out her tongue?"

"No stupid," Gus snarled. "We gonna give her a drug to knock her out. Once they see she's okay they'll pay us then by the time she wakes up we'll be gone."

"What if she don't wake up?"

"That's not our problem, we did what the poster said, the rest is up to them."

"So you're saying we can do what we want with her as long as we don't leave no bruises?"

"Yes," Gus looked down at Rachel. "Get ready for some good lovin' baby, and you ain't even got to die afterwards."

Rachel gasped as warm liquid hit her face. Confused she wiped her eyes and looked up again. Both Gus and Skeet were staring at each other with stunned looks on their faces. Rachel watched as red blossomed on their shirts, and braced herself as they fell forward. She screamed as their combined weight crushed the breath right out of her. By the time Nick arrived she thought she was about to blackout from lack of air.

Nick rushed in and pushed the bodies off her, then he caught her in his arms, and held her as she cried.

Once they were back at the cabin Nick couldn't

help but worry. She couldn't stop shaking. Her whole body trembled, at times she trembled so hard he thought her teeth would break. He started a fire in the old stove and in the pit in the middle of the room. Then he carefully removed her clothes only to discover everything they owned was wet, the only dry piece was one of his shirts. Then he removed his wet clothes, and tossed them on the chair next to the fire. He wrapped her in the only dry shirt. Then he moved their makeshift bed as close to the fire as he could and still be safe. But she wasn't responding. He lay behind her and snuggled spoon style then chafed her arms, and yet still she shivered.

Nick had taken all the clothes out of the saddle bags and laid them near the fire, as soon as a piece dried he put it on her. Then he threw on damp shorts and enveloped her in his arms again. After what seemed like hours she lay still, only her soft breath told him she was still alive. It was only then that Nick fell asleep.

*****

"Nick we need some things," she stood in the middle of the shack days later with her hands on her hips, glaring at him.

Nick had just ducked into the room, it had been two weeks since her near disaster. And he had stayed as far away from her as he could. What he felt for her frightened him. It was dangerous to feel this way and yet he couldn't stop it. His hungry eyes roamed her sleek body, and he laughed when she looked away and presented him with her back, which was an even more enticing view. "You act as if we're staying here."

She turned back to face him. "It doesn't matter

where we're going to be. There are some necessary things that I for one can't do with out."

"Like?"

Her nostrils flared and her hands flew up to rest her palms on her hips. "I need female things!"

He liked the way the outfit she wore fit her. It was a white shirt that had his imagination spinning. It clung to her shapely bosom; the sleeves were rolled up to the elbows, revealing golden brown arms that were just as firm as the rest of her. The tails of the shirt were tucked into a pair of doe's skin pants he had gotten from the carnival. The way they hugged her sweet bottom had to be a sin.

"What are you looking at?" She snapped, and he let a lazy smile lift his lips.

"If I tell you I'd just frighten you with my lustful male cravings as you call them."

"I knew it!" She yelled, and her cheeks flushed a charming shade of red. "I'm sure you can find a professional to take care of that for you."

He moved to her then, and it was pure hell keeping his hands from her luscious little body, and he... Nick caught himself, he stared into her wide sultry eyes, and it brought him back to reality. He couldn't just take what he wanted, and then he'd be no better than his father. "I'm taking you home." Her eyes widened and her lips worked, but no words came out. He bent down and placed a light kiss on her lips. To his amazement she kissed him back. Then she pulled away.

"What do you mean, you're taking me home?"

"I want you to get your things together." He lifted a hand and traced the bruises that decorated her delicate skin. "This should've never happened to you. It was my fault, I was trying to protect you when all the time I was the one you needed protection from."

She reached up, and put one hand behind his head and pulled him to her. She opened like a morning glory to the awakening sun. And he fell in, he took everything she had to offer. One last time, he let his hands run over her until his thumbs trace across her breasts then she was pushing tighter against him and he moaned as his body tightened. Nick caressed her back, then cupped her round bottom and pulled her tight against him. She purred and moved her sweet lips to his neck and Nick closed his eyes and his body trembled with the need to take her where they stood.

He lifted her in his arms and her arms went around his neck and her fingers burrowed into his hair, and she clung to him kissing his face, then wild kisses on his neck and ear all the while her hips rubbed against his raging maleness. Nick let her down and pushed the pants down her legs, she kicked out of them and she pushed open his shirt.

"I want to feel your skin against mine." She said and he almost lost it. He pushed her shirt from her shoulders leaving her totally naked in his arms. She pushed his shirt from his shoulders, but her hands never left his burning skin. Her small cool hands fired his blood like nothing ever had. He was acutely aware of his heart breaking with every kiss, and he knew she felt the same.

Her tears wet them both and she refused to stop kissing him. Nick reveled in her hands in his hair. Her fingers tugging on his curls, her white teeth nipping at his lips, his ear, his neck, it was more than he could take. He captured her in his arms again and lifted her, immediately her legs came up around his waist, and he backed up until her back was against the cool adobe wall. "Take me Nick," she begged. "Take me like you've never done before." The urgency was like a living thing.

He reached under her and found his zipper, letting it lose, he kicked out of his jeans and let her feel his hardness and he growled deep in his throat when he felt how ready she was. His hardness against her softness, Nick rocked his hips back and forward until they were both on the verge of ecstasy. Then he lifted her and positioned himself at her orifice and eased her down. "Hang on love, I'm about to take us both to a place we've never been." He pushed fast and she screamed as an orgasm hit her hard and fast. Nick rode that wave with her, taking her to heights unknown. When she came down to earth he cupped her bottom and found his rhythm. His head on her shoulder, he kissed her neck, and anything he could reach, and she began to purr again. Nick gave thrust after thrust then he held her tight and ground against her then her nails were on his back begging for more. He held tight and pounded her until she screamed her release this time he couldn't stop it. The tingling was there, weakening his knees and turning his every thought to jelly. After he caught his breath he gave her a kiss that was meant to last him a lifetime. "Get packed." He detached himself from her, and set her on her feet, then pulled up his pants. He went and got hers, then he closed her shirt and handed her the pants.

"Is that all you have to say to me?"

He lifted one eyebrow. "What else is there?"

"What was this?" She sneered. "One more time for old times sake?"

"What do you want it to be Rachel?"

"I wanted it to be a beginning for us!" She

screamed.

"There is no beginning for us," he yelled just as loud. "You know there's only one way this is going to end."

"I think that's your way out. You just want a way to let me down easy. Or maybe you don't want me to see what a real coward you are and this is your way of getting out of this without too much trouble."

Cursing under his breath, he turned on the heels of his boots and walked out the door.

"Where are you going?" She cried. "You started this! You can't leave, answer me!" She ran to the door, and stared after him.

Nick could feel her eyes on his back but he refused to stop, there was a river full of cold water waiting for him. "I'll be back."

"When?"

"When I feel like it."

Nick walked to the horses and jumped on the back of his and was about to take off, but he looked at the cabin. The woman inside was more precious then life to him, but he couldn't explain something he didn't even understand. Slowly he slid off the horse and tied it to the tree. Instead of going into the house, he went to a tree not far from the doorway and sat on the ground. It was a nice day, cool out but dry. He had never been more distressed than he was right now. He'd tried to give her the potion. Tried three times, but each time she would say something, or do something and his heart would melt. He didn't know what he thought about the baby. She was no longer sick, as a matter of fact she had a pleasant glow to her that was captivating. Sometimes he would look at her, and smile as he thought of his child growing under her heart.

She would love the baby, that was no doubt, but he had to give her the choice. He had to tell her before it was too late. The problem was, if she hated him as much as he thought she did, would she get rid of the kid just to be done with anything that had anything to do with him? He didn't think she would, but it was her choice, and he had probably taken the choice from her by waiting so long.

After much soul searching Nick headed back. It was later, but not dark yet and she had probably cooked. He smiled; she was turning into a pretty good little cook. He walked into the clearing and stopped in his tracks, it was silent. The kind of silence that tells you something isn't right. His first impulse was to shout her name, but he squelched it. She wouldn't have taken off alone she was too smart for that. Nick slowly moved back into the brush and made his way around the small house.

After a quick inspection revealed nothing, Nick hurried into the house. She was standing at the sink with her back to him. As always he looked for some sign that she was expecting, but there was none. "Don't mind me." He said and walked to the blanket in a far corner and lay down, his skin clammy as he thought of when to tell her.

"I never do." She said and continued with her work.

"You should start packing," he said and put his hat over his face. "We leave for Texas in the morning."

Rachel's hands froze as she worked the beef. Her ears perked up, the sound was familiar, a cross between a bird's call and a whistle. It was almost like when she was a child and Simon... Her heart skipped a beat, and her eyes flew to Nick. He looked comfortable, he lay stretched out on the blankets that cover a small section of the floor. His hat over his eyes and his booted feet crossed at the ankle.

She licked her lips, and her eyes swung towards the door, her heart raced at the possibility. But the chances of her making it out the door without him catching her were slim. Since the attack he was harder to get rid of then gum on the bottom of a shoe in one hundred degree weather. But she had to try. She was afraid of what would happen to him if Simon were to actually get his hands on Nick, it might already be too late for her to save him.

She cleared her throat and put down the knife. "I'll be right back," she lowered her head, and started walking towards the door. Just as she feared, he was on his feet and beside her in seconds.

"Oh, no you don't, I told you not without me."

She wanted to scream at him, but since the attack he had been so different, almost loving in some ways. "I'm not a little girl. What happened was just dumb luck. And because of me, you had to add two more bodies to your list of sins." She snapped, and tried to go around him. "All I need is a handful of those wild onions growing by the river. I'll be right back."

He stopped her, and lifted her chin with his finger and she quaked inside. Loving him was hard work, but if Simon was there then she needed to save Nick's life. Her eyes watered there was no way Nick could fall into Simon's hand and survive it.

"That list was long and deep long before I meet you love. What's two more?" The look in his eyes fired her blood, and his touch did magical things to her, even though she swore she hated him. "I can't let anything happen to you Rachel."

323

He said it so softly caressing that she nearly melted in his arms. "Why Nick?" she wanted to know. "Is it because of the ransom? Are you going to ransom me?" She wanted to cry when his eyes softened, and one of his arms curled around her waist, and then he pulled her flush against him.

"Why are you asking that now?" he asked, and looked at her as if she should know why. "When those thieves had you I wanted to kill. Pure blood lust ran through my veins and all I could see was that blood on your face, it drove me mad with..." Suddenly his eyes rolled back, and he was falling to the ground.

"No!" Rachel screamed, and tried to catch him. "No what have you done to him?"

Simon let Nicks limp body fall to the floor. "What the hell do you mean what did I do to him?"

Ryan caught Simon's arms. "Don't do this. She's been with him for months she probably believes she's fallen in love with him. Remember what the doctor said, it's victims remorse." Ryan said it hushed desperate tones, but Rachel hear him. "Remember we discussed it, don't do this in front of her."

Simon couldn't take his eyes from Rachel's prone form. She lay half over the man who kidnapped and raped her. His lips twitched as an unreasonable laugh fought its way forward.

"You better hope and pray she's not pregnant." Ryan snarled at Nick's unconscious frame.

Simon heard the last words like they were fired from a cannon directly into his brain.

"Aarrgghh!" He screamed and lifted his foot, he delivered a blow to Nick's upper thigh.

"Stop it! Stop!" She sobbed, her hands

everywhere on him as if she could protect him. "What did you do to him Simon?"

There was his baby sister sitting in a broken down shack wearing torn rags. Her hair had been sheared off in ragged clumps and her face bruised, no doubt from a recent beating from this bastard she protected so well. "He's not dead, but he'll soon wish he were." Simon turned to three other men she hadn't noticed and Rachel shivered.

"Take him out of here!" Simon ordered.

"Ryan!" She screamed when she saw him. "Don't let him do this, please Ryan help me!"

They walked towards her and she clutched Nick closer. "No!" she screamed, shaking her head. "Simon no! Don't take him." But Ryan pulled her kicking and screaming out of the way while two other men lifted Nick's feet and dragged him from the room. Ryan held her close to his chest and whispered in her ears, but she wasn't listening.

Dean King

Seventeen

"**N**OOOO!" RACHEL FRANTICLY FOUGHT his hold, scratching at his fingers and kicking at his legs, but soon she tired and became aware of Simon sitting at the table she had been about to share with Nick. His shoulders slumped and shaking. "Simon," she pleaded. "You don't know what happened. It wasn't him, it was Henry. Henry did this. Nick saved me, he only did what he did because he had no choice. He saved us Simon." She said between sobs, as she sucked in great gulps of air.

Ryan sat on the floor with her and hugged her close. He caressed her hair as she cried. "Don't do this Rach, we love you darlin' we love you so much. He'll get everything he has coming to him. He'll pay for this."

"Ryan, he didn't do anything!" She sobbed so hard her chest hurt, and she couldn't see through her tears. "Please believe me. He didn't hurt me."

"I believe you believe that." He held her head pressed to his, as he cried with her. "Darlin, this isn't your fault. You were a victim, he used you. We understand that."

"No you don't," she tore away from Ryan, and stood up to face Simon. "If you understood you wouldn't be doing this. He loves me I know he does."

"Has he said it?" Simon asked, not looking at her.

"No, but he was about to, just before you came he was saying how wonderful I was and how he needed to keep me with him."

Hope bloomed in her chest as Simon got up and walked to her. The tears still on his cheeks, the sadness in his eyes was hard to bear, but she had to hope that he would understand. That he would trust her to know what was best for her. "Please Simon, for me, don't hurt him."

He lifted a hand to touch her face. Her heart sank as his fingers traced the bruises from the other day, panic started to rise as his eyes grew as cold as onyx. "Do you love him?"

Hope, there was hope, her love could save him. "Yes Simon," she said through her tears. "I love him with my whole heart and soul."

"Did he love you enough to tell you he was Henry's son?" She grabbed her chest, her eyes wide. Then she drew back her hand and slapped him across the face.

"How dare you lie just to cover your crime! What you're about to do is a crime, against me, against him and to the world."

"I see he didn't tell you."

"Of course he didn't, why would he? It's just a filthy lie and you know it!"

"I told you, she thinks she understands him, that he is innocent and needs to be forgiven." She looked over Simon's shoulders to see a Hispanic man standing there. "Victims remorse, I knew she would think herself in love with him. It's because she is a good christen girl and she needs to validate what was happening here."

"No, that's not true!" She spoke to Simon. "He saved my life, two weeks ago I was attacked by three men, they wanted the money from some posters, but Nick saved me. He saved me so many times I lost track." But Simon was shaking his head, and her stomach started to churn with fear. "Please Simon, please, I'm begging you, don't hurt him."

He wiped her tears with the pad of his thumbs then kissed her forehead. "I do this because I love you."

"Noooo!" She screamed. "Simon nooo, ooh nooo, please," sobs broke through and she would've collapsed if not for Ryan holding her. "I'm begging you."

Simon let go and headed for the door. "Tie her hands, we'll stay here tonight and leave in the morning." He stopped and turned to Ryan. "Don't let her near the windows, and plug her ears, and put a blindfold on her."

With that he was gone. Rachel lay curled in a ball, her stomach in knots. Despite the earplugs she could hear muffled talking, then a constant thud, a grunt here and there, then hard coughing. With each groan that came from Nick she screamed because she was sure she felt his every pain. Soon all was quiet, and she began to pant in real fear. Her body became cold, clammy, and she was shaking. She jumped as she heard boots scrape against the wooden floor. Male voices, satisfied male voices and they brought tears to her eyes, tears she didn't know she had left.

"What do you want to do with the body?" Someone asked and she stiffened and prayed.

"If he's dead by morning we'll leave it hanging in the tree," Simon said. And she could have sworn she hated him, hated her own flesh and blood.

"And if he's not?" She heard a chair shift and silently wondered if he were looking at her.

"If not then I'll have you take her out of here while I finish. Then I'll meet yall on the way."

Forgive Me, My Love

She sucked in her breath. There was hope. They hadn't out right killed him that meant there was a chance. She gathered her courage and tried not to think about that. She had to get him out of here. With her back to the wall Rachel continued to work at the ropes but soon her fingers were raw and wet, she knew they were bleeding. She had to think of another way.

They removed the blindfold, but she kept her eyes closed and turned her face away.

Cautiously, she opened her eyes; Simon was lying on his back not two feet from her. He was asleep, deeply asleep if his snoring was any testament. She looked around; there were three other men and Ryan in the room, all asleep. She wondered why Tyrell wasn't here. He would've been on her side or at least tried to talk some sense into them.

The room was full which meant there was no one guarding Nick, Simon must think it was okay to leave Nick out there all alone. Her stomach clinched, she prayed they hadn't done any thing crippling to him, if so she'd spend the rest of her life trying to make it up to him.

Rachel wanted to be angry with Simon, but she knew he did what he did because of love for her. He wanted revenge as any man would. Ryan had tied her to a chair and gagged her to keep her from screaming.

Now she lay on the floor trying to come up with a plan to save the man she loved. Rachel looked around the room for a weapon, the knife was on the counter where she had left it. All she needed to do was get it and cut her bounds. Softly, so as to not awaken anyone, she eased out of her covers. She had slept in her moccasins and her clothes so she was ready. She cautiously sat up, and then she eased to her feet.

"Is there something I can help you with Ma'am?"

She jumped at the sound of that sleep filled voice. "Mmmmm," she mumbled through the rag in her mouth.

The man at the door had turned to face her. "Oh wait, let me take that off." As he approached he gave her a worried frown. "You won't start screaming will you?"

She shook her head, and he pushed the rag to her chin, Rachel inhaled deeply and tried to act fragile.

"No," she said in a delicate little whine. "I'm fine."

"I think you should lie back down."

"I need some water, my throat is dry and I have to go to the bathroom."

He looked so terribly uncertain that she almost wanted to tell him everything would be okay. Then he offered her his hand and helped her to her feet. "I'll get you the water, as for the other I'll take you out back."

Rachel watched him as he poured some water in a glass for her, she made a big show of trying to pick it up with her hands tied. "Can you untie my hands? Or hold the cup for me?"

"I can't untie you, but I can hold it for you," He smiled as if to apologize, and she nodded. Her eyes on his, she moved in front of the counter and with as little motion as possible, slowly slid the knife up the sleeve of her shirt. When she was done, she wiped her mouth on her shoulder and looked at him. "I gotta go." She said sheepishly.

"Come on, let's go this way."

She held up her hands and showed him the ropes. "I can't do anything like this."

He seemed unsure again, then he nodded. "Okay, but don't tell them I untied you, there will be hell to pay if you do." Once they were a few feet into the brush he said. "Now promise you're not going to run away."

"I promise."

He untied the rope and she rubbed her wrist. "Thank you so much." She gave him a bashful look and said. "Could you turn for just a second, or should I duck behind that tree over there?"

He grinned. "No I'll turn, just don't run." Then he did as she asked. The minute he turned Rachel thought only for a second about what she was about to do. If she took the knife and slid it across his throat, he'd be dead, and there was no way he could warn anyone, and it would give them a chance at escape. But could she do it? She pulled the knife free of her shirt and looked at it, and then she looked at his thin back. Instead she picked up a fist size rock and brought it down on his head. He fell without a sound. She picked up the rope and tied him up, hands to feet then gagged him with a piece of her shirt.

She got up, she needed that back pack. There were medicines in it that could help Nick with the pain. With her heart raging in her chest, she crept back to the house. She looked in through the window, it was just as when she'd left. She hurried inside and picked up Nick's saddlebags and tip-toed to an open window, with one last look around, she climbed out of the window and crept along the dark path. She hurried to the horses, careful not to spook them.

"Easy boy," she patted the nose of Nick's great black stallion. "It's okay," she whispered. "Let's go get your master."

She untied all the horses and ran them off by slapping their rumps. Then she untied Nick's horse and tied Carlie's reins to the back of the saddle on Nick's horse, which he refused to name. Then she walked them to the front of the house. Her stomach clenched as she readied herself for anything she might see. She told herself she was strong and that she could take anything. She stiffened her back and moved as fast as the horses would let her without making too much noise. She rounded the corner and the reins fell from her numb fingers. Her hand flew to her mouth, and she shook her head. Her brothers couldn't be this cruel. But the evidence was there, hanging by his wrists from a tree. His body slumped when his booted feet could no longer hold him. She gasped, he was naked except for the remnants of his shirt which was hanging past his waist. Her mind shied away from why his pants were down around his ankles.

His arms were stretched high above his head and his feet barely touching the ground. She swallowed hard; the closer she came to him the harder her hands began to shake. Fear and anger warred with-in her, but now wasn't the time to give in to it. She had to get him out of here. Slowly, she walked to him, and cringed. His face was a bloody mess, swollen and discolored, and she was hard pressed not to cry. She reached down and pulled up his jeans, she couldn't look, she shut her eyes and pulled them up but she didn't button them. "Nick," she whispered as she worked to put him back together. "I need your help. Nick wake up." She kissed his bloody chest and then his bruised face. "Please darling I need your help. I can't do this alone." Hope surged as he moaned and tried to move.

Then she reached up and untied one of his hands and put it on the saddle horn "Close your fingers around that." She almost cried as he did what she asked. Then she untied his other hand and helped him lean against the horse. By now she was crying, he was so sticky with blood and his breathing was harsh, his eyes were swollen and he was barely conscious.

"Don..'t don..t look at me," he rasped.

"Baby, don't talk, save your strength."

"Go away Rach...el, leave me alo...ne."

"I can't, I love you and I won't let them hurt you any more."

"Cut...cut the rope."

"I will Darling, just plant your feet and try to hold yourself up for a minute."

"The rope, bind...ing me..."

"I know," she whispered frantically working with the rope at one of his wrist.

"No, lift...my shirt."

She was afraid, she didn't want to see, but he was hurting and he needed her to see it. She swallowed and lifted the shirt tails. A small anguished cry shot from her. A rawhide rope had been tied around his testicules and penis. It was the worst thing she had ever seen. The whole area was black and crusty with dried blood.

"Cut the rope."

Now she understood, quickly she knelt on the ground and grabbed the knife out of her pocket then cringed. She looked up at him and wanted to cry. "I'll try to be careful."

"I don't care. Just do it!"

She caught the rope, but it was so tight she had to push the skin back. As careful as she was the knife still nicked him as the rope fell away. She closed his shirt and leaned in and kissed his chest.

"Can you stand for a second?"

"Yes," his voice was a slow hiss and she knew he

was about gone.

Rachel looked back at the hut; she was torn between staying with her brothers and helping Nick get away. There was no way he could make it on his own, and yet she knew Ryan and Simon would never stop looking for her.

"I'm going to push you, try to pull yourself up." Once she had him in the saddle, she pulled herself up behind him. He was slumped over, and she thanked God he had passed out. She kicked the horse into motion.

She road hard and fast, not sure where she was going, she let the horse have his way. And she sighed to the heavens as a town came into view. It was still dark when she made it to the town. Then she started to recognize some landmarks, and her heart soared. She knew this town. She found her way to Loretta's and sighed with relief. She slid off the horse and made sure Nick wouldn't fall, then hurried to the back door.

She banged on the door. "Help!" The noise coming from the place was horrible. She banged again. "Help me, someone help me!"

Suddenly the door swung open and Tammy appeared. "What the hell do you want?"

"It's Nick," Rachel ran to the horse. "He needs help. I didn't know where to take him."

Tammy was busy looking him over. "Good God what happened to him?" She was still angry for the mess Rachel had left her when she'd helped her. But Rachel would worry about that later.

"I can't explain now, just help me get him inside."

"Wait, don't take him off yet."

Rachel caught his foot and put it in the stirrup. Then the door opened again and Tammy ran out, followed by Paco. Rachel wanted to kiss her.

"Paco," Tammy instructed. "Take him to the downstairs room." The big hulking man lifted Nick as if he weighed nothing, and threw him over his shoulder. "I'll get Loretta."

Rachel followed Paco, her hands clutched together in fear. "Put him on the bed and bring me some hot water." She ordered Paco.

"Go ahead do as she says," Loretta said from the open doorway. She walked into the room and looked down at Nick. "So, your people got a hold of him did they?"

Rachel turned to stare at her. "What are you talking about?"

"Those men who came here asking questions about you, they were your people weren't they?"

"Did you tell them where we were?"

"No, one of the girls must have."

Rachel looked down at Nick's battered form. "Do you have something I can give him to make him sleep?"

"Of course I do, I have a few pain pills that will knock him out." As Loretta turned Rachel heard her tell one of the maids to go and get the kit.

Rachel took the towel from the warm water and began to wash some of the blood from Nick's body. As she did she cried, he had to be cursing her with every breath. It was her fault he was like this and he may not be able to use his manly equipment any more. She shook her head and wondered how her brother's could be so cruel.

An hour later she stood beside the bed staring down at his sleeping face. The Doctor had just left. He was used to these late night visits at this place, so he had come quickly. He examined Nick and found a broken leg, a busted arm and a bloody knot on the side of his head. The attempted castration hadn't been on long enough to do any real damage but he would have to keep an eye on things and see how they go.

After she had him all cleaned up, she pulled the sheet up over him and curled up next to him. She cried until she drifted into an uneasy sleep.

*****

"God Damn it!" Simon growled, "How could this have happened. She's just a girl, how could she get the drop on us? Six grown men!"

"Simon you know how Rachel is. When she gets something in her head, nothing is going to stop her from doing what she wants." Ryan shouted.

"What are you wantin' to do now? They can't be that far ahead, we could catch them, then kill him straight out and take her home."

"No," Simon shook his head. "I didn't want to kill him in front of her anyway."

"You not gonna kill him?" One of the men asked.

"Oh yes I'm going to kill him," Simon promised. "But she won't know it, I'll let her think it was someone else."

"So what now?"

"I have a feeling I know where they're going. I say we get more supplies, call Dad then we go after the brother, Blake. After we get him out of the way we can find out where Henry is hiding."

"Are we going to wait until Dad gets here?" Ryan asked.

"Probably, it is his fight. Besides I'm sure they'll

all want to know that Mom was right and Rachel is at least alive, it not well."

"Well let's get a move on, I'd like to catch her and take her home."

"She'd run from you at the first chance she got." Simon said. "No, we have to get rid of her obstacle first."

"I'm all for that."

"Come on, let's get out of here."

*****

Two weeks later Rachel sat in a chair by the window in her room trying to read a book. The sun was high but she knew by noon the black clouds would be back. Her book lay forgotten in her lap as she thought about these last few weeks. Anger pounding in her head, was the only thing she had left. She was past the pain of Nick's base behavior. He had healed fast and was still healing. It had taken one week for the Doctor to say he was out of the woods. He looked great and he was eating, talking and even laughing with some of the girls. He limped around the house and even invited some of them into his room at night, so she'd heard.

Rachel didn't understand why he didn't want anything to do with her. But every time she went near him, he would turn away. When she touched him, he flinched and moved away from her. He hadn't come right out and say he didn't want anything to do with her, but he made it plain with the things he did.

At first she had understood, she let the other women take care of him even though she wanted to rip their hair out for touching him. But she understood he needed to get over what her brothers had done. She gave him time, but now her patients were at an end.

She stood up and tossed the book in the chair. He was going to talk to her! She headed out her door, then walked into the hall. It was quiet, only the cleaning crew was about. Rachel walked the short distance to Nick's room. She caught the handle and turned then pushed the door opened. She stopped in her tracks. She blinked to clear her eyes. She knew she had to be hallucinating. Nick lay on his back in the bed and two naked girls lay draped around and over him. He looked up and frowned at her.

"Get the hell out and close the damn door!" He roared.

Rachel clutched her stomach and ran from the room. Her hand moved to cover her mouth, and she ran out a door and into the courtyard. The large trees swayed and cast their shadows hiding her from the rays of the sun. But she didn't notice, she kept seeing the man she loved, naked with two whores. He didn't love her any more, maybe he'd never loved her, he wanted nothing to do with her and she didn't know what to do. She looked around without really seeing anything, suddenly she fell to a stone bench beside her. Think, think her mind yelled, but she couldn't get past that horrible image.

"You should think about leaving," Rachel looked up and she stiffened, it was Tammy, she was one of the girls who had been in bed with Nick. Maybe it was her way of paying Rachel back for the attempted escape.

"I was just thinking the same thing."

"You really should," she puffed on a cigarette as she took a seat near Rachel, and crossed her stocking clad legs. She had thrown a white robe around her shoulders and her hair, now black was hanging in disarray around her. She wasn't pretty any more, she was aging fast.

"I need to go home," Rachel said, and she looked

away from the girl.

"I wish I could find a man as fine as your Nick." She gave a wistful sigh.

"He's not mine, you've had him, you could just go ahead and keep him."

"What about yo baby? Don't it needs his father?" Rachel looked at her, her hand automatically going to her small tummy.

"How did you know?"

"What's not to know, I seen it before, these girls always tries to hide a fat belly, but they can't."

"Well," Rachel sniffed. "I won't have a man who doesn't want me. If he loved me he wouldn't have slept with you girls."

"Why not?" Tammy snapped. "All he did was sleep, that man is useless. All he did was talk about you. How wonderful his Rachel is. I did wonder why he didn't just go to you. But it ain't my business."

Rachel frowned. "What are you talking about?"

"I thought your man was a stud, but he turned out to be a dud. Every girl in this house has tried to get him to stand at attention, but no dice. His pecker don't work."

"Don't say that," Rachel gasped, horrified. "I know it still works, the Doctor said it would. He said everything would be fine."

Tammy shrugged. "It might work, if he wasn't so busy trying to run you out of town."

"I don't follow you."

"He said he wasn't a man no more and he didn't want you to find out."

Her heart warmed for an instant. "And you said he hasn't had sex with any of the girls here?"

"That's what I said, he been trying. God he been

trying hard, but it just ain't working. He wants you to think he did so you'll leave. He said something about saving you from him."

"Why are you telling me this?"

"Every child needs his father and that man loves you. He needs you and you need him."

"But he won't let me near him, how can I make him understand if I can't talk to him?"

"Honey please," Tammy waved that away. "You ever tie a man up?"

Rachel felt her face flush as she listened to Tammy explain the best way to grab a man's attention and hold it.

"What if it doesn't work?"

"How can it not work? Men love sex, any sex will get them on their knees every time."

"But you don't know Nick, he's stubborn and he's so much deeper than that."

"All I can say is try. Your people nearly did away with his goods, men don't like it when you touch their package with mean intents. But seeing as you weren't the one who done it, he might forgive and forget. Well, maybe not forget, but he could forgive you."

"What if I can't pull it off, he said once that he needed a professional. That I didn't know what I was doing."

Tammy frowned. "He said that?"

"Yes, not too long ago either."

"He must'a been mad at you. As far as I know to a man one hot box is as good as another."

Rachel cringed and looked away, she didn't want to understand this child. Never in her wildest dreams did she believe she had the skills or the bravery it would take to pull this off.

"Listen sweets, either you throw yourself into it, or you lose your man. It's as simple as that. Now I have a little tonic that can get the juices flowing and help put you in the mood if you need."

"No, no I don't need that, I just need to get my thinking straight. I'll do it, I just have to come to grips with what I'm about to do. And pray God forgive me."

"God ain't got nothin' to do with this, you are all on your own."

Rachel was nervous, she didn't know if she could do it. She had spent all afternoon with Tammy learning the things she needed and now it was time. They had decided to wait until the place was in full swing, and now it was four a.m. and time to put their plan into action. Earlier she had heard Nick leave his room and walk down the hallway. He had gone into the kitchen for something to eat. She wanted to go to him, to hold him and tell him everything would be fine, but she couldn't bring herself to look at him, partially because she was hurt from the scene this morning. But the other reason was what she was about to do to him. Tammy had slipped a sedative in his drink, and then she said every thing else was up to Rachel.

There was a knock on her door, then it was pushed opened. Tammy stuck her head in, "He's all yours, but remember, that potion I gave him will only work for ten minutes are so. You best hurry." Then she was gone.

Rachel took a deep breath, and headed for the door, in the hallway she past a decanter of liquor. Thinking quickly, she uncorked the thing and lifted it to her lips. She took a tiny sip and put it back down. She exhaled hard as the fire kicked up in her stomach. She fanned her watery eyes and exhaled again. Once her racing heart was under control, she sighed again and picked up her bag of goodies then pushed the door open and walked through it. Tammy was at work, so were all of the other girls. It was late, dark outside and the music was loud. Male and female laughter could be heard all the way back here, but she ignored it. By the time she made it to Nick's door her palms were sweaty and her lips dry. She licked her lips to moisten them and wiped her hands on her skirt.

"It's now or never." She whispered and grabbed the handle then swung the door open. The light was on and he was sprawled across the bed, Tammy said the sedative wouldn't last long but it would give her time to set things up. She hurried into the room and closed the door behind her.

Rachel locked the door then went about setting the mood. First, she had to drag him into position, that done she went to her bag and pulled out some rope. It was ten feet long and according to Tammy, it was to be laced through the rails of the headboard, then tied tightly to each wrist. That done, she grabbed the other rope and preceded to do the same with his feet, she made sure they were tied apart. Satisfied that he was secured, she began to relax, the liquor was starting to work and this was starting to feel like fun instead of sinful. She pulled out the tape and looked at his mouth, she pursed her lips in thought, then shook her head. If she taped his lips there would be no kissing and she definitely wanted kissing.

She put the tape back in the bag. Then she pulled out half a dozen candles of varying sizes and heights, after lighting them, she took out her perfume and sprayed it around the room. Rachel took off her pants but left her panties on, she made sure her bare breasts were visible through the long white shirt she wore, then she applied just a hint of makeup to her face. She stiffened when he moaned and tried to move his arm. It was show time, her heart lurched into her throat again, but she walked to the bed and looked down at him.

"Do you know who I am?" she asked.

His eyelids fluttered, and he licked his lips. "What are you doing here?"

"I asked if you knew who I was?" Her voice held a demanding note.

He frowned. "Yes, I know who you are." He snapped. "Now get the hell out of my room, I'm expecting Laura and Carina in a few minutes."

That really hurt. "Really?" She said softly. "I doubt they want anything to do with you."

His whole body stiffened. "And why is that?" He snarled, and then he looked at his binding. "What the hell is this? Get these ropes off me!"

"I told them," she said ignoring him. "You are my man, you're taken. And if any of those women ever came near you again I would slit their throats while they slept."

"What the hell are you talking about? I am not your man!" He gave a harsh laugh. "I would never lower myself to be with someone like you. For gods sake you don't even know how to kiss correctly. All you do is slobber all over my face."

"That hurts Nick," she shook her head and stared at him. "I want you to know, that every time you hurt me I'm going to hurt you in return."

"Is that a threat?" He laughed again. "If you can't take it then you need to give it up. Get out of my life little girl. Go run back to your daddy."

343

"What I'm about to do has nothing to do with my Daddy. You can either let yourself enjoy it, or you can lie there and pretend you don't feel anything. Either way I'm in the mood for some lovin I'd rather get it from you. Now if at the end of this I find you can't give me what I need then I'll let you go and find someone who can."

"Rachel, don't do this," his voice had gone deep, almost urgent. "This isn't what you want."

She ignored him as he started to struggle, he tugged at the ropes with a force that scared her for an instant. She went to the foot of the bed and crawled up between his spread legs. He kept talking, she could hear his desperation, even fear in his voice as he tried to get her to leave. She got up and grabbed the tape.

She tore off a good piece and went to him. "I'm trying to get in the mood. You have to shut up!" She stretched the tape across his mouth, then kissed his sealed lips. His eyes were dark with fury, and he yelled at her through the tape. She cocked her head to the side and stared at him. "Did I ever tell you how wonderful you look when you're angry?" Then she laughed and slid over him to straddle his waist. She grabbed the collar of his shirt and rocked her lower body against his shirt clad stomach. "So this is what it feels like to ride a bucking bronco. Yeee Hah!" She yelled, and then her ride became sensual, with and erotic spin to it. "I wonder what it would feel like if I did this?" She did a grinding motion and his body went taunt. "Oh yes, I think I like that." She lifted her hands to her hair and released the pony-tail, then shook it out and watched him. She ran her tongue over her lips then pulled the elastic of her shirt down until her breasts were exposed. "Come on do the bucking thing again?" She grabbed his shirt and waited, but he didn't move. He was still yelling beneath the tape.

She leaned forward, and opened her mouth on his and she tasted nothing but tape, still she let him feel her tongue running over the surface and the little nips against his lips and she would have sworn she heard him moan. Encouraged, she slid up abit and kissed his neck then nibbled her way to his ear, she nipped his earlobe and suckled it and she moaned. "This may not feel good to you, but it feels damned good to me. You taste like cotton candy. I love it." She let the tip of her tongue dance across the surface of his shell shaped ear and she smiled as a shiver raced the entire length of his body.

She sat up and pulled the shirt from her body and tossed it to the floor. He turned his face away and looked at the wall.

"Its okay," she was saying. "You don't have to look at me. You can pretend you're on a deserted island and the only girl there is the girl of your dreams. Think of her, think of being able to throw her to the ground any time you want. Of taking her, loving her and never having to answer to any one for any thing."

Dean King

Eighteen

SHE UNBUTTONED HIS SHIRT and pushed it off his chest, then she went to his pants and worked the zipper down. He bucked and yelled and tried to kick her off, but he only succeeded in helping her push his jeans and his boxers down with little or no effort. "I'm sorry if I'm not woman enough for you, and I'm sorry my kisses leave you cold, but you are like a fire in my blood and I can't turn off my emotions as easily as you can."

As she spoke she worked her way up his thighs, kissing every inch of them along the way. Then she made it to his still soft man hood and she felt him freeze. Then something like a sob caught her attention. She moved up his chest and looked down at him. He was trying to tell her something, and his eyes were wet, he looked to be in complete agony. Slowly she pulled the tape off then, she kissed him with all the heat she could muster.

"You don't want to do this to me Rachel," he rasped. "I'm not a man any more."

"You look like a man to me," she said, and kissed his chin and his neck.

"You don't understand," he bit out. "I can't give you what you want. My equipment doesn't work."

"I don't believe that, what was that whole thing with the girls in your bed this morning? Why would they be with you if your goods didn't work? I'm sure they don't love you like I do."

346

"I made them, I asked them to help me," he heaved a deep sigh, and looked away from her. "I didn't want you to know I had lost the ability to please you."

"So," she hissed, really getting angry. "You wanted me to think you were a cheat, and a liar rather than have me know the truth?"

"Yes," he snapped. "I can't stand for you to know I'm ruined. You'll see me as less a man now, I don't want to become a charity case to you. You…"

"Number one," she interrupted him. "I could never see you as less a man. Number two; I don't think of you as mine, you proved you weren't when you slept with Loretta. Number three, you don't love me, so why do you care what I think? As far as I am concerned, this is a parting gift, just think of it as you repaying your debt to me."

"Damn it Rachel, why do you have to argue with me? I'm trying to share something with you, and you're trying to fight!"

"Oh the fight has never stopped!" She yelled. "If the only thing I can get from you is stationed between your legs then you aren't going to get out of it with some lame excuse like it doesn't work!"

"It's not a lame excuse, I'm telling you it doesn't work, I've tried."

"You tried with someone else?" She lifted her eyebrows.

"Well," his face flushed under his tan. "Yeah, I didn't want to start with you and not be able to satisfy you."

"How considerate you are."

"Rachel don't get mad, I was thinking of you."

"Really," she said tightly. This night was turning

out to be a bad idea. "I'm so sure you were thinking of my sloppy kisses and my lack of knowledge in the finer things that have to do with sex."

"I'm sorry I said that."

"I don't think you are."

"I am, but it doesn't change the fact that I can't love you."

"Is it physical or mental?"

"What do you mean?"

"Is it that you can't love me with your body or your heart?"

"Put the tape back on my mouth."

"What?"

"Put the damned tape back on."

"Fine, I might just leave you here like you are." She stretched a new piece of tape over his mouth, and stood looking at him. She didn't know how long she stood there, but he did eventually look away. "You are spoiling my fun, I almost don't want it now."

Rachel went and turned on the light. She had started this and she would finish it, weather he enjoyed it or not. She stripped off her panties and walked to the head of the bed. "Tammy told me to do this, she said men liked that kind of thing. What do you think?"

He was slow to turn and look at her but when he did she tried not to laugh at the shock on his face. His eyes went wide as they took in her cleaned shaved genitals. He made a gurgling sound in the back of his throat and she did laugh. She stood before him without a stitch of clothing. "Because I am as you put it sloppy at this, I took some lessons. I won't tell you from who but I will tell you they were very interesting. If at anytime you don't like what I'm doing, you just raise your hand," she giggled and said. "That's right you can't, oh well lay there and take it."

She got up on the bed and stood over him, and eyed him from head to toe. "Umm, all mine to do with what I want. I love it. I've never had a sex toy before." She shivered when his body seemed to convulse, there was movement in his manhood and she had hope. Her feet on either side of him, she walked to his chest and sat down, then rolled her hips back and forth. "Ummm, doesn't that feel good?" She felt him shaking and smiled down at him. "I hope I'm doing this right." Her hot center against his hard stomach was electrifying. She leaned forward and kissed his chest, she dropped kisses all along the hard plains, then she took one of his little nubs between her lips and nipped it with her teeth and he did shiver, he shivered badly, but then so did she. She reversed her position and traced her tongue down his stomach and to his pelvic bone and he stiffened again. She turned until her shaven area was resting on the tape covering his mouth, and he groaned and moved his head trying to rub against her. She looked back, "Would you like to play?" He nodded his head hard. "Are you going to be a good boy?" Again he nodded. "Okay, but the tape goes back on if you start spoiling the mood. You can tell me how you like my new skills later."

She pulled the tape off his mouth, and he said. "Come here." The roughness of his voice thrilled her and she went to him. He caught her mouth in a kiss that had her leaning against his chest. It was wild and wet, almost dangerous and she loved it. He pulled away and stared at her. "Bring my friend back up here. I need to get reacquainted with her."

Rachel smiled and turned, she straddled his chest

and brought herself close to his lips. He blew on her sensitive skin and she jerked with pleasure. "Oh God that feels good." She moaned.

"Come closer," he rasped and she smiled as his shaft was slowly gaining life. She wiggled until she felt his lips on her, and then she sighed as he played with his strong tongue and wonderful lips along her nether regions. Then she was moving on him rolling her hips back and forth and all else seemed to fade. The room became smaller and darker and she could think of no one, but him and she had to taste him again. Quickly she grabbed his manhood and loved it like his lips were loving her, and he groaned against her and she felt it all the way to the tip of her head. He started to tense up and she exploded in ecstasy, her cries were loud and long and she pushed herself against him and still he continued. She had to pull away, and when she did he begged.

"Untie my hands. Please Rachel I need to touch you."

"No, not yet, I want to have you just like this." She flipped around and straddled his hips. She looked into his deep blue eyes. "I love you Nick, and I do believe at least your body loves me." She reached down and grabbed hold of his manhood and he sucked in his breath. She brought him to her orifice and slid down, inch by slow wonderful inch. She bit her lip as he pushed up and filled her so completely.

"Oh God!" He yelled. "God Rachel. Let me go I need to touch you."

"Am I doing this right?" She hissed.

"Yes, Goddamn it, yes!" He practically snarled. "Let me touch you sweets."

"I like how you are right now, raging hard for no

one but me." Once he was fully sheath, she began to gyrate her hips and she leaned forward.

"Kiss me," he said in a harsh whisper. And she did. It was a wild kiss full of desire and new scents to fuel their raging passions. "Ride me baby, move those hips." And she did. Her head thrown back and her fists clenched on his shoulders, she let her body take over and his every words egged, her on making her wild with desire. She nipped at him and kissed his chest. She lavished his taunt peaks with her tongue, until he stiffened under her and her bottom slapped against him. Then he was pounding into her as hard as the ropes would allow. Suddenly there was a surge of raw desire as they both reached the pinnacle of passion together.

Rachel lay on his chest and listened to his raging heartbeat as it slowed. She had never felt so wonderful, so at peace, then she did right now. She was dizzy from the lofty heights he'd taken her to. A slow smile eased to her lips and she realized they were covered in sweat both hers and his. She didn't want to think about what would happen when she untied him, the moment was fast approaching. He probably did hate her, but she had to at least tell him about the baby. Then they could go their separate ways.

It pained her to think of a life without him, but life was never fair. It was time to come down from her cloud. She lifted her head, folded her arms on his chest and looked at him, but she found him staring at her. "I call that a miracle of science." She said and he actually smiled.

"You are a miracle," he said, with so much emotion her eyes watered. "I can't believe you did this."

"Was it bad?" She wrinkled her nose and gave a

small giggle. "I wanted to shock you and let you know who was boss all at the same time."

"I believe your point has been well received."

"Would you like to stay like this for a while longer?"

"No, but I wouldn't mind returning the favor."

"Maybe one day," she winked. "But not now, we need to talk." She got off him, and untied his feet, and then she worked the ropes and untied his hands. "You were pulling so hard the knots are almost permanent." She struggled, but she got him loose. The minute he was free he tackled her and pushed her to the bed.

"Now little girl, it's my turn." He kissed her deeply and had her moaning into his mouth, he lifted his head and looked at her. "Who did you learn your tricks from?" At her blank look he said. "Was it a male who showed you what to do or a female?"

"Does it matter?"

"Hell yes it matters," he roared. "I told you I didn't want any man touching you."

"Even though, you didn't want to touch me?"

"What the hell does that mean?"

"Am I to sit by and let you sleep with any and every available female and do nothing, just wait for you to come back to me?"

"Was it a male?" His hands tightened on her arms.

"It was Tammy, she told me, she didn't show me."

He tossed her from him, and pulled up his jeans. He sat on the edge of the bed and stared at the walls. "Why did you do this?"

"Because I wanted to show you how wrong you were. We belong together, one without the other isn't complete."

Forgive Me, My Love

He turned and looked at her. "I can't stay with you."

"I could only hope."

"No, don't hope, there is no hope."

She moved to him, and flattened herself against his back, her arms looped around his neck. "You don't love me?"

"Honestly," she held her breath and waited. "No, I don't." She pulled away from him and slid off the bed. Rachel picked up her shirt and put it on, then she grabbed her pants, but he caught her hand.

"Liar!" She screamed. "You said, 'I love you, my heart, my soul, my forever. You said it in the cave I heard you! Why are you lying?"

"You lie just as well as anyone!" He railed. "I thought you didn't speak Spainsh. Aparentlt you don't speak it very well because I didn't say that!" Nick stormed.

"You did, I know what I heard. I love you and I know you love me."

"Don't beg anyone to love you Rachel, it's too desperate. It's beneath you."

Her heart was far too broken to try and speak right now. "You deny everything we had?"

"Not everything," He shrugged, carelessly. "It was fun for me, that's all. Wasn't it fun for you?"

She looked away from him. "I could say it's okay, you don't have to love me. I can live with that, but that would be a lie. Would you like me to ignore the fact that the man I love with all my heart, with all my soul can't bring himself to love me the same way? That isn't me! With me it's all or nothing."

"Then it's nothing."

"Fine," she slipped the shirt over her shoulders and brushed her hair with her hands. "I'll remember tonight, it was great. I'll try it on my fiancé when I get home, maybe he isn't so self righteous."

"What the hell are you talking about?"

"I need a father for my child," she yelled. "If I can't have the real father, then I'll have to settle for someone who's understanding of the situation, and loves my father's money enough to take over that roll."

"So you know?" He asked.

"You know?" She said in astonishment.

"Yes, I've known since the sickness."

"And you never said a word!" She cried, terribly hurt.

"Hold on a minute," he went to his satchel and dug around, he pulled out the vial and turned to her. He held it up. "This is why I came to Loretta's that night, I didn't have sex with her. She gave me this."

"What is it?"

He went to her and placed it in her hand, then closed her fist around it. "It'll help you get rid of the baby." She shrieked and tossed the vial to the ground.

"How dare you! How dare you! Do you hate me that much?" She turned and ran from the room.

"Rachel!" he was about to follow her when Paco showed up in his doorway.

"Someone is here to see you," he said in Spanish. And Nick frowned, it had to be Miguel. He pulled on a shirt, and buttoned his pants, then followed Paco out of the room.

Caldwell was leaning against the doorframe smoking a cigarette. "Beast!" Nick hurried to him. "What are you doing here? Did everything go okay?"

Forgive Me, My Love

"I had to find you," he pushed off the doorframe and met Nick half way. "There's trouble at Blake's."

Nick grabbed his shirt sleeve, "What are you talking about, what happened?"

"When I got there the place was crawling with men. All of them armed. I stayed for a while and checked things out. It looks like Blake and the blond chick with him are being held hostage. Some old Mexican woman took the children. It didn't look pleasant."

"I have to go," Nick hurried into his room and threw his things in his satchel. "I want you to take the girl in the room down the hall back to Texas. She'll tell you where to go from there."

"There are a lot of girls here Nick, which one?"

"She's beautiful, young, and her skin is a soft butternut brown. Her name is Rachel. She'll fight you, but take her anyway. And be careful, she's pregnant."

"Will do, we can square up when you get back to Texas." Caldwell left the room, and Nick searched the floor for the vial but couldn't find it. He gave up, it didn't matter anyway she obviously wanted the child, which gave him extreme joy. He threw the satchel on his shoulder then thought about the quickest way to get to Blake's. He would have to steal a truck. As he headed for the exit he saw Caldwell searching the hall then looking out the door.

"What are you doing? I told you her room is…"

Caldwell pointed to a woman carrying a bag over her shoulder and marching down the street. "I think that's your pigeon down there. Do you want me to get her?"

Nick thought about it for a second. Where he was going wasn't safe, she'd be in the way and she could get hurt. But the farther away she got the more desperate he

355

became to have her back. Living without her was just going to have to wait. He would take her with him, and have Caldwell keep her out of harms way. "Go get her, grab her hands and pick her up gently. Oh, and put your hand over her mouth, she likes to scream."

"You owe me big time for this."

"I know." While Caldwell went after Rachel, Nick grabbed the keys to Loretta's truck and hurried back outside. He drove up beside the struggling pair and yelled. "Get in!"

Rachel looked at him with wide eyes, and started fighting again. But Caldwell put her into the back seat and slammed the door shut, then he got into the front seat and Nick took off.

"I don't want to see you, I don't want to talk to you..."

"Then shut up!" Her mouth slammed shut and she turned away from him.

"Nick what are we going to do when we get there? I counted twelve men."

"Did anyone look hurt? Could you hear what was being said?"

"Apparently you were spotted on a tape. Someone thought you were dead, but it turns out that Blake was hiding you. It made this Henry fellow very mad." At the sound of Henry's name Nick saw Rachel's attention peak.

"Henry?" She scooted forward in her seat. "Are we going to find that rat?"

"I said shut up!" Nick yelled.

"If that's where we're going then great I have a bone to pick with him. He ruined my life, that Bastard almost killed Bianca and..."

"Rachel if you say one more word I'll..."

"You'll what?" She sneered. "You've already broken my heart and killed our baby what more can you do to me?"

"What? I did not kill our baby. You didn't even take the stuff."

"Who said I didn't?" She countered.

"Rachel," he said with a sinking heart. "Tell me you didn't."

"Why would I tell you that? I wouldn't want you to have to make some death bed confession just to save your soul when you're ninety."

"When I finish out here I'm going to kill you with my bare hands."

"I'm not scared of you."

"I believe we have company." Caldwell said.

Pulling up on the side of them was three big black SUV's. They were trying to box them in, but Nick floored the gas petal and the big truck took off. "With any luck we maybe able to use one side against the other."

"What do you mean?" Caldwell took out his semi-automatic gun and made sure it was loaded.

"I'll lay you odds those are her relatives in those SUVs." Nick said and his tone was grim.

"This is turning into more fun by the minute. Don't tell me you kidnapped her and got her pregnant now her father and your father are after you both?"

"Now, if that were the issue why would Blake be involved? Why would I have you here to smuggle his wife and kids out of town?"

"Listen man," Caldwell said. "If I'm about to die I want to know why?"

Nick looked in the rear view mirror and Rachel was staring at him with a peculiar look on her face. "I'll explain, but you won't be in the line of fire. I want you to baby-sit. Your charge is right there in the back seat."

"I'd like to know what's going on too?"

"Henry has Blake and Sophia."

"What about the children?

"They've been taken away?"

"Because we were spotted there?"

"Yes."

"We have to help them."

"How are we going to do that when your relatives are right on our tail?"

"My relatives would've been shooting at you by now."

"Not if they saw us put you in here. They'll wait until we all get out, then they'll try and take you."

"And I'll gladly go with them."

"No you won't!"

"Yes I will at least they love me, they're willing to kill you because of what they thought you had done."

"You should've let them."

"Why, so you wouldn't have to look at me again?"

"Where is that tape? You need a gag."

"If you two can stop the arguing for a moment I think we need to do something about them."

"Let's give her to them."

"Then they'll kill you."

"At least I'd be out of my misery."

"If I have to live in misery than so should you," Rachel yelled.

"I think we should take out the tires, that would slow them down enough to give us a head start."

Beast raised his gun and pointed it out the window, but Rachel reached over the seat and grabbed the barrel of the gun and yanked hard. The blast was deafening.

"Rachel!" Nick yelled panic blinded him, and he tried to stop too fast sending the truck into a tailspin that sent it toppling over on its side. By the time the dust settled and Nick could think again, they were surrounded by boot encased feet. Nick frantically looked in the back seat and saw Rachel laying on her stomach, blood running down her face and her eyes closed. His brain went into action, he grabbed at his seatbelt, and wrestled to get free, finally getting it off, his body fell hard onto the broken glass that used to be the windshield, the dented metal of the roof poked into his skin. He glanced at Caldwell and he seemed to be moving. Rachel was the only one without a seat belt.

"Darling," he said as he crawled towards her. "Darling can you hear me?" He pulled her into his arms, and wiped the blood from her eyes, he felt for a pulse and smiled, it beat strong and hard. "You'll never know how much I love you Brat." He whispered against her hair.

"Get them out now!" Nick heard the harsh tone and knew his days were numbered. They had almost killed him once, this time they wouldn't hesitate. He dropped a kiss on Rachel's battered brow and yelled. "Rachel needs your help! I'll get her as close to the windshield as I can, but you're going to have to pull her through."

"You better hope she isn't hurt."

"Why? Because you'll kill me?"

"You're dead any way it goes."

"My thoughts exactly," Nick cradled her close, and crawled to what was left of the window. Then hands were reaching in and pulling her from him.

"Oh God Rachel!" It was a female voice and Nick had no clue whom it could be. "Oh honey." The woman cried.

Nick emerged in time to see Bea bending over Rachel and brushing her hair out of her face. She stared at him and he wished he knew what she was thinking. If nothing else Rachel would be happy to see the girl. Caldwell was on his knees beside the wreckage with his hands tied behind his back, he looked none to happy. Nick turned just in time to catch a well place fist, the pain only added to the pain in his heart. He didn't flinch and neither did he fall to his knees.

"Get on your knees maggot!" He stared at a younger taller version of Rachel.

"This isn't the military son," Nick said. "Try to use something a little more degrading." He received another blow for his efforts.

"How was that?"

He looked straight into the eyes of the man who had tried to castrate him and wanted to laugh. "You know this would be funny if it weren't so damned hot."

"Do you think this is funny?" The Rachel twin said. "I'll show you funny!"

"Stop it Ryan," the voice came from an older man who had been looking Rachel over. Now he stood up and headed towards them.

"Let me hit him Dad, please just one more."

"No Ryan, this is bad enough as it is."

Nick tensed as the man stopped in front of him. *What a way to meet your girl's parent?* The mans' eyes ran the length of Nick and he tried not to look away. The sadness in those gold eyes, so much like Rachel's, was almost too much to with stand.

Forgive Me, My Love

"Why?" was all the man said.

Nick shrugged, now was time for some truths. "Because I love her."

The blow to his stomach wasn't what he expected. He doubled over and fell against the older man, he was promptly pushed away.

"You don't think we do?" The man railed. "You don't think it killed us thinking she was dead? Do you know what its like to have a child and to bury that child? Do you have any clue what hell you put us through?"

"Sir," Nick rasped. "All I can say is I'm sorry. I thought I was saving her life. I thought..." Another blow, and his head was ringing. "I wanted to protect her." He gasped.

"You didn't think we could've done that?" Simon yelled. "You think we would've let someone come in and take her again? All you had to do was bring her home, now look at her." All eyes turned to Rachel who was now sitting up.

She was a sight, bloodied and her clothes torn. Nick had to admit he hadn't done well by her.

"Daddy?" At her small cry, the man ran to her and pulled her into his arms.

"Darling," he squeezed her tight. "Darling, we missed you so much." He kissed her cheeks and she cried and pulled Bianca into the embrace with them.

"I love you," Rachel cried. "I love you all so much you don't know how I missed you."

And Nick received another blow to the head. He staggered but refused to fall.

Rachel's eyes clashed, with Nicks and she froze. She pulled away from them and hurried to his side. "Stop hitting him," she placed herself in front of him and glared at her brothers. "How dare you! I told you before that I would have none of this! You better not throw another punch. How could you dowhat you did to him?"

· "See Dad," Ryan said. "She's crazy, she thinks she is in love with him."

Rachel turned to John. "Daddy, forget about all that. We need your help. Nicks friend…"

"No Rachel," Nick covered her mouth with his hand, but three sets of guns were immediately pointed at him, he dropped his hand. "Rachel," he said in a low tone. "Don't tell them that. I'll help Blake later I'm sure they'll be fine until we get there."

"How are you going to get there if you're dead? Besides my Dad will help I swear he will."

"I don't want his help!"

"Well, I liked Blake and Sophia and I won't let scum like Henry hurt them."

She turned from him and he wanted to take her hand and run, but now it was too late.

"Dad, we were on our way to help a friend of Nicks. His name is Blake, he and his wife Sophia were taken hostage by that awful Henry and…"

"You mean you know where Henry is?" Tyrell asked.

Rachel shrugged. "I don't know how to get there but Nick does."

Simon walked to Nick and grinned in his face. "So you know how to get to Blake's?"

Nick refused to speak. "You better answer him boy." John said. "Your silence won't save your father, and it could get your brother killed."

Rachel let that sink in then frowned at John. "What are you saying Daddy."

"I'm sorry precious, but Nick is Henry's third son, Blake is the youngest."

Rachel felt the bottom drop right out of her, she spun around to face Nick, and she felt as if she were seeing him for the first time. The resemblance was there, but only slightly. "It all makes sense now."

"No Rachel," Nick said. "I don't know what you're cooking up in that brain of yours, but it's wrong."

"Yes," she whispered, the pain in those few words was hard on his ears. "It's wrong. You only wanted to hold me until your father got his money from my father. You were helping him."

"Goddamn it!" Nick yelled, the hurt in her voice was so painful he cringed inside. "That isn't it, I knew you'd jump to the wrong conclusion."

"Then you tell me why?" She yelled, her eyes glassy, he knew next would be tears, and he didn't have time for them right now. "Why did you keep me? Why not let me go home?"

Nick sighed in frustration, he didn't want the whole world to be in on this conversation. "I've asked myself the same thing many times and the answer is...I just don't know."

"Oh I know!" she sneered, her bright eyes turning stormy. "You are just your daddy's henchman. You had me fooled, at times I thought you really cared for me. Of course the vial confirmed that you didn't." One lone tear spiked her lashes and escaped to run down her cheek. "Good-bye Nick, I never want to see you again."

"Rachel please," with those few words Nick felt as if all the joy had been removed from his life. "Rachel let me explain."

"You've already done that. Now you go to the

bosom of your family empty handed, and I'll go back to mine broken hearted."

"Come on honey," Bianca wrapped Rachel in her arms and they walked away. Nick watched until they disappeared inside one of the SUVs. It was hard not to go after her, but with three guns pointed at him, he had no choice. But he vowed if he made it through this he'd find her and make her understand.

"Now tell us where…"

"It's okay Dad," Simon said, and Nick didn't like the smug look on his face. "I know exactly how to get there."

"Listen to me," Nick tried. "Blake has nothing to do with this. He's innocent he's as much a victim as Rachel and I are. You've got to listen to me."

"Everyone get in, we're moving out." Simon directed. He looked at Nick. "You come with me."

"No," John said. "I want him with me."

"What about Rachel? We can't have him in the same truck with her."

"Rachel and Bianca will go with Ryan and his crew. Simon, you take this man with you and Tyrell." He pointed to Beast. "And I'll take Dominick with us."

Simon growled something under his breath, before he walked off. Nick breathe a sigh of relief anything had to be better than being in Simon's tender care. John summoned Nick to follow him. Once they were all inside Nick said.

"Sir, I have to tell you everything that's been going on."

"All I want to know is how you came to be involved in this?"

"It was an accident. My father has always been

into slavery and drugs and prostitution. But I just stumbled into this, I wanted to protect her, I love her."

John shook his head. "You won't mind if I say I don't care. Bianca told me what you did and how you rescued them. She also said you took them back to Henry's. I think on your part it was an honest mistake, but why didn't you bring her home? Why let us think she was dead?"

"I had to think, I needed time to figure out how to beat Henry at his own game."

"So you were going to use my daughter to do that?"

"No, I wanted to make sure she was safe. I couldn't leave her with you, Henry would just take her again. What was I supposed to do? Your daughter isn't the easiest person to live with, but now I can't imagine living without her."

"You better start imagining it. You'll never have her."

Nick nodded, he had known that, but to hear it made it a reality. "I don't deserve her."

"Why lie to her?"

"I didn't lie, it was just an omission." Nick explained. "Sir if you knew anything about me you would…"

John gave a bitter laugh. "You think I don't know about you? The minute Henry grabbed my daughter and Bianca you don't think I grabbed every bit of information I could about him? I know all about you son, even things your father doesn't know. That is the only reason you're not dead. I've figured some things out but I don't know why you did what you did. You put us through hell."

Nick hung his head for a moment, and then

nodded. "I was selfish and I didn't think, I'm sorry for your pain."

"And I'm sorry for yours. I guarantee some one will die today."

The closer they came to Blake's the more dread coiled in his stomach. Quiet had fallen and darkness was here. Perfect for tonight's events. If he could get Blake out of this alive then his life would've been worth it.

"This place is wired like fort Knox." Nick whispered. "There are movement sensors and cameras on every inch."

"Okay, but I believe Simon has a plan."

"Sir?" John looked at Nick. "Will Rachel be alright? I mean you have to watch her, she liked Sophia, she might get it into her head that she can help. Whoever has her will have to be very careful."

"She's going to be fine, Ryan can handle her."

"Blake is just Henry's account and investment officer. He hasn't ever hurt anyone. I'll kill anyone who hurts him."

"Point taken, but turning a blind eye is just as bad as doing the deed. Sin is sin." John got out of the truck and Simon met him half way.

Rachel watched through the dark glass of the SUV as the men met, there was no sign of Nick, but the man named Beast was there and they all stood around talking and nodding. She felt Nick's betrayal like nothing she had ever experienced. Then she tensed as he was pulled from one of the trucks with his hands tied in front of him, his black curls were tousled and he looked grim. She wanted to hate him, she knew she would never see him again. But just because he was a liar didn't mean Blake and Sophia had to die for it. *But Blake was Henry's son too. Had Nick lied to Blake and Sophia? Did they really believe she was Nick's wife, and that they were a happy couple that had just come here for a visit?* Maybe Nick hadn't told Blake the truth, maybe Blake was innocent of all this.

Too soon the men disappeared from sight, Rachel turned to Bianca. "I'll get a gun and go after them. You wait here."

"No Rachel," Bianca gasped. "The last time we were involved in gun play I was almost killed."

"I know but so was I, they need my help. Simon and Ryan aren't playing, they could probably talk Dad and Tyrell into killing Blake and Sophia as well."

"You mean we have to make sure they don't kill Nick?"

"That too," Rachel didn't see the point in trying to deny it.

"Rachel forget him, your parents won't let you two be together."

"I can forget him easier if he's alive. Dead, I'll be living with the memory of a ghost and I don't need that."

"Rachel I'm not getting out of this truck."

"I need you, come on Bianca."

"I'm only here because I love you, and dad thought I could comfort you in your time of need."

"Look either you're with me or your not, either way I'm going."

"How are we going to get in there?" Suddenly the sound of gunfire interrupted the night. They both ducked, and then Rachel opened the door and slid out. The grass was soft under her bare feet and it cushioned her steps.

"Wait, I'm coming with you," Bianca slid out behind her and hurried to where Rachel stood.

"Bianca, when you love someone like I do, it

doesn't matter what they've done, I couldn't breathe if he were no longer alive to share that breath. Do you understand?"

She nodded, but Rachel doubted she did.

"I can't let Nick die, even if I never see him again, at least I know he's alive, and I can live with that."

"Fine, lets go see if we can join the party."

Rachel led Bianca towards the back and away from the house.

"I don't understand," John was saying. "Where are they, I know those men weren't guarding a empty house." They prowled room after room, and came up empty handed. Then they were all in the living room, Nick was shoved to the couch.

"Where are they?" Simon asked, and Nick didn't answer.

"I said where are they?" he repeated and lifted his gun.

"If I knew do you think I would tell you?" Nick said.

John held up his hand, "Search again. It's a big place and Henry is as slick as a snake, we'll find him."

Nick continued to work on the ropes that bound him, hoping he could get free. He knew they were probable in the hideout, watching every move these people made. He had to get free before a blood bath started.

Rachel tucked her shirt inside her pants and kissed her fingers, then placed it on her small tummy. "Be good for Mommy darling, we have to go save daddy."

"What are you doing Rachel?" Bianca asked.

"This place is out of range of the cameras. I can swim from here to an under ground room, then go in from there."

"Have you been here before?"

"Yes, I know these people, most of all I think I know Henry. He's probably watching the monitors and laughing at the crazies trying to find him. But when I come up behind him, he won't be laughing." Rachel waded into the cold water.

"What do you want me to do?"

"Wait over there behind that well. If you see anyone but me come out shoot."

"What if something happens to you? What will I tell your father?"

"Tell him I love him, and I'll see him on the other side."

"Damn it Rachel, I'm coming with you. I won't be the one to tell him that." Bianca took off her shoes, and followed Rachel into the water.

"Fine, but hold onto my shirt, its far. We'll hit the well and come up for air, then we go under again, until we get into the tunnel." Rachel turned and tucked a large knife into Bianca's belt.

Half fearful Bianca stared at it then at Rachel. "What's that for?"

"You'll need it," Rachel explained. "We may have to be quiet, if there's a guard we'll have to kill him quietly."

"Ewww," Bianca squealed and pulled back. "What happened to you? You can't just kill people, we aren't like them."

"You would be amazed at what one would do when your life is on the line. Just do as I say, and we may get out of this alive." Rachel couldn't help, but smile, she sounded like Nick.

"Are you sure you want to do this Rachel?"

"Yes, now do you have the flash lights?"

"Yes."

"Here, give me one. Turn yours on when I turn mine on, be ready to use the knife."

Bianca nodded.

"Let's go."

The water was cold and it was dark, nearly impossible to see. But Rachel focused on the meager light in the distance, anticipation strengthened her strokes as she pushed towards life giving air. Her lungs were starting to burn and her head felt as if it were about to explode, but she had to make it. Suddenly her head burst through the water, and she gulped the air, then Bianca joined her, they dragged in a lungful of air. After they caught their breath Rachel said. "You ready for the last leg?"

"I'd rather not."

"Come on girl, our folks need us."

Bianca nodded, they dragged in air and, she wrapped her hand around Rachel's belt loope and followed her under.

This time wasn't so bad, the distance was shorter. They emerged slowly out of the water, and Rachel took the lead.

Ninteen

"HENRY!" BLAKE SCREAMED FROM the chair he had been tied to. The bloody whelps across his bare back burned as sweat ran into them. For days he had been held up against the wall on the far end of the hidden bedroom, the same wall that was now splattered with his blood. "Don't do this!" His stricken eyes went to Sophia who lay crying on the floor in front of Henry. Tony wield a belt clenched in one fist, every time she made a sound he beat her. "Tony stop it she doesn't know anything."

"I saw them on the monitors." Henry snarled. "You think I don't know what's going on?" He yelled, and then pointed to Sophia. "Tony, put her on the bed."

"Dad," Blake whispered, his worst fears coming to life in front of him. "Daddy please don't do this! If you ever loved me please don't hurt her like this."

"I'm done with hurting her. Now it's you I'm gonna hurt. Tony, strip her."

"Oh, God!" Blake screamed, as he jerked and bucked in his chair nearly overturning it. "Don't you touch her. You fuckin' bastard don't you touch her!"

"Blake! Blake, don't look at me." Sophia screamed. "Don't see this." She sobbed.

"I'll kill you," Blake seethe, "I'll kill you both."

Henry walked to Blake and smiled. "Now we're

getting somewhere." He turned to look at Sophia. "Tie her hands to the headboard.

Tony snickered, and did as Henry asked. "Can I be first Dad?"

"No, I'm first, this beauty needs to know a real man."

"Please daddy," Blake could only beg, it was all he had left. "I don't know where he is, I'd tell you if I did, I swear to God I would."

"It doesn't matter," Henry caressed Blake's face with a gentle hand and Blake closed his eyes and turned away. "I'll teach you the same lesson I taught your brother. Robert thought he could get away from me. I showed him what total obedience really is." Henry laughed as Tony readied Sophia. "I had his wife ten times. By then he'd decided that he loved me above all others, and that it was me he would serve. It's too bad she killed herself, but after having me and then going back to your brother it had to be a shock to her system. She couldn't have me any more and she couldn't stand it."

Blake threw his head back and laughed as he had never laughed before. When he wouldn't stop Henry backhanded him. But even that didn't stop him. "You..." Blake laughed on the point of hysteria. "You're not a man, you're a fucking coward. You are the scum of the earth. When you die I hope I'm the one holding the gun."

"Dad," Tony murmured. "They're all in the library; it'll be like shooting fish in a bowl. Come on."

"No," Henry snarled. "Leave them, we're about to..."

"This can wait, Nick's up there with them, see. The fucking trader!" Tony pointed to the monitors. "We can take them off guard, I'll take them from the west, if you'll get them from the east. We could kill them all before they even know what hit them."

"Fine, I'm gonna finish here."

Tony shook his head. "She's just a piece of meat Dad, I may need your help."

"Get the fuck up there and end this!"

Tony picked up two of the guns from a nearby dresser and stormed out of the room.

Rachel coughed and gagged as she tried to get her breath, the trip was longer then she remembered. She pulled herself up, one hand on the slimy wall, the other on the mud covered ground as she entered the tunnel. She was relieved to see Bianca coming up behind her. Once they caught their breath, Rachel turned to Bianca. "Turn on your flash light."

"What now?" Bianca asked as she followed close behind Rachel.

"There's a door, it leads into the back room, we'll go in through there, then once we see how many people are in there. We'll make our move."

Bianca caught Rachel's arm and spun her around to face her. "What's after that? I mean, say we find some bad guys, then what?"

"We do what comes natural Bianca. Now give me that knife."

"No Rachel," Bianca backed up a step. "I can't let you."

"You can't let me what?" Rachel said in a fierce whisper. "We have to do something. I can't let this asshole kill everyone I know and love. For all we know he may have killed Blake, Sophia and their kids."

Bianca wiped the tears from her eyes. "Please Rachel, this isn't you. You're not talking about killing

373

anyone are you?"

Rachel sighed, and went to Bianca, she slid her arm around Bianca's shoulders, and kissed her cheek. "No, I'm not talking about killing anyone, just saving a few lives."

Bianca accepted that, and nodded. She reached around, and pulled the knife from her belt. She handed it to Rachel. "No killing?"

"No planned killing." Rachel took the knife, and headed for the door. She opened the door and peeked inside. The room was empty. She motioned to Bianca. "Come on." They snuck into the dark room. Rachel motioned to Bianca to stay quiet, then she looked around the room for a weapon. But she couldn't find anything useful. Rachel cut a look at Bianca, she didn't want to scare her, but she knew there would be bad dealings tonight. She stiffened her spine, it didn't matter that Blake was Henry's son. He was in trouble because he had helped them.

Rachel pushed open the door to the bathroom, again the room was empty. Her heart was now in overdrive. It banged so hard against her chest, she didn't know if she would be any use when the time came. She swallowed hard, and grabbed the handle to the last door. She heard horrible screams coming from the room she had shared with Nick. She squeezed her eyes shut and mouthed a silent prayer then slowly pushed the door open. Her stomach turned, the scene was more horrible then any she could've imagined. Sophia lay screaming as she tried to fight off Henry who was climbing on top of her. Blake's head hung to his chest as he sobbed.

Rachel's frantic gaze fell to a forgotten gun. It lay on the dresser. Without a second thought, she pushed the door open and grabbed the gun.

"Get off her Henry!" Rachel screamed as she turned to face them. Blake's head popped up, and his joy was to painful to witness.

"Give me the gun!" He begged, almost hopping in the chair. "Rachel, untie me and give me the gun."

"Well, well," Henry cooed as he slid off the bed, and righted his pants. "You always find a way to ruin my day don't you?"

"That's what I'm here for," she waved the gun, and handed the knife to Bianca. "Get away from the bed Henry!" Rachel commanded, then to Bianca, she said. "Go untie Sophia."

Henry raised his hands and moved slowly away. "Why are you pointing that thing at me?" He mocked. "We both know you don't have it in you to use it."

"Then why are you doing what I asked?"

"Because I need…" he jumped behind Blake, and pulled a knife.

Bianca had made it to the bed, she was untying a hysterical Sophia.

Rachel cursed as Henry put the blade to Blake's neck. "Kill him," Blake yelled. "Rachel kill him, shot him. If you have to kill me to do, then for god's sake do it!"

"Shut up son," Henry yelled, his hand around Blake's neck. He stretched Blake's neck so far that the front legs of the chair lifted off the floor.

"Put the gun down, or I'll slit him from ear to ear."

"You are a wicked son of a bitch!" Rachel shouted. "Let him go."

"Drop the gun." Henry countered.

"Blake!" Sophia sobbed. "Don't kill him, please Henry don't."

"Then you come here Sophia." Henry commanded.

She didn't think twice, still sobbing she slid off the bed.

"No Sophia, don't do it." Bianca cried.

A small cut opened up on Blake's neck, and Sophia cried out as if she were the one in pain. She wrapped a sheet around her body, and walked towards Henry, when she was close enough he grabbed her and let go of Blake. The chair clattered on it's side to the floor and Blake struggle to right it. "No, Sophia!" He yelled.

Sophia gave a strangled sob as Henry pulled her close.

"Now you put that gun down sweetheart," Henry said. "I'm taking this little lady with me."

Sophia stood with Henry's hand wrapped around her neck. Her face was calm, and her eyes nearly black, then it happened. No one saw it coming, as if in slow motion, she lifted one hand, and brought it down in a clean ark. Then Henry was screaming, and he shoved her away. She landed on the floor beside Blake. Henry grabbed the handle on the knife that was buried in his thigh, and was about to pull it out when he looked up.

"Gottcha!" Rachel held the gun pressed against his forehead. "Now, let's go get your other sons." Rachel looked at Bianca. "Untie him, and get her some clothes. I'm taking this Bastard upstairs."

*****

There was chaos in the house as they searched

every inch. "I say we kill him now." Ryan said.

"No, if we kill him we would be as bad as Henry." Tyrell said.

"Who the hell cares? This is Henry's seed."

"Stop it son," John snapped. "This lust for blood isn't like you."

"Dad," Tyrell grabbed his chest, then lifted his hand a small dot of blood blossomed on his chest, and then it trickled from his lips as his mouth filled with blood.

"What the hell?" Simon cried as Tyrell fell into John's arms. Simon turned, and gasped as the wind was knocked out of him by Nick who had jumped from the couch and knocked Simon to the ground.

Tony stood in the doorway his gun raised ready. "Get up all of you!" He snarled.

Nick looked down at his arm, it dripped with blood. But he got off Simon and stood facing his brother.

"Tony don't do this. These people have done nothing to you." Nick tried to ignore John's sobs as he held his fallen son.

"Get over here you trader!" Tony hissed.

"Don't do this Tony. You can't think to kill a whole family then just get away with it."

"No, I don't expect you to get away with it." Tony sneered.

Nick lifted his hands and slowly moved to where Simon now stood. "Tony listen to me, this has got to stop..."

"It will stop!" Tony snapped. "You," Tony pointed at Simon. "Get on your knees. Shut that shit up!" He swung the gun towards John and fired. John fell backwards blood pouring from a wound to his head.

Simon charged forward with a pained snarl, but Nick punched him in the ribs, and then delivered a blow to his head. Nick grabbed a lace runner from the nearest table and wrapped it around Simon's hands, and then kicked him in the back of his knees sending him to the floor in a cursing, snarling rage. "I'll kill you, damn it, I'll kill you!"

"Tony," Nick ignored Simon and turned, he placed himself in front of Simon, and faced Tony. "I can't let you do this."

"You think you have any pull here little brother? This is my world, these people will do what ever I tell them to do. I'll kill you all and say you went crazy, and wiped out your whole family and these visitors. It will be such a sad story for so long. It may even go down in history as some kind of haunting tale of greed and passion."

"How about I kill your father?" Everyone turned to see Henry, his hands held high, and Rachel behind him with a gun at his back.

"How about I kill him for you?" Tony turned, and blasted Henry three times in the chest. At Henry's stunned look, Tony said. "You taught me well Pop, now its time I take your place. You have gone as far as you coul…d." Before Tony could finish talking, Nick picked the gun up off the floor and fired. Tony look down at the blood stain on his shirt, confused he looked around the room and saw Nick with a gun pointed at his chest.

"Well I'll be damned," Tony grinned. "You got the jump on me. I should've just killed you and been done with i…it." He slid to the floor, and stared with sightless eyes.

Rachel screamed, and ran to her father and

378

brother. Nick wanted to go to her, but he had to see how many relatives he had left. He ran down the hidden stairs and froze, Bianca sat on one side of Sophia and Blake sat on the other. He was crying, but Sophia stared into the distance with blank eyes. She was wrapped in a sheet and her lovely hair was matted and tangled, her face was as bruised and bloodied as her husbands. Nick walked into the room. Bianca helped Sophia stand, together they walked out of the room, and Nick let them go.

"Blake," he whispered, and Blake looked up as if he didn't know him. "I'm so sorry Blake."

"They wanted to know where you were, but we didn't know. God I wish I had. I would've told them, to save her I would've given them the world on a silver platter, but I didn't, Henry and Tony…" Blake cried, his shoulders shaking. "They beat her, every time I couldn't tell them where you were they beat her some more. They were about to take her in front of me, but Rachel and her friend saved us. They saved my wife. And I wanted to die, I couldn't help her, I couldn't help any of them."

Nick took Blake into his arms and held him as Blake beat at his back with closed fist. "It wasn't your fault Blake, you know how they are. I'll try to help you two get over this."

Blake pulled away. "How can you help? Look at her, she's gone, they broke her. She'll hate me forever."

"The Sophia I met was made of tougher stuff than that."

"But you didn't see what they did. My poor beautiful Sophia."

"Do you still love her?"

"Yes! I'd never stop loving her, but can she forgive me?"

"I don't know, but I know she loves you. Given time, I'm sure she'll forget all this."

John moaned, and Rachel looked down. Her heart took flight. "Daddy," She whispered. "Daddy can you hear me?"

He nodded and tried to sit up. "No," she said. "Stay still, you've been shot, and you have to stay still." Simon and Caldwell had wrapped Tyrell's body in a sheet and carried him to one of the trucks. Ryan had come running from upstairs and stood staring at all the blood. Rachel barely recalled Bianca walking by with Sophia tucked under her arms. Nick had come out of the hidden room and he bent down beside her.

"I'll take your father to the Truck."

Rachel nodded. "Put him in the front one, the sooner we get them all to a hospital the better."

Nick helped John to his feet them tossed the older man over his shoulder. He headed off towards the trucks. The repercussions of tonight would be heard for a long time to come.

*****

It was late afternoon, and Pat stood at the head of the main stairs in the upper hallway. In her fists she clutched an old doll of Rachel's, she didn't realize her fingers were crushing the delicate fabric of the twelve year old doll. She stared towards Rachel's closed door, and with a heavy heart she walked away. Pat had wished her baby back, but the person who lived behind that door wasn't her baby. That person was just a shell of a girl. She was private now, moody and silent. Pat wanted to help, but Rachel had closed herself off from the family.

Forgive Me, My Love

Even Bianca couldn't get close to Rachel. She'd finally agreed with John to bring in a therapist. Rachel needed someone to talk to, and apparently she felt she could no longer talk to her mother. It hurt to think she had lost her baby in more ways than one. Pat wondered how long Rachel would wait before she told them about the baby she carried. Sighing hard she ducked into her own room determined to think of a way to help her child.

Rachel sat on her bed in her room. She had been home three weeks and still she couldn't get used to sleeping on the soft mattress. Even eating was difficult, it was as if she didn't know how to be Rachel any more. The old Rachel would laugh and tell funny stories at dinner. She would sit up straight and use the correct salad fork, fold her napkin across her lap and extend her pinky when taking a sip from her goblet. This new person was someone only Nick would understand, and she missed him terribly.

Restless, she slid off the bed and went to her dresser. She lifted the lid on her jewelry box and immediate tears sprang to her eyes. The vial sat on the white satin staring back at her. It was proof of Nick's betrayal. *Was it betrayal when someone you loved didn't love you?* In her book it was just as bad. He had led her to believe he felt something for her, and then when it was all over, he walked away.

Three weeks wasn't a long time, but it was an eternity to a lonely heart. Hope still lingered, she looked at the letter that lay on her bed, it was ready for the mailman. She was hesitant. Maybe he didn't love her, but she'd poured her whole heart into that letter. All her hopes for them, all her dreams were in that letter. It was the last one she would send. So far she'd heard nothing from him. She wondered how she would go on if he didn't feel the same way. She clenched her teeth against the tears that were ready, because deep in her heart she knew he didn't love her. Despite what he'd said in the cave.

She refused to give in to despair. So many people had died useless deaths. What hurt most was her brother was no longer with them. His presence, his smile, his energy, his sweetness, all gone and every time she thought about it she became sick. She regretted what happened to Sophia and Blake, they should've never been involved, but Nick had put them in the middle of the whole thing. As far as Rachel knew Sophia and Blake were still in Mexico. They had sent the kids with Miguel and Maria to Sophia's relatives on a small island in Spain. By now Miguel and Maria would be reunited with their children.

Rachel remembered the last day she had seen Nick. *Remember,* she scoffed. It was all she could think about. She had escaped the hotel her father had stashed her in and hurried to the only Hospital in the small village. She asked for Sophia and was directed to her room. As she approached, her steps had faltered. Nick and Blake stood side by side, with their backs to the wall. They both looked at her. Now she could kick herself for not seeing how alike they were. Two sets of gulf blue eyes stared at her. They were the same height, Blake had straight hair, but it was just as black as Nick's curls. Rachel looked away from the sorrow in their eyes.

"Blake," she whispered. "May I see Sophia?"

"Sure Rachel," he pushed off the wall and knocked on the door. He stuck his head in and said something, and then he nodded and held the door open for

Rachel.

She ducked in, too conscious of Nick's searching gaze on her. The instant her gaze landed on the fragile beauty laying on the bed her heart went out to her. "Oh Sophia," Rachel cried as she went to the bed.

Sophia looked up and burst into tears as she was enveloped in Rachel's embrace. "I'm so…rrry," she cried once she had calmed a bit. "I'm so sorry." Sophia had taken Rachel's face between her cold hands and stared into her eyes. "If I had known you were a victim in this, that they were holding you captive I would've helped you get away. I would've…"

"Stop," Rachel caressed Sophia's hair and calmed her. "You couldn't have known. Besides, do you think Nick would've let me go?"

"No, but I could've talked to Blake," Sophia gave a defeated shrug. "Who am I kidding? I didn't even know what kind of family I had married into. I knew I hated Henry and Tony, but I had no idea they were this wicked. It saddens me that Blake didn't trust me enough to confide in me."

"How bad were you hurt?" Rachel changed the subject, not sure how to answer that.

"Only my heart has been seriously wounded. You arrived in time to save me from Henry's sexual depravities. They were convinced we knew things we did not know."

Rachel hugged her again and kissed her cheek. "I'm so glad you were speared that. I was astonished when you stabbed Henry in his leg, where did you get the knife?"

"I took it from your friend." She grinned, then winced. She smiled and gently caught the side of Rachel's face. "I did learn something from your stay with us."

"And that would be?"

"How to protect myself, before I met you I was use to being taken care of, now I can do it myself."

Rachel actually smiled, she hadn't thought she could do that any more. "Why is Blake in the hallway?"

"I don't know if I want to see him yet." Her eyes started to water again. "I don't know if I can trust him. He's done nothing but lie to me."

"Oh darling, I don't know what to say, but from what I can tell he loves you so much."

"I know he does, and I love him, but what is a marriage without trust? How could he keep this from me?"

"Look at it from his side," Rachel caressed Sophia's hand. "What if you were head over heels for Blake? You wanted to marry him at all cost. Do you think something like this could've spoiled things for you?"

"What do you mean?"

"Would you have told Blake about your family? If they were this bad what would you have done?"

She shrugged and looked away. "I don't know, but the children could have been killed. We could've all been killed."

"True, but if he'd told you would you have left him?"

"I don't really know."

"It may have been a chance he was unwilling to take."

"Why are you on his side?"

"Because I know how bad Henry was, if he were my father I would've hidden it from the world."

"Like Nick did?" Sophia asked quietly.

Forgive Me, My Love

"That's different, Nick had other reason's for keeping the truth from me."

"Like what?"

"I don't want to talk about it right now."

Sophia nodded. "My parents are coming into town," she said quietly. "They should be here tomorrow, they are bringing my children back. I need to hold them so bad."

"Oh, I'll be gone by then," Rachel sighed. "My Father has us booked on the next plane out of Jalisco."

"What are you going to do about Nick?" Sophia wanted to know.

"Nick doesn't love me and yet he didn't tell me he was Henry's son. As it turns out, all I know about him is what I can see. I don't even know how old he is, or his correct name."

"Oh Rachel, Nick loves you, I know he does, it's in his eyes every time he looks at you. I don't know why he hasn't talked to you about things but I'm sure now that it's all over he will."

"No, I don't think he will. He doesn't love me, at least not like I love him. I'm not going to tell him about the baby."

"What!" Sophia gasped, and Rachel flushed under her happy smile. "Are you pregnant? How far along?"

"I don't know how far, but I'm starting to show. Nick thinks I got rid of it."

"Why would he think that?"

"That rat gave me a potion that was supposed to abort the baby. Now what does that tell you? He doesn't want it, and if he doesn't want the baby, he can't want the mother."

"I can't believe he'd do that!" She murmured.

"There has got to be a reason."

"Yes," Rachel mumbled. "He doesn't love me."

"Well, I love you and I'm sure once Blake gets to know you, he'll love you too."

"What do you mean?" Rachel asked her brow creased in a curious frown.

"Don't be silly," Sophia waved it away. "You are part of our family now. You're having a Rawlins baby! Oh how wonderful, my children will have a cousin. This is great, you have to tell him."

"Don't you mean Dennison?"

"Oh no, Blake did like Nick. He took his mother's name. They are Rawlins; he said he would never claim to be a Dennison. At the time I didn't know why, but it was his choice. You really should tell Nick about the child."

"If he doesn't want me for me, then why should I tell him about our child?"

"Because it's his child too. If he truly doesn't want you then he has to be held accountable for the child's sake, you can't do it alone Rachel."

"I won't be alone. I have my family, they'll help."

"Are you sure?" Sophia asked. "I know if I came home pregnant with no husband, my father would kick me out for shaming the family name. What about yours?"

"They'd understand but they wouldn't be happy about it," Rachel bit her lower lip. "If my father hates me for this, then Bianca will help me raise the baby."

"What if Bianca wants her own life?"

"You act as if I can't do this," Rachel snapped. "I can do it with, or without help. Help would be nice but I'm prepared to go it alone."

"Write down your address, I would still like to be there for you. Blake has always talked about possibly moving to Texas, but I've always wanted to live next to my parents. Now I think it's time I grew up, if he wants to move there, then I will be closer to you, I can help."

"Are you going to forgive him then?"

"Of course, I just want him to sweat abit. He lied and I feel as if I barely know him."

"Yes, it's not a great feeling, but I can see why Blake lied, Nick is another issue, he had nothing to lose and still he didn't tell me. That shows a lack of respect."

"But what if it's like you said to me? What if he was trying to protect you by not telling?"

"Our situation is different, you and Blake are married. He should've told you what you were getting into, given you a chance to back out if you wanted to. I was kidnapped, forced into this, why wouldn't Nick tell me all of it? If their lives were that bad why not just come out with it. He doesn't feel anything for me so what's the difference?"

"He's just like all men, they don't talk, you have to pull things from them. I'm sure you don't go around telling complete strangers about your life."

"If I had kidnapped that stranger then I might be inclined to share just a bit."

Sophia nodded. "What are you going to do when you get home?"

"Jump back into my old life, at least as best I can," Rachel said, not wanting to expound on the subject.

Sophia caught Rachel's hands and gave a small smile. "Write your number too, that way we can chat."

"I will, when you know where you're going to be I'll need your address too. I'd love for you to meet my mother." Rachel said, truly meaning it.

"Maybe I'll see you soon." They kissed each

others cheeks, and Rachel said her goodbyes with a heavy heart. She dreaded going back into the hallway, facing Nick was too hard. With any luck he would be gone.

But luck wasn't with her. He stood with his shoulder pressed against the wall quietly chatting with Blake, both men stood up when they saw her.

"How is she?" Blake asked, and it had been hard to ignore the eagerness in his voice. "Does she want to see me?"

"She's doing fine, she smiled a few times." Rachel touched his arm. "You have to give her some time Blake, I'm sorry to say she doesn't want to see you just yet. Give her a day or two. When her parents get here maybe…"

His eyes stretched wide. "Her parents are coming?"

Rachel nodded, wondering at the panic in his eyes.

"When?" He grabbed her arms. "Do you know when?"

"Any day."

"Oh God no!" He let go of her and slumped against the wall. "I can't let her talk to her mother. That woman hates me she'll turn her against me, I know it."

"What about her father? Is he on your side?"

"No, the whole damned bunch of them were pissed because I'm not from Spain. They wanted her to marry a Spaniard with money. They didn't care that I have money."

"I'd say you have a problem." Rachel said, and her eyes slid to Nick who stood watching.

"Damn it all!" Blake said then winced at the pain in his back. "Now they have weapons against me."

"But you have two beautiful children doesn't that count?"

"Not with them."

"How are you holding up?" Rachel asked Blake. She wasn't ready to face Nick, her stomach was in knots, and she didn't know why. "I heard from my father that you were badly beaten. Should you be out here?"

"It wasn't the first time Henry beat me, I'm fine, or I will be soon. It'll take a while to heal, but when I do I'll be as right as rain. It's Sophia I'm worried about."

"You don't sound very bitter?"

He actually grinned, or it looked like a grin through the swelling on his face. "Because I'm free, we are free, for the first time in my life I can open my nostrils and inhale, I can lift my arms to the sky and scream as loud as I want. I don't have to worry if I did it right or who's watching me. I'm not happy about how things are with my wife, that I believe we can fix if I get to her before her mother. Forgive me, but even at this dire time I can't stop smiling."

Her eyes swung to Nick and she was glad to see him stiffen. "I take it you're equally happy?"

"Yes and no."

She lifted a brow at that. "Why?"

"I'm free, but I no longer have my captive to drag around, I may find that I miss it." He said quietly, and she had to fight not to look away from his intense gaze.

"I'm sure you can find another one."

"No, I think one was enough." She tried not to react as he came to stand in front of her. His hands on her arms, he pulled her close and allowed his eyes to caress her rapidly heating face. "Go home brat, live your life, forget this happened."

"If only I could," she whispered her eyes on his.

"You can and you will." He bent and placed a

small kiss on her lips, and then he released her and turned to Blake. "I'm leaving in the morning, but I'll stop by before I go."

Rachel was devastated, she had been right. He didn't love her. She turned and with as much dignity as she could muster, and started to walk away. Then her lips tightened and she turned back to stare at his retreating back.

"Give me a reason to stay," she had yelled at his back. "Don't you walk away from me Nick."

He stopped, and her heart took off, then he turned to face her. "If you don't have one, then I won't give it to you."

"So," she hardened her voice. "I'll never see you again? You can just turn away from me, and never look back?"

Neither noticed Blake's retreat into Sophia's room. Nick had sighed, and looked at the floor, then his eyes shot back to her. "Look for me."

"What?"

"Look for me, when this is done I'll come to you."

"Nick," she started forward, but he held up his hand.

"Go home Rachel." With that he turned, walked down the hall and closed the door behind him.

That was one of the most difficult days of her life. She had had a few, but that one hurt her heart. Rachel wiped at a tear, and then she laid her hand on her still small belly. The life in there was struggling to survive, but at three and a half months her doctor had her under close supervision. She had forbidden her doctor to tell her parents. She wanted to do it at the right time. They would be angry, but she was willing to face facts. After what happened to her, her days as the cherished sweet heart of the family were over. Now she was a grown woman with decisions to make. She went to her bed and curled up, and then clutched a pillow to her chest.

She reached for the letter and clutched it in her fist, she had to believe he would come.

*****

John paced the Persian rug in his study. His hands were clasped behind his back and deep furrows laced his brow. At the knock on his door, he shouted. "Who is it?"

"It's me Pop," the door opened and Simon stuck his head inside. "You asked me to come. Is this a bad time?"

"No," he grumbled. "Come in and close the door behind you."

Simon came into the room and stood next to John. "What's wrong?"

"Your sister," he snapped. "She's changed."

"Of course she's changed look at what she's been through."

"But I want her back."

"There's no way, an event like that can scar a person for life. She's never going to be the same."

"I'm not stupid Simon!" John growled. "She's still holding onto the thought that he will come for her."

"How do you know?"

"I over heard her and Bea talking. She swore he said he was coming for her, and she can't wait. It's sickening."

"Do you really think he'll come, you think he loves her that much?"

391

"Who gives a shit if he loves her?"

"I thought you did!" Simon yelled. "You want her to be happy don't you? If having him makes her happy then why fight it?"

"Because Henry will not win this!"

Simon blinked, and then shook his head. "I thought we were talking about Rachel."

"That boy isn't right for her."

"He's not a boy, and she's not a child. She hasn't been for a while."

"I need Rachel to find herself before she tries to become a wife."

"What do you want Pop?"

"I'm going to Mexico, I know where Nick is hold up with his brother. I'll get Ryan to go with me. I'm going to tell Nick to come here and tell Rachel, to her face that what they had is over."

"Are you sure that's a good idea?"

"Of course, it'll give her a chance to come to her senses. And him a chance to find his."

"What if he doesn't agree? What if he loves Rachel, and comes here then takes her away?"

"That's where you come in. I'm going to tell him I have Rachel under lock and key. If he came here he would find you as her body guard and if he tried to contact her in any way she would be put under house arrest, and he'd never see her."

"That won't work," Simon scoffed. "He knows you love her too much to do that."

"He'll probably come here to check if I'm lying or not, but when he gets here he'll see you dogging Rachel's steps then he'll know I meant what I said."

"Is it that bad Pop? They could be good together.

You should've seen how they fought for each other. I think they'd make a good couple."

"No one paid you to think." John turned and left the room.

Twenty

IT WAS JUST PAST THREE IN the afternoon
and the sun was high and bright. Nick stood in front of the
window of his bedroom. He was about to add his last
letter to Rachel to the pile of out going mail. This would
be the fourth letter to her in as many weeks and there had
been no reply. He'd been about to lose hope when her gift
had arrived with a small note that read. 'Losing a friend is
never easy. I hope this one will help ease the pain.' Nick
hated to think he was heart sick, but that was the only
thing he could think of. She never once mentioned love.
Had she already forgotten him? Surrounded by her
family, she probably never thought of him or the time
they spent together. He looked down at the letter, this was
the last one. If she didn't respond then he would take the
hint and leave her alone.

Nick looked around the small room of the house
he shared with Blake and Sophia, it was Miguel and
Maria's old home right behind Henry's burnt out
Hacienda. From the window Nick could see the only
thing left standing, the tree of truth. It was a beautiful
tree, long sweeping limbs. It was almost graceful when
the wind blew. Right now everything was silent, which
meant little Dominick and Vanessa were having a nap.
Blake's children had come with his in-laws. The in-laws

couldn't stand to be in Mexico, and since Sophia had decided to stand by her man they had left in disgust. They told Sophia she and the children could come to visit anytime, but Blake was not welcome in their home. Nick wondered if it would be like that with Rachel, if she did love him, would her parents make her choose between her love for him and them? It was likely, maybe it was a good thing she didn't love him.

It was time for him to think about going to see her. He had waited, just to make sure that when she got home, if she had time away from him, would she still claim to love him. He still didn't have a clear answer. There was only one real way to find out, he had to ask her. He was nervous, and his hands grew sweaty just thinking about it. The possibility that she could say no was high on his mind. So he had thrown himself into his work here and put it off. But putting Henry's affairs in order was a job that would be never ending. They had repaid people, closed down bordello's and cantina's that had high crime. But first, they had gotten Cara back into the arms of her family. Now, they needed to find ways to put this blood money to good use.

Sophia had already gotten started on building a community hospital for the poor. Blake had gifted one hundred thousand dollars each, to twenty families in town. Nick had set about building a school it was Sophia's idea and it was a good one. He got the distinct feeling she didn't like him. But she was tolerating his presence very well. There was still millions left so Nick decided he would invest it in small businesses. But he would do it in Texas.

Nick's lips tightened as he recalled the day Rachel'd been ushered onto the plane with the arm of her father wrapped around her. It was the day he realized her love for him might change. She said she loved him, but did she mean it? Would she care that he himself was penniless? Would his one bedroom apartment in Houston be enough for her? He doubted it, but he had to try. Once he was finished here, he would be free to go get her.

Sophia bit her lower lip and hurried down the hall to Nick's room. It was late afternoon and like usual he was shut away in his room doing God knows what. She knocked lightly on Nick's bedroom door, and jumped as the door was immediately flung open.

"Yes," Nick said, and she tried not to flush. She was still uncomfortable around him. He wasn't the same man she'd met when he was with Rachel. Back then he'd been so different, happy and at ease. Now he walked around the small house with a permanent scowl, he seemed tense and angry. Even the kids had been afraid to go near him. Which made her think he just didn't like kids. Maybe that was why he'd wanted Rachel to abort their child. That conversation she'd had with Rachel was always on her mind.

The only smile she had seen on his face since Rachel left had been when the delivery man had come by. She remembered the look on his face. It had been the look of a man in love, there had been a perfumed note and a package. She felt horrible every time the mailman came Nick met him at the door, and there was nothing for him. She wondered if he were waiting for a letter from Rachel? Maybe she should tell him she'd been talking to Rachel almost every day. Then she decided not to, she had promised Rachel she wouldn't.

"What is it Sophia?" She gave a small squeak of surprise as the little puppy Rachel had sent him ran out of the room and passed her feet.

"Oh no," she giggled as it nipped at her toes through her sandals. "Shoo, go away."

"Come here you little bugger," Nick picked the golden Labrador puppy up, and she proceeded to lick his face. He held her away from him and she wiggled to get free.

Sophia laughed. "I thought you were going to get rid of her?"

"I was," Nick said, as he put the dog back in the room and closed the door. "But Rachel owed me one dog, among other things. So I think I'll keep her."

"Oh," Sophia clasped her hands in front of her and smiled.

"Can I help you?"

"Oh yes," she blushed prettily. "A Mr. John McKinney is here to see you."

At the first mention of the name Nick was at a loss, and then he remembered Rachel's father's name was John. His heart rate picked up. "Tell him, I'll be right there."

"Okay, I put him in the salon." She clutched her hands together and hurried away.

Nick forgot her, the instant she was gone. His mind on Rachel's father, what if... *No,* Nick shook his head, *why borrow trouble?* He would just go in there, and make sure it was her father and not another of Henry's victim's wanting to find a taken family member, there had been too many of them to count, once news of Henry and Tony's death had been released. He straightened his clothes, and ran a hand through his hair, then cleared his throat. Then he headed down the hall. Nick opened the door and his heart froze. It was him. His eyes made a quick scan of the room, and he let out the breath he was holding. She hadn't come with him. His gaze went to the red scar on the right side of John's head. It had healed, but the hair had yet to grow back.

"John," Nick held out his hand. "To what do I owe this pleasure?"

John looked at the offered hand, and turned away. "This is no pleasure visit. Let me get to the point. I want you to give my daughter back to me."

Nick lifted a brow at that. "What do you mean? I've already done that."

"You gave me a shell!" John thundered.

"I'm not understanding you."

"You told her you would be back for her, call her and tell her it was a lie."

"Why would I do that?" Nick's eyes narrowed. *Is she waiting for me?* It gave his heart a pleasant leap just to think it.

"Because she won't eat until she sees you again. She thinks she's in love. You and I know she isn't. This was forced on her and she took the only way out she knew. Now, because of how stubborn she is, she's probably decided to have you or die. I won't let her do either."

"Is that what she said?" His heart jumped, and in his mind he was already packed and ready to go get her.

"No she hasn't said it!" John yelled. "Hell she swears she doesn't love you, that she wants nothing to do with you, and yet she still won't eat, she won't become a part of our family again."

"She went on a hunger strike?" Nick was thoughtful, that wasn't go news.

"Don't be stupid," John snapped, anger in every

word. "She just doesn't eat, she sits at the window seat in her room and stares out the window. Her therapist thinks she may be waiting for you."

"Wait a minute," Nick snapped, now he was pissed. "You have her seeing a therapist? For what?"

"What did you think I would do?" John yelled, his face dark with bitterness. "You had her for two months in the wilds of this God forsaken country. I'm just glad she didn't end up pregnant from what you put her through. If she had been you'd be dead right now."

"If she were you would have no say in it, she'd be with me right now."

"If she were pregnant you wouldn't know it. The minute she gave birth I'd have the doctor take it away and tell her it died, and then it would be disposed of."

Nick was starting to become ill. "You would kill Rachel's child?"

"No," John snarled. "Your child!"

"You are insane."

"There is nothing I won't do to make sure my daughter has a happy healthy life. You don't fit in any part of that."

"So you are having her brain washed?"

"If that's what it takes."

"So, she's seeing a head doctor, any progress?" Nick planned to be on the next flight. She may not know it but she needed him, her father had gone off the deep end. "You can do what you like, but the girl I knew was too strong for that."

"I won't reminisce with you," John spit out. "You may have had fun dragging her through that nightmare, but for us it was sheer terror every day she was gone."

"I understand." Nick said quietly.

"No," John shook his head. "I don't think you do. Henry wasn't the only one who could play hard ball. If you force me to I can be a real ass."

"What do you want from me?"

"Tell Rachel that you don't love her, you never have. The only reason you kept her with you was incase Henry needed to use her."

Nick frowned. "I'm not telling her that."

"Yes you are, because it's the right thing to do. You'll do it, or live in hiding all your life. I won't rest until you give her back to us."

"But she's my heart, I love her, doesn't that count for anything!"

"No, it doesn't."

"I can't, I won't do it."

"Fine, I was just giving you the chance to say your goodbyes. Like this you'll never see her again." From the look on John's face Nick knew he meant every word. "If you force it, by the time I get home she'll be gone. You can search the world over and you'll never find her."

"Is that fair to her? You want to make her life hell just because you think she maybe in love with me?"

"It's your choice, she can live a happy normal life. Get married, have kids, be really happy with someone she chose. Or you can force me to keep her under lock and key."

Thoughts of ways to take Rachel away without her father's knowledge ran through his mind. How could he free her so they could be together?

"Don't think of that," John said as if reading Nick's mind. "Simon is with her every step, every day. She doesn't know why but he is there."

"I don't believe you."

John pulled out his phone and dialed a number. "Yes, hello Pat darling, how is our little girl?"

"So she's the same? Okay honey let me talk with Simon." John looked at Nick. "Simon where is Rachel, let me talk to her. Hello Darling how are you?" As he spoke Nick couldn't get rid of the need to pull the phone away from him. He waved Nick over and let him listen, her voice was pure heaven. "Now let me talk to your brother." Hearing Simons voice convinced Nick that John wasn't joking.

Nick nodded and moved away, he stood by the window, his hands resting on the seal as his world crashed. He had already picked out where they would live, and how he would ask her to marry him, now this.

"Fine, I'll see you all in a few days." John hung up the phone.

"I'll do what you ask." It was the hardest thing he'd ever said.

"Great, I expect you at my home in one week. Take this check for your services. After you're done I never want to see you again." John tossed the check to the desk top, and turned, then left the house. Nick crashed his fist into the wall and ignored the pain, it was nothing compared to the agony ripping at his heart.

*****

"Nick."

He stiffened. "Not right now Blake." He didn't want to face any one. Knowing Rachel might love him, and was right this instant waiting for him made him the happiest man in the world. But knowing he could never be with her tore him apart. He did know one thing, he'd never do what John wanted. If he saw her, he'd take her in his arms and ruin her life with her family because he knew they'd never accept him.

"I heard what he said Nick," Blake walked into the study and closed the door. He went to where Nick stood with his head hanging and clasped him on his back. "Don't listen to him Nick. You have enough money here to buy an island and take her away with you. He'd never find you."

"It's not my money." Nick growled and shook off Blake's hold. He walked to a chair in front of the desk and dropped into it. "It's blood money."

"Blood money when it's used that way."

"Listen to your self!" Nick snapped. "Henry killed people and ruined lives, are you of all people going to tell me that kind of money is ours free and clear?"

"No," Blake countered. "Not free and clear, fought for with our pain, our blood. You remember what he did to mom, to me! And don't forget Cara, Miguel and Maria, they suffered for years under threat of death from that Bastard."

"Miguel and Maria have four million dollars they should be very happy."

"But what about you Nick?" Blake pleaded. "Take the money, be happy."

"What are your plans?" Nick turned the table on Blake.

"I bought four hundred acres in south east Houston, Texas. Two hundred of that I'm giving to you. Do with it what you will. I'm building a house for Sophia and the kids. We'll raise horses, and have a few chickens, maybe I'll breed bulls."

"What are you smiling about?" Nick wanted to

know.

"I can plan things, Nick. You don't understand what that means," Blake thumped his chest. "You don't know how it feels to plan things, I've never been able to do that before. When I married Sophia, I thought I had it all planned, but I was wrong. I brought the woman I love into a death trap. I gave Henry a weapon to use to keep me controlled. But now I can stand here and say what I want to do, and do it without fear." A tear crept from Blake's eyes and Nick went to him. He caught his arms and when Blake smiled, Nick pulled him into his arms and hugged him tight. "I never thought I would live long enough to really live. But here it is." Blake hugged Nick tight then let him go, and wiped his eyes. "I'm sorry, it's just so unreal right now. All this freedom is going to take some getting used to."

"Believe me I understand." Nick sat on the edge of the desk and looked at Blake. "Two hundred acres huh?"

"Yes," Blake beamed. "Right next to us. We're leaving in a day or two to look at it and start planning. For some weird reason Sophia has decided Texas is the only place she wants to live. Can you tell me where I can get a good place to stay while the house is being built?"

"Sure," Nick said. "Stay at my place. I'm rarely there, but I do keep up with the rent. The landlord has the key, I'll call him and let him know you're coming."

"Okay, now what about you? What are you going to do about Rachel?"

"I don't know? Either she got rid of our child or she hasn't told her parents about it yet. If she got rid of it that means she wants nothing to do with me. If like her father says she loves me and is just waiting for me to come to her, then maybe she wants us to tell them together. I'll have to go and see for my self."

"Do you believe her father about locking her away?"

"Yes and no. I think he hates me enough to do anything to keep her away from me. But he loves her enough to want the best for her, he could Shepard her off into a quick arranged marriage. God knows what kind of crap the shrink is feeding her."

"Going down there is your best chance to see what's really happening."

"Listen," Nick said. "Can you and Sophia wait one week? Help me get this mess together then I'll go to Houston with you. Whether I become a family man, or not I still need a place to lay my head. I'll look at the land and buy some from you."

"No Nick, I just told you I gave you the land."

"I don't want a gift, I'll buy it from you. I've had this plan for a house in my head for years," Nick shrugged. "Now is as good a time as any to get started on it."

"Then it's settled, in one week we close down everything here and we all move to Texas." Blake said smiling from ear to ear. "I take it you're not going to listen to John."

"Once I get this house built, he can kiss his daughter good bye, because she's moving straight into my arms."

"Not to throw cold water on your party but what if she doesn't want to?"

"She'll have no choice, I could kidnap her."

"You are joking aren't you?"

"Yes," Nick laughed. "I'm going to wine and dine

her and make her love me again."

"Now that sounds like a plan! What woman wouldn't melt with gifts and constant attention?"

"Let's hope this woman will, sometimes I swear she's as tough as nails."

*****

Three weeks later, it was late evening, just after dinner and Rachel walked into the living room. Both her parents, Ryan and Bianca were all settled in playing a board game.

She stood just inside the doorway and cleared her throat. "Can I have your attention please?" Everyone turned to her and she almost chickened out. She had hoped to have Nick by her side when she made this announcement but apparently that wasn't to be.

"What is it darling?" Pat asked.

"I don't want any of you to blow a gasket or anything. Just stay calm I have every thing under control."

"What is it brat?" Ryan said. "I'm winning and you probably just broke up my streak."

"When I'm done you can go back to it." She looked around at the sea of faces, and said as quickly as she could. "I'm four and a half months pregnant."

The shock wave that went around the room was phenomenal. No one spoke. And then John grabbed his chest and fell forward.

"Daddy!" Rachel screamed.

"Call 911!"

Rachel was at the phone in record time. By the time the ambulance came John's lips had a white ring around them, and his skin was colorless. Either he couldn't talk or he wouldn't talk all he could do was stare at Rachel. And she refused to look away. When they took him away she didn't go with the family. She went to her room and started packing her things.

"Where do you think you're going?" Ryan said from the door way.

"When Mom gets back home with Dad, I'm leaving." Rachel refused to look at him, if she did she knew she would fall apart. She needed to be strong.

"Where are you going?"

"I don't know," she sniffled. "But I do have friends."

"Is it that woman you talk to on the phone almost every night?"

Rachel gasped and turned to stare at him. "How do you know who I talk to?"

"Don't be stupid, Dad knows everything about you."

"Apparently not everything."

"How can you still be a smart ass when you just sent our father to the hospital with probably a heart attack by saying you're going to have a bastard?"

She turned quickly, pulled back her hand and delivered a stinging slap to his cheek. He grabbed his cheek and then grabbed her arm.

Rachel threw her chin up and dared him. "If you hit me I'll tell and no matter how mad Dad is he'll still get you for it."

Ryan tossed her arm from him. "You've done it now Brat," he said softly, his brown eyes soft. "What ever you do from here on out will be with my help. Dad has probably disowned you."

Forgive Me, My Love

Her lower lip trembled, and she fell into his arms. "Oh Ryan, I don't know what to do?" She looked up at him through watery eyes. "I love Nick so much, just saying it makes my heart squeeze with agony."

"But you have to know it wasn't really love." He caressed her hair, and she put her forehead on his shoulder.

"I'm beginning to see that." She whispered.

"It was just your need to make good of everything, honey we all understand, no one is going to judge you."

"I don't know," Rachel turned her head, and stared at the wall. It felt so good to have someone comfort her, and not pass judgment. Talking to her mother had been hard enough but talking to Bianca was almost painful. Bianca had been there, she had witnessed the whole thing. *What a sucker she must think I am.* Rachel gave a small watery laugh, and Ryan's arms tightened on her.

"He loves me Ryan, I know he does."

"Then why isn't he here? Why hasn't he called or tried to see you?" Ryan grabbed her arms and pushed her from him to stare into her eyes. "It was just a fling. Men do it all the time, this time you got to do it. It's rare that women get the chance to live in a man's world, but you did. Now it's over, let's get back to living."

She nodded and he wiped her eyes, she gave a wet smile and sniffed hard. "Okay, you're right. I'm on my own. My first move will be to move out of here."

"Where you gonna go?"

"Maybe, I'll live with Simon."

"Uhh, I wouldn't do that if I were you, he hasn't been in the best of moods. Have you noticed he hasn't been around lately?"

"Actually, I haven't noticed much of anything."

"I think he had a fight with Bianca, they've been avoiding each other like the plague."

"Can I move in with you?"

"Sorry, but that's a bachelor pad, can't have you around scarin' away my honeys. I'll cut you a loan to get your own place, and when you finish school you can pay me back."

"It sucks that I'm older then you, and yet you finished school first and got a good job."

"That's what comes from not having high aspirations. I'm happy with being a draftsman. If I invest right I'll have everything that pops has."

"So I'll get an apartment."

"What about the bambino?"

"I'll raise it alone."

"No you won't, not if I'm around."

"Thanks Ryan."

"I'm going to the hospital. If the look in dad's eyes is anything to judge by, he'll need a stern talking to before he gets back here."

"Leave that to Mom."

"Nite brat," Ryan kissed her cheek.

"Nite stinker," Rachel kissed his cheek, and watched as he left her room. She turned back to her suitcase, her look thoughtful, then she closed it and sat on her bed. She looked up as her phone rang. She went to it then looked at her caller I.D. quickly she lifted the receiver and said. "Hey Sophia how are you? How is Mexico?"

"I'm fine, Mexico is divine, I never knew what I was missing. Now that Henry is gone Blake is such a different person. He is so open with me and he smiles and laughs so much more then before. I have fallen in love with him all over again."

"I'm so happy to hear it."

"How are you?" Sophia asked. "I had a dream last night that you weren't doing to well, I thought I better check in and see for myself."

"I'm glad you called," Rachel sat on her bed. "I think for the first time, I'm growing up. It's been hard but I think I'm ready to stand on my own two feet."

"That doesn't sound good."

"What do you mean? It's wonderful, I feel...I don't know, relieved maybe? I've been waiting on something that will never happen. Now, that I've accepted it I think I can move on."

"Rachel." There was hesitation in her voice.

"What is it?"

"Nick..."

"Nope," Rachel cut her off. "If you called to talk about him, then I must tell you don't. I understand many things, and he is one of them. I don't want to talk about him ever again."

"But Rachel he..."

"Is he dead, hurt, missing?" As much as she missed him she wished there was a reason why he hadn't come to her.

"No but..."

"No buts," Rachel swallowed her pain. It was wonderful to know he was safe, but it was gut wrenching to have proof that he didn't care for her at all. "If he's okay then I'm fine with knowing only that, apparently he doesn't need or want me so I'm not wasting any more of my time on him."

"Okay."

"Is there something you wanted to talk to me about?"

"Blake and I are moving to Houston tomorrow."

"Oh, how wonderful!"

"It is wonderful," Sophia agreed. "I can't wait to see you."

"Oh, you've made my day!" Rachel gushed, genuinely happy for the first time in a long while. "What made you decide to come?"

"Blake liked it, and it's official my family has told us both that they hate him. I can't live in that country next to them knowing he isn't happy. I love him, so in a way I've grown up too. I am willing to follow my husband any where. Once the house is built we will be ranchers. And of course I wanted to be close to you, we have to keep all the cousins together you know."

"Sounds like heaven."

"Guess what?" Sophia whispered.

"What?" Rachel whispered back.

"I'm with child."

"No!" Rachel cried with excitement. "You're lying!"

"No, I swear it must've happened the week before everything started. I'm surprised the baby survived, for a while in the hospital I thought I would die, but the doctor told me I was having morning sickness, and that I needed to stay off my feet because of all the abuse I received, but so far all is well."

"Ohhh, I'm so happy for you." Rachel said with tears in her voice. "How far along are you?"

"We guess I'm about eight weeks."

"That's wonderful Sophia," Rachel paused, and then said. "Well I'm four and a half months now."

"Maybe when I get there I'll come to see you?"

"Of course by then I'll have my own place. I just told my parents I'm pregnant."

"How did they take it?"

"Not well, my father is in the hospital."

"Oh Rachel," Sophia was quiet for a moment. "Are you okay about this? Is he going to be okay?"

"He's going to be fine, he was glaring at me when they took him away. But I'm a little scared, even while I'm so terribly happy. Even though Nick never loved me I loved him. And this baby will feel all the love I have for it's father, and it'll never feel unwanted."

"I'm so happy we'll be near you, maybe we can be birth partners. Blake can help us both."

"No, I don't want Blake to know."

"Oh I'm sorry, you are right not to trust him yet. But just give him time, you will see he isn't really a bad guy."

"It's not that, it's just he'll tell Nick, I don't want Nick to ever know. He didn't want the child, he wanted me to get rid of it remember?"

"Yes," Sophia sighed. "Are you saying never tell him?"

"Never."

"Oh how heartbreaking," Sophia cried. "I've tried to be nice to him. He seems so gloomy all the time, are you sure he doesn't love you? I really thought he did."

"I have no doubt if he knew of the child he'd do the right thing. But I don't want the right thing. I want him to want me. Just me, for me. And if he's not ready, then I don't need him. Anyway I poured my heart out to him in my letters and he hasn't answered one."

"But you should tell him, give him the chance."

411

"The chance to do what, hurt me again? If I told him now he'd feel trapped. He'd hate me and our child. No, I know what I felt for him was false now. There was nothing real about it, I imagine he was glad to be rid of me."

"Don't say that!" Sophia snapped. "That baby is real and you know your love was real."

"I thought mine was, and now it's over." Rachel changed the subject. "When will you be in town?"

"We fly in at three thirty p.m. tomorrow."

"Maybe you can sneak away and meet me for lunch sometime this week."

"It maybe hard, I'd have to be very careful. But I will find a way."

"Okay, let's make it soon."

"Very soon, call me okay?"

"I will, good night."

"Good night mommy." Sophia giggled.

"That sounds strange," Rachel murmured, she was filled with an unexpected joy.

"You better get used to it." Sophia sighed. "In about two years it will be your only name."

"Sounds good to me, goodnight mommy."

"Goodnight new mommy."

*****

"This can't be happening." John groaned from his hospital bed. "She didn't even care, did you see the look on her face. She didn't even care."

Pat caressed his brow. "She cares that's why she's not here. If she were here you'd be fighting with her, and she knows that wouldn't be good for you."

"She didn't even come to me when I fell to the floor. She just stood there." He moaned.

"She called emergency, then she went to let them in. Rachel loves you John you have been her world for as long as I can remember. Maybe she was ashamed of having let you down? Maybe that was her escape; she didn't want to face your pain."

"I don't think so, I think she was daring me to do something about it."

"Don't think like that!" Pat spat. "If you do anything to make her feel unwelcome or even mention one word about her not keeping that child you and I will have serious problems. This will be our first grandchild..."

"You stop right there!" He roared. "That is a bastard forced on our child I will not have it..." Pat did something she'd never done. She drew back her hand and slapped him hard across the face. At his stunned look, she turned on her heels and marched out the hospital doors.

Twenty-One

WEEKS LATER, JOHN GOT OUT OF HIS
bed at home. He got dressed and walked downstairs to the
breakfast room. Pat wasn't talking to him and he'd not
seen any of his children since he'd come home from the
hospital three weeks ago. They may hate him, but he was
determined to find away to get rid of that child.

He walked into the room and was vaguely
surprised to see everyone there. He took his seat at the
head of the table and summoned the server. "I'll have my
usual."

"Yes Sir."

"Are you supposed to be out of bed?" Ryan asked.

"Of course, it was a mild stroke nothing to be
concerned about."

Pat spoke up. "Rachel is determined to move out
next week. She's found an apartment in town."

"Yes daddy," Rachel said. "I won't burden you
any more than I have. It's already arranged."

"Unarrange it," John barked, and everyone
jumped. "I'm sorry, I didn't mean to yell. Darling I lost
you once, I won't lose you again. Stay home, you are no
burden for me."

"See honey," Pat was saying. "I told you your
father loves you, he'd never want you gone."

"Still," Rachel shrugged. "When the baby comes

you may not want…"

"So you're going to keep it?" John asked.

"Yes." Rachel said, her tone hard.

"I wish I'd have known this I wouldn't have given Nick that check." John laughed, but it was cold and calculating. "I would've kept it and given it to you to help with raising his child."

Rachel stiffened, and her eyes shot to him. "What check? And when did you see Nick?"

"A while ago I went to Nick, and begged him to come and see you. I asked him to put your heart at ease that if he didn't love you to at least come here and tell you so. But he wouldn't," John shook his head sadly. "I wanted to strangle him. Then he asked me for the money he spent on you."

Rachel gasped, and her head began to swim. "How much did he want?"

"Two hundred fifty thousand dollars."

Rachel's lips tightened, he had to be telling the truth, there was no way he could know the correct amount, Nick had to have told him.

Pat started to get up, but Rachel waved her back into her seat.

"Did he say anything else?" She had to know.

"Only that he'd think of you when he spent it."

Tears sprang to her eyes, and any love she'd felt for Nick was now crushed, along with all hope.

"John," Pat said. "Do you know for sure he cashed it?"

He reached into his pocket and pulled out the cancelled check. John handed it to Rachel. She took it with wooden fingers. "It was cashed the very next day."

"I have to go to my room."

415

"Rachel, wait I'll go with you."

"No Bea, I want to be alone."

Once she was gone Pat stared at her husband. "Why did you do that?"

"Do what? Tell her the truth?"

"I'm sure it's your version."

"You don't trust me now?"

"After all these years of marriage," Pat cried. "I don't think I know you at all. You're like some revenge crazed jerk, it's a side of you I never knew existed. I'm not sure I like you any more." Pat got up, and headed for the door.

"You'll thank me when we have our little girl back. You'll see!"

"Pop," Ryan said. "I think you've lost it."

"All of you, think what you like, but this is my fight and Henry will not win."

Bea and Ryan stood up and left the room. John was sure they would all understand what he was doing. When Rachel became the sweet little girl she had been, they would understand everything he'd been forced to do.

✶✶✶✶✶

Four months later, Nick was worried that too much time had past. But he had been so busy putting his life together. He needed to make sure John had nothing to use against him when he went to get Rachel back. Nick built a home that he hoped was good enough for Rachel. This afternoon he stood in his yard beside Blake and Sophia, and smiled as the last shrub was put in place. He turned to them and smiled, Blake returned his smile, but Sophia turned away. She had been acting strange for months now. Not that they had ever been close, but at least when they'd met she had seemed to be trying to get to know him. Now it was as if looking at him made her physically sick.

"It's going to be hard not having you underfoot." Blake laughed.

"Yeah right," Nick said, and laughed at Blake's referring to Nick living with them. Blake's home had been finished months ago. "With me always under foot your poor wife never had her husband. Now that my place is finished she can have you back. I have to go catch my own Philly."

"You think she'll still have you?" Blake asked.

"I don't know. They may have brain washed her so bad that she treats me like Sophia does, and never wants to look at me again." Nick paused to look at Sophia, but she turned up her nose and looked away.

"And if that happens?"

"Then I'll spend a good bit of time changing her mind. I can wine and dine, her until I get a ring on her finger and her back in my bed."

"Wow, you really love her don't you?"

"You just don't know. That girl is like a fire in my veins. It's been hard sleeping without her tucked under my arm. I can't seem to get through one day without thinking of her."

"Have you been by to see her?"

"No he hasn't!" Sophia snapped, and folded her arms cross her bulging tummy and stomped off.

Nick looked at her, then at Blake, but Blake gave him the ignore her look and Nick continued.

"No, if I did I'd never leave without her. Hell I might just kidnap her, I can't trust myself. I had to wait until this was ready. Now I can woo her right. She can see I'm a man with something to offer her."

"Ahhh," they both looked up to see Sophia a few yards away lying on the ground. They ran to her, but Nick reached her first, he went to his knees in front of her and reached out to her. "Are you…"

"Get away from me!" She screamed, and Blake hurried to put himself between Nick and Sophia.

"Honey, it's okay it's just Nick."

"I know who it is, and I don't want him to touch me." She hissed, her eyes boring into Nick.

Baffled Blake looked at Nick's stunned face, and shrugged. "What happened, honey are you okay?"

She nodded. "The grass is still wet and I slipped, that's all."

Blake helped her to her feet, and Nick got to his. "The baby's okay?"

She nodded again, and peeked at Nick from behind Blake.

"If I've done something to offend you I'm sorry Sophia." Nick said meaning every word. "If you tell me what it is I can try to fix it."

"No you can't!" She yelled and both men jumped back. "Even if you could it's too late."

"Tell him honey," Blake pleaded. "Tell us what's wrong."

"There's nothing wrong, just leave me alone."

"Look," Blake said in tones he rarely used with her. "I'm tired of this, it's been going on too long. Since you first met him you've been standoffish, and judgmental. Nick is my brother. I won't be forced to choose between you two. Let's fix this right now."

"Don't you yell at me for the likes of him!" She

yelled back and pointed at Nick.

Blake immediately became concerned as tears ran from her eyes. He went to her, but she stepped away.

"He has no soul! No heart!" She thumped her chest. "He's a mean beast, and I will not have anything to do with him ever again."

Blake looked at Nick. "What did you do?"

"The hell if I know."

"You know!" She screamed. "You told Rachel to get rid of your child!"

Nick froze. "What?"

"You hear me!" Her Spanish accent became strong as it always did when she was upset. "You gave her something to get rid of the child you didn't want. How could you?"

Blake held up his hands. "If Nick did that it's his own business. Leave it alone Sophia. He has his reasons."

Nick held up his hand. "Let her finish."

"I can't stand the sight of you. I despise you, you coward!" She hissed. "How could you break her heart like that?"

"How do you know I broke her heart? Maybe she broke mine."

"I know you are not the one about to give birth all alone." Sophia realized too late what she said as the color drained from his face, and then he fell to his knees staring at her in astonishment.

"Say that again?"

"No, I'm sorry I didn't mean too…" She turned to run, but Blake caught her arms and spun her around to face Nick.

"Tell him again." He yelled.

She sniffled and looked away from Nick's burning

eyes. "She is my friend."

"When did you talk to her last?"

"Last night, she's been to the hospital three times with false labor."

Nick sat flat on the new grass. John's words came back to haunt him. *If she were pregnant we would take the child and tell her it died at birth.* Nick shivered, desperate panic shook him.

He didn't look at Sophia who cried on Blake's shoulder. "How is she? Have you seen her? Has she asked about me?" He hated how eager he sounded, but he couldn't keep the hope from his voice.

Sophia wiped her face and looked at him. "She thinks she doesn't love you any more. Her therapist has taught her how to push you from her heart. But she's in perfect health, with the pregnancy she has gain forty pounds."

"You have been friends all this time and never told me?" Blake asked, shocked and a little hurt.

"There were many things you never told me Blake, so don't look at me like that. At least my omission can't get you killed."

"So," Blake caught her arms. "It's going to be like that?"

"Excuse me," Nick said. "Can we get back to me? The baby, do they know what it is?"

"No she didn't want the doctor to tell her."

Nick swallowed hard. "And me, she didn't want me to know?"

"She thinks you don't love her. She doesn't want you if you want her only for the baby."

"What do you think I'm doing this for? Does it look like I want to be without her?"

Forgive Me, My Love

"You never said a word. How am I supposed to know what you are thinking? I didn't even know what my husband was up to. Am I supposed to figure out the brother too?"

"Blake," Nick said. "This has to soak in, I need time to think. Let me find out a few things, and then I'll get back to you."

"Are you moving in here tonight?"

"Yes, I'll have my things out of your place before night fall." Nick walked a way.

*****

It was well past midnight and Nick was frantic, if Sophia was correct the baby was due in two weeks. *His baby.* Just the thought gave him chills of happiness. He had to make every second count. But if he went to her now she'd think it was only because of the baby. The thought of her hating him was easier to take knowing how she must be suffering with her father breathing down her neck. He wondered if she ever went back to school. Probably not. But he'd make sure she finished after she had the child.

He opened his wallet and pulled out her phone number. He debated calling her, then decided against it. No one there would help him, besides it was too late, they'd all be asleep. He would go to her parent's home, and see if he could get a glimpse of her. That decision made he fished the address out of his wallet. With it clutched in his hand, he locked the door to his new house and jumped into his truck.

*****

"Mom," Rachel puffed hard, she was in the throws of false labor again, but this time she wouldn't go to the hospital. "Mom?"

"Yes darling?" Pat wiped Rachel's brow. She worried that the baby would come too soon. She had never delivered a baby before, and she didn't want her first grandchild to be the first.

"If I yell his name again, could you please not tell any one?"

She didn't have to ask whose name. Rachel had been calling for Nick even in her sleep. "I promise baby."

"Even Bea, don't tell her." Rachel panted as the pain came back. "Ho...w how... long was wa...s tha...t?"

"I won't tell Bea and that was ten minutes."

"Have they evened out yet?"

"No dear, they're still staggered."

"Damn!" she said. "Why can't we just get this over with?"

"Maybe the baby is just like it's mother and father, stubborn?"

"Don't mention him to me."

"Okay," Pat fell silent.

"What's taking Bea so long? I could really use that crushed ice right now."

"How's it going?" They both looked up to find John standing in the doorway. He had been less than supportive during her pregnancy, but since she first started with having false labor he had seemed to be trying to understand. He had even picked out the doctor Rachel would go to, and the nursing staff. He made sure she had the whole wing to herself and for that she was thankful.

"It's going well." Pat said, and Rachel looked at

her. It hadn't escaped her noticed that her parents were in some kind of a battle, she hoped she wasn't the cause of their trouble.

"Good," he walked into the room. "I made those arrangements just for times like this. I don't want my only daughter to suffer when there is no need. Dr. Paydar will induce labor in three days."

"What?" Both Rachel and Pat sat up straighter. "What do you mean?"

"I told you," he said the hard tone in his voice giving Rachel pause. "I'll have him induce you. You do know the more you have these false alarms the more danger the baby will be in?"

"What kind of danger? The doctor at the emergency room said everything should be fine. Every woman has these."

"Yes John," Pat snapped. "I recall having two months of false labor with Ryan and he was fine when he finally came."

"That's a matter of opinion." John joked, but the ladies weren't laughing. "Okay, at the time I didn't have the resources to make sure you were taken care of. Now I do." His gaze turned to Rachel. "If you keep going like this you could stress the baby's heart and never know it. By the time you give birth that child could have been dead for weeks without you knowing it."

Rachel gave a sharp cry, and Pat hugged her tight. "Don't listen to him." She cooed to Rachel, and then to John she yelled. "Since when are you an expert in child birth?"

"Since my baby is about to have one," he snapped back at her, and Rachel tensed. Her parents never behaved this way towards each other, she had to assume this was her fault.

"You may not know this," John continued. "But I love that girl, and I'll do everything possible to protect her and if that means inducing her labor to save that child's life then that's what I'm going to do."

Pat looked at Rachel. "What do you think? Do you what to do it?"

Rachel looked at John. "You think it's the best thing to do Daddy?"

"Yes darling," John murmured. "I hate to say it but it maybe too late already."

"Okay, I'll do it," Rachel said. "Can he do it tonight?"

"No," John shook his head. "Everything has to be ready. I just talked to him about it today, and he said Sunday is the only time he can do it."

"Fine," Pat conceded. "As long as the baby is still kicking, then you know she's okay."

"She, huh?" Rachel smiled. "I wouldn't mind having a girl."

"Well, let's just hope she's healthy." John said, and he left the room.

"Hey sorry I took so long with the ice," Bea hurried into the room. She handed the ice to Rachel. "Simon is here."

"Simon?" Pat said with a smile. "What is he doing here?"

"I called him," Bea said, in a breathless tone. "I thought Rachel was about to have the baby and I thought he might like to be here for it."

"Good thinking," Pat said.

"Not good thinking," Rachel said between bites. "He can't stand looking at me, why would he want to be here for this?"

"Because you're my sister and anything that effects you, effects me." Simon walked through the door and Rachel noticed how Bea moved as far from him as the room would allow.

"I'm glad to hear you say that. It's hard enough enduring Dad's forced smiles, but to think you despised me too was just getting to be too much."

"I don't despise you and you know it." Simon sat on the couch next to Rachel and held her hand. "Look at that gut!" He laughed and it was an honest laugh.

Rachel tried to throw her arms around him, but she couldn't reach, so he met her half way.

"I'm big, aren't I?"

"Big isn't the word."

Rachel let go of him and cupped his face, then kissed his cheek. She caught his hands and looked at the other occupants of the room. "I have a favor to ask."

"Sure what is it?" Simon said.

"Dad set it up for me to have the baby this Sunday."

Simon frowned, "They can do that? I thought the little ankle biters just came when they wanted."

"They do it for emergencies."

"Are you in that much of a hurry to see her?" Bea asked.

"Why do yall keep saying her?" Simon asked. "You gonna give the little man a complex you keep calling him a girl."

"Okay listen," Rachel said. "I have a friend who wants to be at the hospital with me when I have the baby. She is six months pregnant so she can't come in the room but she wanted to be there for moral support."

"Fine, why tell us?" Simon asked.

"Because it's Sophia."

"Are we supposed to know Sophia?" Pat asked.

"No, I guess not," Rachel took a deep breath. "She's Blake's wife and Blake will probably bring her."

Simon's fingers tightened on hers for just a moment. And Rachel flinched at the fire in his eyes.

"No Simon," She said. "Before you ask, he doesn't know about the baby and I don't want him to know."

"You still think you love him?"

"No, I know that I don't." Some of the pressure on her fingers lightened and he nodded.

"And you think Blake won't tell him?"

"Blake loves Sophia, she said she made him promise not to say a word. This means a lot to me to have her there. I know I have Mom and Bea," she smiled at the two then turned her eyes to Simon. "But Sophia was there, she was as much a victim as I was. I think it would make me feel more at ease."

"I don't like this." Simon was saying. "What if he comes back, what if he finds out and tries to get dual custody?"

"Nick," Rachel bit her lip. She had promised herself never to say his name. "He maybe many things but a father isn't one of them. He never wanted this child, so even if he found out he wouldn't come. And if he did it would be just to see what his seed looked like."

"Are you so sure?" Pat asked.

"Very."

"Fine," Bea said. "But have you told dad yet?"

"No, and I'm not going to."

"You know he'll be upset to see them."

Forgive Me, My Love

"I know, but I'm counting on you all to keep him from upsetting her. She is pretty far along, Blake won't take kindly to anyone making her cry."

"Yes darling, we can do that," Pat said. "Now let's get you up stairs and to bed. You should enjoy your last few days of blissful quiet."

*****

Simon looked up from the pool table briefly as the door to the family room was opened. And Ryan came in. He went back to his solitary game. His lips tightened when Ryan fixed himself a drink without saying a word. He recognized the stiffness in Ryan's shoulders and waited.

Ryan tossed a quick look over his shoulder as he tried to figure out how to proceed. Talking to Simon was never his favorite thing to do. It has been Tyrell's job to keep the peace between them, now they would have to do it themselves. Simon was formidable, not only in size, but he was smart he knew how to turn every conversation to his advantage. But this was one conversation Ryan intended to win. After he made a show of putting ice in his tumbler, then splashing bourbon into it, he took a big swig, then exhaled. He turned and went to stand in front of the table, then leaned back against the wall with his arms crossed.

"What do you want Ry?"

"That brain washing session Dad set up for Rachel worked."

Simon stopped, what he was doing and stood up, he looked hard at Ryan and it made Ryan clench his teeth. "And?"

"And what?" Ryan shrugged his broad shoulders. "I'm just saying, mission accomplished."

"Spit it out!"

"Her brain is warped now," Ryan spat, and pushed off the wall. "She's about to have a child, and you two made her doubt herself, you made her believe she was crazy to love that man. You made her into an emotional cripple."

Before he finished Simon was on him. He grabbed the front of Ryan's shirt and slammed him against the wall. Ryan threw his drink across the room, and grabbed Simon's hands.

"You were there!" Simon snarled in to Ryan's angry face. "You saw what she looked like! You saw what happened to Tyrell! And you act like we're the bad guys? Like we had a choice! She had to forget. She needed to forget."

"No she didn't, she needed to remember," Ryan yanked Simon's hands from him and pushed hard. "You two have ruined her for life. My sister will never be the same. Why couldn't you let her handle this her way?"

"Because she would've went to him."

"Is that so bad? He had losses too, his father, two brothers and from what Rachel told me he loved her, from what I saw with my own eyes he loved her."

"Then why hasn't he come to see her?" Simon snapped. "That's kinda odd for a man in love not to at least try to see the woman he's in love with."

"Not in this house it isn't."

Simon stiffened. "What does that mean?"

"You know exactly what that means." Ryan put distance between them. "If I were Bea I'd have left here a long time ago, god knows you wouldn't know love if it hit you square in the face."

"Get the fuck outta here Ryan!" Before Simon finished the door was closing behind Ryan.

Simon stood looking at the empty doorway. Had they acted to hasty in getting Rachel into therapy? No, it was what she needed, it offered her someone to talk to. She did look better. Was she really in love with that fool? And what was that Ryan was sprouting off about Bea? *That boy is just stupid.*

Simon went back to his game, he never noticed he was hitting the balls much harder then necessary.

*****

It was two a.m. and Nick sat in his truck outside Rachel's home waiting. He was getting worried. According to his calculations she was well past her due date. At least a week passed and still the baby wasn't here. He knew exactly when the baby was conceived, it had to be that night in the cave. He remembered it like it was yesterday. But this was great for him, it had given him three solid weeks to get everything together. His thoughts went back to when he'd first seen her weeks ago. It had been like coming home. He had followed their car as she, her mother and Bea went shopping. When she'd stepped out of the car he'd been glad he was hidden because stunned joy was the only thing he could think of. Once he'd gotten his wits back he'd settled into following them all day. He was glad to see how happy she was. They bought all kinds of baby things. Both for a boy and a girl, it filled him with joy to see that he was right. She would love his child no matter what.

Since he had learned she was still carrying his

child, he had set about making sure he would be involved in the birth. He had gone to Blake's, and together they donated million's of Henry's money to a new women's center that had been built at the hospital where Rachel's doctor practiced. Then he set about making himself known as the benefactor and ingratiating himself to all the employees. It was no easy task to have everyone know him, but now he had them all eating out of his hands. He had learned who her doctor was and had made arrangements for him to be else where when Rachel gave birth.

So in the extra few weeks he had been given, he had become almost a regular. There wasn't much the nurses and midwives wouldn't do for him. He had told them his story, and they were very sympathetic. Then he threw Henry's money around as if it came from a never ending source. Everything was arranged, right down to his being in the delivery room, pretending to be an intern. Now he sat back and watched the house, or what he could see of it from the road. It was large and entirely gated. The fence was all brick, so he couldn't see much and it didn't help that the house was so far from the road. The house he'd built was no match for this one, he just hoped she would like it.

Suddenly Nick tensed, there speeding down the road was an ambulance. His heartbeat went out of control as fear and excitement hit him at the same time. The ambulance arrived at the house and at the same moment his cell phone went off. Just as arranged, the nurse called to let him know Rachel had gone into labor and they were bringing her in.

He also knew the exact date and time she was to go in and be induced. But apparently she had gone into labor on her own. *That's my girl!* He didn't know how she would feel if he showed up, but he knew he couldn't let her go through it alone. He needed to be at her side. John wasn't about to get his way. Nick wasn't happy with John for planning to give his child to a childless couple who wanted to adopt. They were willing to take Rachel's child without her consent or knowledge. If anyone was going to get his child it would be him. He started up his truck and followed the ambulance at a distance. He knew her family wouldn't allow him in the room, or anywhere near Rachel, but if his plan worked he may get the chance to see his child born. And make sure Rachel was okay.

*****

Rachel waited until the very last moment to tell anyone of her labor pains. They were constant, and at even intervals. She was in true labor. It scared her. Secretly she prayed Nick would come back, that he would show up, and take her into his arms and tell her that her father lied, that he didn't take any money from him, and that he loved her. But she had seen the canceled check, it had been made out to Nick and cashed. *God, how that had hurt.* Now it was too late, she sucked up her heart ache, and called for the ambulance. The only ones who would be by her side was her Mother, Bianca, and hopefully Sophia, without the three of them she would've been lost. After months of waiting for him, she was now prepared to do this without him. It was just as the theropist said, all in her mind. She hadn't really loved him, it was just a convenient way to escape what had happened to her. It was just her brain rationalizing everything so that it would be easier to deal with. She could accept that now.

In the ambulance Rachel squeezed Pat's hand and fought the tears that trekked down her face. "He's not coming is he Mama?"

"It'll be alright Darling," Pat whispered in her ear. "You don't need him. Women have babies' without their men everyday and they have no problems."

"I know Mama," she sniffled. "But I'd die just to see his face, to hear his voice. I miss him so much. Even though I hate him, I would feel better just knowing he was near."

"I'm here for you Rach," Bianca held her hand tighter, and Rachel nodded as another pain hit. "Try not to think about him. You have more important things to do right now."

"Ma'am," the attendant said to Pat. "She's already dilated six centimeters, as soon as we get her to the hospital we'll have to take her straight to the birthing room."

"I understand," Pat nodded. "Will I be allowed to go in with her?"

"Yes Ma'am, but we have to prep her, we'll send someone out to get you when she's ready."

They nodded and fell silent the rest of the ride.

*****

Nick hurried down the empty hall way and into a room marked employees only. He hid behind a far corner and waited. He looked at his hands and wasn't surprised to see they were shaking. But he didn't know if it were from the thought of being a father, or the need to kill the man who was going to try and take his child. He stiffened as the door on the far end opened. Nick peeked around the corner and thanked his lucky stars. It was Rachel's doctor.

Nick straightened, and walked to the man as he hurried to remove his jacket.

He looked up. "Oh," he looked confused. "Who are you? I didn't know…" That was as far as he got. Nick drew back and his fist plowed into his face.

"You," he said over the prone man. "Are lucky I have other things to do right now." Nick pulled out the tape and stood over him. "For now you have to go in the closet, I'll call you when it's all over."

After tying Paydar in a chair and wrapping tape around his mouth, Nick rolled the chair in the closet, then closed and locked the door. His only problem would be if someone found Paydar before Rachel could have the baby. The doctor on call would just have to deliver this child. He went to the locker that was to be his, and took out the uniform that was left for him and changed as quick as he could. With his hair covered by a blue mesh cap and a mask covering half his face in place, he walked out of the room. With a stethoscope around his neck and a clipboard in his hand, Nick put on a blue mesh gown over his kaki slack and the netting over his tennis shoes. He looked the part of the eager intern.

He even had an official nametag labeling him as an intern. He walked into the birthing room he had arranged for Rachel to be in and stood in the back in a dark corner. He planned to watch everything from his corner. He was so excited to be near her he couldn't stand the wait. Holding the clipboard he pretended he was busy when they wheeled Rachel into the room.

Rachel and Bianca looked at him, and he ducked his head even though he was sure they couldn't recognize him. Every time she made a sound his heart jumped, he wanted so bad to go to her, his fingers hurt as they clenched the clip board. He tried to close off the sound of her suffering, but he couldn't and he hurt with her, Nick found himself staring at her averted face. Then she started saying his name, and his heart melted, he started to go to her but the nurse caught his arm and pushed him back into his corner.

"She needs me." He snarled.

"You can't go to her," she whispered. "As hard as this is, you promised us you would stay in this corner. Please Nick, our jobs are at stake."

"I can give you enough money so you'd never have to work again, just please let me go to her."

"I love my job, don't jeopardize it. It's sad I know and we are all trying not to cry for you, but please control yourself."

Nick's heart was bursting, but he nodded. He was unable to look away, he willed her to see him. But she didn't.

Rachel had never been in such extreme pain. She huffed and puffed just as she was taught, but it didn't help. The only thing she could think of was Nick. If he were here this would be that much easier, he'd hold her and kiss her and her tears would be of joy not this heart pounding fright. "Nick," she cried real tears then her watery gaze went to Pat. "Please forgive me mama, but I need him. I promise I won't think of him again, but I need to say his name, I need to."

"Ssh," Pat kissed Rachel's sweaty brow. "You say whatever you like." She murmured fiercely. "Scream his name if it make you feel better."

Rachel nodded and squeezed her and Bea's hands so hard it hurt. "Owww, oh God it hurts!" She said through clenched teeth. "Nick! God where are you?"

Rachel knew a moment of panic. How was she going to raise a child alone? Before when she thought to go through with this it had been so easy to say she could do it. Easy to say she could handle everything without him. But now she admitted to herself, she had doubts. What if she couldn't do this alone?

Nick had been on her mind, so when the man walked into the room her eyes went straight to him. Instant joy shot through her, and then a crashing disappointment took hold. It wasn't Nick, he may be Nick's height, and size, he may have black hair, but Nick wouldn't come here. He didn't care about her or his child. He had made that clear. It was all she could do not to burst into tears again. It made that day he'd given her the potion clearer, he had meant it.

But she couldn't keep her eyes from the doctor in the corner. She tried but the atmosphere in the room had changed. She felt different, more at ease and she turned her face to Bea. "That man looks...owww...ouch..."

"Don't hold your breath..." Pat instructed. "Remember your class. Breathe Rachel."

She did, puff, puff, puff. It was the most embarrassing thing she'd ever done. But for some reason all that went out the window. They had her gown pushed up to reveal everything she owned, then they smeared her stomach and pelvis area with iodine then set about shaving her. All the while they kept saying, breathe, breathe. Rachel felt as if she was about to burst. The baby was right there, she was sure one more push and the baby would pop out. But now when she needed to push they told her no, wait don't push. How in heaven's name was she going to manage that?

435

The room Nick had them put Rachel in was an all inclusive room. Labor, delivery and the rest of her stay would be in that one room. The bed she lay on was a birthing table which meant the lower half would fall away, then when everything was said and done it would be lifted and turned back into a bed. His heart beat picked up as they started lowering it. And his heart contracted. She was in so much pain, her hair was plastered to her head with sweat. She clenched her teeth and had been pushing like a champion, until the nurse had said stop. Silently he cheered her on, he was so proud of her, he could've hug her.

"Where is the Doctor?" Pat yelled. Nick looked around, he had been so into Rachel's suffering that he hadn't noticed the doctor was absent.

"I'm sorry Ma'am, but we have three ladies giving birth at the same time. The mid-wife is going to have to deliver the baby."

"You can't be serious!" Pat screech. "This is important, she has been through to much to chance something happening now. We need a doctor in here."

"But it's impossible, the Doctor is with a breech birth he can't get in here. Her doctor hasn't made it here yet."

"Don't you have a back up? Someone around here, I refuse to believe there is only one doctor on night duty."

"We have two and we are trying to call another in for you, but by the time he gets here the baby will be here."

"Why is it my daughter gets stuck with no doctor yet everyone else gets a doctor? She had her own private doctor, are you telling me you didn't call Dr. Paydar the minute you knew she was in labor?"

"Yes Ma'am, we did, he said he was on his way. But he hasn't made it here yet."

"What!" Pat screeched. "You've got to be kidding me, we are paying that man an arm and a leg and he's not here? I can't believe this! Find someone!"

"Ma'am one doctor is with a breech birth and the other we are trying to reach. Your daughter is having a natural birth she has no complications. She'll be fine, our mid-wife can deliver her."

"What about him?" Bianca pointed to Nick and his heart froze. "He's a doctor isn't he?"

Nurse Wade, was one of the nurses who had helped him get everything arranged, but now she shook her blonde head. "No, no he's an intern, he can't deliver a baby."

"Then what good is he, why is he here? Intern means he's a doctor already."

"He's here only to observe." The nurse stated, but Nick waved for her to come to him. As the nurse headed for him she grabbed the midwife, Ms. Palmer's hand.

"What is it?" Nurse Wade asked.

"What happened to Doctor Hamm?"

"I don't know, we can't get in touch with him."

"So everyone is occupied?" Nick asked and they nodded. "Can I do it?" he whispered excitement in his voice. "Ms. Palmer, you can do most of it, all I want to do is catch the baby when it comes out, then you can show me what's next."

"It's not that simple," Nurse Wade said, fidgeting with her glove. "There is so much more to it than that."

"That sounds fine, I'll do it," Ms. Palmer was saying. "I'll make it look like you're doing everything.

Once I get the baby out, I'll hand it to you and you can cut the umbilical cord, and hand it to the mother. But you have to stay impartial, you can't do anything to give us away, or our jobs will be on the line."

"Deal, but you have to tell them."

"Okay," Ms. Palmer turned back to the three. "Fine, he'll deliver the baby, but I'll have to stay close. I don't want to lose my license."

"How many have you delivered?" Pat asked and Nick dropped his voice.

"I've witnessed thirty."

"I said delivered, I almost lost my daughter once, and I don't want to lose her again. Are you sure you know what you're doing?"

"He's one of our best interns Ma'am."

"How do you know that when he hasn't delivered any babies?" Pat snapped.

"Can someone get this baby out of me!" Rachel screamed as a wave of pain washed over her.

Twenty-Two

NICK STOOD TO MS. PALMER'S right side. But he found his hand on Rachel's leg in a gentle caress as she came closer and closer to expelling the baby. The nurse pushed his hand off but not before Rachel gave him a strange look between pants.

"Who…are…yo…?"

"No time for talking I see the baby's head." Nick said and forgot to change his voice. Her eyes widened and then she was crying and she pushed the child free.

Nick gave a shout of surprised laughter as he caught the squirming crying baby. All he could do was stare at this little miracle, all warm and wet, fresh from the womb. He was so entranced that he couldn't answer their questions.

"What is it?" Pat asked.

"Can I cut the cord?" Bianca wanted to know. But it was Rachel's voice that brought his head up.

"What are you doing here Nick?" The air in the room stood still as his eyes clashed with hers.

Nick cut the umbilical cord and handed the baby to Ms. Palmer. She took the baby, and cleared the lungs allowing it to take a good healthy breath and let loose a precious scream and passed it back to Nick.

He looked at Rachel and a tear escaped one of his eyes. "You did good Rachel," he said with so much emotion she cried even harder. "Thank you sweetheart, she's beautiful."

"What did…you…what…di…d I…?"

"It's a girl," he walked to the head of the bed and removed his mask. She shook her head and looked away from him. Shock filled the room as Bianca and Pat stepped away from the pair. Nick handed the baby to Rachel and kissed her tear stained cheek. "She's so beautiful," he whispered, with his forehead against her ear. "Just like her mother."

"Go away," Rachel spit out, through her tears. "Please go away, and never come back."

Nick closed his eyes, and then nodded; he turned and left the room. For now he would give her what she wanted. There would be enough time later to tell her how he felt. And even if she hated him, he intended to stick around forever.

*****

Nick hurried down the hall. He wanted to get out of there before any more of her family spotted him. He needed to get his thoughts together, and find a good way to approach her father. As he rounded the corner, he stopped dead in his tracks. Simon was standing in front of him, with Ryan at his side.

"What are you doing here?" Simon growled.

"Visiting my family," Nick said in a tone that booked no argument.

"You have no family here." Simon grated.

"Yes, he does," Blake countered as he rounded a far corner with a very pregnant Sophia at his side. "I see we made it just in time."

"Did she have the baby yet?" Sophia asked, her voice filled with anxiety.

"Yes, it's a girl," Nick said, not taking his eyes from Simon. "Go to the front desk they'll tell you where you can go to see her."

She hurried off as fast as she could.

"Are you okay here?" Blake asked Nick.

"I'm fine, go with your wife. I'm sure Rachel would love to see her."

Blake went after Sophia. And Nick refused to move as Simon took a step closer.

"You are one sorry son of a bitch to come here like this. What the hell are you doing here?"

"I'm trying to keep your father from selling my child to the highest bidder. The proof is locked in a closet in the doctors lounge."

"What?"

"You heard me!" Nick snapped. "Your father was going to tell Rachel that her child died, then turn around and give it up for adoption."

"You lying bastard!" Simon grabbed Nick's shirt but Nick caught his wrists and tossed him off.

"Oh you think my father is the only man in the world who has ever done anything under handed. You think your father is so honorable and special that he can do no wrong?"

"My father would never do that. You can spout lies until you're blue in the face, but it doesn't erase the fact that you left Rachel pregnant with your child, not to mention everything else you did to her. You can't ever call yourself a man. You think I'd believe anything you say?" Simon laughed. "If you weren't so pathetic, I'd feel sorry for you."

"You're the one who's pathetic, I love your sister. I love her and your father was about to…"

Simon grabbed Nick's shirt again and slammed him into the wall behind them. Nick pushed him off and shoved him into the chair next them.

"You're not fit to lick my father's boots! You stand there all self righteous and sprout lies like you were born doing it. My father is not like you Nick, he's an honorable man. My father would never do something as under handed as that. Where as your father would do that and much more, right?"

There was nothing more in this world Nick wanted to do than punch Simon right in the mouth. But he had to think of Rachel, fighting her brother wouldn't get her back in his arms. "I know what my father was, now you need to know what your father is capable of. The truth is in the doctor's lounge. In the closet all tied up. That's the doctor your honorable father paid to take my child."

"God damn you! To think I was having second thoughts about you," Simon pushed himself up out of the chair, and straightened his clothes. His gaze shifted past Nick's shoulder. "What do you what me to do Dad? You heard the lies he's been spreading. He probably can't wait to tell it to Rachel. Let me kick his ass."

"No," John said, his voice strangely raspy, and everyone stared at him, but he could only stare into Nicks eyes. "Just kick him out of here before your sister sees him."

"She already has," Nick said, and his tone grew hard as he met John's gaze. "I delivered our daughter."

"Simon," John snapped, his tone more urgent. "Get him out of here!"

"Don't touch him." Blake said, as he came around the corner. "Or you'll have two of us to deal with."

"As sorry as I am to say it," Ryan said, no one had seen him come up. He stood at the fringe of the crowd holding the arm of a struggling Dr. Paydar. "The minute Nick started talking I went to check things out, and I found this in the closet." Ryan's face wasn't that of a young man, his eyes held the tragic look of a man who just realized his father was not God. "I'm going to take the tape off his mouth, and when I do I want total silence. Dad that means you and Simon, I know you two want the best for Rachel, so do I, but I won't have it at the expense of her heart. Now," Ryan ripped off the tape. "Spill it."

"Sir," Paydar said, in an ugly whine directed at John, but John refused to look at him. "It wasn't my fault, I didn't know you changed…"

"Don't say a word." John growled, looking at his sons. Simon couldn't look away, his nostrils' started to flare and his eyes held a hint of glassiness. "Nothing happened…"

"Dad?" Ryan said, and his tone spoke for them all.

"I said nothing happened!" John turned to Nick in angry desperation. "You may want to take your brother and his wife and leave my family to me."

"No," Simon said, the trimmer in his voice brought all eyes to him. "Dad, is what he said true?"

"Don't you dare question me!"

"I dare!" Simon thundered. "Did you plan to do that to Rachel?"

"I don't answer to you!" John shouted. "I can't believe you would ask me that kind of question."

"Dad," Ryan whispered in stunned disbelief. "How could you?"

443

"Who said I did anything?" John tried, even though he knew it was a loss cause. "All you have is his word, is that all you need to turn against your own father?"

"You're not much better then Henry was." Sophia cried, and buried her face against Blake's chest.

"All I wanted was to protect my child." Now he was begging them to understand, but he still wouldn't admit to doing anything wrong.

"From what?" Simon yelled, his face red with fury. "Her own offspring? Do you even realize what you almost did? Do you have any idea what would've happened if you had succeeded?"

"I almost got rid of him." John pointed at Nick. "If I had succeeded..." He clamped his lips tight as he realized what he had said.

"You almost lost your family." Nick growled. "Just like you're trying to make me lose mine."

"You have no family, that girl and her child are my family, Henry will never touch them again." John hissed.

"Dad," Ryan said softly. "Henry is dead."

"Mom's coming." Simon snarled.

"We'll continue this later." John hissed.

"And what makes you think I won't tell your wife?" Nick threatened. "Maybe she would see things my way."

"Please," John said, but his hard tone belied the word. "Don't you do it, if I lose her you'll never rest, I'll track you to the ends of this earth."

"You won't have to, because I'll be on your door step every second of every day." Nick promised, as he spoke he walked closer to John and Ryan stepped between them. Blake grabbed Nick's arm, and pulled him away.

"Let's go Nick, this is beneath you don't hide behind a woman's skirts."

Nick shook off his hold, and glared at John. "Do you know how I felt when he came to me and told me to come see Rachel and tell her we were over? You don't know how that ripped my heart out." He turned fully to face John. "You cold hearted bastard! You planned to keep her locked away just so I wouldn't see her. Now, it's my turn, lets see how you like it."

"No Nick," Ryan said. "If you love Rachel don't do this. She won't thank you for it."

"Don't do what?" Pat said.

Blake pulled Nick towards the exit while Nick and John continued to glare at each other.

"Oh now I see what all the yelling is about." Bianca said. "You all spotted him."

Simon looked at Bianca, then his mother and turned and walked out the same door Nick and Blake had just exisited.

"What's wrong with him?" Pat asked. "He's not going after Nick is he?"

"No mama," Ryan said. "He's just going to blow off some steam."

"He was that mad," Pat asked totally mystified. "When are you all going to get over this?" She snapped. "Her delivery was the most beautiful thing I've ever seen. Rachel loves that man and he loves her, and that child needs its father. I won't have any of you getting in the way of that."

"Yes mama," Ryan said, but he couldn't keep the anger from his voice. "Dad I think this belongs to you."

He shoved Paydar towards John and walked away.

"Oh Doctor," Pat said, but her voice held a hint of reproach. "You missed the whole thing, but the midwife did great. You may want to check in on Rachel though just to make sure she's okay."

Dr. Paydar looked at John. "Is that okay with you Sir?"

"Yes, make sure she's alright, and don't go near that child."

"Yes Sir," he squeaked then hurried off.

"What was that about?" Pat asked, staring after the retreating man.

"Nothing, when can I see Rachel?"

"Not until they get her cleaned up."

*****

"Mama!" Rachel screamed. "Mama!"

"Ma'am, you've got to calm down, this isn't good for the baby."

"Mama!" Rachel was beside herself. All she could think of was being in her mother's arms.

"I'm here baby," Pat hurried back into the room. They were almost finished getting Rachel cleaned up.

"Where did you go? I need you here. Why did you leave?" She cried huge tears, and even she didn't know why she was crying.

"Hush," Pat said. "I went to make sure Nick got out of here all right. If your father and brothers ran into him it would probably bring down the whole hospital. But everything was okay."

"Did he leave? Nick, I mean…is he gone?"

"Yes darling, he walked right through the whole

lot of them and everyone lived."

"Hold me Mama," Rachel asked. "Could you just hold me for a second?"

"Yes darling," Pat put one arm under Rachel's head, and held her close to her heart. "I'm so proud of you honey. You did wonderful."

"She is beautiful isn't she?"

"Yes, and you'll make a wonderful mother."

"You think so...I held her and she's...she's so wonderful. I..." Rachel couldn't seem to stop the tears.

"Ma'am I'm going to have you get up and walk to the chair and have a seat so we can clean the bed."

"What?" Pat asked, "She doesn't get her own room?"

"This is a birthing room. She does every thing here."

"But when we took the tour, they didn't show us this."

"This wing was under construction. Mr. Rawlins, made the arrangements. But he said if you don't like this room you don't have to stay here. There are other rooms available."

Rachel was deeply touched. It never dawned on her that they were in a special room. She had thought it strange that she hadn't been moved to the delivery room, but then she had been in to much pain to really care. "This is fine. I'll stay here."

"The room is designed for the mother and child to stay here from labor to post partum, but you do have a choice."

"No, I'll stay."

"We'll bring the baby in just a moment."

"Okay."

Dean King

The nurse left and with Pat's help Rachel eased
out of bed and wrapped the gown securely around her,
then walked to the chair. "This baby having stuff is
difficult." She tried to laugh, then clutched her stomach.
"That feels awful."

"It will for a while, but don't worry. You'll be just
like I was, I lost my baby weight with in six months of
each child."

"I hope I'm as lucky as you Mom."

"Do you want to talk about Nick?"

"No," Rachel shook her head. "Not yet, I know I
have to, but I can't yet."

"Let's just get you settled. Then you can deal with
the other things when you get out of here."

"Thanks for understanding Mom. Do me a favor?"

"What is it?"

"I can't see him yet. Can you make sure he
doesn't come in here?"

"But Rachel,"

"No Mom, I can't do it. I may say some things
that…never mind. Just don't let him in here."

"It's not fair to him."

"I know, but if he comes to see her, I'll leave the
room."

"But he has the right to be here."

"It would be easier if you told him to leave."

"You want me to do that?"

"Please?"

"So, he can't see her, and he should leave the
hospital all together?"

"Yes."

"Alright, I'll talk to him when I leave here."

"I know it sounds mean, but I don't feel strong

448

enough to face him.”

"I understand, it's your choice.”

"But you don't agree?”

"I haven't been through what you've gone through. You know that man better than anyone, but I wouldn't be able to sleep at night if I didn't tell you this once again. It seems to me he did what he did to protect you. He was as much a victim as you were. If he had given you back what do you think your father would've done to him knowing what Nick had already done to you? Either way Nick probably thought he was going to die. But he hung onto you, and tried his best to keep you safe. I believe his letting us think you were dead was cruel, but it saved your life…”

"Mom, we've discussed this before, can you just find him and give him my message. Tell him when I leave here he can call and we can set up a good time for him to see her.”

"Alright,” Pat was quiet, but Rachel knew that wasn't the end of it. But she couldn't take any more. Not right now, not when her heart screamed to be in his arms and her brain denied the need. All she wanted was to hold her child.

*****

Bianca stood at the entrance to the waiting room. She had just left Sophia with Rachel. They seemed to be the best of friends. Sophia offered a shoulder to cry on and Rachel accepted. Feeling this side of left out, Bianca had decided to give them some alone time. She knew she would always be best friends with Rachel, but now she felt a strange distance between them. Rachel had changed.

And Bianca was trying hard to understand it. Now here she stood, staring at Simon's broad back and wishing she could turn and walk away before he could see her. Their fight weeks ago was still fresh in her mind. Again she wondered how men could be so pigheaded. Just when you think you've found a sensible one they go off and do something stupid and make you question your own sanity. She had been leaving the kitchen with Rachel's glass of crushed ice, when Simon had walked in.

He had looked at her with something she couldn't name. She had been trying her best to ignore him since they had gotten back from Mexico. But just the day before she had decided to stop hiding from him, there was no point. If he had something to say to her, then he should just come out and say it. She already decided that she would try to understand anything he had to say, then she would pack her bags and move out. It was time, she could've graduated a year ago. She had already gotten a Bachelor's degree in history. But she had decided to get her masters degree just because Rachel was still in school. But now Rachel was moving on without her, so it was time to put her degree to work. Last week she applied for a teaching position. It was in a high school on the outskirts of Houston. If she got the job, she had planned to rent an apartment and get on with her life.

But just when she was about to beat a hasty retreat out of the kitchen he surprised her by speaking.

"How have you been?"

She turned so quickly she spilled some of the ice. "Oh," Bea put the glass on the counter top and looked for a towel. When she looked up she found Simon standing in front of her with a towel in his hand.

"I'll get it." He said, and bent to clean up the

mess.

"No, no," she said trying to keep the nervousness from her voice. "Don't do that, I'll get it." She reached for the towel but he was already done.

Bea looked down at his gorgeous bent head and had to look away when he looked up. "You didn't have to do that." She whispered, her heart fluttering like a wild bird.

"It's nothing," he tossed the towel in the stainless steel sink, and leaned back on it. "Just wanted to help."

She clenched her teeth against the flush she felt flooding her cheeks. "Thanks."

"So," he looked at her with an intensity that made her look away. "I asked how you are?"

"I…I'm fine, never better."

"Really?"

"I'd be better if Rachel and Nick would stop being so stupid, and go ahead and get back together."

"Why would you say something stupid like that?" he roared.

"Why is that stupid? They love each other. If I loved someone like that nothing would keep me from him. I think she's afraid to disappoint you and dad, that's why she won't go back to him."

"You know nothing about what happened out there when he had Rachel do you? You said yourself he took her against her will. What they had wasn't real. They were living in a fantasy world Nick created."

"So you admit he loves her?"

"I admit he may think he loves her."

"And why do you say they shouldn't have the chance to prove their love?"

"That bastard can suffer for the rest of his life for

what he did to this family."

"Is that what all this is about? Revenge?"

"That and then some."

Her heart sank. "I thought you were better then that Simon." Her eyes began to tear, and her lower lips started to tremble. "I didn't think you were the type to judge people. I had hoped you would have an open mind, and be able to accept anything that was thrown at you."

"Of course I can, I do have an open mind."

"Except when it comes to love, right?"

"Their love."

She shook her head and left the room, she was glad he didn't try to stop her.

Here he was again. When she had stood still as stone in that huge kitchen facing him, she realized she still loved him, she couldn't stop no matter how mean he was or what he did, she still loved him and the only thing she could do about it is to live with it. When they were children he had never been an easy person to know, he always had his nose buried in a book or he would be running around outside. She remembered when she'd heard the news of his engagement.

She had been twelve years old and deeply in love with him. It had been the worst time in her life. She'd thought she was going to die. That had been the moment she realized he didn't see her as anything but a sister. She hadn't wanted to be his sister, she still didn't. But that day she'd wanted to run away and hide from the world, from his grinning face as he told his tale of love and broke her young heart.

Yesterday, it came back to her and she understood her feelings. It was as if a light bulb had gone off in her brain. Today, could she face the beast that held her heart?

She didn't want to, but she had to do it. She walked into the room and went to the window and stood next to him.

They were quiet for a moment, and then she broke the silence. "I love the way the sun bounces off the deep green of the tree tops at this level."

"It's kinda like looking down at the clusters of broccoli. Rich, thick, green."

She looked at him, and he looked at her. They both laughed.

"I must be hungry." Simon murmured.

"I don't remember the last time I ate." Bianca said.

"Do you want to go down to the cafeteria and get a bite?"

"Sure." She nodded, and turned she fell into step beside him. "Have you seen the baby?"

He nodded.

"What do you think of your niece?"

He smiled. "I got to hold her." His whole face seemed to glow. "Her little hand curled around my pinky and she looked right at me, it was as if she knew who I was."

"What do you think?"

"What can I think? That sweet bit of life is the most beautiful thing I've ever seen. I love her already."

"I take it you want some of your own?"

"Of course," Simon said, and he seemed surprised she would even think otherwise. Bianca's heart crashed. "What about you?" he asked. "Don't you want your own children some day?"

"No," she shook her head. "I mean yes, but I can't have kids. Besides, what kinda parent would I make? I haven't had the best upbringing. I wouldn't know what to do, or not to do. My kids would probably turn out more messed up then I did."

"There's nothing wrong with you Bea."

She laughed, but it was weak even to her ears. "I'm not like you guys." She turned her head to look at him. "You were raised to be honorable, steadfast, trustworthy, responsible... I could go on and on..."

"Yes," he said in a tight voice and she didn't understand the undercurrent she was getting from him right now.

"But so were you, my parents have had a hand in raising you since you were little. Are you saying they did well by us, but not you?"

"No, I'm saying what we are, we are at birth. No one can take certain things away. If you were born with anger problems, your parents would teach you how to manage it, unless they don't know themselves. If that's the case then all is lost."

"What are you trying to say Bea?"

"I'm leaving when Rachel gets home." She waited, on the one hand she wanted him to take her in his arms and tell her not to go, but on the other hand she wished he would kiss her forehead and tell her to be happy, then walk away.

"Why?"

"Because I'm all grown up now. My best friend is now a mama. I'm so happy for her, but it's time for me to get out from under foot."

"Can you just walk away?" He asked, and she looked at him.

"I'd never just walk away. I love you," her heart caught as she admitted her true feelings, but she continued to deliberately mislead him. "I love your whole family, I'll come back. I'll visit my little god child as often as I can."

"You can just pick up and leave?" He asked again, he seemed mystified, she couldn't make him understand. To do that would mean telling of her illness and there was no way she could do that. "We've had too much turmoil lately. This is the last thing Rachel needs." He sounded angry now. "How could you be so selfish Bea? She needs you, don't run away."

"She has her whole family. I believe she'll be happy for me. Besides, she and Sophia have more in common then she and I have, it's time for me to get on with my life."

"So you haven't told her?"

"No, not yet, but I plan to tonight."

"Christ!" He snarled. "Not you too." She wanted to shrink away from the look he gave her.

"What are you talking about?"

"I'm not hungry, I'm going home, tell Rachel I'm there if she needs me after you break her heart."

"That's not fair Simon." She yelled at his departing back. "Come back here!"

Bianca stood in the nearly deserted hallway, and stared as his image became smaller and smaller. She was doing the right thing, leaving to start her life wasn't the same as running away. She turned and headed back towards Rachel's room.

*****

"Honey," Pat said as she ran her hand lovingly over Rachel's freshly combed hair. "That baby is so lovely. I swear she has your nose and your strong chin."

455

"And his eyes, his hair, his ears and she even has his dimples."

"That may change you know," Pat tried to ease some of the tension coming from Rachel. "The eye color could take up to a year to change. But sometimes it does change."

"She even frowns like him."

"Oh Rachel," Bianca sighed. "It was so romantic. Nick there ready to catch the baby with a tear in his eye, and that smile he gave you. Didn't it make you happy that he was there?"

"Bea," Rachel said, as she brushed the baby's hair with her hand. "If I said it once I've said it a thousand time. I DON'T CARE!"

"Of course you do."

"No I don't!"

"Say what you like, but I know you still love him."

"Is that so bad?" Pat asked.

"Has he been by to see her?" Rachel said.

"He hasn't left the hospital since she was born. That first day, he went home and changed then he came back. He's been pretty good about staying away from your father and brothers. He and Blake just disappear when Sophia is here."

"How do you know he hasn't left?" Rachel tried to keep the eagerness from her voice.

"I've talked to him." Pat said.

"What, when?"

"When you told me to, and every day since."

"Why are you still talking to him?"

"Because he's the father of my grandchild, and when I go to the nursery he's in there holding her."

"He was in the nursery?"

"Yes, and I might say he has that place buzzing at how protective he is. If I didn't know better I'd think he would make a fine father."

"What do you mean know better?"

"You've told me how cruel and hateful he is. I wouldn't want someone like that to raise my grandchild."

"He…he…well he wasn't that bad."

"What do you mean?"

"Nothing, when you talking to him next, tell him to stop sending all this junk. There are so many flowers in here it's starting to stink."

"If you think this is bad wait until you get home. Between Nick and your father the house is almost filled with every kind of flower you can name."

"Tell the Nurses in the nursery, I want her to stay in the room with me from now on."

"That would be mean, to do that to him is wrong."

"Wrong?" She snapped. "What about what he did to me? Wasn't that wrong? Did I ask to be dragged half way across Mexico? I'm not going to let him fond all over my child. He didn't even want her, and he hasn't even tried to see me."

"But you told him not to. Anyway, your father and Simon won't let him near you."

"Thank god for that, I don't need him in here filling my head with all his lies. I still can't believe I was that naive. How did I let him hoodwink me like that?"

"You weren't naïve," Pat assured her. "You're young, and I think you made the right choices."

"No I didn't, I shamed the whole family by falling in love with the enemy. I feel so stupid."

"Look, you're coming home tomorrow lets talk

about it then."

"No, there's no need, I'm done talking about this."

"Have you filled out the birth certificate?"

"Yes, her name is Dominque Patrica McKinney."

"Oh Rachel, you do love him, you named her for him." Bianca gushed.

"No, I don't love him," Rachel snapped. "I named her that so that everytime I look at her I remember never to make the same mistake again."

"Rachel that is a cruel thing to say!" Pat snapped.

"I don't mean it that way," Rachel sighed. "I love this child with all my heart, and she'll never know what a creep her father is. But I have to have a way to protect myself. This will keep me strong."

"Well, I think you did it because you love him," Bianca snapped. "And you'll never convince me otherwise."

Rachel didn't look at her, "I'm done mom, I really need to sleep."

"All right, I'll be back in the morning." Pat placed a kiss on Rachel's head then gathered her things and they left.

Twenty-Three

NICK FELT HER PRESENTS, but he refused to look up. "I love your daughter."

"I know that," Pat said, he turned away from the nursery window and looked at her.

"No matter what you may think of me," he whispered. "I love her."

"It's not about what I think, it's about what she thinks."

"Your husband won't accept it."

"I know that too."

"I'll fight him."

"You'll have to fight her too."

"I know, but I'll win with her."

"How do you know?"

"Because she loves me as much as I love her."

"Should I start planning the wedding?" Pat joked.

"Yes, just make sure you plan to have it outside with whatever color flowers she likes. Anything else you want to add do so and send the bill to me. I'll give you my address and phone number."

"Are you serious?" She frowned.

"Yes, I've never been more serious."

"When do you think I should start?" Pat was starting to get excited.

"Give me six months, if it looks like it'll be sooner I'll let you know. But Rachel is very stubborn, so it may take a while."

"You're very sure of yourself aren't you?"

"I'm fighting for my life, without Rachel I have no life. I have to win."

"I'm happy to hear that. I'll help as much as I can, but what I've come to tell you isn't good."

"Let me have it," Nick braced himself, he had hoped she wanted to see him, and talk things through but from the sound of things that wasn't the case.

"The baby will be moved into Rachel's room permanently, she asked me to ask you to stop sending the flowers. You are to call her when she gets home from the hospital, to make arrangements if you are still interested in seeing or being a part of your daughters life."

His heart flipped at the word daughter. He still couldn't believe he was a father. It was beyond reason, and despite what he had thought earlier in life, now he was the happiest man alive. Now if Rachel would come back into his arms, his life would be complete.

*****

Pat was at her whit's end. Something was wrong, not only with Rachel, but with everyone in the house. Weeks had gone by since Rachel and Niki had come home and everyone seemed to walk passed each other as if they didn't exist. That wasn't her family. This was going to have to stop.

Pat grabbed everyone she passed and told them to meet her in the family room. She stuck her head into Rachel's room and saw both girls on the bed playing with the baby. "I want you two in the family room right now."

"But Mom," Rachel started but Pat held up her

hand.

"No, this is an over due conversation. That child is two months old and everyone here is walking on egg shells. Get in that family room."

She closed the door and marched down the hall.

John sat in his chair at his desk in his office. He was working on his third bourbon, and it was only two in the after noon. But he couldn't help it. He was as much a monster as Henry had been. John put his head in his hands and shook it. A sob caught on his lips. Now his children hated him. He had taught them to be honest and trustworthy and now they saw every thing he'd done as false. They didn't believe him any more, and worst yet they didn't believe in him. That stabbed him straight through his heart. He couldn't even touch his wife without feeling as if he had contaminated her. As for Rachel. He stopped and sucked in a shaky breath. He was man enough to realize he'd ruined her life. Dominick had suffered the lost of so many family members. And from all he knew about the boy, he seemed to be as solid and trustworthy as one of his own sons'. "Why!" John raged in silent distress. "Why did I do it to them?" He had no answers. He needed the answers if he were going to get his family back. As it was Pat barely talked to him. After everything he'd done he deserved everything she gave him.

There was a loud banging on the door. "John I know you're in there and I know what you're doing. I need to see you in the family room. Be there in five minutes."

He sighed as she stomped off. She was angry, and she had every right to be. He was glad he had an apartment in town because, after tonight he might need a permanent residence. He wiped his face then pulled out a small key. He inserted it in a lock on a drawer in his desk and pulled out two stacks of letters. He tucked them into his jacket pocket. Then wiped his face again, this time he picked up the tumbler and downed the rest of the drink. He picked up the phone and made a call, then John walked like a man headed to the gallows, out the room and towards the family room and what could be the end of the family he fought so hard to build.

*****

Nick was done waiting. After months of playing the good guy and waiting for Rachel to come to her senses he was bone tired of this limbo. He'd promised Blake he wouldn't go to Rachel's' home alone. But Nick didn't need anyone to go with him, this was his fight and his fight alone. Blake was at the hospital with Sophia for her doctor's appointment. So if he were going to do this, he had to do it now. He needed to talk to John, then he would talk to Rachel. So far every time he went to their home to see his child Rachel was absent, either Bianca or a Nanny brought the baby out to him, and it was the worst feeling in the world to know that Rachel couldn't bring herself to look at him. Today he was going to be the bully. He would talk to her if it were the last thing he did.

*****

"Sophia I don't think we should be doing this." Blake said as they arrived at the McKinney gate that led to their drive.

"It's okay, I'll only stay for a moment. It's just

that I can't shake this dream. I think she needs me. You know I'd never come if I wasn't sure."

"I know," Blake fretted. "But you are so close to delivering. I don't think you should be out and about."

"I've had two children already, I know what I'm doing." She reached over and patted his arm. "I swear we won't stay long."

"Alright," Blake sighed as he took in the stately house in front of him. This was the first time he had brought Sophia here. Every time she and Rachel met it had been at their home. Rachel had insisted he not be there when she came over. Blake was okay with that, he'd go to Nick's and wait for a call when he could come home. He'd actually spent the night at Nick's when Rachel and Sophia had one of their sleepovers. It helped that his children loved it when Rachel and the baby came to visit. It also helped prepare them for when they get their own little one. He couldn't shake the feeling that coming here today wasn't a good idea.

*****

Pat stood in front of the brightly lit windows. It was two thirty in the afternoon and the sun was making it's way to this side of the house and lighting the room in a pretty rosy glow. It didn't phase the occupants of the room one bit. Simon sat in a winged back chair near the piano it was as if he didn't want to be there so he was as close to the door as he could get. Bianca sat on the settee with Rachel softly chatting about something, and Ryan stood at the window behind Pat staring out at something. Pat clasped her hands in front of her. She didn't know where to begin. She wanted to wait for John, but he

463

seemed at odds with everyone in the room. Briefly she wondered if she should go on without him and just talk to him later. That seemed a more likely idea, the two hadn't really talked since Tyrell's funeral.

"Ryan," Pat said and he looked at her. "I need you to have a seat in the chair next to the settee." He nodded and went to the chair. "Simon, you too, take the other chair."

"I'm fine where I am," Simon grumbled.

"I asked you politely Simon," Pat snapped. "If I have to say it again you won't like the way I say it, get your butt in that chair."

"What's the point?"

"That's the point!" She snapped. "Your attitudes are what's wrong. Now, do as I asked."

With a huge sigh Simon took the seat next to Bianca.

"I can say the only good thing that has happened to this family has been Niki's birth. That baby has brought some much needed joy to our sagging faces. It's been hard with Tyrell's death. This family has always been strong, and I don't want to let what happened in Mexico ruin what we had." Pat folded her hands in front of her, and looked at each one of them. "I want each of you to tell me what's wrong? What is it that keeps you all from talking to each other?"

No one said a word, neither did they look up. "Alright," Pat said. "I'll go first." She walked to the desk and sat on top of it, her legs swinging in front of her. "I feel lost. I don't know how to explain it, but there's a hole in my heart and I feel as if I'm empty. I love you all, and I know I'm surrounded by your love, but I lost one of my children. For a while I lost focus of everything else. I think Niki pulled me out of that. Seeing her, preparing for her birth, gave me a reason to live again. She helped me in the same way I want to help you all." She stopped when all eyes were on her, and dabbed at a stray tear. "I haven't shared this with anyone not even your father. But I think Tyrell's death is putting a wedge between your father and you children. I know ya'll need us, but if he's anything like me John's heart hurts. He's heart sick and he, like the rest of us, can't handle this alone. We need each other."

No one spoke.

"Please say something." Pat cried.

Bianca cleared her throat and spoke up. "I applied for a job in Houston as a History teacher just before Niki was born."

"What?" Rachel cried. "When, how? Why didn't you tell me?"

"I wanted to see if I'd get it before I told anyone."

"Well?" Rachel prompted.

"I got the job." Rachel jumped up, and screamed with joy, and Bianca followed suit.

"Oh my god!" Rachel cried. "Oh my god! You're a teacher." Rachel squeezed her tight and swayed in her joy. "I'm so happy for you."

Bianca pulled away, and looked at Rachel. "Are you sure you're happy? I thought you might be upset."

"Why would I be? We're sisters, that bond is never broken. You could move to the end of the earth, and I'd still call you and you'd have to come home for all the important events. And I'd have to plan your wedding." Rachel caught Bianca's head between her hands, and kissed her cheek. "Together forever?"

Bianca's eyes watered, and she nodded.

"Well," Ryan said. "We're going to have a teacher in the family. I never thought that would happen."

Bianca broke away, from Rachel's embrace and her eyes went to Simon only to find him staring at them, and he quickly looked away. "Now," she said. "For the bad news." She sucked in her breath and continued. "I'm moving out. I rented a small condo off highway six near Richmond road. It's close to where I'll be teaching. I'll start moving my things by Friday."

"So soon?" Pat asked.

"Yes," Bianca said. "It's time I did something with my life. We never know how long we have on this earth and I'm ready to start living."

Ryan stood up and walked to her. "You're not trying to escape us are you?"

"Never!" She said and smiled as his arm snaked, around her waist and he gave her a squeeze.

"I should've asked you to marry me when I had the chanc..." He didn't finish. All eyes turned to Simon as he jumped from his chair, and headed for the door.

"Simon!" Pat yelled. "Sim..."

He stopped in his tracks as the doors were opened and John stood staring at him, with Nick standing behind him.

*****

John's head lifted at the light tap on his study door. "Who's there?"

"Sir," Malcolm, the butler said softly. "Your guest has arrived."

"Bring him in." John stood up and waited.

Nick didn't know why John had called him and

demanded he come here. But he did know either way he was going to be in this spot. It was time they spoke like men, face to face.

"Sir," Nick began, but John waved him to silence.

"Call me John," At Nick's raised eyebrow he went on. "I'd like you to have a seat."

Nick gave a tight nod and took a seat in front of the desk. At first glance things seemed different. Less hostile, but Nick didn't want to let his guard down. Any thing could happen.

John sat and clasped his fingers on the desk in front of him. "Let me start by saying I'm sorry."

Nick froze, and swallowed hard. Maybe this wasn't going to be too painful.

"I had no right to do what I planned to do to you, and Rachel. All I can say is I'm sorry. If you want you can come with me to speak with my family."

"But Sir..." Nick started, but John cut him off.

"I was about to separate you from your family, the least I can do is let you watch as my family separates from me." John stood up, and walked towards the door and out the room.

Nick jumped up, and followed. His mind was full of what he wanted to say, but now what was there left to say?

John opened the door in time to see everyone standing and Simon ready to escape the scene.

John walked past them all, and Nick followed, but he had eyes only for Rachel. She looked lovely in her gray shirt and pants. But she looked away from him, and he took that as a bad sign.

"I want everyone to get in here and close the door."

Simon sighed and closed the door. Everyone took their seats, but Nick stood near the window. He didn't feel the need to be there. This had nothing to do with him.

"Pat," John said, and already Nick could see tears in John's tired eyes. "First, I want to say I'm sorry to all of you. I hurt everyone in this room. The only way I can explain it is male pride." John bowed his head, and his shoulders began to shake. All the women stood up, ready to go to him, but he slammed his fists down on the desk top, and they all jumped back. He looked at them all with such fierce pain Nick had to look away. "I'm so damned sorry." John looked at Rachel, and he did cry. He held his hand out to her and she came to him.

Rachel looked around, her heart ached for her father, but she didn't know why he was so torn up. It was hard to concentrate on anything with Nick standing so close. Now that she knew what she really felt for him it was almost funny, how he must have laughed at the little girl as he called her, for believing she loved him. It was funny even to her. But now her father needed her. She went into John's arms, and hugged him tight. She rubbed his back in a caressing motion. "It's okay daddy, we all do things we're not proud of. It'll all work it's self out."

He nodded, and lifted his head from her shoulder. Pat handed him a handkerchief, and he let go of Rachel and wiped his face. "Ryan, it was you who snapped me out of my insanity." He gave a choked laugh, then looked at them all. "I have loved everyone of you since the moment I knew your mother was pregnant with you. I understand what you felt Rachel, and you too Nick when you first held that tiny bit of life up stairs." He gave a watery laugh. "Simon, the second you came out all warm and wet I held you and you urinated right in my face."

Everyone laughed, but it was a tense laugh as they all waited. John wiped his face. "First," he reached into his pocket and pulled out two stacks of envelopes. He handed one to Rachel, then looked at her. "Give this to Nick for me darling."

Rachel's hands trembled as she recognized her writing. "These are my letters."

John nodded. "And those are his to you. I want you to keep his and give him yours." Too numb to think she nodded and went to Nick. Rachel handed him the letters, and her eyes clashed with his, then she turned and took her seat next to Bianca, his letters crushed in her sweaty palms.

John continued. "I did so many things wrong. I want you all to know what I did, and why I did it."

"But Honey…" Pat started.

"No, no you don't know Patsy, I would never hurt any of you. Nick, I don't even know you, but what I do know of you tells me you are a good man, despite who your father was."

Nick was touched by that, and he looked at Rachel but she refused to look his way.

"I don't deserve any of you," John continued, his tone heavy with self reproach. "I had Malcolm pack a suitcase for me. After I'm done here I'll leave. And if we can get passed what I've done…we'll see where it goes."

"Are you leaving me John?" Pat asked in a voice that brought more tears to his eyes.

"I'd rather not," he gave a small wet chuckle. "But I don't know myself any more. Just let me say this, then you tell me if I need to go."

She swallowed hard, her eyes on him.

Nick felt a moment of panic for John, he knew

469

what John was going to say. He pushed off the ledge and hurried to John's side and whispered in his ear. "You don't have to do this Sir. It's over, they don't need to know."

John whispered back. "I can't live with myself, I have to tell them. It's tearing me up inside."

Nick nodded, and went back to his place.

"I'm ashamed of myself for having done this, but," John announced. "I hired doctor Paydar to be Rachel's private physician."

"But it was wonderful to know you cared so much." Pat said.

"It wasn't that I cared Pat," John bit out. "I hired him to keep the baby quiet when it was born, and tell Rachel it had died." He ignored the gasped that filled the room and pushed on. "I had a couple waiting to take the baby and adopt it."

Rachel's disbelieving gaze flew to his tortured face. "No," her face crumpled as the words sank in. "No, daddy…no…" she shook her head against his words and Nick wanted to take her in his arms, but Pat beat him to it.

"I'm so sorry, if it wasn't for Nick I would've made a horrible mistake." John said.

Pat looked at Nick. "How did you know?"

Nick looked at John with a question in his eyes and John nodded. "John came to me in Mexico, he threatened me and told me to come here and break things off with Rachel, but I wouldn't do it, that's when he mentioned that he would do if Rachel were pregnant."

"How could you John?" Pat asked in total disbelief. "Your own child?

Rachel lifted her head from Pat's shoulder, and stared at Nick. "Was that when he paid you off?"

"He never paid me off." Nick denied.

"You liar!" Rachel shouted through her tears. "He showed me the canceled check with your signature, two hundred fifty thousand dollars. You said you wanted your money back, I guess you got it."

"I swear to you I didn't cash any check." Nick shouted. "He offered but I told him I didn't want his money."

"It got cashed and I never saw you!" She screamed. "It was as if we never were. You didn't even try to see me."

"I cashed it." They all turned to the small voice that came from the open door way. Sophia stood next to Blake, her cheeks ruby red.

"Why?" Nick said.

"I was doing laundry and I checked the pockets of one of your shirts, inside I found the check, and I deposited it for you. We were trying to get all Henry's money together and I thought if I took care of this for you I'd be doing you a favor."

Rachel started laughing, it was a laugh that bordered on hysteria. She shook loose of Bianca and Pat and ran past Blake and Sophia and out the room. Nick ran after her. He caught her at the base of the stairs.

"Rachel!" She froze, and turned to face him, her chest heaving. "Please talk to me."

"About what?" she all but screamed. "About how I waited for you? How about you never wrote me not even to say thank you for the dog! Maybe we should talk about how you knew what my father was doing and never told me!"

He caught her arms, and pulled her close and kissed her softly. She pulled away and drew back and slapped him across his face, and then she turned and ran up the stairs.

Nick rubbed his cheek and shook his head. He turned and walked out the front door with Blake and Sophia close on his heels.

Pat turned to John, and watched as Bianca ran out after Rachel. Ryan and Simon had also disappeared. She fell to the settee. "Why John?"

He came and sat next to her on the settee. John was careful not to touch her the look in her eyes was so devastating he wanted to hide from it. "I thought about it Patsy, I've thought every second of every moment since Niki was born. I think, I felt cheated. Deep down I wanted to kill Henry with my bare hands, but I couldn't. His own child killed him before I could get the chance, yet my child kept suffering. I can't stand what he did to her and Bianca, I felt as if he got away with hurting them. I may have gone a bit insane with vengeance. All I can do now is pick up the pieces. I need to know that you'll stand by my side. Help me through this, God knows Rachel must hate me."

"I...I don't know what to say. I'd never have thought you would be capable of something like this."

"I know, I didn't know I had it in me to do this to one of my own grandchildren. But you have to see where I was at the time. I was seething inside, I needed to get even with Henry, I needed to take away some of the hurt Rachel had gone through."

"But this kills me John, it... would you have really gone through with it if Nick hadn't stopped you?"

"No," John shook his head. "At the last possible moment I cancelled the contract. I was on my way to tell the doctor that all bets were off, and to just deliver the baby and give it to Rachel. But Nick beat me to it."

"Don't move out John, I need time to think, but I don't want you gone, I don't think I could live with that."

"No, I have to go. I want Rachel to feel safe." His voice broke on that word, and she touched his hand. "I need to give her space."

"Please don't move out, I'm sure she'll forgive you."

"This is my own doing, I have to go, and hopefully it'll only be for a short while." He kissed her cheek and stood up. John walked to the door and through it.

*****

Bianca hurried into Rachel's room. "Oh Rachel I'm so sorry I don't know what to say."

"What can you say," Rachel said through her tears. "My own father was going to sell my child."

"Rachel he wasn't thinking, he was hurt and angry. I'm not trying to make excuses for him, but he did say he called it off."

"Yes," she snapped bitterly. "Only after Nick saved us."

"Nick did save you, didn't he?"

"Don't say it like that!" Rachel fumed. "He may have saved his daughter, but he's still not a nice guy."

"He looks good."

"So," Rachel wiped her eyes, and sat on her bed preparing to feed Niki. She refused to look at the stack of letters she'd tossed on her dresser.

"What did he want? Why was he here?"

Rachel looked at Bianca through lowered eyes.

473

"What is wrong with you?" She snapped. "He probably couldn't wait to tell me what a creep my father was."

"Oh Rachel, he didn't say anything about dad that dad didn't say himself."

"Nick made it plain that there was no love between us any more. I can live with that."

"I can't," Bianca said. "I'm tired of this. I love you Rachel, but you've changed. You don't smile, you don't joke, and you don't enjoy life any more. You still love him and your fighting it."

"I don't! It was sympathy and that's all. I thought I was in love because of our never ending contact with each other, because he was my only way to survive, and I convinced myself that I loved him."

"Oh, don't give me that psychology bullshit. You may have let that psychologist talk your head out of loving him, but you can never talk your heart out of it."

"That is ridiculous. If he loved me why did he abandon us so quickly?"

Bianca entreated. "Nick doesn't seem to be the kind of man that would take you away from your family. If your father said no, and ordered him away what do you think he would've done?"

"I would've hoped he would've fought for me. That he would've come to me and talked it out, not run away like some coward."

"Does that man strike you as a coward?"

"Yes!"

Bianca sighed. "He's no more a coward then you are, even though at this moment you're acting the part of the coward very well."

"You're a fine one to talk!" Rachel stood up, and buzzed for the nurse. She headed for the nursery with a fuming Bianca on her trail.

"What are you talking about?" Bianca demanded.

Rachel held up her hand. "Wait," the nurse came. "Jamie, could you feed Niki for me? How many bottles of breast milk do I have left in the freezer?"

"Two Ma'am."

"Fine, I'm going out tomorrow so I'll pump as many as I can tonight." Rachel kissed the baby's head and caressed her soft cheek. "Mommy will see you later darling."

The nurse turned and left the room. Rachel headed down a long corridor that led to the stairs and would take her to the library. She needed some time to think. She sighed in frustration when Bianca followed.

"Tell me what you meant?" Bianca demanded.

"This isn't the best time for this conversation."

"The hell it's not," Bianca grabbed Rachel's arm, and pulled her to a halt. "I am no coward!"

"How can you look at me and say that? You have loved Simon since the day you first laid eyes on him!"

Bianca gasped and her face drained of color. "I have not!"

"Liar."

"I don't!"

"Yes you do," Rachel accused. "Why are you fighting it? Why don't you go to him and tell him? I know why? Because you're a coward!"

"Stop it Rachel!" Bianca yelled. "You know I don't love him, and even if I did I shouldn't, I could kill him."

"Bullshit Bianca!" Rachel yelled, then turned and hurried down the hall. "You just don't want to get hurt, so you're playing it safe. You'd rather live a lie than take a chance on a man who may not love you."

"Why are you doing this? You know I'm sick, you know what could happen if I told him how I feel. Do you want me to do that to him?"

"Whom are you living for? Us? Him? Or yourself? Take the chance Bianca, let him know, then you can move on. Don't run away like some coward. You've been hiding in this house, close enough to touch him, look at him, but never love him. He's my brother and I love him. I love you too. He deserves to know the truth."

Bianca fell into the nearest chair and buried her face in her hands. Rachel went to her knees in front of her and took her hands from her face then held them. "You have to be honest with yourself. This thing with Nick has taught me that love is a wonderful thing, if you love for the right reason. You have the right reason, go for it. Tell him and let the chips fall where they may."

"But what if he hates me?"

"He doesn't hate you. He could never hate you. But if he doesn't love you like you love him, then it's better to know now. Then you can get out of this limbo. Go on with your life, for gods sake at least someone in this house can be happy."

"But I don't have a life Rachel. My life is over, and what if he does love me? How can I live with myself if I pass this on to him, to our children?"

"You could always adopt," both girls gasped, and both jumped.

"Simon." Bianca gasped, and shook her head in disbelief. She turned stunned eyes to Rachel. "I'm not ready.

"Here's your chance, get ready," Rachel whispered. "Don't blow it." She kissed her cheek, and gave Bianca's hand a small squeeze.

Bianca and Rachel stood up. Bianca straightened her shoulders, and faced him even though her heart was raging and she thought she might pass out. "How much did you hear?"

"Enough to know that you're in love with some guy, and you think he may hate you. It's none of my business, but I'd like to talk to you if you can spear a moment." Anxiety trembled through her, the anger in his eyes wasn't particularly pleasant to behold.

She gave a somber nod. "Let's go in the library Simon, I need to talk to you too."

"It's okay," Rachel whispered in her ear. "Remember, it's just big head Simon. He's still extremely ticklish and he's a big baby."

Bianca tried to smile, but her stomach was in to many knots. She watched Rachel hurry up the stairs, and wished she could go with her. Bianca turned and headed for the library, she was extremely conscious of Simon breathing down her neck.

Twenty-Four

RACHEL LOOKED UP FROM her packing. The door to her room stood open, and standing beside her was her father. He was the last person she wanted to see, but she was sure he knew that.

"You don't have to leave Rachel." He said in a tone, she had never heard him use. "I'm leaving, I've already had Malcolm arrange it."

"Why daddy? How could you do something like this?"

"I was desperate," John explained. "I thought I was doing what was best for you. I felt as if I had let you down."

"You have, I don't know if I can ever look at you the same way."

"And that hurts me more then you'll ever know." She looked away, but his words brought her eyes back to him. "You need to read these." She looked down, in his hand was the pack of envelopes tied together with a string.

"No, it's too late now. I had planned to burn them."

"Please,"

"Why?" she turned burning eye to him.

"Because," John said softly. "I want you to decide.

Forgive Me, My Love

You have to be the one to say if you love him or not."

"I already know how I feel. I didn't and don't love him."

"He wrote you two letters a week for four months. I kept them from you. Read them if you like if not toss them in the trash." His tone was almost pleading. "I love you, and I want you to see that he loves you too. Everything I did, I did because I didn't want you hurt anymore. I lost sight of so many things Rachel, I lost myself in my need to avenge my children. If you never want to see me again I understand, just remember I love you, and I'll never stop."

She held out her trembling hand and took the packet, and threw it on the bed. With a sad cry she tossed her arms around his shaking shoulders, and buried her face in his shoulders. "I love you dad." She cried through her tears. "I know why you did what you did, but it still hurts." She mumbled against his shirt. "I don't know what to think, or what to do."

He caressed her back. "I know darling, I feel as lost as you do." He lifted her chin until her tears stained face was looking up at his. "Could we find our way back together?" Her eyes flooded again as his voice cracked. "I…I want us to be a family again. Believe it or not I love that little girl. I see you all over again when I look at her." His hand caressed her back, and she was reminded of when she was a young child, and needed his comforting touch. "I have so many reason's why I did what I did, but the fact remains, none of them are good enough."

"We'll work through this together." She said. "Don't leave, we'll both stay put and try to fix this."

"Okay darling," he kissed her forehead, then gave her a small squeeze. "We'll talk again later?"

"Yes daddy," he nodded, and then she watched him walk out the door. She looked down at the letters that lay on the bed and her heart ached. Had Nick really cared? What would she find in those letters? There was only one way to find out.

*****

Simon followed Bea into the room, his eyes on her stiff back. It never occurred to him that she could be in love with someone else. In his mind she was his. He'd always imagined her in his arms until recently when she'd told him other wise. *So why talk to her? Did she know he loved her and wanted to let him down easy?* His lips twisted in anger. He wasn't some college guy who needed to be dealt with.

As soon as they walked in, she turned and closed the door. "Whatever the hell it is you want to say, say it so I can get outta here."

Her skin lost some of it's color, and her lips tightened. He hoped she was uncomfortable, he would never make it easy for her to break his heart.

"You may want to sit down for this," her voice squeaked as she waved him to a chair.

"I'm fine," he growled, and took a threatening step towards her. "Tell me what's going on Bianca, so I can get the hell out of this mad house."

Bianca clasped her hands in front of her, and began to pace, his tone was making this difficult. "I just wanted to say that... well... that I'm ill."

"What's wrong with you?" He frowned deeply and his heart picked up speed.

"I...I...I don't know how to say this," she turned

stricken eyes on him, and his expression softened at her obvious distress. "I've been sick for a long time. I know I have no reason to tell you this, but I want to. Now that I'm moving out, there's no reason to keep torturing myself. I don't want you to hate me."

He went to her and caught both her arms. "I could never hate you. Just tell me." Hope clogged his throat. Did she finally trust him enough to tell him the truth?

She gave a watery laugh and lifted glassy eyes to his face. "Yes you could, once you know my secret you could and should hate me."

"Just tell me."

"I'm dying." Stunned quiet met that comment. "I don't want to leave here without you knowing why I've been avoiding you."

His heart stopped. He hadn't thought she would put it like that, he almost wished she would tell him she was in love with some other guy, but then that may be still to come. He braced himself and frowned. "What? What do you mean, and I didn't know you were avoiding me."

She gave a small laugh and shrugged. "Of course you didn't why should you even notice if some one like me were talking to you or not."

"I would notice, stop being stupid, and tell me what this is about."

"Alright fine, I...I was careless with some guy when I was sixteen. Rachel and I went on double dates. We dared each other, well, we bet on who would be the first to make love with a guy. I wanted to win so I did that night. It was stupid, he was so much older than me. I should've done what Rachel did. Just get up and run away. But I didn't, and that one act of stupidity has cost me the love of a wonderful man and the life of any child I may have."

Simon felt so bad for her. This man she was so in love with had better treat her right. Simon knew he'd never get over the pain of losing her, but as long as she was happy then he could live with it. Gently he clasped her head between his hands, and looked into her eyes. "It's okay Bea, I'm sure your man will understand. Tell me the rest. I'm the closest thing you have to a big brother, use my shoulder to cry on."

Her eyes watered and she wanted to look away. "Oh God, this is hard."

"Tell me Bianca." He whispered his grip on her fierce.

She nodded, then whispered. "I have HIV."

Slowly he said. "Look at me." She turned tear filled eyes to him. "I know," he whispered against her quivering cheek. "I've always known."

"What?" She stiffened, and pulled slightly away from him. "How?"

"I over heard you and Rachel talking to Mom about it. I was angry at first, then I was hurt, not for myself, but for you. To have something like that happen to such a wonderful person is so unfair. I was ready to find that guy, and kill him with my bare hands, but in the end all I could do was leave. I wanted to… "

"Do you also…" she gave a shuddering sigh and looked up into his eyes, and Simon could feel his heart melting. "Do you also know that I love you? I've always loved you, and now I've ruined everything." She started to cry.

Simon closed his eyes as immense joy took hold of him. His heart took flight, and he kissed her eye lids, and then her cheeks. "Are you sure Bea?" he said between kisses. "Please tell me you're sure?"

"I am," she whispered. "I've always loved you and I always will."

And last his lips found her lips. Simon paused when she refused to open, he sighed and said. "Open for me baby."

"I can't," she whispered. "I have to protect you from me."

"Let me worry about that. Open for me," slowly, she looked at him, then did as he asked. She moaned as he plundered her depths, it was everything he'd imagined and more. To soon the kiss ended, and she sagged against him.

"So this is what real love feels like." She whispered against his shirt.

"Tell me what you feel? Is it anything like what I'm feeling?"

"I have this fierce urge to rip off your clothes and discover what's been hidden from me for so long."

"Is that all?" He chuckled, she was indeed feeling what he felt.

"No, I want to wake up in your arms everyday, and stay by your side forever." She detangled herself from his arms and walked away. "Those were the thoughts I've had of you for the past ten years. I wanted you to be my first and last." She paused, and then turned back to look at him. "But that year you were rumored to be engaged to your girlfriend Tamara. And I was so hurt, angry and confused. I wondered why you didn't like me? Why did you always treat me as if I never mattered?"

"It was because I loved you," he said and she turned to face him.

"What?"

"I've loved you since you were ten. I couldn't face the fact that my heart had betrayed me. You were just a child, I knew I couldn't have you, and besides you were almost my sister. If my parents had had their way they would've adopted you. I couldn't have you, not then, and over the years I convince myself that it was wrong. So when you became a teenager, and then a woman, I needed someone to take my mind off you. So I had planned to ask Tamara to marry me. But not because I loved her, it was to cleanse my soul of all the impure thoughts I had of you."

"But you never said," she murmured. "You loved me?"

"Yes, I've always loved you Bianca. I'm willing to take any amount of time God is willing to give me with you."

"But I can't do that to you Simon, I love you too much."

"I won't let you do anything else. I won't lose you. Just let me hold you, let me love you. We can go to your doctor and see what precautions we need to take. As for children we can cross that bridge when we get to it."

"No, no I can't, I can't do this to your parents. You can't put your life in jeopardy like this, they'd never forgive me."

Simon went to the phone, he quickly dialed a number. "Mom, is Rachel with you?"

"Yes, we're talking."

"What about Ryan is he home?"

"I think I saw him. What is it sweetheart?"

"Has dad left yet?"

"No, he's not going to leave. Rachel talked him

into staying."

"Fine," Simon said. "I have something very important to say to the family tonight so if you don't mind I want dad to be here to hear it. I'll tell cook the whole family will be at dinner tonight."

"But that only gives her two hours to prepare."

"She'll do it, I don't care what she prepares, I probably won't taste it anyway."

"Alright Darling,"

Simon hung up the phone and turned to Bianca. "This is where our lives begin. You and me, will you marry me?"

"I...I have to think, this isn't as simple as two people getting married. I could get sick, and die or I could make you sick then I'd have to watch you die. I couldn't do that Simon I just couldn't do it."

"No one is going to die," he assured her. "There are ways we can stay protected. I'm willing to try them or you?"

"Yes, I am but,"

"No but's," he kissed her lips again. "We'll announce it tonight, then you and the ladies can start your plans."

"Don't I get a say in this?"

"You said yes, I love you Bianca I'm not going to let anything stand in the way of that."

"Let's hope we're doing the right thing." She sighed and laid her bright head on his chest.

*****

"Rachel honey?" Rachel turned at the sound of Pat's voice. She quickly wiped the tears from her eyes as

Pat came to sit beside her.

"Why is it all I seemed to be able to do is cry?"

Pat laughed. "You and I seem to have the same problem."

Rachel held up the opened letters. "Did you know about these Mama?"

"No, your father just told me everything. I'm so sorry honey, I know he was trying to do the right thing for you, but that doesn't excuse everything."

"No it doesn't," Rachel looked down at the letters.

"So, what did he say?" Pat wanted to know.

Rachel shrugged. "In the first letters he said how he loved me and wanted me to be patient, that he had to take care of his father's estate, then when he had a house ready for us he'd come, he said he had something to ask me. Then in the last letters he said he understood why I never wrote, or called him." Her voice started to waver. "He said "With this time apart logic had returned, and I probably realized I didn't love him. He said it was the same for him, but that he could handle it. If I never wanted to see him again he would stay away. It was signed, Love Nick.'" Rachel shrugged again because she didn't know what else to do. "I guess you all were right, it wasn't love after all."

"But I thought you had already figured that out."

"I had held out a little hope. It was tucked away inside my heart. Dad succeeded, Nick doesn't want me any more."

"You can't say that, you have to talk to him before you close the door all the way."

"I just want to close the door on this hold awful experience."

"You can shut out your heart, just like that?"

"I've been trained well. This will go away."

"What will you do with the letters?"

"I'll put them away, and maybe one day when Niki is a mother I'll tell her what happened and show them to her."

"Will you let Nick see her?"

"When ever he wants."

"Alright darling, listen, Simon wants us all to come down for dinner if you can, will you?"

"Yes Mama, I'll be there."

"Good." Pat stood up and caressed Rachel's cheek. "I love you sweets."

"I love you too mama." Pat turned, and left the room closing the door behind her.

*****

Nick stood inside his newly finished home. It wasn't a big house, it only had four bedrooms, three baths and two living areas. It was exactly what he wanted. It felt good to stand in the center and know it was his, this was where he'd planned to bring his bride. He rubbed his face, he could still feel her finger prints against his skin. Now it looked as if he would have no bride.

It was late and he'd just come from Blake's. He was in a foul mood, and he was tired of this, he actually thought about giving it up. He could be making a fool out of himself by trying. He had given himself two more months to get her back in his arms, but what if she didn't want to be there?

Nick looked at the phone. He picked it up and dialed her number.

"Hello?"

"Hello?"

"Hi, this is Nick Rawlins may I speak with Rachel please?"

"Oh Nick, this is Pat, how are you son?" For a second he froze.

"I'm okay, how's Rachel?"

"This night isn't over for us yet. We're about to sit down to dinner. Can you call her tomorrow?"

"Yes, yes I can."

"Great, please call I'm sure she wants to talk to you."

"Are you sure? I mean I didn't get that idea."

"Just call her."

"Alright, good night Ma'am."

"Good night son."

Nick hung up, and stared at the phone. *What the hell was that?* Did it mean she approved of him and would help him? At the hospital he'd gotten that idea but since then there had been no indication that she wanted to help. He'd been by to see the baby eight times and Pat was never there.

*****

Simon took in the group around them. Dinner had gone as well as could be expected. John sat at the head of the table, but he barely spoke and his eyes were deep set and dark and his lips tight. Rachel sat with her fists wrapped around the handle of a knife as if she were ready to plunge it in some one's heart, her eyes were trained on her plate. Pat sat at the other end of the table she and Ryan tried to have a normal conversation, but it fell flat, and poor Bianca sat next to Simon unable to look at anyone. Her face was pale and her pretty nose beet red.

"Janet," Simon waved the maid over to him. "Can you bring the champagne I had you ice and flutes for every one." They all looked up at that. Simon forced a laugh. "Rachel, if you could unass the knife it would make what I have to say that much easier."

"Simon watch your language!" Pat snapped.

Rachel flushed, and put the knife down.

The champagne arrived and when every glass was filled Simon said. "Mom, dad, this last episode not withstanding, I've always envied the marriage you guys have. I've looked at you two as the perfect couple. I want what you have." Now he had every ones attention. "Dad, I understand what you did and why. Everyone who loves as deeply and as great as you do, would be tempted to do just what you did. I truly believe you lost your mind for a while, and as a man, I felt what you felt. After what they did to our girls I wanted blood. But Nick saved my life, I'd been trying not to recognize it. I wanted to hate him for what happened. I wanted to deny that day, and how he pushed me out of the way. He would've taken that bullet for me. Then when Rachel came out, and she was the target I saw the look on his face. It was the look of a man about to lose his heart, his life. It was the look I would've if anyone denied me my love."

"What are you saying Simon?" Rachel said tears running from her eyes. Simon looked around the table, and notice everyone except Ryan had tears, Bianca's shoulders were shaking. Simon reached for her hand, and pulled her to her feet.

"I'm saying that I would die with out this woman by my side." There were gasps around the room. "I asked Bianca to marry me, but she won't have it unless you all say it's okay."

"Of course…" Rachel began but Simon held up his hand and Bianca dried her tears.

"I'm sick," she said. "Rachel and Mom know how, and why, and I've just shared it with Simon. Now I should tell all of you before you say anything else."

"No Bianca," Rachel said. "What goes on between you and Simon is your business, you don't have to tell them anything."

"She's right Bianca, you don't have to," Pat said softly.

"That would be true if I didn't love you all. But I love you too much to hurt you." Bianca turned to John. "I know how fiercely you love your children, you've proved it over and over. I'm sorry to say, I'm one more challenge, if you say that I shouldn't marry Simon then I won't do it."

"What the hell," Simon yelled. "I don't care what he says…"

"Stop it Simon!" Bianca snapped. "Of course you care, you love that man, he's everything you ever wanted to be. Don't you stand there, and tell me you don't care. That's a bold faced lie. If he won't have it then I won't marry you. I love him, he's been the best and only father I know and I will not disrespect him like that."

Simon closed his lips, but his nostrils flared and his hands clenched on the napkin he'd picked up.

"Sir," Bianca began and all eyes were on John. "I have HIV. It happened a long time ago, but the doctors say I'm just a carrier. I may never get sick, but I could pass it on to any partner I have."

The silence was deafening. John stood up so fast his chair fell behind him, his face was white.

"John," Pat's urgent voice came across the table. "They are adults let them live their life."

"Dad, there are ways for Simon to protect himself." Ryan yelled.

"What about children?" John asked in a strangled voice.

"We'll adopt." Simon answered.

"Are you well Bianca?" John asked, his voice hushed. "Is that why you took so long to heal?"

"Yes Sir to both, I'm well and I love Simon. I've loved him for years."

"And I love her Dad."

John walked around the table and came to Bianca's side, he caught her face in his hands. "You poor child," he hugged her tight. "I didn't know."

"I wanted it that way. I didn't want to worry you."

"Did you think I wouldn't understand?"

"No Sir, I...I..." she broke into tears. "I didn't want you to know I'd been so stupid. I didn't want you to hate me."

"How could I hate you?" He kissed her cheek. "You are like my own child. I could never hate you."

She lifted her head, and looked at him. "And now, I tried to tell Simon that this wasn't fair to you. That we shouldn't do this, but I do love him so much."

John looked at Simon. "You'll take care of her?"

"What kind of question is that?" Ryan said. "He's your son, of course he'll take care of her."

John pulled Simon into his embrace and hugged them both. "Then let's have a wedding."

Pat immediately set into wedding mode. Sudden joy brought happy smiles to every face. Only Pat saw the shadow in Rachel's eyes.

Twenty-Five

RACHEL FINGERED THE ENVELOPES that sat on her dresser in her bedroom. She'd read them so many times she knew each word by heart. She turned and walked to her bedroom window. It was wet outside, dark thunderstorms ran through the area. Everything was finally coming together. She couldn't help but smile when she recalled the look on Bianca's face. And she'd never seen Simon glow like he was doing earlier tonight. It's as if the real Simon had finally come out to play and she was so happy for them.

The phone rang, and Rachel picked it up. "Hello?"

"Rachel?" At the first sound of his voice her blood turned to lava. "It's me Nick, can you talk?"

She looked around the room, she wasn't ready for this. Everything he'd done flew right out of her mind. His voice was the only thing that mattered at this moment.

"Yes, I can talk." She cleared her throat as her words came out husky.

"How are you?"

"I'm as well as can be expected."

"Good," he paused and she wondered what he was doing, where was he?

"Did you enjoy your visit with Niki today?" She asked him.

"Yes and I wanted to thank you for naming her after me. Dominique is a beautiful name."

"Yes well I thought if she wasn't going to have her father at least she could have part of his name."

"I plan to be a big part of my daughter's life." He said quietly, when there was no response he continued. "I think we need to get together and discuss this."

"You're right."

"Can I pick you up tomorrow night?"

"No," she hesitated. "I don't know if we should...I mean I'm not ready to..."

"For God's sake Rachel," Nick snapped. "I'm not some stranger. I want to see my daughter all I want from you is to make plans. You and I are stuck with each other for the rest of our loves. Even though you don't love me we can still be friends right?"

"Yes," she sighed. "I suppose you're right. I'll meet you."

"Fine," he gave her the name of the place. "Be there by seven, I'll be out front waiting for you."

"I'll be there."

"Good night."

"Good night."

She looked down at his letters. He'd said some things that melted her heart and brought tears to her eyes. And as she'd read on she had seen his heart breaking. Then he'd give up on them altogether. Now she understood why he'd acted that way. He thought she didn't love him and he'd given up on them. Just as she'd done. But was it the right thing to do? He'd been here almost every day. She'd told the Nanny to stay with him as he played with Niki. But Rachel was ashamed to say she'd watched them and she ached to be a part of their play sessions. Niki seemed to recognize him instantly and she would smile and gurgle up at him. Rachel wondered if she could join them, after all she couldn't hide from him forever. She was woman enough to admit she was hiding.

But just being near him broke down her logic. He actually turned her brain to mush. If he came tomorrow to see Niki, she had to tell him about Simon and Bianca. And maybe she'd make a special trip to Sophia's and tell them. That decided, she smiled and got ready for bed. She made a habit of getting Niki from her crib and letting her sleep cuddled in her arms all night. It made for a very peaceful night.

*****

The next day Rachel laughed as she played with Niki's pretty pink toes. The baby cooed up at her and gave her the biggest dimpled smile, but her blue eyes hurt Rachel's heart every time she looked into them. "Come on Niki, let's go and see what Aunt Bea is doing?"

Rachel turned at the knock on her door. "Come in!" She yelled.

Pat walked into the room, she went to the bed to stand beside Rachel. "Oh, isn't she adorable?" Pat cooed as she touched Niki's hand and toyed with her little fingers.

"Why thank you," Rachel beamed. "She is such a treasure."

"What do you think about Bianca and Simon?" Pat asked. "I must say I'm a bit surprised. It never dawned on me that they were attracted to each other."

"I've known for years. She tried to hide it, but her eyes always gave her away. I do wonder why Simon never saw it. It was written all over her face."

"Maybe he was as blind as I was."

Rachel shrugged. "Men are usually the blind ones."

"Sometimes we women can be equally blind." Pat paused and kissed Niki's petal cheek. "I heard Nick was here again."

"Yes, he came to see the baby."

"Is that the only reason?"

"I've decided to meet with him and discuss visitation."

"You have a date?"

"No mother, just talking shop."

"Don't do that Rachel. I think he still loves you and I know you still love him. You know now that he was innocent of all wrong doing, that man's deserves another shot.""

"I'll always have a fond affection for him but any chance I had with him is gone. He wouldn't give me another chance and I won't ask him to."

"Do you really believe that?"

"Yes, he said he knew I didn't love him, but that he wanted to be a part of his daughter's life. We are having dinner tonight to discuss the particulars."

"Are you going to give him joint custody?"

"I have to or he'll probably take me to court. I don't think I'm up for that kind of battle."

"What if I told you to marry Nick? To make him fall in love with you again and marry him?" Pat whispered. "What would you say?"

Rachel laughed with very little humor. "Mom, have you lost your mind? All this wedding planning has gone to your head. I told you I don't love him. Why would I want to make him love me?"

"Because I have heard you crying at night," Pat

said quietly, her hand lay on Rachel's back in a gentle caress. "I heard you whisper his name too often and I see the dreamy look that comes to your eyes when ever you look at Niki."

Rachel gasped and her skin paled. "That isn't so!" She denied, and she pulled away. "I could go the rest of my life without ever seeing him again."

Pat prayed she hadn't over stepped her bounds. "It would be a short life, you'd waste away to nothing. As it is you barely eat now. I know you love him. Stop denying it. Just go get your man."

"Mom," Rachel sighed. "If I wanted him I swear I'd go get him, but I don't. Now that I know the reason behind my obsession with him, I know how to fix it. All I have left to do is face him and tell him how I feel."

"And you think you can tell him to his face that you don't love him?"

"Think?" Rachel laughed. "Mother I know I can. He's a lair, and a thief, I don't know why I didn't see it earlier. He had me fooled right down to the every end. I know I fought therapy, but now I'm glad Dad made me do it. Now I can get on with my life, I can raise my daughter with a peaceful heart."

Pat kissed Rachel's forehead and looked into her eyes. "I pray you're right, but if you have any doubt about what you feel, don't shut him out yet. Give him a chance to…"

"To what mom? He gave up, we are both adults, it's over," Rachel interrupted. "You want me to throw myself at him? I don't think so. I don't love him, end of story. When I meet him tonight I'll tell him what I just told you, then he and I can move on to other things."

Pat nodded. "Alright darling, I guess I can assume

these late night tear sessions will be over soon?"

"As soon as I confront my demon."

"My poor sweet darling," Pat kissed Rachel's cheek then she kissed Niki's. "Make the right choice Rachel. That's all I ask, make the right choice."

Later that Nick stood outside the hotel and waited. Patience wasn't his best attribute but for her he was willing to wait forever. He had arranged everything. First he would impress her with all he'd done, then he'd stay close to her and maybe she would remember what they'd had. He knew to confess his love wouldn't bring about the hoped for results. So he planed a sneak attack. Rachel being the person she was, would never admit to loving him. Her wounded pride wouldn't let her. But he knew she had to feel something for him and if she didn't, his plan tonight would reveal it all. He looked at his watch, she was thirty minutes late. He shoved his hands deep into the pockets of his tuxedo pants and hunched his shoulders. Deep in thought he didn't see the limo drive up, he turned just in time to take in a sparkling wine red dress, it's split revealing sleek tone legs, the burgundy heels seemed custom made for such elegant feet and his body stirred.

Nick slowed his gait as he walked to her, and tried to appear causal as the driver helped Rachel out of the car. She was stunning, her hair was full and hung down her back in glossy curls. And her's was the face that haunted his dreams. His eyes traveled her body and he was hard pressed not to fall to his knees and beg her forgiveness. She had matured, her body before the baby had been sleek and bordered on thin, now she had lush curves and his hands ached to caress them.

But he knew that kind of thing would never work.

He had to play hardball if he were going to win her heart.

"Hello," he said in his most casual tone. "You look nice."

Rachel could only stare, he was more then she had ever dreamed. This was a Nick she didn't know, had never met. He looked well beyond nice he was stunning. His hair was tamed, it lay in soft, glossy wave on his head. His face was clean-shaven and he was dressed in a black tuxedo. When he said it was formal dress tonight she had no idea what to expect from him. She looked down and smiled, she had expected to see his cowboy boots but instead he wore mahogany loafers. Her heart quickened, his blue eyes sparkled like sapphires and she could feel herself drowning in them. She shook herself and accepted his offered hand.

"You look nice also."

Nick nodded. She was giving him the cold shoulder, but the look in her eyes had been all too hot until she had frosted it over. "I'm taking you to the presidential suite. It will give us the privacy we need."

"Why do we need privacy? And why in a hotel?"

"It's not just any hotel, I own it. And I don't want to be seen in the restaurant arguing with you. If you'd like I can have Bianca brought over so you can feel safe."

"Are you laughing at me?" She raised a brow at him.

"No, I just want you to be comfortable."

"You're just rolling in blood money aren't you?"

"It was blood money, now it's being filtered, put to better uses you could say. But I'll tell you about that later. I'd like to know that you feel comfortable here, with me."

"I'm capable of taking care of myself. Beside, you

know better than to harm me, my family has already proven they can take care of their own. You wouldn't be that stupid."

"You're right, I wouldn't harm a hair on that pretty head of yours."

"See that you don't."

They made the trip up to the fortieth floor in silence. When the elevator door opened, Nick stepped aside and allowed Rachel to precede him.

"I hope you like it, it's not much but I like to call it home."

Rachel walked around in stunned awe. Hundreds of pictures of herself and Niki lined the walls. A few giant posters, but most were small portraits. She looked at him as he came in from the entryway.

"What is this?" She didn't know if she were angry or flattered.

"Oh, I wanted to watch my child grow so I had photos taken of her."

"Why am I in every photo?"

"Because you can't seem to let her go, all you do is carry her around so I couldn't help getting you."

"So you've been following us around for the last three months?"

"No," he went to a bar and poured a drink. "Would you like one?" She shook her head. "I've been following you around for four months. I wanted to watch my baby grow."

"You mean my baby." She countered.

"Dominique is our child, we can't put her through a tug of war. That's why I asked you here."

She pointed to some of the pictures. "There are photos of me without Niki."

"You didn't give her my last name?" Nick countered.

"Your last name?" she laughed. "I don't even know it."

"Come on, you know my name," he waved her towards an elegantly attired table for two. Crystal and china, glittered in the low light. Rachel caught her gown in her sweaty hands and walked ahead of him to the table. He held out the chair for her then went to his own. Once he was seated, he picked up a bell and a waiter appeared.

"Sam, please bring the lady a white wine, make it light, sweet."

"How do you know that's what I want?"

"Because you daydreamed about a cold glass of white wine back at the cabin."

"You remember that?"

"I remember a lot of things," he cleared his throat. "Here are the menus if you would like to order something."

She picked up the menu and glanced at it, then back at him. "What are we doing?"

"We're having dinner like civilized people do."

The wine arrived, she stood up and picked up her glass. "There is nothing civilized about us Nick, there never has been." She took a sip of her wine and stood up, she went to stand in front of a photo of Niki. "This isn't you. It's not the Nick I know." She turned and looked at him. "The man I knew wore dusty jeans and a black Stetson. He wouldn't be comfortable in this." She looked around the room, then back at him. "I'm not comfortable here or with this new man." She turned and set the glass on a nearby table then headed for the door.

Nick was out of his chair in an instant. He caught

he arm and swung her around to face him. At her surprise gasp he sealed her lips with his and pulled her tight in his arms. And it felt like heaven. He held her tight as she struggled for a moment, then she stopped and soon she was kissing him back. Her purse fell from her fingers then she buried those fingers in his freshly combed hair pulling him closer.

"God, I've missed you." He murmured against her lips. "I've missed everything about you."

"Don't talk," she rasped. "Don't say a word." She ran her hands up around his shoulders, then down his back and Nick felt his knees go weak. He picked her up in his arms and carried her into his room. Gently, he laid her on the bed and stared down at her. Slowly he removed his tie, and then slipped off his jacket. She stood up on the bed and unbuttoned his shirt and pushed it from his shoulder. Her lips traveled along his neck and up to his ear then to his mouth and Nick drank from her sweetness, he kissed her with everything he had in him. Then his hands reached around her and found the zipper of her dress, he pulled it down and slid the dress from her shoulders.

Nick buried his head between her beautiful breasts, the same ones that fed his daughter. He caught one nipple between his lips and loved it, he smiled just a bit as he tasted milk on his tongue. He caught the other one between his fingers and squeezed softly and more milk came he lapped it up and she moaned. Her head thrown back and her fingers clenched on his shoulders she held him to her.

Rachel had known the minute he kissed her that this was what she waited for. This was what she needed. His arms around her felt so good she never wanted it to end. He was everything she wanted in a husband, but she couldn't have him. One tear slipped from her eye as she held his head close and let him love her in the only way he seemed capable of.

Rachel let him go and stepped back. She wondered what he thought of her new figure. Whatever he thought it had to be good because the look in his eyes didn't change. She walked to the head of the bed then turned to face him. She eased down and kicked off her shoes. She was so ready for what he offered.

Nick kicked off his shoes and undid his belt and pulled it off. She looked great like a dream standing on his bed waiting for him. His body hardened instantly, and he pulled on all his reserves to hold steady and not pounce on her. She wore nothing but thigh high black stocking and a smile, then she lowered herself to lay on the bed and his whole body flushed and his head filled with his need. He knelt on the bed, then made his way up her body kissing every inch, the smell of her filled his nostrils and his body hummed. He lowered himself to her and he shivered as she purred and wrapped her sweet arms around him.

Nick had known it would be like this, they were free to show their love and no one stood in their way. He leaned over her, then went to his elbows and buried his hands in her hair holding her still as he took his fill.

Rachel didn't want to think of tomorrow, this was here and now. This was Nick, not some rich playboy bent on showing off his ill gotten gains. This was her Nick, the man who caught fish with his bare hands, the man who rescued her time and time again. The man who loved her. She opened herself to him, and he slid between her spread legs and nestled there. Her eyes drifted closed, and her legs hooked around his hips trying to pull him closer. Her breasts tingled and ached for his touch. And her nether regions burned from the heat of him there. She could feel the bulge in the front of his pants, and knew he was feeling the same way.

She reached between there bodies and worked with his zipper, as he kissed her like there was no tomorrow. When she finally got it loose, she quickly pushed his slacks down his hips and his hard heat fell exactly where she wanted it most. She opened her eyes and pushed her hips up against him and the breath hissed from him. She smiled and did it again and again, until he was kissing her as if she were everything he wanted in this world. He let his weight add pressure and she thought she had died and gone to heaven. Her fingers gripped his arms, then traveled around his waist and down his back until she gripped his strong bottom. She squeezed and he jumped.

"Nick," his name hissed from her. "Please don't make me wait. I need you inside me." She leaned up and traced kisses down his throat and her hands ran up and down his back.

"Are you ready for me baby?" He growled against her lips as he rocked his body against hers, and she shuddered as wave after wave of pleasure raced through her.

"Yes," she shouted. "Oh yes, please."

He eased back and let his shaft find her sweetness and he pushed forward. The breath hissed from them both as passion claimed them. Nick rocked his hips until he was fully sheath inside her delicious heat. He lowered his head and took a deep breath, control was a hard thing to hang onto when you were with the one you loved. He looked into her dreamy eyes and knew she wouldn't leave this room without his ring on her finger. It was a promise he had made a long time ago, and after this he was sure it was a done deal. She would marry him and he would take her away.

He ran his hands over her hair as he stared into her face, then he shifted his hips and she moaned and lifted hers. Nick began to thrust hard, then harder until she was gripping the sheets above her head and crying out for mercy. He shifted as her wetness flowed over him testifying to the great pleasure he had just given her.

Rachel needed to show him just how much she loved him. She felt a deep undeniable need to give him as good as he'd just given her. She slid her fingers in his hair and cupped his head. Then pulled him down until his ear was close to her lips, she nibbled the edges and was delighted at his response.

"Roll to your back." She whispered then tickled his ear with her tongue. He inhaled and gave to few more thrust that had her shaking before he gathered her in his arms and rolled. With her legs tucked on either side of him he caught her waist and held her tight.

Rachel loved the feel of him like this. She offered him everything she owned. With her knees firmly in place she leaned over him and caught his nipple between her lips and suckled, his body became as taunt as a bow and she began to ride him like a new toy. Rachel reveled in her love for him, she rose and fell as fast as her hips would let her. The stars were right there waiting to take her to paradise. He bent his knees and held her tight as he took over and pounded her over and over until she screamed her release. Then he threw his head back and yelled as he found paradise with her.

Forgive Me, My Love

Hours later, Rachel woke up to find herself nestled in his arms. For a brief second she smiled as she remembered loving him twice in as many hours. But that was over, it was time to face reality. She moved his arm from her and stood up. After gathering her clothes she went to find the shower. Once she was done and dressed, she went back into his room and found him still asleep. She leaned over and kissed his forehead, then brushed a stray curl back behind his ear.

"Another time another place, we might have worked." She kissed him again then turned and walked out of his apartment.

*****

A few days later, Nick sat in a rocking chair with little Dom on one knee and Vanessa on the other. But his mind had gone back to two nights ago when he'd held Rachel in his arms. It had been like coming home, he'd had some hope that she would be his, until he'd found her note. It read 'I like my way of saying good bye better than yours.' If she could still deny what they had after the night they shared, then she didn't love him, he'd been right. It still hurt, and he knew it would take forever to get over that kind of pain.

The doorbell rang and he looked up. "I'll get it."

"No, no," Sophia waddled towards the door. "I need to do all the walking I can. It helps when the baby gets ready to show up." She laughed, but Blake fell into step next to her. Nick wondered if his face had looked like Blake's did now when Rachel had given birth. Nick had volunteered to be the baby sitter when Sophia went into labor and they had accepted, only Nick didn't know

505

if he could handle it alone, but he was willing to give it a try.

"So what brings you down here?"

Nick looked up to see Rachel standing in the doorway, and Blake holding Niki.

"Aunt Rachel!" Both children jumped from his lap, and ran to her, she knelt to hug them. But her eyes clashed with Nick's and neither one could look away.

"Hello munchkins, look at how big you've gotten."

"Did you bring us anything?"

"Of course."

Blake cleared his throat. "As you can see Nick is here. He just stopped in to say hello."

"Hi," Rachel said.

"Hello," Nick answered. "How's my girl?"

"I'm fine," Rachel started then flushed. "You meant Niki, how stupid of me."

"Not stupid…"

Rachel cut him off. "I came by to tell you the news." She looked at them all. "Simon and Bianca are getting married in two months."

"What?" Sophia cried. "I didn't know they even liked each other."

"They've been in love for years, but they hid it from everyone including each other."

"That's great news Rachel, how's your father taking it?"

"He's changed a lot, he's taking it very well."

"Great," Nick nodded, not really interested. "Can I show you something Rachel?"

"Sure."

"Blake, Sophia, do you mind keeping an eye on

Niki?"

"What?" Rachel asked, flustered. "Why can't she come with us?"

"Because, I need to show you this alone."

Rachel's stomach clenched, by his tone she was sure it wasn't going to be good. "No, I don't think I'll go with you."

"Blake?" Nick growled.

"Sure we'll watch her."

"I don't want the children traumatized so I suggest you walk." Nick murmured.

"I said no!" Rachel snapped.

"Walk or be carried?"

"I'll do neither you can't do that to me any more Nick."

"Sophia, can you take the kids out of here?"

"Don't you dare Sophia!" But it was too late they were already gone.

Nick approached her and Rachel backed away from him. "You can't man handle me, Nick I just had a baby and...and...aahhhhh!" She screamed as he picked her up and tossed her over his shoulder. She clenched her fists and beat on his back. "Let me down!"

His hands rested on her upper thigh and he caressed that area and she screamed louder. He turned his head, and kissed her leg. "I'll let you down when we get to where we're going." He delivered a slap to her bottom. "Now shut up."

Nick deposited her into his truck and locked the door, when he got to the drivers side he unlocked the door and got in. He grabbed her arm just as she opened her door, he pulled her back inside and locked the door again. He looked at her. "Trust me."

She looked away and folded her arms. About five minutes later they pulled up to a stone fence with and iron gate. Across the top was a circle with RD inside. A few minutes later they pulled up to a nice size house. It looked like a log cabin, it had lots of windows and an screen encased wrap around porch.

Nick got out, and Rachel refused to even wonder why they were here. He came around to her side and held the door opened for her, she hesitated for a moment. Then she got out and stood staring at him.

Rachel's heart felt heavy and sadness caught her. "Why am I here Nick?" she asked quietly.

She shivered, and closed her eyes as his presence overwhelmed her. She felt warm, and safe all over again and it brought back memories of the life they had shared all those months ago. And she had a desperate need to have them back.

"My name is Dominick Rawlins, I'm the third son of Henry Dennison. My father was insane with pride. Most people cherish their family's history, they're proud of where they came from, and who they are. My father was no different. His ancestors were murderers, thieves, prostitutes, grave robbers, pirates, and lastly, con-artists. Any vice known to man my family has dabbled in it."

"Nick, I don't need to know this, save it for who ever you decide to marry."

"You are the mother of my child, you should know all about me." He caught her free hand. "Come on." She pulled free of him, and he sighed, but she did follow him. She was surprised when he pulled out a key and inserted it in the lock. As soon as the door opened a big ball of fur leapt through the door and into the yard. Rachel screamed, and then on instinct jumped into Nick's arms. But she looked up and saw he was laughing.

"You mean you don't remember your gift?"

Rachel looked at the dog as it came to settle next to Nick's leg. "Sugar puff?"

"Sugar Puff?" He laughed. "Tell me that's not what you called him."

"Is he a boy?" Nick nodded, and she looked surprised. "But they told me he was a she." They both became conscious of her body against his.

"It doesn't matter," Nick said and his eyes focused on her lips.

"Well," Rachel broke free of him, and put some distance between them. "What ever works. What's his name?"

Nick opened the door wider, and waved her in. "Sal."

She laughed. "Should I ask why?"

Nick shrugged. "It fit."

Rachel stepped inside, and her mouth fell open, their footsteps echoed through the empty house. "Wow, this is beautiful, whose house is this?"

"Mine." He said, and she lifted a brow at him.

"This and a place in town? Livin' it up aren't you?"

"Not really, the place in town was just to impress you. I hate it there. This is my true home."

She looked away from him and walked around. "Where is the furniture?"

"Would you like me to show you around?"

"If you think it's necessary."

Nick shook his head. "Wait, come, sit with me." He led her into a great room off to the left, and straight to a set of metal chairs, and then he sat down beside her.

"Now, where was I? Oh, Henry had lots of money. As best Blake and I could find out, he killed our mother's parents and married her. She thought she was in love, everyone, but her knew what was happening. Henry wasn't her rescuer, he was her captor."

"Sounds familiar," she got up, and walked away.

Nick ignored that. "Henry has a great and disturbing track record in Europe, which is why he relocated to Mexico. Like I said he was extremely proud of his lineage and he wanted us to be proud also. I rebelled; I ran away from home and crossed into Texas. I finished school with forged records, and then I joined the police force. I was on the force for five years, then I spent two years in jail because I knew too much about the workings of certain parts of the police force. Then I was released, with the promise that I knew nothing. That was when I became a bounty hunter. I was chasing a bounty when you happened."

"So in trying to save me, you lost every thing."

He shrugged. "If you look at it like that."

"Tell me about your new found wealth."

"Blake and I split everything, and we decided to do only good with it. I took only the money that I paid to get you and that is what I live off of. The interest from Henry's money is being deposited in an account for charities. But most of it was donated and has gone to fix the lives that have been shattered by Henry. But right now I'm a venture capitalist."

"What exactly is that?"

"I look for small businesses that need money, and if I think it's a good idea I fund their projects, then I get repaid when they make it big, plus some."

"What if they flop?"

"It doesn't matter because it isn't really my money any way."

"Why am I here Nick?"

He paused, and then it was his turn to stand up. He paced for a moment, and then stopped to look at her. "I thought you should know. I've fallen in love."

Her heart skipped a beat and she felt light headed. "I don't know what to say… I can't return the sentiment," She turned back to face him, and her eyes narrowed at the smirk on his face.

"I'm in love with someone else Rachel. I wanted you to know since I'm going to have contact with my child. I didn't want to have any hard feelings that may linger."

For a moment she couldn't speak, her head felt as if it were about to explode, but she managed a small smile. "Oh," she said in high tones. "Who is she?"

"You don't know her, she doesn't run in your circles."

"When did you meet her?" Rachel casually walked back to a desk that stood in the corner of the room, and absently ran one finger over a letter opener. "When can I meet her?"

"You can meet her anytime you like. You'd like her Rachel, she's fun, easy going and a joy to behold. She puts all other females to shame. And I think she makes a wonderful mother."

"What?" Before she could think her fingers had curled around a paper weight, and it was sailing through the air. It crashed against the wall and fell with a loud thud to the hardwood floors.

"What the hell was that for?"

"How dare you?" She seethed. "Here I am fresh

from having your child, still fat and swollen with milk and you're in love with some skinny bitch you just met?"

"Who said I just met her?"

But Rachel wasn't listening. "My father put me through weeks of deprogramming and you never came. I thought you took money to stay away! What was that about? Why did you show up in the delivery room? Why am I standing here right now? You know, I thought you may have one loyal bone in that body of yours, but I was wrong. I was wrong to put my faith in you, I was wrong to love you and I'm wrong for crying right now. You don't mean anything to me."

"Then why are you?"

"Because there's a knife in my heart six inches long, and I think it maybe fatal." She turned away from him, and put her hands over her face.

"Do you want to meet my fiancée?" He whispered, but all Rachel could do was shake her head, as she continued to cry.

Nick stood behind her, he caught her arms and propelled her out of the room, and down the hall and stopped. "Here she is, Darling, this is the girl I've been telling you about."

Rachel clenched her teeth, and her fingernails dug into her palms, she dropped her hands and screamed. "Don't do this to me Nick... Do you hate me so much that you would..." She stopped when she found herself looking into a mirror. She saw his reflection behind her. "What kind of trick are you playing?"

"No, trick," he pulled her back to him, and whispered in her ear. "The girl I love is here, she's staring at me from the eyes of a stranger. But I know those eyes, the girl that is locked away deep inside you. She's the girl

I fell in love with, bring her out Rachel, let us be together again."

Her face crumpled, and she turned in his arms, and then looped her arms around his waist. "She's here and she does love you, so very much"

"Oh God," he breathe into her hair. "I prayed I hadn't lost you. But for so long it looked as if you were gone from my life for good."

"I didn't want to be, but I had no choice. It broke my heart when I thought you took that check and left me standing there like a fool."

Nick pulled away just abit. "You know that was a mistake."

"I know now, but I didn't then and it hurt so bad. Why did you wait so long to come to me?"

"I wanted to show your father I could support you in the style you were raised. And I believed you didn't write because you had realized you didn't love me."

"And now?"

"I'm tired of being lonely, more than that, I want to be with you." Nick said, and his eyes caressed her tear stained face. "I want what we had at the cabin. Is it possible?"

"Not only is it possible, we can start the second you say the word."

"I spoke with your father." Nick said. "He said if I could get you to talk with me and you want me I could have you."

"And Simon?"

"Same thing, but even if they objected I'd never let you go again. I love you too damned much to do that."

"Oh Nick, I feel the same way."

Dean King

EPILOUGE

"Mom," Rachel said, as she fanned herself. "Is it really that hot outside? I can't seem to catch my breath."

"It's just your nerves." Pat assured her.

"But I'm not nervous, I'm so happy I can't stand it."

"Believe me, you can be happy, and still be nervous."

"You think that's what it is?" Rachel huffed as she stood near an open window.

"Yes dear, you are about to marry a man you love more than life itself. It's hard not to be nervous."

"You think I can do it?" Rachel turned stricken eyes on Pat. "I love him Mom, what if I make a horrible wife. What if we start living together, and he decided he doesn't really want me, what if we…"

Pat caught Rachel's arms in a firm grip. "You listen to me young lady. That man loves you, and you love him. You two have a beautiful, little girl together. Everything will work out. Just calm down, everything will be fine."

"Do you think so?"

"Yes, I was just as nervous as you are."

"Were you?"

"Of course, I didn't have my family with me. It was just me, your father and the justice of the peace. I

514

vowed that my children will always have the best of everything. And I believe you and Bianca got the best men out there."

"Thanks Mom," Rachel pulled Pat close, and gave her a hug, then there was a rustle and a frantic knocking on the door.

"Mrs. Pat come quick, the caterer needs you."

"I'll be back darling, just calm down, you'll make it through this just fine." Pat kissed her cheek, and left the room.

As soon as she was gone the door opened again, and Bianca stepped through. Rachel looked at her and broke into tearful smiles. "You look like an angel."

"So do you!" Bianca squealed and they fell into each others arms.

"I knew that dress would look like heaven on you."

"You too, step back so I can see." Bianca stepped back and they each turned and posed in their dresses. Both girls wore white, and each had had their very own designer. Rachel had gone for the sleek sexy look that was class in it's smilpicity. While Bianca had wanted the traditional big skirts and tinh bodice.

"Are we really doing this Rachel?"

"Don't tell me you're getting cold feet."

"No," Bianca smiled. "Mom talked me out of that last night."

Rachel laughed. "She just talked me out of mine."

Bianca giggled. "Do you feel better?"

"Yes, what about you?"

515

"Yes and no," Bianca lifted the skirts of her white gown and adjusted the sleek folds of material so that she could sit with out wrinkling anything. "I'm still not sure about this, dear god I love him. But I'm not just doing this to Simon, I'm doing it to his whole family. If he were to get sick would any of you be able to forgive me?"

"Oh my God!" Pat yelled from the door way. "How could you say something like that?" Both girls jumped at the sound of her voice.

"I had to say it, I have to know…"

"Know what Bianca? Simon is a grown man, do you think we would turn our backs on you, or even hate you if he got sick, and heaven forbid if he died? How could you think it? How could you? As much as we love you how could you doubt us?"

Bianca got up and went to her. "I'm sorry." She hugged Pat.

"Yes Bianca, you need to let that go," Rachel said as she joined them in a group hug. "We love you both end of conversation."

The three stood hugging, "I wonder how the guys are doing?" Pat asked, and then the door creaked opened.

"Can I come in?"

"Dad." Both girls said, and it was the sweetest sound John had heard in a long time.

"It's almost time, Pat they need you to go downstairs, the music is about to start."

She nodded, and kissed each of their cheeks, then she went to John, she looked at him for a moment then kissed his cheek and left the room.

516

Forgive Me, My Love

"How are you two?"

"We're okay, just a bit nervous."

"How are the guys?"

"Let's see," John said. "There was one busted nose, one black eye, a cracked rib."

"No!" Both girls screamed, and picked up their trains and started for the doors.

John laughed, and caught their arms. "Wait a minute I'm just joking with you they're behaving like nice little boys."

"Dad, how could you?"

"It's what you two expected, but they're fine. They may even like each other after all is said and done."

They stood looking at him not ready to forgive his little joke, and he flushed. "Okay I'm sorry." They came to him and pulled him into their arms.

"I love you Daddy." Rachel said.

"Me too Daddy," Bianca chimed in.

"You two ready to get married?" John asked with a suspicious sniffle. "I know two young men that can't wait."

"We're ready."

"Man you ladies look good, reminded me of when your mother and I got married."

"I thought you two wore jeans and t-shirts?"

"I was talking about the look on your faces." He sniffled again then dabbed at his eyes. "There's the music, as planned we'll all walk out together."

*****

Nick stood in the pool house of Rachel's family home with Blake getting dressed, he straightened his bow tie and wondered why he had to ware the thing. It was a beautiful day for a wedding, and he was so happy he didn't mind sharing the day with Simon.

"Blake, do you have that damned thing that's supposed to go around my waist?"

"What thing?" Blake said from his corner, he sat putting on his shoes.

"It's a cumber bum, and I have it." Simon said as he and Ryan walked through the door.

Nick turned to look at him. He hadn't spoken to either of Rachel's brothers in a long while, and now wasn't a good time to get reacquainted. Even during the wedding preparations they had ignored each other.

"Simon, Ryan," Nick said. "You know my brother Blake?"

"Hi Blake," Ryan went over to him, and shook Blake's hand. "How's the new baby boy?"

"Getting big fast," Blake grinned, always the proud father.

"And your wife? Is she doing well?"

"Yes," Blake's eyes narrowed as old fears came rolling back. "Why?" He growled, and took a step towards Ryan, but Nick jumped between them.

Nick grabbed Blake's lapel and whispered. "What the hell is wrong with you? He was just being polite, I'm sure he could care less about your wife."

Blake shook his head. "I'm sorry, for a moment

there I had the ugliest flash back, and I jumped."

Nick palmed Blake's head and said. "Let it go."

Blake shook free to find both men looking at him. He went to Ryan and held out his hand again. "You have to excuse me, I'm a little protective."

Ryan visibly relaxed, and grinned. "I didn't mean anything man. I guess all of you are protective like that."

"You could say we have a lot to protect," Blake laughed.

Simon chuckled, and tossed a look at Nick. "Which is the only reason he is allowed to look at Rachel."

They fell silent as Nick walked to Simon. Nick drew back his fist and delivered a blow to Simon's chin. It spun Simon around, and he fell against the wall.

"What the hell?" Both Blake and Ryan ran forward but Simon waved them off.

"It's okay, I deserved that and a lot more." Simon shook it off and stood up. He went to Nick and held out his hand. "Peace?"

Nick shook his hand. "Peace."

"I was wondering when you'd get me."

"I had so many things planned for how I'd pay you back," Nick shrugged as they finished dressing. "But since we are going to be brothers, that's going to have to do. I don't want anything unsaid between us."

"I consider that conversation finished."

"Done," then Nick smiled. "Let's go get married."

Each man walked out of the room with his best man at his side, and headed for the alter at the head of the stairs that led into the house. They each took their places and Nick scanned the crowd. The wedding announcements had gone out the very next day after Rachel had agreed to be his wife, as did the invitations. There were enough people here to fill a concert hall. And he didn't know any of them, he was sure Simon knew them, but it didn't matter. The only thing that mattered was that his girl was would be wearing his ring at the end of the day.

Suddenly the music started to play and the crowd became hushed. Nick felt his stomach tighten as he waited for a look at her. He looked over at Simon and saw the same tight expression. Simon looked at him and winked. Nick grinned and turned back to the isle.

A pretty little girl with shiny black curls and a dress as white as a cloud came strolling down the isle tossing flowers in every direction, then she was followed and a whole bunch of other girls. Nick found himself growing impatient, then finally there was a murmur in the crowd, and his heart jumped at the sight of her. Rachel held on to one of her father's arms while Bianca held the other. Nick speared a passing glance at Bianca but his eyes were only for Rachel. She was a vision, she floated down the isle in her clinging white gown, the scooped neck line leaving the tops of her breast bare. She didn't seem to walk, it was as if she were floating, and then the priest asked 'Who give this woman to this man?' Nick heard John say. 'I do." And his heart swelled. Nick held out his arm to her, and her small hand curled around it and she pressed close. He had to stop himself from kissing her.

Then the service began and Rachel couldn't recall what the priest said. All she heard was you may kiss the bride, she didn't even hear the shouts and whistles as Nick bent her over and plundered her lips. It was a kiss that promised so much more, and she was ready to cash in on that promise.

Rachel stood beside the wedding cakes. They had not been able to decide, and Pat suggested they each have their own cake. Rachel smiled as she felt strong arms circle her waist from behind, she nestled into those arms and sighed. "I love you Dominick Rawlins."

"And I love you Rachel Marie Rawlins," he kissed her ear then nipped it.

"I like the sound of that."

"So do I," he murmured against her neck and she closed her eyes and moaned, then reached up, and cupped his cheek. "I can't wait to get home."

"Me either, I want you all to myself." She turned in his arms, and smiled up at him. "When I saw you at the alter I nearly melted. You looked so good, I can't believe I almost threw us away."

"You my dear are a vision come to life, just holding you in my arms seems too good to be true. You have made me the happiest man in the world just by saying two simple words. I do."

"Let's make this promise to each other, we'll always trust and confide in each other."

"This I do solemnly swear."

"I love you Nick."

"I love you Rachel, always. Never doubt that."

"Let's get our little girl and go home."

"Music to my ears," Nick turned her around and lightly tapped her bottom, she laughed and picked up her gown and they hurried away.

Forgive Me, My Love

Check out these other Rogue books:

By S.D. Valyan

Whispers from the Heart	ISBN 0-9719751-7-5	$7.99
Hearts of Fire	ISBN 0-5952016-8-7	$20.99
Promises Unspoken	ISBN 1-4196-2869-0	$20.99

By Dean King

Bed of Lies	ISBN 0-9719751-4-0	$20.99

Amazon.com
www.rogueromance.net

Dean King